Teeth

of the

Wolf

Teeth of the Wolf

The Path of Ra Book 2

Dan Rabarts   Lee Murray

Teeth of the Wolf © 2018
by Dan Rabarts and Lee Murray

Published by Raw Dog Screaming Press
Bowie, MD

First Edition

Cover Image: Daniele Serra
Book Design: Jennifer Barnes

Printed in the United States of America

ISBN: 978-1-947879-07-2

Library of Congress Control Number:

www.RawDogScreaming.com

Acknowledgements

Lee: Dan, it's that time again.

Dan: Wine o'clock? Thank god.

Lee: No, it's time to write our acknowledgements. You know, blow kisses to our friends.

Dan: Right. Hat tips to all the amazing folk who helped make this second book happen.

Lee: We should start with our talented pool of beta readers, who gave us our first wave of feedback. People like historical fiction writer Charlotte Kieft, who pored over the text for us while suffering a double dose of flu and jet-lag!

Dan: And there's former detective Phil Weeks who helped tighten up our procedurals, and long-time Aussie friend and editor Jodi Cleghorn, with her advice on birthpunk, which I didn't even know was a thing. Sandra Dusconi, who has the dubious honour of having read early drafts of pretty much everything I've ever written. Bet she needs a wine right now. What time is it in Canada?

Lee: If you're opening a bottle, pour one for Simon Fogarty. Not to mention Daniele Serra for the gorgeous cover art.

Dan: Everyone who supported *Hounds of the Underworld*. There were a lot of those.

Lee: Let's not forget Raw Dog Screaming Press: Jennifer Barnes, John Edward Lawson and their team. How do we explain to everyone how it feels to be part of this little publishing house with so much heart? Maybe with the words of our most famous compatriot, Sir Edmund Hillary, who said, "there is something about building up a comradeship—that I still believe is the greatest of all feats—and sharing in the dangers with your company of peers. It's the intense effort, the giving of everything you've got. It's really a very pleasant sensation." Our editor J.L. Gribble is responsible for a lot of that intense effort, with her supernatural ability to zero in on my missing words, your word echoes, and our incomprehensible Kiwi colloquialisms.

Dan: I have to thank my long-suffering wife Chrissy, who has adjusted to my being there in the room with her but really not being in the same place at all when I'm down the writing rabbit-hole. My kids for being a constant source of fear and inspiration.

Lee: Smooth move, getting in there first, Dan. To David Murray, the reason for my most heartfelt existence (he told me to say that), who shares my office, tolerates my incessant mumbling, and is my instant research tool for anything sciencey. And to our children, Céline and Robbie, my best fans.

Dan: And you, Lee. This wouldn't be much of a collaboration on my own, and Penny continues to put her foot down and keep it real while Matiu goes flailing off on mad tangents. Thanks for carrying on down this dark path with me, it continues to be a wild adventure.

Lee: Same! It's been epic. I couldn't have done this without your shadowy flair, and those unexpected explosions. But don't roll up your crime tape just yet because Auckland is in the middle of a crime wave. I heard Detective Inspective Tanner has eighteen active cases on the go…

Publisher's Note

Because the region this novel takes place in is so much a part of the story we have chosen to retain the British spelling conventions that are the standard in New Zealand. This work also incorporates New Zealand phrases and words from the indigenous Māori people so we have included a brief glossary in the back for anyone not familiar with these terms.

PROLOGUE

Mārama drifts in the *waka* on a sea of rippling black.

She lies in its belly, the paddle flat on her chest, her hands folded over its carved wooden handle. The sky expands above her in shades of blood and fire, curls of colour twisting through each other like lovers' fingers entwined, or ropes thrown out to hold back the sun. She knows this place. She has been here before.

She aches.

There is a warmth, a memory of something that should not have been. She wants to curl into herself, crush her hurt down into a small cold ball and bury it deep inside, along with all the rest. But if she closes up now, like a *kōwhai* flower retreating from the chill of night, she may not have the strength to unfold again. And this is no place for weakness.

She doesn't question how she came to be here. Once you've been, it's easy to find your way back. Or to be brought back. There are rules. Someone wants her here, but she has a choice. Either let the *waka* carry her, or take up the paddle laid across her chest, fight the current, this other desire that calls to her.

Yet the burden is heavy, pressing down her bones, speaking of the black depths beneath, the burning expanses above. Fighting is hard, and she has fought so long already. Fought the pull to return. The dreams have haunted her, the whispers taunting, always there in her thoughts, in the shadows that flicker wherever she looks.

If she could run away, she would have by now. Running isn't an option, not when she has people to care for. So she must fight. Pushing against the awful weight, choking back the cries that flutter to her tongue like trapped birds, she comes to her knees and into a crouch, clutching the paddle in both hands.

A gravid moon peeks above the skyline behind her, rising as she rises, shrouding her in silver light.

The *waka* floats on, outriggers slicking across the waves, the twilight painting the glassy sea in red and black whorls. The horizon is not an unbroken line. She tenses, and grips the paddle tighter. The sea boils and splits, something huge rising from the deep, waves cascading off its back. Coils and spikes and fins breach the water, shredding the sea to a fury of white wake.

She straightens her back, lifts the paddle over her head, and screams out her challenge to the beast, the *taniwha* she knows so well. Then she plants the paddle in the waves, and drives the *waka* forward, surging towards the monster.

Because when you can't run, all you have left is the fight.

CHAPTER 1

- Pandora -

"Well, what do you think? Can you do it?" Tanner demands.

Penny has hardly had time to take in the scene, let alone open her satchel and get out her sampling tape, but as to whether she'll do the work? No question. Over the past month since Sandi Kerr went on her sacrificial killing spree, the only contracts on offer have been some discreet chlamydia testing for one of the inner-city brothels and a bit of algal bloom monitoring for the local council. While the humdrum work allows her to cover the payroll, those withdrawals leave next to nothing in the coffers. Coffers. Ha! Chance would be a fine thing. Only one employee and things are that tight, she's getting close to checking the back of the sofa for spare coins. She needs the work. Desperately. Although Tanner doesn't need to know that, and nor do her parents for that matter. Heaven forbid, she could do without *that* particular lecture.

"Right now, we need the extra hands," Tanner is saying, his bellow startling an approaching jogger, who veers away in fright. "What the hell are these people doing here?" He directs his question at a couple of uniformed policemen milling near the pathologist and his technicians. "Close the ruddy park, will you? Use some common sense!" They scuttle away, like slaters from sunlight.

Tanner turns back to Penny. "My own science guys are completely swamped. This godawful heat doesn't help. Impossible to concentrate. Have you ever known it to be this fucking hot in January? At this hour?" To make his point, he picks at his shirt with his fingers, pulling the damp fabric away from his skin. Just 8:30am and the park is like a hothouse. Penny checks her watch for the temperature, then does the conversion in her head: 35°C...that would make it...308.05K.

"Can't stand the heat myself," Tanner goes on, his question obviously rhetorical. He lets his shirt droop. "Bloody awful. And this humidity! It makes everything a thousand times worse. Not to mention the speculation. The way they're telling it at the station, it's the weather that's fuelling the crime wave."

Penny nods. She's heard that, too. Among other things. According to the news media, it's our wasteful environment-polluting bourgeoisie coming back to bite us. The online tabloid, *Dish-It*—always economical with the truth—had gone a step further, proclaiming that the climate change apocalypse was upon us.

"Look at us, we're drowning in our own sweat," its news presenter had gushed only a couple of nights ago. "The worst recorded heat wave since 2032. Fresh water sources are becoming unpotable," she'd said. "Sorry, someone's talking in my ear. What's that, George? *Non*-potable. Well, I don't know, do I? Oh, OK. That was my producer, George, telling me that non-potable means our water isn't suitable for drinking. Wow, that's terrible. If you're one of those people who prefer water, then that's going to be a problem. What? The teleprompter? Oh right.… Experts agree that the increased temperatures have contributed to the unprecedented algal growth in and around the harbour area with algal mats expected to continue expanding if temperatures persist. It's symptomatic, it seems, of the ongoing eutrophication of our water courses. The lines are now open for your comments… What's that, George? You want me to keep talking? But the words are… Oh yes, well, this eutrophication is worrying, isn't it? I, for one, am interested in what our callers have to say about the Europeans' involvement in all this."

Penny had turned the report off.

It isn't just the temperature that's risen, tempers are heating up too, with people looking for someone to take their frustrations out on. Even the more respectable pundits—more respectable than *Dish-It* anyway—believe citizens are on the verge of rioting. Sensationalist reporting, but with a smidgen of truth. Penny had done an online search and found a number of studies linking a hike in temperatures to people's testosterone and adrenalin levels, with corresponding peaks in the violent crime statistics. Some of the research had pointed to associative causes, with people gathering for social activities in warmer weather, but that wasn't the whole story, because most crimes tended to occur at night.

Like this one: the victim's body discovered a little over an hour ago, in the early morning, by a passing jogger.

"The heat does tend to make people a bit crotchety," she concedes. It's an understatement. Several of Penny's neighbours have been arguing into the night. Delivery men have been more curt than usual. Even poor Cerberus has been fractious, the Labrador barking at the slightest provocation.

Penny flicks her pony tail off her neck, hoping a breath of air from the harbour might cool her.

"My department has fifteen suspicious deaths on the go," Tanner says wearily, "this one'll bring us to sixteen. Sixteen investigations! It's crazy. My go-to science consult is up to his ears in backlog."

Penny's head snaps up in spite of herself. That 'go-to consult' would be Noah Cordell, Penny's former lover, former boss. Formerly, she'd thought he was wonderful too, but that was a long time ago. Months.

"That's right, you know Cordell, don't you?" Tanner remarks. "Apprenticed to him, weren't you?"

In a manner of speaking.

"Uh-huh." She purses her lips, resists the urge to say more. It isn't professional to diss a colleague—even a dork like Noah—and he had been the one to recommend Yee Scientific to the police, which had led to Penny picking up her first solo case as lead researcher. That contract had been timely too, her little company stumbling before it got properly out of the blocks. Of course, she isn't that naïve. She knows she'd only been awarded that first case because LysisCo had rejected it—Noah was hardly magnanimous, he'd been throwing her the crumbs—but still, Penny hates being beholden to him.

If the big detective notices her discomfort, he doesn't show it. Instead, he steps up to the yellow police tape and, without stepping over it, puts his hands on his hips. Penny sidles over to join him and they take in the scene: a man in grubby clothes sprawled on a park bench, a bare foot, deathly pale, dangling.

"Well, this one doesn't look too cerebral," Tanner concludes. "You should be able to handle it. Homeless guy ODs. Happens often enough. Or maybe he rubbed someone up the wrong way and they slipped him a bad fix."

Penny's spine tingles. In science, it doesn't pay to make assumptions off the bat. That way only leads to false starts and inaccurate results. She says as much to the detective.

Grabbing his belt buckle with one hand, Tanner tugs up his pants, gazes out across the water to the Auckland skyline. The pants immediately fall back under his belly where they were a second ago. "That might be so, although I've been in this game for a while; you get a nose for these things. In my experience, if it looks like smoke, then it's probably smoke, you know?" He lifts a stubbled chin at the corpse, which is already visibly wilting in the summer heat.

"So, same deal as last time," he says with finality, even though Penny hasn't agreed to anything. "You'll operate through Clark." He inclines his head towards the constable, who's directing the sticky beaks away from the foreshore and back to the car park. "I'll expect you to keep Clark informed of any developments. You tell him, he tells me. I take it you still have his contact details?"

Penny nods. She likes Toeva Clark.

"And Ms Pandora?" Why must Tanner call her that stupid name? She hates it. Even if it *is* her given name as listed on her birth certificate, it still raises her hackles. Can't he just call her Penny, like everyone else does? Apart from her parents, of course, and Matiu, when he's trying to get a rise out of her. And Beaker, when he's flustered. And... Oh, for heaven's sake. She grits her teeth.

"Yes?"

"I hope I don't have to remind you that you are the *science consult* on this case and not a sworn-in detective inspector."

Her hackles rise. "Of course not. I—"

Tanner cuts her off with a wave of his wookie hand. "This should be an open-and-shut case, but in the event that it isn't, I don't want to hear any stories of your pretty little arse being hauled out of any burning buildings. Are we clear?"

"I couldn't help that," Penny retorts hotly, her pony tail bobbing in irritation. "We had no choice but to follow up on a legitimate lead. Going to the surgery was vital to the investigation. We—"

"You were there after hours."

"We were being conscientious!"

Tanner raises his eyebrows. "Ah yes, *we*. I forgot your brother was with you. Matiu Yee. Convicted crim." He pulls a look of distaste as if Matiu were a piece of gristle he'd just picked out of his teeth. Penny's relieved her brother isn't here right now. Thankfully, he's taken Cerberus off for a bit, the pair of them loitering at the edge of the trees on the other side of the park.

"None of that was Matiu's fault. His counsel clearly demonstrated how Hanson set him up to take the fall. Matiu wouldn't have been convicted if the witnesses hadn't been too traumatised to testify. Everyone knows they were manipulated. Matiu isn't a bad person, just impetuous and perhaps a bit easily led. In any case, he wouldn't be the first to get himself mixed up in a bad crowd and—"

"Yes, yes, I'm sure he was innocent."

Penny doesn't need a net to catch his sarcasm. She squares up, pulls her shoulders back. "Matiu's done his time, Detective, paid his debt to society. He shouldn't have to pay again because of certain people's prejudices. All my brother needs is a chance and if..."

She trails off. Tanner doesn't say a word. Come to think of it, it's been her doing most of the talking...

Damn it.

She's only fallen for a tactic straight out of the manual. Policing 101: keep schtum, let the silence yawn outwards until your interlocutor runs off at the mouth, saying things that—in their case anyway—are better left unsaid.

Stiffening, she lifts her eyes to Tanner's. She has to crane her neck because at over two metres, the man's a behemoth. "Anyway," she says with as much defiance as she can muster, "he's only my driver, and in case you haven't noticed, I don't bill you for my travel."

The detective's eyes narrow and he grunts. "So long as you keep it that way." Then, turning on his heel, he stalks off past a line of upturned dinghies in the direction of the parking area. "Remember, keep in touch," he calls without a backward glance. Penny nods anyway. She wouldn't put it past Tanner to have eyes in the back of his head.

With the detective gone, she takes a deep breath and steps over the crime scene tape.

- Matiu -

Matiu scratches his arm. It's been weeks since it stopped hurting, but the skin under his dressing still itches like hell, and the clammy heat isn't helping. The Harbour Bridge is a murky silhouette in the haze, lurking like the hump of some mythical sea monster. He drifts from one shady patch to the next, Cerberus padding at his heels, and tries not to rub himself raw. Tries not to think about how he earned this healing wound, hunting down that woman, Sandi Kerr, stepping into a place that should not be and screaming into the gaping maw of something eternal, and eternally hungry. So he drifts, floating along the line of the crime scene tape that hangs limp in the heavy, moist Auckland heat, kicking at stones and tugging Cerberus along with him.

Across the yellow tape that divides the public parkland, a swarm of cops are studying a corpse. Among them, Penny is taking evidence samples for processing back at the lab. Under no circumstances, she had told him very firmly, is he to cross the tape and approach the crime scene. Last time he did that had only led to more trouble than either of them could handle, and to be honest, he doesn't want to get dragged into anything like *that* mess again. Hell, they're not even cops, sure as shit aren't getting any danger pay for tracking down brutal criminals in a merciless underworld which Matiu has one foot in and which the police struggle to infiltrate.

So he's content to hover on the fringes of the scene and watch. There's no longer a voice in his head goading him on to do things he shouldn't. Hasn't been since that day at Hanson's farm. It had been a relief to have Makere depart, but it left Matiu with a gnawing worry as well. He saw Makere walking away, not a shadow but a form, a man. Whatever had happened between the farm and the museum basement where Matiu had stepped into that *other* place, the ghostly presence who had haunted him since childhood had taken its leave. But he doubts that means Makere is gone. Just changed, somehow.

Released?

In any case, there's now a new voice in his ear, this one lower, less articulate, and just as insistent. Cerberus growls low and rumbly as they circle the crime scene, moving from one dappled spot of shade to the next. Oddly enough, the cops hadn't wanted a dog slobbering all over their evidence, but that shouldn't have upset Cerberus. The Labrador's got it in his head that he's Penny's guardian, and he's not happy about being taken from her presence. Cerberus seems to have a sense for many of the same things Matiu does; *other* things, things that lurk in the periphery, stalk the shadows. Things that hunger.

If Cerberus is feeling unsettled, then maybe it'd be wise for Matiu to share that disquiet. If Makere were here, he'd probably be whispering to him, telling him he needs to get closer, needs to see the body, needs to touch it, look into its cold dead eyes and fall into whatever hell the poor homeless guy saw in his last mortal moments. He leans back against a tree, tugging Cerberus' leash so the dog has to settle by his feet, and closes his eyes. The heat blankets him, thick with the smell of the bloom that fills the harbour, and he just breathes.

Not so long ago, he'd realised that breathing was something he took for granted. He'd lived through moments that would haunt him forever, when his breath had tasted of cold sand and ancient horror. What he'd taken away from those few short, sharp alien breaths was the knowledge that what had gone before was only the beginning. This hot Auckland day, when some folks will be at the coast swimming in between mats of floating algae, while others are firing up a barbecue in the back yard or throwing a ball around the park, is an interlude. A calm before the storm. The deep quiet inhalation of the sea as it draws back its fist in a tsunami rage.

There's more to come. Does it start here, in the park, with some dead homeless guy? Or is this just another symptom of the sickness that runs through the population like a cancer? Another killing over drug money, or a difference of opinion over the outcome of the latest fiasco on a rugby field taken too far, or something just as ridiculous? Something itches, more than just his healing arm. A sense in the back of his skull, quieter now than it used to be yet somehow more insistent, more precise. Across the crime scene tape, something is screaming out to him to be seen.

He ignores it, keeps his eyes closed, breathes deep, and screams back at it inside his head.

- Pandora -

Making a slow circle about the bench, Penny records her observations on her phone. "January 12, 2046, 8:34am: Little Shoal Bay Reserve, North Shore. Victim is a Caucasian male, estimate mid-thirties, discovered approx. 7:15am by a jogger and phoned in to the station, stop."

Like a Raggedy-Ann doll dumped in favour of the toy of the moment, the victim is slumped face-down across the park bench, his left hand twisted beneath his hips. It almost looks as if he were holding up his trousers when he'd fallen.

She presses record again. "Jeans, business shirt—a button-down—and missing one shoe. The victim presents prone on a bench at the southwest corner beneath a…" She looks up. "…a *kōwhai* tree, stop."

Had he meant to pee against the trunk and lost his footing? Maybe he'd been drunk? He'd have to have been drunk to even *think* of desecrating a tree as graceful as this.

"Possible fall," she says. "Question alcohol, stop."

She lowers her face to the corpse and sniffs gently. She wrinkles her nose: no detectable scent of alcohol, but even over the smell of salt it's not hard to tell it's been a wee while since John Doe here enjoyed a bath.

Stepping back, Penny balances her phone on the back edge of the bench, then takes a pair of gloves from her satchel and, snapping them on, checks his scalp for contusions. Nothing obvious. She'll have to follow up later with the pathologist. Although, looking closer, his jeans appear to be bagging at the waist, and he's missing his belt, which might explain why he was holding them. Perhaps his tenure on the city's streets had caused him to lose some weight. A diet of burgers and fries scavenged from rubbish bins can do that. His skin is peeling in places too, evidence that he's been living outdoors a while. Stepping around the body again, and without touching her phone, she leans in to record the new observations.

Perhaps Tanner's right: there's nothing of interest to note. No obvious foul play anyway. Just a sad case of a homeless man taking leave of this life in a suburban park. Penny takes a moment to admire the curve of the mudflats edged with mangrove lace, the gentle slope of the boat ramp as it enters the water, and the flotsam of little craft with their brightly painted hulls in blue and orange. The seaside park is a moment of calm at the edge of the city. There are worse places to check out.

But she can't stand about day-dreaming. She needs to get on. The forensic pathologist will want the body moved soon, the heat and humidity hastening its decomposition.

Resuming her assessment, she moves closer to examine the man's face. His chin is perched on the armrest, tipped upwards to meet the sun.

Penny draws in a breath.

This is no yoga sun salutation, and nor has he gone gently into that good night. Instead, the victim's mouth is slack and gaping, and his eyes, bizarrely, are still open, gazing at her with an expression so haunting, *so fearful*, that her heart lurches.

If Penny didn't know better, she'd swear he died of fright.

She exhales gently, letting her pulse slow. "Expression of fear, stop." As soon as she's said it, she shakes her head. Tuts.

So subjective, Penny.

Successful scientific consults make objective observations, not wild conjecture based on their emotions. Nothing can be determined from the victim's facial expression. More likely, Penny's projecting her own feelings about the poor man's last moments. Extreme fear is expressed by contracture of the risorius, a muscle only found in two thirds of the population. Which means a significant minority aren't capable of pulling a frightened face. And even if he possessed the necessary musculature, filaments loosen and slacken in the moments after death and before rigor sets in.

The observation simply isn't relevant.

Using her knuckle, Penny deletes the comment from her phone. Yet she can't help but wonder: what would cause a John Doe to look like that? Pain? A bad trip perhaps? It wouldn't surprise her, not given the garbage drugs are cut with these days, and since he was likely short on cash, well…

Gently, Penny lifts the victim's free arm, already stiff. Even with the sea breezes, conditions are stifling which is accelerating the rigor process. Penny puts the death somewhere between 3:00am to 7:00am. She records her estimate. Only a ballpark at this stage. The pathologist can take the rectal temperature. She'll content herself with a glance at the exponential decay curve, thank you very much.

She moves on to examine the inside of the victim's arm. "No visible needle tracks, or evidence of adhesives," she says, loud enough to be picked up by the phone's recorder. Again, the pathologist's report should provide more detail.

Removing a roll of sampling tape from her satchel, she takes a couple of skin surface samples anyway, in case any residues are wiped away when his clothing is removed. She tucks the samples in her satchel, then lifts the victim's arm again, pulling away his shirt to look at the skin of his side and back. A tell-tale purple haze is creeping up his side. "Lividity appearing on the torso," she says. "Suggests victim died *in situ*."

"Good morning, Dr Yee."

Crouched beside the victim, Penny is holding his arm in the air. "Officer Clark," she says from under the dead man's armpit. "We have to stop meeting like this."

Clark gives her a grim smile. "We don't always meet in the best of circumstances, do we?" He stoops to bag up something that has tumbled in the grass, the movement drawing Penny's attention. It's the man's missing shoe.

Hang on, that's strange.

Lowering the victim's arm, she straightens up. "Officer Clark, if you wouldn't mind, could I take a look at that, please?"

"Of course." Clark passes her the bag. Penny turns it over, the transparent plastic crinkling. It's a loafer, in buttery-soft tan leather. She recognises the brand: Saveas. "Pretty posh shoe," she remarks, handing the evidence bag back to Clark.

"Yes, does seem an expensive choice of footwear for someone living rough," Clark muses.

"Only $3,000 a pair."

"You're kidding." Clark wipes his forehead with the back of his forearm.

"My mother got Dad a pair for Christmas. I suppose our John Doe could have got them at a charity shop. Someone's unwanted gift perhaps?"

"Or he could have stolen them."

"Or he could have stolen them."

Penny doesn't like to speak ill of the dead. Clark must feel the same because they're both quiet for a moment. Behind them, Clark's colleagues are ushering the onlookers away, their voices carrying over the quiet plop of water on the mudflats.

"At least we have an actual body this time," Clark says after a minute. He's your glass-half-full type. "It's a starting point, isn't it? Although you have to feel sorry for the poor fellow. You wouldn't wish it on your worst enemy, would you? Going like that. With no family or friends to see you off."

Penny nods. As intolerable as her family can be at times, she'd hate to die alone.

"Hey you. Come back!" This time the shouts are coming from the other side of the park. Her heart already plummeting, Penny glances up to see Matiu cross the police line to stride across the grass verge, Cerberus in tow. Speaking of family…

What the heck, Matiu. Stay out of the way!

"That's your brother, isn't it?" Clark says.

"Yes, sorry," Penny says, her face suddenly hot. "It must be important. He wouldn't cross the police line otherwise."

Not if he knows what's good for him.

"I think we're going to have to wind it up here, anyway," Clark says, waving the evidence bag towards a vehicle which has just pulled into the grounds. "The pathologist's keen to move the body, get it out of the heat."

"But I'm not quite finished—"

Already the van is backing up to the edge of the grass. The pathologist's staff, dressed in their white paper suits, surge across the site like a posse of abominable snowmen. Penny grabs her phone from the bench and she and Clark take a step back as the men in white converge on the body.

"On two. One, two."

All clinical efficiency, they flip the body over and place it on a stretcher. They're about to move off when Penny spots something.

"Wait!" she cries. "Sorry, I won't be a second. I just need to look at that hand."

Clark nods at the snowmen and they stop where they are, allowing her to approach. Penny lifts the victim's hand, the right one, the one that had been squashed under the body, turning it over and peering at the fingertips.

"Look," she says to Clark. "What do you make of this?" Two of the man's fingertips are solid blue-black, the border a straight line drawn just below the first knuckle. "Is that ink?"

"Looks like it. Maybe he had a tattoo done recently," Clark surmises. "Yes, look, there's one there; just above his wrist." Penny had nearly missed the tiny motif, the man's sleeve partly obscuring it.

The snowmen shuffle in impatience. Outside the police cordon, Matiu is signalling to her. Cerberus is riled up too, yanking at the leash and trying to get under the tape.

"Dr Yee… your brother. He seems… agitated."

She brushes the constable off. "It's fine. He can wait another minute. This tattoo isn't recent, but I think it could be significant…"

She looks again at the tattoo. Etched into the skin on the ventral surface of the man's wrist, it's circular, about the size of a roll of dental floss. Comprising several concentric central whorls, it could possibly be Māori, a stylised version of the koru, but the outer ring resembles a cog and there's a dark slash across the centre of the image which suggests an eyelid. Just an attractive design, or is it a symbol of some sort? Or an emblem? Perhaps John Doe was part of a gang, or a band of musicians? That might explain the expensive shoes, but not the ink stains on his fingers. Still, this is good: a mark like this could identify him to friends and family if he doesn't show up on any fingerprint database. That side of the case isn't her responsibility of course, but it's interesting…

Cerberus woofs.

"Dr Yee," Clark says quietly. "The pathologist would like to leave now."

Penny drops the wrist, embarrassed. She'd been in la-la land. "Oh, yes, of course." She catches Matiu's glower from the side-line. "Um… I might have to head off soon myself."

She needs more time with the body, but the snowmen are leaving, carrying their prey back to the lair. Quickly, Penny whips out her phone and, running alongside, takes a quick photo of the tattoo. It will have to do.

- Matiu -

"Come on!" Matiu stops short of the crime scene, afraid of what he might find if he gets too close. Cerberus strains against his grip, eager to get to the park bench. Muscles along the dog's back and down his legs ripple, like he's on the verge of a fight, though there are no other dogs nearby.

"What's the problem? I'm trying to work here!"

"It's Mārama. Mum called, said she's been admitted to hospital. She had a…" He glances at Clark, bites his tongue. "She's had a fall. On the bus."

"The bus?" Penny asks. "What was she doing on the bus? I didn't think she went out at all."

20

"Can we just get out of here?"

Penny's jaw tightens. She lowers her voice. "Matiu, I know how important she is to you. She's my aunty too, remember? But I have to finish processing the scene. It's what I'm being paid for. There could be important evidence and if I rush and miss something—"

"You'll never know. Guy's a bum, Penny. Tag 'em and bag 'em. We've gotta go."

Penny stamps her foot, just a little. Not so much that Clark might see, but enough that Matiu can infer she's irritated. Her next words come out through gritted teeth. "Is she dying?"

"What?"

"Seriously. Is she dying? Did the hospital call and say, 'Come quick, she's dying and you have to say goodbye because she might not be with us much longer'?"

Matiu steps back. Something's changed in Penny these last few weeks. Not surprising, given what they've been through, but still, the acid in her tone is new. "No, they—"

"Then go wait in the car, and I'll be along as soon as I'm done."

Matiu tugs at Cerberus, still straining to get a sniff at the bench. He nods slowly. "Righto. But just so you know, you're right."

Penny throws out her hands in exasperation. "Of course I am."

"About the bus."

She stops, befuddlement replacing the moment of indignant victory she'd allowed herself. "What?"

"Mārama never takes the bus. She doesn't leave the house unless one of us takes her out. Why was she on the bus, Penny?" He spins away, yanking on Cerberus' leash harder than might've been fair, and stalks back toward the carpark. He should stay, watch her back. Bad things are brewing, and they need each other. But how can she rank the death of some hobo over Mārama's well-being?

Because something's not as it seems about this apparently random death. He can feel it, just like Cerberus can, and so can she. Whatever there is to find here, they might be better off not finding it. Ignorance may be preferable to falling down the rabbit hole again. Sure as hell won't be rabbits down there.

He ducks under the yellow tape and waits.

His phone pings, a photo from Penny. *What do you make of this?* He opens the image.

An eye stares up at him from the screen, looks into him. Blinks.

He drops the phone with a cry, as something cold burns through his fingers. Cold as a winter river.

Cold as death.

CHAPTER 2

- Pandora -

No, no, no, no, no! Not right now.

She needs this case. Really needs it. And not just financially. She needs it intellectually, emotionally, and…OK, if she's really honest she wants it *vengefully*. Noah Cordell is breathing down her neck, watching and waiting for her to fail. Wouldn't he just love that? Well, damned if she's going to give him the satisfaction. She'll just have to be quick. Get the samples and get away…

Turning back to the scene, she takes out her sampling tape, preparing to process the bench seat where the John Doe's body had been. It's odd that he should die here. How many bottoms have sat on this bench in the shade of the kōwhai's dewdrop leaves? Hundreds? Thousands? It's a popular spot, if you consider the way the green park furniture is chipped and worn, its bowed wooden boards hinting at layers of white, orange, even more green paint underneath. It's as if he came here for company, so he didn't die alone.

Using a grid sampling formation, Penny takes a series of systematic swabs, finding comfort in the repetitive nature of the work. In some ways, this paint is a metaphor: pulling back the layers to reveal a crime's true form, perhaps even a perpetrator's true colours. Although, maybe Matiu's right. It's likely this is just a bag 'em and book 'em situation. Just a bum, who happens to have expired on a park bench.

She labels the tape, Matiu's glower creating a hot spot on the back of her neck, reminding her that he's waiting.

As if she didn't know.

Well, even if this is just an open and shut case as everyone seems to think, that doesn't mean she shouldn't give it her full attention. No one should die in a public park without an explanation. John Doe's family, whoever they might be, deserve that much.

Matiu will just have to wait. It won't kill him. It's only going to take her a few minutes to finish sampling the scene, half an hour at most. Besides, what could happen in half an hour? Mum's at the hospital with Whaea Mārama, and when it comes to dealing with the authorities, Kiri Yee is a force to be reckoned with. If something's going to happen, the hospital is the best place for her. It'll be nothing anyway. Just a little lapse. Some routine tests and a bit of bedrest will be all that's called for. It isn't like this is the first time Mārama's been unwell. According to Mum, Penny's aunty has been mentally unbalanced on and off for most of her adult life.

"But you should have seen her before, Pandora," Mum said once in a rare unguarded moment. "When your Whaea Mārama was young. You wouldn't think so now—to you and Matiu she's probably always seemed this…this…broken—but there was a time when my sister was the most beautiful thing you ever saw. Her laugh was like a fantail's, like a stream. The sound of her giggle: it bubbled and tinkled and chattered, and you couldn't help but be drawn to her. She was so full of life. A picture of happiness. Our grandfather used to say that even the gods envied her. I used to envy her a little myself. My own sister…"

There'd been something wrenchingly sad in her voice. Penny had wanted to reach out and touch her, but she wasn't really sure her mother had been speaking to her at all. She'd been looking at Penny, but not really. It was as if she'd been mesmerised by a water droplet forming on a fern frond. Next thing, the droplet had smashed and Mum had snapped back to her usual self, all business, scrubbing at her eyes and rabbiting on about how she needed to get Carlie to schedule services for those vehicles in the fleet still overdue for maintenance.

That's what this visit to the hospital would be, just some overdue maintenance for Mārama. A few more minutes won't hurt.

A few minutes…

She glances towards the car. Except, her brother isn't there. Instead, he's hovering outside the tape. His jaw ripples with tension and his hands on the lead are clenched white. He's even got the dog on his side, Cerberus yanking at the leather restraint and growling low in his throat.

Ah shit. Who is she kidding?

"Officer Clark." Penny steps over to where the officer is labelling the bag containing the shoe. "Can we keep a couple of uniforms here for the rest of the day?"

Placing the plastic bag into an evidence box, Clark puts the cap back on his marker pen and slips it into his breast pocket. "Hmmm," he murmurs while shaking his head theatrically. "Tanner won't be thrilled. It's all about cost-benefit with him at the minute."

"Sixteen cases…"

Clark raises his eyebrows. "Yes, and that's just this morning's count. The way things are going with this heat, we could have four more on our hands by this afternoon."

"Please. It's just…" She lowers her voice. "The thing is, I've got a bit of a personal emergency—a family member's been hospitalised."

"Oh? Why didn't you say? That's no good. No good at all. Of course you'll want to head off. I'll do what I can to extend the cordon. At least, I can call you straight away if Tanner tells me otherwise."

"You mean if he tells you to go to hell."

"Well, I wouldn't put it quite like that."

"I'm an independent, so you can blame me if you like," Penny says, snapping off her gloves.

Clark snorts. "Very brave, given that Tanner's not here, and you won't be the one giving the report."

Smiling, Penny pulls the gloves inside out and pops them in the waste section of her satchel.

"You still here?" Clark says. "Go on, off with you to the hospital."

"Um…" Penny purses her lips.

Clark sighs. "There's more?"

Penny nods. "Is there any chance you could arrange for me to examine the body later, too? At the morgue?" She looks out from under her eyelashes. Gives them a bat or two.

Clark laughs, the subterfuge not lost on him. "Boy, you ask the hard questions, Dr Yee. OK, since you've asked so nicely, I'll check with Mather, the pathologist. He's not keen on crowds in his labs, but I'll see what I can do."

"You're a lifesaver. Thank you."

"Huh. If only Mrs Clark agreed with you."

But Penny is already swinging her leg over the tape, the sampling satchel banging at her side.

- Matiu -

Penny has barely shut the door before Matiu accelerates into the service lane, past the parked cop cars.

"Slow down!" Penny protests, struggling to secure her satchel around her feet and clip her seatbelt at the same time. "This is a private service access, not a racetrack."

"Places we need to be, sister," he grumbles. *And places we need to be away from.*

"At least let me get my seatbelt on!"

Matiu relents, easing off the gas while Penny completes the process—apparently quite complicated, given the huffing and puffing and dirty looks thrown his way—of snapping her belt comfortably into place. All very precise and measured, as is Penny's way. "You done?"

She glowers. "Yes, I am."

"Good." He floors it, the engine howling as the Commodore whips around the narrow, winding lane. Penny grips the dash.

"Oh, that's just excellent, Matiu. Way to leave an impression of unflappable professionalism when departing a crime scene. Have I told you how much I appreciate your dedication to helping make Yee Scientific Consultancy a successful business venture with your amazing PR skills?"

"We're in a hurry."

"Not impressed, little brother."

Matiu holds up a hand, grinding his teeth. He needs to be away from this place, this bright open garden of life and vitality corrupted by something dark, dangerous. Tainted with the stink of murder, and worse.

Penny's mouth forms a small 'o' of indignation. "Don't give me that 'talk to the hand' BS, buster."

"Shoosh, I'm ringing." He taps the phone in its holder to receive the call. "Erica," he says, turning on his warmest, fuzziest voice. "Are we still on for this afternoon?"

"Hello, Matiu. Just calling to make sure you *remembered*. Since you've *forgotten* the last two appointments we had booked."

Matiu purses his lips. "I didn't forget, I just had things come up. Busy-busy, you know how it is. Gotta keep the clients happy to keep the job to stay out of trouble with all the wrong kind of people. We've talked about this, sweetie."

"Don't call me that. It's inappropriate and it pisses me off. You don't want to piss me off. Be here today, Matiu. Or my recommendation to the Board will be that you need a little more time deprived of personal freedoms in order to learn some respect for authority."

"That's a bit harsh, don't you think? I'm holding down a job. Not getting into any trouble. That should speak for itself. No need to worry."

"Really? Then how come your name has cropped up on no less than two police reports which have crossed my desk in the last two months? Cases of property destruction and suspicious death? That sort of thing *worries me*, Matiu. A lot. I think it's time we had a very clear discussion about what is and is not appropriate behaviour for an ex-convict in your situation."

"That's not fair. I wasn't the culprit in those cases, I was an innocent bystander in the wrong place at the wrong time. If anything, I was trying to help."

"You were *involved*. That's enough. I don't want to hear that you're involved in anything more than an argument with your shoelaces when they won't do up nicely. Got it? I'll see you at 1 o'clock." She cuts the call.

"Bitch." Up ahead, the carpark barrier arm raises slowly at their approach. Matiu scans the few other cars in the lot. It's become a habit of late, always looking over his shoulder. Probably from a lifetime of doing so, and there always having been something there. Now there's nothing he can see or feel, but it doesn't ease his disquiet.

"You really need to stay on her good side."

"That's because without me to drive you around, your business is sunk."

"Yes, Matiu. That's why. Not because you're my brother and I'd prefer it if you stayed out of jail."

Matiu pulls onto the street. There aren't many cars around, as usual. Only the rich or the powerful can afford to drive for pleasure. Penny's just lucky their parents happen to run transport operations for the government and can afford the fringe benefit of allowing Matiu a car to shuttle her about from job to job, so long as he can still make important pickups for clients when need be. Really, he's a glorified taxi driver, but he doesn't let that niggle him. Not like the niggle he got going through the carpark. There was something familiar back there, but between Erica in his ear and Penny on his back, he can't quite place it.

As he eases the Commodore around a bend, there's a flicker of movement in the rear-view mirror. Another car on the deserted streets? A grey Ford Mustang, maybe? There was one in the carpark. Now that he thinks about it, it looked a lot like the one he and Simon Kingi rebuilt back when they used to work for Hanson. Matiu grimaces. He hasn't seen Si for a while. Be glad if he never does. Simon Kingi was one of those guys you could pretty much guarantee you'd get into trouble with if you ever got on the turps together, fuse shorter than a bee's dick and all testosterone and flying fists at the drop of a hat. Matiu earned himself a lot of scars and a few collars running with Simon Kingi. Hanson got Kingi in line, though. Took all that potential rage and channelled it for... Well, not for good, but certainly for profit. Polished that rough bastard up until he was all sharp and vicious. The thought spikes a chill through him. What happens to a guy like Simon Kingi when there's no Hanson in the picture? So much tightly wound anger, and no one to direct it. There's a recipe for trouble, right there.

Sweeping around another corner, Matiu glimpses the other car, still tailing them. Coincidence? He hopes so. It's a short drive from the North Shore to Greenlane Hospital, maybe twenty minutes following the motorway south, and he doesn't want any trouble. Not today.

Penny's phone rings, and she answers with a roll of her eyes. "Hi, Dad."

Matiu grins. If he had to choose between Simon Kingi with a wasp up his arse, or a phone call from Dad, he'd take Kingi any day of the week.

- Pandora -

"Pandora. Good," Dad's voice booms through the speakerphone. "I've got you at last. I don't appreciate not being able to contact you when I need you. This is the third message I've left this morning." Penny checks her screen where three angry red blips indicate missed calls.

Oops. She'd assumed those blips had been from Matiu.

"Ignoring calls is the height of bad manners," Dad rants. "A sign of disrespect."

In the driver's seat, Matiu sniggers.

"But Dad, I was at—"

"Your mother and I need to be able to get hold of you in an emergency."

An emergency. Penny's stomach turns to tofu. It has to be Mārama. What other emergency is there? She steals a sideways glance at Matiu. His smirk has melted away, leaving only tight-lipped tension. Even his tatts look sharper. She should have come straight away. She'd known Matiu was agitated, deduced it from his body language when he'd stalked across the park. Even the bloody dog had been trying to send her a message—all that straining and tugging on the lead. And yet, she'd put her work first.

Fat lot of use having highly tuned observation skills, Penny, if you're going to ignore the cues.

Penny prays nothing happens to Mārama. It mustn't. It would break Matiu: they're so close, their relationship as fragile as a single thread of a spider's silk and yet weight-for-weight, stronger than steel. Her brother lives his life balanced on that thread. If anything has happened to Mārama…

Feeling as heartsick as Thomas Midgely—that is, if the wretched inventor were able to look back—Penny keeps her voice even for Matiu's sake. "Dad, is this about Whaea Mārama? Have you heard someth—"

Dad cuts her off. "Are you with your brother?" he says sharply.

"Yes. Matiu's right here. We're in the fleet car. Here, let me bring you up on screen and that way you'll be able to see us."

Matiu's head snaps round, his pupils blacker than Dad's bank balance. He makes a couple of quick throat slashing gestures.

As it turns out, they can make all the rude gestures they like because Dad isn't interested in eyeballing his children right now, "No, no video feed, please Pandora," he says. "Speakerphone only. I'm in negotiations—tricky ones—I've only stepped away briefly. Certain guests get a bit jittery around recording devices. They prefer to remain anonymous. At least, until we know the outcome. I just wanted to be sure you were on your way."

"To the hospital? Yes, we're heading there now."

"Good, good. You should support your mother. Seems things with your aunt have taken a nasty turn. Is that you in fleet car 55?"

"Yes, sir," Matiu replies, looking over his shoulder to check the blind spot.

"Well, what are you doing turning off there? You've gone and missed the motorway on-ramp."

"Caught sight of a bit of congestion up ahead," Matiu says, his voice tight. "Thought I'd avoid it. Make better time."

Penny frowns. Congestion. What's he on about? The road's clear.

"It's not showing on my feed," Dad replies, clearly not seeing it either.

"It just happened," Matiu says. "Too soon to show on any agency feeds."

What just happened?

Cerberus thrusts his doggy snout into the gap, his paw poised on the console. Penny pushes him back.

"Off, Cerberus," she whispers.

Rambunctious laughter sounds, followed by Dad's voice, too muffled to hear. He comes back on the line. "I have to go. Get to Greenlane: don't stuff about," Dad says. "Tell your mother I'll be there as soon as I can."

"Bye, Dad," Penny says. "Hope the talks…" She trails off. Dad has already closed down the call.

Matiu sighs. "You're such a try-hard, Penny, you know that?"

"Shuddup." She swats him with the back of her hand. "And don't change the subject. What's going on? Why are we going this way?" she asks as Matiu ducks down a side street.

"We're being followed." He tilts his head, indicating the rear.

"We are not."

"Dark grey Mustang, rolled-down windows."

"Oh for crying out loud, Matiu, we are not being followed. You can't help yourself, can you? So I'm the lead scientific consult on a case: it's my *job*. Quit making out like I'm some B-list crime show detective. Didn't you hear Dad use words like 'emergency' and 'Mārama'? Stop dicking around. We need to get to the hospital."

"Check the side mirror, sis. About a block back. I think you'll find the guy in the passenger seat is a Simon Kingi. Prize badass. One of Hanson's lot."

Penny closes her eyes. Opens them again. "*Pleeease* tell me there is no gangster tailing us. I don't believe it. You promised us that was all over. No wonder Erica's on your case. Come on, out with it. What did you do?"

"I didn't do anything," Matiu splutters. "Why assume it's anything to do with me? He's following us. Both of us. This car!"

Penny shakes her head. "He can't be."

Matiu snorts. "Well, he is, and he's been on our arses ever since the cops tipped your John Doe into a body bag."

"Don't be crass. That was a person."

"A person of some interest to Kingi from the looks of it."

Penny folds her arms. "That's ridiculous. I don't even know why we're having this conversation. The person in that car looks like someone you know—"

"And drives the exact same car."

"Drives a *similar* car."

"Exactly the same car. I ought to know, I helped the bastard rebuild the engine block, back in the day."

Aargh. He is *so* annoying. Then again, his Mārama was rushed to hospital this morning and Matiu has never been great at expressing himself. She softens her voice. "Look, it's a coincidence, OK? He just happens to be going the same direction as us."

Turning the Commodore into a side street, Matiu arches an eyebrow.

"It's *possible*," she insists.

Matiu shakes his head.

Well, there's a way to find out.

Leaning to her left, Penny puckers up, making showy fish-kisses at herself in the wing mirror.

"What are you doing?"

"Shhh." She snaps off a photo, then feeds the image into the facial recognition app on her phone. "I'm going to prove to you that the person in the car behind us is just a regular citizen going about his business. Someone who happens to look like your King-pin fellow. Then we'll know for sure, won't we?" She taps the screen. "It's a bit grainy, but it shouldn't take long... it's searching now..."

The results appear. Penny purses her lips.

"Well?" Matiu demands.

"I guess the photo was too grainy."

"Let me look."

"No, it's fine. It was a long shot, anyway. The accuracy of these things is marginal at best. Relies on the acuity of the image..."

"Penny, give me the damn phone!"

She tilts her shoulders away from him, but he leans over and yanks it from her hand. He checks the screen. "What do you know? Simon Kingi," he says wryly.

"It might not be him. There's a margin of error—"

"In his prison uniform. I'd know those dreadlocks anywhere."

Penny wishes she could stop the tremor in her knees.

- Matiu -

What the bleeding hell? Why would Kingi suddenly be following him? To be honest, Matiu can think of any number of reasons, but none of them make any sense. Not since he got away from that crowd. He's got nothing to offer them, owes them nothing. Didn't steal from them. Sure as shit can't sell them anything. Therefore, whatever Kingi wants, it probably has to do with the stiff in the park. Which is disturbing. "He was waiting, in the car park. It's a shakedown."

"Matiu. No more drama. Let's just get to the hospital." She can't conceal the quiver in her voice.

"You're a civilian, a weak point. There's something about this case they want, and you're the way in." He's not sure about that, but it's the sort of reasoning that'll make Penny zip up and let him do what he needs to do. He swings around another suburban corner and hits the gas. Damn it! Now he needs to be on the motorway. Needs the open road, space to put between himself and the Mustang. He throws the Commodore into a hard turn, tyres screeching as the back end fishtails.

"Matiu!" Penny shouts, as she holds on for all she's worth.

"What? You've got your seatbelt on." Another hard corner, and Matiu smirks in triumph as he checks the mirror. Clear, so far. Still, he doesn't slow down. Two more screeching corners, the car thrumming under his palms as it tears up the streets like the performance vehicle it is. Even on biofuel, the engine still growls like a trooper. Despite the comparable power of the Mustang on his tail, Kingi will probably be running a poorer quality fuel than the good stuff Dad sources for the fleet.

Hurtling around another corner, Matiu lines up the onramp. He races towards the motorway, the suspension creaking as he hits the ramp and enters the southbound lanes.

"Matiu!" Penny says, her eyes wide as she looks in the side mirror. "Behind us!"

He glances back. The Mustang fishtails around the last corner, a cloud of black smoke billowing off its tyres as it straightens up and races towards the onramp. "Damn," he mutters. "Damn and fuck and damn."

The Commodore climbs the arching ramp and swoops down onto an open curve of motorway, the harbour muddy green to the left, and Matiu lets the car roar. A horrific waste of fuel, he knows, but letting Simon Kingi catch up is not an option.

There's hardly any traffic on the motorway, as is typical. Matiu swerves around a smoky delivery truck and speeds towards the bridge. All four southbound lanes are clear up ahead, with a row of reflective barriers running down the centre where the additional two lanes were clipped onto the bridge in the 1960s, hanging off the side of the towering arches which run red with corrosion and neglect. The Commodore gathers speed, the safety rails blurring. Matiu glances back. Kingi's undertaking the lorry, then he swerves right. Crap. In a dead run downhill, neither car will have an advantage. Matiu won't be able to shake Kingi unless something on the Mustang breaks, which you'd expect under normal circumstances because it's a Ford, but in this instance, when it really matters, probably not.

"Matiu! What are we going to do?"

"In the dash there's an old tablet I was going to reprogramme for music. Grab it out." He veers the car to the left, and winds his window down. Wind howls through. Kingi stays in the right lane, trying to come alongside.

"A tablet? Why?"

"Questions later. Right now, help me get this homicidal maniac off our tail!"

"We don't know he's homicidal," Penny mutters, but rummages around until she finds the tablet, its black touchscreen dark. "Now what?" She puts it in his outstretched right hand. "Are you going to video this for the police? Why not just ask me to do it?"

One shot. Matiu has to balance pulling this off with not having Penny screech in alarm and try to stop him. He weighs the tablet in his palm, flat and sleek; remembers times gone by, years ago, down by the sea, skipping stones. Weighing the good stones, the smooth and flat, those that would hit the water and just keep bouncing. Rushing air is a lot like water, right? Just up ahead, the soft reflective barriers end and the rusted arches rise up between the second and third lanes.

He eases off the gas suddenly, watches Kingi swell in the wing mirror. Then he yanks the wheel to the right, and for a second he's got a view of the Mustang's grill alongside, and the tablet leaves his hand, spinning. The Commodore slices between the barriers, clipping one which bends and snaps back into place as he passes. Cerberus skids off the back seat and into the footwell, yelping. Matiu whips back to the left before he hits the concrete centre rail, tyres screeching as he finds the car's centre of gravity and accelerates away. The arches scroll skyward, in between the Commodore and the Mustang.

"Matiu! You..."

He checks the mirror. The Mustang swerves, weaving like a drunk, the windscreen shattered into an opaque spiderweb of fine cracks. He smirks. There's an offramp on the far side of the bridge, which will lead them into the maze of central Auckland. He can lose him down there.

Penny glares at him. "Matiu, that was very dangerous! You might've caused an accident. You're going to get us killed!"

Matiu groans. "Seriously, sister? Look, I—" But when he checks the mirror again, the words die on his lips. Looks like someone's kicking out the smashed windscreen, and the Mustang is closing the gap. "Fuck's sake." Matiu hits the gas, one eye on the broken asphalt ahead and one on the car screaming up behind. He hadn't seen anyone else in the car. How can Kingi be holding down the gas and kicking out the window at the same time? "Hold on," he mutters, and drops a gear. The engine shrieks, pulling revs the delicate biofuel was never intended to create. Matiu ignores the climbing temperature gauge. Organic oil, not designed for this sort of shit. Still, it gives him a momentary boost, and he veers around a rusty orange sedan. The Mustang drops back, the windscreen spilling out onto the motorway in a rain of shattered glass. In the mirror, Matiu sees something misshapen writhe, twist, though it's hard to get a good view inside the Mustang with the steel framework of the arches blurring past between them.

Then the arches are gone, sinking back into the bridge. In both directions,

Waitemata Harbour spreads out in a hot, hazy murk. Matiu slams the gearstick back up. The offramp is close, closer.

There's a bang, followed by a horrible flapping noise. The steering wheel jumps in his hands, and the car slews uncontrollably left, back through the reflective barriers which snap and clatter along the car's belly. Grunting with the effort, Matiu corrects towards the centre of the road, but the car is grinding along on a shredded tyre, most steerage gone, his speed evaporating.

"Fuck. Fuck!" Matiu would slam the steering wheel, if he could afford to let go of it. Sparks flying from the front left wheel rim, the car careens across the left lane and into the safety rail. Penny covers her face, right as the passenger airbag bursts and she vanishes behind it. Cerberus howls.

Matiu hits the brakes, and the car has barely stopped before he's out the door.

Kingi skids across the lanes around in a cloud of black smoke, back end sweeping around, coming to rest facing the crippled Commodore. The orange sedan swerves around the Mustang, horn blaring.

Matiu wrenches the boot open, hunting for what's buried in the bottom. Maybe not as good as a shotgun, but for someone like Kingi, good enough. A crowbar will still break bones if he needs it to.

The Mustang's door opens and Kingi steps out, but it's not Kingi, it's... something else. Something with more limbs, more appendages than there should be. Matiu flashes back on Hanson, all sinuous shadows in the dark of the room that smelled of death, but this is broad daylight, the middle of Auckland Harbour Bridge, and there's Simon Kingi striding towards him, with two, maybe four, maybe more tentacles twisting out of his back. And his eyes, black pits. Grinning.

Cerberus barrels across the road, charging straight at him, a snarl curling from between bared teeth. Kingi swings a boot and sends the dog skittering over the asphalt.

"Cerberus!" Matiu shouts, but then all thought of the dog is stripped away. The smoky delivery truck tries to swerve, but it's going too fast. Matiu flinches, ducks, as the lorry collects both Kingi and the front end of the Mustang. Simon hurtles backwards, up and over the safety rail, a smashed tangle of limbs, and vanishes over the side of the bridge, while the Mustang spins around twice, a whirlwind of shattered metal and glass. The truck screeches to a stop in a haze of diesel fumes and hot brakes.

Matiu breathes. Dimly he hears Penny, yelling something incoherent as she practically falls out of the car. The Commodore's a mess. Hell of a time they're going to have explaining this to the depot, aren't they? No matter. Matiu knows some people who can sort it out. Polish it up good as new. Never mind that someone was trying to kill them. That Simon Kingi is probably dead. That Simon Kingi was *not* Simon Kingi.

Never mind that it's not over.

CHAPTER 3

- Pandora -

The Commodore slams into the barrier. Sparks fly and the passenger side airbag bursts, enveloping her. There's the grinding shriek of metal on metal as Penny's door scrapes against the barricade. The shrill goes on and on. Still going. The note pulses in the back of her teeth. Penny holds her breath, swathed in the deflating airbag. Clamps her mouth closed. She covers her eyes and waits for the burn.

Matiu brakes hard and she's thrown forward, then whiplashes back as her seatbelt snaps taut. Cerberus howls, but Penny can do nothing for him.

There's an awful interminable moment of stillness…

The car jerks to a standstill and they're engulfed in a swathe of black smoke, the stench of burning rubber hot in her nostrils.

Penny exhales. Inhales again.

It's OK. I'm OK. We're not dead. Matiu stopped us. Her heart pounds on her chest wall as if it wants out.

"Matiu—"

But Matiu has flung open the door and is already diving out of the car. A horn blares. Cerberus clambers forward, Penny sandwiched between the airbag and the dog's flank. Cerberus' claws scritch on plastic in his scrabble to get over the console. Suddenly, he's in the driver seat and the lead is trailing past her. She makes a grab for it, but, fighting to get free of the billowing parachute, she clutches at air. "Cerberus, no!"

There's a thump on the back of the car. Matiu? What's he doing? The fuel crisis means there are fewer cars nowadays. Once upon a time, cars would be bumper to bumper on this bridge, authorities altering the lane directions over the day just to cope with the traffic flow. But it's still the motorway, fewer cars doesn't mean Matiu couldn't get hit. You're supposed to move away from a vehicle after an accident in case your car's rear-ended. Her blood runs cold with suspicion. What's in the car boot? A gun? Hanson's gun? No, that can't be right. Hanson's gun was bagged up and put in police storage after the ruckus at the museum. Besides, Matiu knows if he's caught with a firearm he'll be marched straight back to prison.

But if Kingi's still after them, and Matiu has a gun…

She has to get out! But this blasted airbag has her cornered. Penny can't see a thing. Desperate, she fumbles with her seatbelt, her fingers tripping on the clasp. The airbag's everywhere, in her face, like a cloud of cotton candy.

Come on, come on!

Hands shaking, she grasps blindly. At last, the belt clicks open. Penny gasps in relief. She gives the airbag a final push and clambers over the console, all hands and knees.

Through the angle of the open door, she gets her first look at the accident, at the Mustang. Facing back towards them, it appears untouched, aside from the smashed windscreen. Cerberus is already across the road, snapping at the car door, baring his teeth and growling. A car whooshes by in a streak of colour, blocking the Mustang and the dog from view. Penny cringes. Cerberus! He's going to get run over. The road clears and the door of the Mustang swings open. Is that Kingi? A foot descends. Cerberus is going berserk, barking and snarling, trying to hurl himself at Kingi. Kingi barely notices him. In a flash, he kicks out, sending Cerberus flying against the barriers. Cerberus bashes the barrier and slumps to the ground in a heap of golden doggy fur, stunned.

No!

But she hasn't got time to worry about Cerberus because Kingi is coming. He's crossing the road. *Coming for Matiu. For me.*

Panic hits. Her heart lurches. Goes into palpitations, shot full of 4,5-β-trihydroxy-N-methylphenethylamine. She can't get free. Her foot is caught on the console. Penny kicks back to free herself. In the end, she practically falls out of the car. One foot on the tarmac, she puts a hand on the door frame to steady herself and gets a flash of Cerberus, against the barriers and getting to his feet, and of Kingi, still coming.

Black eyes…

Whump! A truck hurtles past and he's gone. Brakes scream, or maybe it's her screaming, and all she can think is Cerberus could be under the wheels.

Penny and Matiu wait for the traffic to pass before dashing across the road.

Matiu goes after Cerberus, who has recovered from the kick and is 100 metres down the road, in the direction of the city, rushing back and forth at the railing. Penny can hear him howling from here. The poor baby's beside himself with fright, but at least he hasn't been bowled away by a passing vehicle.

Not like Kingi.

But where is the man? Where did he go? Penny's sick with worry. Kingi's a bad egg, there's no doubt about that, but to have caused his death? Penny doesn't want to think about it. She scans the roadway. Further along, the truck—Wyatts Couriers, marked on the rear doors—has limped over to the median and out of the way. No sign of Kingi on the road. Could he have gone over the side?

Quickly, Penny leans over the edge. The pedestrian SkyPath is slung under the clip-ons, its transparent ceiling allowing pedestrians to observe panoramic views of the harbour and the city, as well as the bridge's construction. There'd been talk of removing the Japanese clip-ons, the lack of road user revenue not justifying maintenance of the 1960s relics, but the 2020 SkyPath addition had become a public favourite that, given the cost of scrapping the extra lanes, the Council had voted to leave well enough alone.

Mid-morning and there are several people on the scenic walk. Below Penny, a woman carrying a toddler gazes upwards at the girders supporting the century-old structure. Another day Penny might have waved at the baby, but today she's intent on scanning the SkyPath for a sprawled body, or a crack or tell-tale splotch of blood which would indicate where Kingi might have bounced off the Perspex before falling 43 metres into the sea. Nothing, and the pedestrians don't seem perturbed either. Wait! The toddler is grabbing at his mother's chin, demanding she look. Has he seen something? Penny follows his finger.

He's pointing at Cerberus. The mother smiles. Penny reads her lips: "Doggie."

Straightening, Penny turns and looks back the way they came. Kingi isn't on the SkyPath and he definitely isn't on the road. Which leaves only one place: he must be plastered to the front of the truck.

Like a fly.

An image flashes into her head, of Kingi's bones smashed, his organs splattered across the fender, black eyes staring. Penny's legs sag. She grasps the rail. She isn't hurt. At least, she doesn't think so. Just the body's normal response to shock. And she hasn't had a chance to look at the front of the truck yet.

The cars have slowed. Rubberneckers hoping to see some blood. A couple of Good Samaritans have pulled over and are erecting orange safety cones the ones they give away at service stations—around the crash vehicles.

Still grappling with Cerberus, Matiu joins her at the railing. It's all he can do to hold the Lab in check. Penny sinks her hands into Cerberus' fur and kneads gently, hoping to calm herself as much as the dog. "Matiu, did you see where he went?" Even to her, her voice sounds thin. "Kingi? After the truck hit him?"

As if she didn't already know.

"It didn't hit him." He gazes out over the ocean.

"What? Matiu, no. It hit him. I saw it."

"Must have just clipped him," Matiu says, gazing out to the horizon. "It all happened pretty fast. I saw him run off down the motorway."

On the road shoulder, the truck driver is approaching, weaving as if he were drunk.

Rushing over to meet him, Penny gives him the once-over as she nears: his overalls—Wyatt Couriers embroidered on the breast patch—are solid red, so any injuries would be hard to pick up. No sign of anything major. Nothing external anyway. "Are you OK?"

"What the hell just happened?" the driver blurts. "Why was that guy on the road? He had... he had..." His face pales. The walk from the truck has been too much for him. He leans heavily against the railing, then plops bodily to the ground, one shoulder jammed against the concrete. He's about to get up again, but Penny drops to a crouch and puts a hand on his arm. "You know, I think... sorry, what's your name?"

"Chand."

"You know, Chand, I think you should stay where you are," she says. "The ambulance will be here soon and we can get you checked out. Our vehicle has instant HELP."

Matiu's head whips around.

"They have to come," Penny explains. "My airbag deployed." She turns back to Chand. "Do you remember what happened?" Well, they can hardly leave him. He's in shock. And since they have to wait for the ambulance, she may as well find out what he knows.

Chand clutches at his knees, rocking gently. "He was in the middle of the road. Just stepped out of nowhere. I... I hit him."

"I don't think so. You can't have. My brother says he ran off."

"I hit him. There was a thud." He drops his head into his hands and starts to blubber. "Oh jeez, I'll lose my job, my licence."

"Nah, you're fine, mate," Matiu says. "The guy took off down the road."

"See?" Penny says gently. "No harm was done. If you'd hit him, he'd still be on the road. Take a look. There's no one."

Chand lifts his head. Watery eyes stare out over the road.

"His back, there were... tentacles..."

Tentacles? Penny shivers, but, still holding on to Cerberus, and out of Chand's line of sight, Matiu draws a little circle in the air with his index finger. Mouths the word, "Loco."

Penny nods. He's probably right. The man isn't making any sense. Halloween was months ago. He has to be concussed. Only, he doesn't look confused. Slumped against the rail, his body crumpled in on itself, the look he gives her is one of pure fear.

"He was there," Chand babbles, his voice quiet. "I hit him. Smacked right into him. Anyone else would have died. But not him." He shudders. "Tentacles... he had *tentacles*. On the road... I swear I saw... a demon!"

Penny glances along the road. Someone's coming.

Chand's right. It's definitely a demon.

Penny stands up to meet him. "Detective Tanner."

"What are you doing here?" Tanner says, signalling to his off-siders to deal with the traffic.

Penny lifts her chin. "I could ask you the same thing. I didn't think traffic was your brief."

Tanner smiles. "Touché, Dr Yee."

"Matiu and I were first on the scene."

No one was hurt. That's the main thing. If Matiu's being dragged back into a bad scene, Dad will get injunctions slapped everywhere. On everyone. There's no way Matiu's going back to prison. So, there's no reason to tell Tanner any more than necessary.

The detective looks at her shrewdly. "You mean, you caused the accident."

"We…we…"

Tanner doesn't wait for an answer. He stalks up the road towards the Mustang. Penny throws Matiu a don't-you-dare-interfere glance and follows the detective. Tanner doesn't muck around and Penny's forced to add in a little run-skip every second or third step to keep pace. "No point denying it," Tanner declares. "I've already viewed the bridge CCTV—saw it on the way here. Looked to me like your brother was playing boy racers with the Mustang. A game of chicken. Seeing who had the biggest balls."

Penny's about to protest, but the ambulance passes, the blare of its siren making conversation impossible. When it has pulled in and two paramedics in Hi-Viz yellow are attending to Chand, Tanner continues, "I asked you why you were here. Shouldn't you still be with Clark at Little Shoal Bay Reserve? Better yet, you could be back in that lab of yours, already analysing the case samples."

Penny bites her bottom lip. "I've had to step away for an hour on a personal matter: my mother's sister has had a—"

"Mummy called, did she?"

Penny's face burns.

"Ah. Not Mummy: it was Daddy then." Tanner has met Penny's parents, but it wouldn't have mattered if he hadn't: her father's fleet is well known in the city.

"…medical emergency…" she trails off.

Tanner slows his stride. He fiddles with the button of his shirt pocket. "Sorry," he says curtly. "I didn't know." Penny nods. When he goes on, she imagines his voice is softer. "I expect you'll want to get away, then. Before you do, can you give me a quick heads up about what happened?" He leans in to look through the Mustang's shattered windscreen. Tiny blocks of glass litter the seats.

So much for only telling him what's necessary.

"This vehicle followed us from outside Little Shoal Reserve."

Tanner circles the vehicle, looking through the windows. "You're sure about that?"

"Yes, I am. Matiu noted the vehicle's make and colour before we left. He suspected we were being followed and took a convoluted course. They were definitely following us. When they knew they'd been spotted, they tried to run us off the road."

"They?"

"He. A man."

"Someone trying to impede the investigation? I'll have Clark check the Mustang's plates. Did you see what happened to the driver?"

"The courier truck hit him—just clipped him, Matiu said—and the driver ran off back towards town."

"Wyatt Couriers." Tanner cranes his neck to read the back of the truck. "Their guy should be able to fill in the gaps, then."

Penny shrugs. "Actually, I don't think he remembers much. Too shocked." They look over to the rail where, like a couple of Christmas baubles on either side of a candy cane, the two paramedics are helping Chand into the ambulance.

Penny searches the road for Matiu, finds him back on the far side of the bridge, changing the tyre on the Commodore. Cerberus is in the front seat, his paws on the dash. He pushes his muzzle into the windscreen, as if trying to tell Penny something. Probably 'get a hurry on'. At least he doesn't appear to have suffered too much from the kick. What kind of a monster kicks a dog anyway?

"I'll have uniforms look at the CCTV again," Tanner says, pulling Penny back to the moment. She has something else to ask him.

"Detective? Our John Doe, and now this. Is there a chance the death could be gang-related?"

"It's possible. Most serious crime in the city is. The gangs have their fingers in a few pies."

"Hmmm."

Tanner kicks at the Mustang's crumpled registration plate with the toe of his boot. "Why? You have some special reason to think a gang might be involved?" His phone rings. He turns away from Penny while he answers it. Runs a hand through his hair. "Tanner. Fuck. Another one?"

While he's speaking, Penny hunts out the image of the tattoo on her phone. She waves it in front of his face. Still on his call, Tanner holds her hand steady a second, then shakes his head. She puts the phone back in her pocket.

Waiting on Tanner, Penny walks the length of the Mustang again, taking care not to step in the glass on the roadway. Most of the windshield is gone, but the circumference is still rimmed in shattered glass, like salt crystals on a margarita glass. She peers into the car, careful not to cut herself on the jagged edges. That's when she sees the dark smudge, a tiny smear on a diamond of glass. Blood? Looks that way. It has to be Kingi's. A scrape caused when he pushed out the windscreen. If it is, and the Little Shoal samples include similar samples, that would put Kingi at the scene and not simply loitering in the carpark. It would put Matiu in the clear.

She looks over at Tanner. Facing away, towards the ambulance, the detective is still on the phone. Quickly, slipping the spare piece of sampling tape out of her shirt pocket, she dabs it on the edge of the glass, folding the tape over to ensure its integrity. Then she tucks it back in her pocket.

Tanner's winding up his conversation. "Where? Nah, nah, tell him I'll meet him there," he bellows. "Send the co-ordinates to my vehicle. Yeah, I'm leaving now." He rings off, sliding the device into his pocket, then points to Penny's phone. "That design's new to me. Doesn't mean it isn't a gang patch." He grunts. "Hey, I have an idea. Why don't we ask your brother? He's better connected than both of us."

"This has nothing to do with Matiu."

But Tanner is already striding away towards his vehicle. "Let's hope not, Dr Yee."

- Matiu -

Matiu cinches the last wheelnut tight, and whistles quietly. Took him almost four minutes to change the tyre. Was a time when he could jack, block and strip all four tyres off a car in two minutes flat. Sort of shit him and Kingi used to pull, in fact. Two guys, a ute, a couple of jacks and a hand-compressor. But to be fair, he never used to put the tyres back on. That's the bit that takes the time.

Sweat runs down his back, drips off his forehead. Looks like Penny's got the cops tied up for the moment, and Cerberus is safely out of the way in the car, with the windows cracked so he doesn't parboil in the heat. Tossing the jack and the tyre iron into the boot with the shredded tyre, he crosses to the rail, casts his eye over the harbour. More bloody police tape, stretched out around the Mustang and the truck. Damn it. Matiu sure would like to get a closer look at the safety rail, where he saw Kingi go over the side. Did he go into the harbour? Smash apart when he hit the water?

Matiu glances down. There's a Chinese kid in the covered walkway, staring back up. Not at him, not quite. Eyes wide, mouth open. His olds are ignoring him, lost in whatever it is wealthy Asian tourists talk about while they take photos of the slush we call Waitemata Harbour. The kid's looking at the underside of the bridge.

Despite the heat, a chill goes through Matiu. He saw Kingi go over that rail, he *knows* he did, those black tentacles whirling about him as he tumbled through the air.

Tentacles. Like a fucking octopus. What's the chance those things on his back whipped out and snatched at the rail, caught him before he fell, lowered him down, and he's still there, hanging, lurking. Waiting for shit to go quiet so he can take his shattered ribcage somewhere to get stitched up. Matiu can picture him there, broken limbs hanging useless, blood leaking from torn skin, and those appendages, something *other*, sprouted from him like tumours, like...parasites. Clinging to him. Keeping him alive.

He fights the urge to duck under the tape and go look closer. Nope. Best thing he can do is get the hell away. He turns and strides back towards the car. "Penny, come on. We're out of here." Cerberus turns around twice and settles in the back as Matiu throws himself into the driver's seat and guns the engine. Pulling away from the barrier slowly, with a shriek of metal on metal, he noses the car around the edge of the police cordon. Penny hurries over, waving at him, and he slows down almost to a stop. Almost. Penny grabs the door handle and jerks at it, but the door catches, bent panels jamming against each other. Matiu jerks a finger over his shoulder. "Hop in the back."

"What? Have you seen how much room that dog takes up?"

"Can't sit in the front 'til we've cleaned up the airbag anyway."

Glowering, Penny yanks open the back door and slides in, squeezing alongside the Labrador who doesn't seem inclined to make any extra room for her. "Don't you think the police might want to inspect our vehicle before we leave the scene?" she asks, fumbling to clip her seatbelt around the dog's bulk.

"No-one's telling us to stay, sister, so we ain't staying. We're not inside the police tape."

"We were involved in an incident!"

"And the sooner the cops get the road cleared, the happier everyone'll be. If anyone wants to check out the car, they've got your number." Waving to the uniform assigned to manage traffic flow, Matiu eases out into the fourth lane, the only one still clear for vehicles.

"Matiu—"

"Pandora. We've got places to be."

A hundred metres down the road, the other lanes open up. Matiu veers left and accelerates, putting the bridge behind them. It recedes in the rear view, like a *taniwha* sinking into the harbour.

"Seriously, Matiu. Why?"

"Why what?"

"Why was your old mate Simon Kingi waiting for us in the car park? Why did he try to run us off the road?"

Matiu stares straight ahead, chewing the inside of his cheek. "You need to find out who your dead guy was mixed up with."

"Really? That's your answer? You think it's more likely that some random guy lying dead in a park on the North Shore—a guy who wears three-thousand dollar Saveas—has gang connections, than the guy Simon Kingi was chasing?"

"Look, I don't fucking know, all right. I swear I've had nothing to do with Kingi for years. Thought he was still inside. Really, I got nothing." He's quiet for a minute as the Auckland CBD, layers of fluted needles of glass and steel, scrapes across the horizon. "OK, I got two things. You listening?"

Penny sits forward, her face in the rear-view mirror crinkling in unexpected anticipation. "I'm all ears."

"First thing. Something's changed, maybe Hanson being taken off the scene. Guy like that kicks it, leaves a hell of a void in the power structure. Could be any number of people making moves to fill his shoes, and maybe some crazy fucker like Simon Kingi, or someone who's got something over Simon Kingi, has a reason to come after me. I'll have to make some enquiries."

"OK," Penny presses. "What's the second thing?"

Matiu watches the skyline slide by, all those towers reaching for the clouds. All that real estate, all those people. So much going on, a million tiny struggles to survive in a city slipping into the sea. "Your stiff. What sort of shit can a guy like that be mixed up in? Guys like that don't just end up dead in a park wearing shoes worth three grand. Maybe he went on a bender, drank himself stupid, got into a fight he couldn't win, but if he did he walked a fuck of a long way even from the Devonport bars before he keeled over. Something about it stinks, right? All I'm saying is, before you write off the idea that a guy like that couldn't be mixed up in some nasty shit, it might be worth considering all the bad shit he *could be* mixed up in. Look at this place. Lot of desperate people out there. Lot of predators."

Penny shakes her head. "He's a victim, we know that. I'm not sure—"

"Nor am I. I don't know what else is out there, under the surface, but you don't have to scratch very deep to find the rot."

She sighs. "Let's just swing by the lab on the way to the hospital so I can get Beaker to start processing the evidence. You know, the stuff the science is based on? And leave the speculation to the police, OK?"

It's Matiu's turn to shake his head as he veers towards the offramp, the descent into the guts of the beast. "Just saying it might be a good idea to keep an open mind, eh. Evidence is fine, but someone has to interpret it."

"Yes. The police. We just deliver the facts."

"Facts," he repeats, and laughs. The fuck do the facts have to do with anything?

CHAPTER 4

- Pandora -

"Wait here," Penny says. The back door is sticky. The accident must have dinged up the door frame. Swivelling on the seat, she forces it open with quick jab of her heel. "I won't be long. I'll just get Beaker running these samples and be straight back down. You can turn the car about if you like."

Matiu raises an eyebrow. "In ever decreasing circles, you mean?"

"Matiu…"

"Penny, I'll be here," Matiu says, impatient. "Stop gassing and hurry up, OK?"

"Right." Scuttling across the road, Penny punches the code into the archaic keypad and hauls open the heavy fire doors. One flight of stairs and another set of fire doors and she's in the lab. She sucks in a breath, tasting Cleanase and butyric acid, overlaid with the fake lemon of floor cleaner, and feels her shoulders relax, a nasty knot between her shoulder blades easing. It's the best kind of stress relief. She loves this lab, loves everything about it, right down to the individual gas outlets. She throws her satchel on a benchtop, then grabs her lab coat from her hook by the door.

"Penny, is that you?" Grant Deaker, aka Beaker, is her technician, filched from Noah Cordell when she left LysisCo. His safety goggles covering half of his face, he pokes his head around the end of the bench where he's setting up an assay.

"I'm going to assume that was a rhetorical question," Penny replies, pulling her arm through the sleeve of her lab coat. Given she and Beaker make up the entire workforce of Yee Scientific Consultancy, who else could it be?

Beaker ducks behind the bench so only the top of his hair is visible. "The landlord."

"Not without providing me with 24 hours' notice," Penny says. She opens her satchel and begins unloading the samples.

"He came an hour ago."

"What?" Penny's head jerks up. Please don't let the landlord have a beef with her. She's barely getting by as it is. She can't afford to change premises. "What did he say? Have the other tenants been complaining? I'll bet it was that arsehole on the ground floor—the one who hates dogs."

"Just kidding," Beaker says. Bobbing up above the cabinets, he grins. With the goggles on, he looks like an oversized fly.

"Beaker," Penny wails. "Quit mucking about." Chuckling, he disappears from view. Penny dips her hand into her shirt pocket and examines the smear of black blood taken from Kingi's Mustang. "I can fire you, you know," she says sternly. "It's in my power."

She won't. Beaker's the best there is. A distant descendant of Rutherford, Beaker is a stickler for experimental rigour. He'll have deduced that while it wasn't probable someone other than Penny had entered the lab, it was still possible. It's one of the reasons Penny is determined to keep him on: he's so thorough, always questioning assumptions. In science, you can never prove anything right, and Beaker's one of those rare sorts to test and re-test hypotheses, often employing different methodologies, comparing the results and ensuring that there are fewer chances of being proved wrong.

Penny turns the sample from the Mustang over in her hand. For some reason, she doesn't want Beaker to process it. Why? It's just blood, and Simon Kingi is a convicted felon. Why not trust Beaker to run the assay?

"Actually, I thought it could be your dad," Beaker says, walking past her with a tray of cuvettes. Startled, Penny thrusts the sample into her satchel. "Because he's phoned three times already this morning."

"Yes, I got his messages, thanks," she says, smiling a little too brightly. Beaker pinkens, his freckled skin glowing against the starched white lab coat. If Matiu were here, he'd tease her about encouraging the boy, since he seems to think Beaker has a puppy dog crush on her. That's total rubbish.

No. 1: Blushing is a normal stress response experienced by everyone. It's only because redheads have pale complexions that the relative changes in skin pigmentation are highlighted.

No. 2: Beaker's not a boy. He's thirty-two!

No. 3: Last, but not least, Penny's Beaker's boss, so of course he jumps to and does everything she says. It's got nothing to do with infatuation and everything to do with fulfilling the terms of his employment contract. A crush? They share a professional admiration and mutual respect for each other, that's all.

Mutual respect. So why are you hiding this sample from him, Penny?

"Your father seemed pretty agitated," Beaker's saying. "More than his usual... um... more than usual."

Beaker must have copped an ear bashing from Dad.

"I hope everything's OK?" The cuvettes safely in the fridge, Beaker turns, pushing his safety goggles to the top of his head so his red hair sticks up. The look he gives her is so earnest, she almost giggles.

"You know how parents are, Beak," she says, buttoning up her lab coat. "Not having four extra rolls of toilet paper on hand constitutes an emergency."

"Yes, I thought it would be something like that, but then Carlie, from Despatch called, wanting to know why you weren't where you were supposed to be."

That niggly knot returns to stab Penny in the back. She sighs. "It's my aunt. She's been hospitalised. Matiu and I were on the way to Greenlane Hospital when we were in an accident and that delayed us so—"

"Hang on. Back up, back up. An accident? Penny! Are you OK?"

"I'm fine—we're all fine—although we might not be when Dad sees fleet car 55. It wasn't our fault, but it got squished up against the barriers in the collision. Right now, it looks like one of Salvador Dali's elephants has stomped all over it."

Beaker stares at her. "You're sure you're fine?"

"Absolutely."

"Well, if you're fine, why are you here? Shouldn't you be at the hospital?"

"Samples, Beak." She flaps the Little Shoal samples in the air. "I have to get them started. I can't risk Tanner giving the work to someone else. I can barely afford to pay you as it is." She stalks to the microscope, yanking the stool from under the bench. Its legs scrape on the ground. "It was irresponsible of me to take you from Noah…"

Beaker places his hand on the microscope, stopping her from hauling off the dust cover. "Penny, firstly, I would not work for that snake in the grass even if he paid me."

"Technically, that's what working for someone means."

Beaker ignores her. "Secondly, your aunt is in hospital. This is not the time to be talking about things like pay packets. We'll discuss it when the time comes. Give me those samples. I'll get on to them while you go to the hospital. What are we looking for? Bodily fluids? Hair samples? Soil and residue? The normal stuff?"

Penny lets her shoulders drop. She relinquishes the sample packages. "Beaker, thank you. Honestly. I'll make it up to you."

The technician's blush is as crimson as his hair. "Don't be silly. We're a team."

"You're sure about this? You don't mind?"

Beaker makes a shooing action. "Go on. Get."

"Thank you." Penny slides her satchel off the desk and makes a show of hanging up her lab coat, but as soon as Beaker is back at the bench, she sneaks into the chemical store, placing the windscreen blood sample into plastic packaging and slipping it behind a row of reagent jars. There. It should be safe and stable until she has time to get back and test it.

"Penny?"

Penny whirls.

It's just Beaker. His brow furrows.

"Oh…um…just thought I'd cool off a second before I go outside in that heat." She blows out theatrically, fanning her hand in front of her face. "Phew, it's hot out there. Well, that should do it. Bye, Beak." Leaving him standing there, she flees out the fire doors and down into the street.

If there aren't many cars on the road these days, it's because they're all in the Greenlane Clinic carpark.

"For fuck's sake." Matiu bangs his fist on the wheel.

"What about there?"

Matiu zooms forward, but a little smart-car is already occupying the space. Annoying. It didn't need a full park. You could park a bus in there. A pedestrian, seeing their beaten-up car and Matiu's scowl, gives them a wide berth. By the time they've found an empty space, and a shady spot to tie up Cerberus, Matiu's like a ripe tomato left in the sun. She has to run to keep up.

"Matiu, sweetie, you need to calm down. You're not going to be any good to Mum or Whaea Mārama like this."

Whoops. Bad move. Matiu pivots on his heel and grabs her by the arms. "And whose fault is that, Pandora?"

"Not mine!"

"Really? Who took her sweet time swanning about the park with her crime tape, then? Who had to stop on the bridge and blather on and on to Tanner, and then if that wasn't enough, fart around another half an hour making doe-eyes at lover-boy at the lab?"

She twists, trying to throw him off. "I was not making doe-eyes at anyone. I was dropping off samples for my colleague to get underway, because that is my job, Matiu. This might surprise you, but I've worked hard for this: it's how I make a living."

Letting her go, Matiu pushes his sunnies up onto the top of his head and looks her squarely in the eye. "Yep, that's right. It's always about you, isn't it, Pandora?" He stalks off towards the hospital entrance, his jacket slung over his shoulder.

"All about me? All about me? Hey!" Dashing forward, Penny flicks him in the back. He turns. "I'm not the one who got us in a car chase. I didn't go smashing in a windscreen, wrecking a perfectly good tablet and several perfectly sound vehicles. And don't forget who was following us, Matiu: only Simon—" She jabs him in the shoulder with her finger. "Bloody—"

Jab.

"Kingi—one of *your* former associates. If I was dallying at the Mustang with

Tanner, it wasn't to pass the time of day: it was to make sure he didn't suspect *you* of anything. Anyway, Tanner's the least of your worries. What about Dad? He's going to be ropeable enough when he sees the car, wait 'til he finds out you're back running with Hanson's old crowd—"

She's about to jab him again, but Matiu catches her hand. "I'm not back in the gang, Pen."

"So you say."

"Penny, I'm not."

In her bones, she doesn't believe he is—doesn't want to believe it—but damn it, she doesn't want to give him the last word either. Shrugging, she steps into the hospital lobby. "Whatever."

- Matiu -

Matiu stalks through the overpoweringly white hallways like a wounded angel. His footfalls are heavy, shoulders stooped, eyes downcast as he attempts to leave Pandora behind—or at least make her do that silly skip-jump-step she has to do to keep up with him. Still, he's livid at her, for suggesting he might be running with the pack again. When would he have the time? What would he have to gain? Holy shit, the people he used to know keep turning up dead, or corrupted by something from the other side of the veil. He wants no part of that. At the thought, his arm itches again. With all that's happened since leaving the park, he'd almost forgotten the constant, painful itch under his bandage. But here, surrounded by doctors and trollies laden with medical supplies to trigger the memory, the tingling, burning sensation comes back in force. It should've healed by now, but it's taking its goddamned time. Like it's not just a burn, but something burrowing into his skin, chewing on his flesh. Something no amount of antibacterial spray or saline solution is going to wash away. Something he brought back with him from *over there*. Is this how it started for Hanson, too? For Kingi?

He resists the urge to scratch, and hopes he's just being paranoid.

Mārama's ward is on the third floor. Matiu strides past the lifts and hurdles up the stairs two at a time.

"Seriously?" Penny groans. When he glances back, she's pushing the call button for the lift, staring daggers at his retreating back. He allows himself a sour grin. Stairs are good, helping him burn up the leftover adrenalin from surviving a run-in with a murderous aberration intent on...what? Killing them? Or something worse? He was pleased to be driving when they left the scene. He'd seen Penny's hands, shivering like leaves in a breeze. His would've been trembling too if he hadn't been gripping the steering wheel.

At the third floor, he pushes through the smoke door and looks both ways. To his right, the lift doors, nurses' station and a little waiting room. And there's Mum, standing at the desk arguing with a charge nurse. Good old Mum, always able to find someone who should be doing something for her. According to the signage, Mārama's ward is to the left. Slipping through the door, Matiu slinks down the hallway without giving himself away. When Pandora steps from the lift, she won't have a chance. That's good. Mum's sure to tie her up for a bit, give him a bit of time alone with Mārama. *Just don't mention the car, sis, whatever you do.*

Opening the door to Ward 312, Matiu scans the beds and drawn curtains. Mārama is in the corner by the window, her privacy curtain pulled around to block out the room but allowing her a view over the greensward and carpark below. Matiu crosses the room and pauses at the edge of the curtain, looking her over. She's resting, pillows laid back, eyes shut. She's not hooked up to any machines, just a drip that might be saline or some painkiller. The sight of her there, so thin and vulncrable, tears something inside him. It's worse, somehow, than watching her potter about her cluttered little flat in a daze, or paralysed by tormented memories of things she can't speak of, and completely wrong on another level entirely. She's strong, not this frail thing before him. Hers is a strength he has depended on, clung to. Knowing she would always be there, one way or another—even if most the time her *there* was some other place, some hiding hole where she would bide her time against the turning of the tides—has been one of the pillars that holds him up, above the dark.

He lowers himself into the chair beside the bed, the sun through the window warming his back. Takes her hand in his. It's cold, but she grips his fingers in return. She rolls her head, cracking her eyelids to regard him.

"Matiu," she croaks, and squeezes. A thin smile flickers on her lips, then fades.

"Mārama," he forces a smile, glad she's alive and cogent. Just recognising him is a good sign. "How are you feeling?"

Her eyes drift closed again, her grip firm. "He was here."

The warmth on his back drains away, like a curtain of ice has dropped across the sun. He sits forward, tension spiking. "Who? Who was here?" But he knows. There's only one she can mean, only one who would bring that chill to her voice.

"He said he will find you, Matiu. Said...it's your turn."

Her breaths become slow and deep as she sinks away, a stark contrast to his own sharp, shallow inhalations. *His turn.* What the hell did that mean? His thoughts skew from one dreadful possibility to another, each worse than the next. He pushes back the chair and stands, reaching out to grip the windowsill, holding onto something solid, something that won't fall away beneath him.

He will find you.

The pieces fit together with a sickening thud. Hanson gone, Mārama falling ill. Kingi hunting him, corrupted by something from beyond the veil. And now this insidious little message. This threat. His arm itches and a memory flashes by, a landscape of black sand and boiling clouds, a creature vast and twisted curling against the sky, all tooth and jaw. The eternal, echoing cold.

It's your turn.

Matiu pushes away from the window and hurries out of the ward, head down, heart thundering. He needs to get out of here. The room feels tainted, crawling with unspent anger. A feeling he remembers so well, that itch in his spine when Makere used to hang there on his back, taunting and tempting him, urging him to bend, to break. He needs to breathe.

- Pandora -

The lift doors ping open. Penny steps past the security guard onto the third floor Mental Health Ward to the smell of...nothing. No melange of cabbage and disinfectant, not even the slightest hint of plasticizers. Well, that's a surprise. Sensing an odour is a complex matter, dependent on the concentration and solubility of the hydrocarbon in question, the pH and hence the relative volatility of the substance, and its partition coefficient with the surrounding air, as well as the number and functionality of Penny's own olfactory receptors. To sense nothing, either Penny has a dreadful cold, or the hospital's using advanced membrane filters to ensure its air quality, since any aerosolised hydrocarbons are well below odour detection limits...

"Pandora!" The elevator doors have barely closed before Mum runs to meet her, her vintage Manalo Blahniks clacking on the polished linoleum. "Darling!" Mum wraps her in a cloud of custom perfume. Penny suppresses a smile. Even a hospital-grade membrane filter has no answer to Kiri Yee's signature scent of mānukā and mint. "Thank God, you've come," Mum murmurs over Penny's shoulder. "I've been so alone." She waves her hand in the direction of the nurses' station. "The nurses are no help. It's hopeless."

A creep of fear steals up Penny's back and the hairs on her nape stiffen.

Please, no. Don't let it be hopeless.

She pulls away to search Mum's face, noting the dark smudges under her eyes, and the mesh of hair at a tangent from her normally perfect bob. "Hopeless? What have they said, Mum?"

"Nothing! I can't get anything out of them. Well, nothing I can understand. Your aunt hasn't woken up all morning, Pandora. She's not just sleeping either, she's unconscious. I can't bear to watch her—she's hardly breathing." Mum clasps her hands together under her chin in a muted prayer.

Gently, Penny surrounds her mother's hands in her own. "Let me see what I can find out, shall I?"

Mum bites her bottom lip, then nods. "I'll wait over there." She points to the wide bench seat intended for visitors. Made from bright yellow leather, it's the sort of furniture you see all over hospitals, intended to be cheery and welcoming, but only accentuating the hopelessness of the place. The Manolo Blahniks clack away.

"OK, I won't be long…" Penny trails off.

The nurse behind the counter has blue-black hair and a nose stud in the shape of a unicorn. "Can I help you?"

"Good morning. I'm Dr Yee. I got a call…I'm here about Ms Mārama Ngata."

"You're the GP?" the nurse asks, the unicorn breaking into a trot as she speaks.

Penny gives her a broad smile, inclining her head just a little, but says nothing.

"Of course, let me get you her chart." The nurse passes Mārama's patient tablet over the counter. Well, Penny can't help it if the nurse got the wrong end of the stick, can she? She didn't actually say she was Mārama's GP. Anyway, no point looking a gift unicorn in the mouth. She's closing her hand over the tablet when the nurse frowns. "Sorry, I have to ask you to read it here, though," she says. "You know, regulations."

Penny rolls her eyes in empathy. "Rules. Of course."

Her back to the nurse, Penny brings up Mārama's chart. Ignoring the patient history, she jumps straight to today's event:

Female, 55 years, admitted 6am by ambulance following severe psychotic panic attack during which patient reported hallucinations of demons. Mr Visser suggests possible bi-polar disorder with psychotic features. Long-term history of schizophrenia.

Ah. Looks like it's more of the same. Poor Mārama. Penny searches the tablet for a list of current meds—risperidone, venlafaxine, and clonazepam, and in doses sufficient to tranquilise an elephant. No wonder Mum said Mārama was out of it. A full raft of physiological and psychometric tests had been ordered for when her aunt is stable.

When has she ever been stable?

Penny returns the tablet to the nurses' station, thanks the unicorn girl, then makes her way to where Mum is waiting.

Mum stands up. "What did they say?"

"It's nothing to worry about. A severe panic attack, that's all."

Crossing her arms over her heart, Mum runs her hands up and down the sleeves of her cashmere cardigan. "But why? I don't understand. Why would she suddenly have an attack? What's changed?"

"I don't know. It might not be anything much. She might have forgotten to take her meds."

Mum stops mid-rub. "Not taken her meds? That's unacceptable. Un. Ac. Cept. Able." She paces the length of the bench, shaking her head, then turns and stalks back. "I can't believe it. The money we pay for good care. I'll have to hire a new nursing service."

"Mum, I said she *might* have forgotten, not that she did. I don't know what happened. It doesn't really matter."

"Doesn't matter?" Mum's voice rises.

"I didn't mean doesn't matter. Of course not. That's not..." Penny takes a deep breath. Why does Mum always make Penny so tongue-tied? It's as if she's a kid again, explaining the accidental ink stain on her white duvet cover. Who gives a white duvet to a nine-year-old anyway? "What I meant was, the important thing is for us to focus on getting Whaea Mārama better, and right now she's in the very best place to get the care she needs. Mr Visser and his staff are going to do everything they can to get her back on her feet."

"How can you say that, Pandora? My poor sister is lying in that room, unconscious. Unresponsive. She's so... so... floppy! For all I know, she might never wake up."

"Now, Mum—"

But once Kiri Yee is on a roll, she's like a marble let loose on Dunedin's Baldwin Street. "You know she could die in that room and no one would be any the wiser. They've just left her there. Left her!"

"They've left her to *rest*, Mum. The specialist has her sedated, so she can recover from the trauma of the attack. As soon as she's stabilised, they'll reassess her and make an ongoing treatment plan."

"But Pandora..." Mum sits heavily on the bench, covering her face with her hands so Penny has to crouch to hear her speak, "you weren't there. It was horrible." She closes her eyes. "My baby sister wanted to kill herself. Mārama wanted to die!"

"Mum, please, don't."

Her eyes fly open. "I think she means it. Really. I think she intends to kill herself. You should have seen her, screaming and scratching at herself with her fingernails. Tearing at her hair. I've never seen her that way before. She was hysterical—beyond hysterical."

The yellow leather whines as Mum drops her head to her knees. "She kept saying it was my fault for not looking after my family better. How can she say that, Pandora? How can she possibly accuse me of neglecting her? She knows I've done everything I could. Everything."

"Of course you have, Mum. No one could reproach you. You've been the best sister anyone could want."

Penny rummages in her satchel for a tissue, but Mum's quicker, getting one out of her own handbag. She dabs at her eyes, careful not to smear her make-up as she continues her soliloquy.

"I tried to comfort her. I put my arms around her and pulled her to me, and that's when she told me she would rather die. She said the demons were already haunting her, she might as well go to hell. She kept saying it over and over. How we'd be better off if she were underground. Pandora, it was as if I'd been stabbed in the heart. I was so scared for her."

Sitting on the bench, Penny places her hand in the middle of Mum's back and rocks her gently. Certain studies suggest invoking a person's parasympathetic nervous system can be as effective as a tranquiliser. "I think that's what the doctors meant by a severe panic attack, Mum. Whatever Whaea Mārama might have said, you mustn't take it to heart. What she's saying isn't real, it isn't rational. It's just part of her psychosis."

Mum gives a series of hiccuppy little nods. "Yes, yes, I know that. It's just so hard to hear." Tucking the tissue into her sleeve, she breathes deeply. Then, shrugging off Penny's ministrations, she stands up and smooths out the seams of her brocade skirt. Not that she needs to: there isn't a wrinkle in sight.

"Where's Matiu? Didn't he come with you?"

Penny has to hand it to Mum, she's one tough cookie. "He arrived just before me. Came up the stairs. I expect he went straight in."

"Hmm. I must have missed him while I was at the nurses' station." Mum starts for the room, her heels decisive, but Penny clutches at her arm. "Maybe we should let them have a moment alone?" She drops her voice, making it as soft as she can, knowing the words will hurt her mother. "If anyone can persuade Whaea Mārama not to give up hope, it'll be Matiu."

For a second, Mum's face crumples, but just as quickly she shores it up again. "Yes, yes, you're right. They're very close."

As close as a mother and her son.

The elevator doors ping and Dad rushes in. "Kiri," he says. "We came as soon as we could."

We?

"It's fine, dear. Mārama's fine. No need for all this fuss. Turns out it was just a little panic attack. Matiu's in seeing her now."

The elevator doors open again and Penny's heart sinks as Craig Tong sweeps onto the third floor. With his slicked-back hair and too-perfect suit, Craig is as smooth as a caramel latte and just as sickly. Penny can almost hear the hospital's membrane filters cranking up to cope with his cologne. She closes her eyes and breathes through her mouth.

"Craig brought me," Dad announces as if it weren't already obvious. Penny opens her eyes. "Decent of him to let me off at the lobby, while he found a park. Honestly, you'd think there was an apocalypse: the car park was completely full. It was an a-park-alypse!"

"Hello, Pandora," Craig says, striding over and taking her hand. His fingers are clammy.

"Um… hello, Craig," Penny says. "It's kind of you to come." Penny's cell rings. She almost jumps in delight. She's never been so pleased to get a call. She plasters a look of regret on her face. "Excuse me one moment. I'd better get this." Resisting the urge to wipe her hands on her jeans, Penny steps to the window. She checks the number. Unlisted.

"Ms Pandora. I think you need to get yourself out here."

"Detective Tanner? Yes, I'm nearly done here. I'll head back to Little Shoal as soon as I can."

"Not to Little Shoal. To Karaka Bay. I'll have comms forward you the address."

"Another case?"

"Actually, I've got an inkling it might be the same. That tattoo you showed me on the bridge—our latest Jane Doe is sporting the same insignia, or at least it looks that way. Inside left wrist, same as this morning's stiff. You want the job?"

Penny's thoughts race ahead. It's dreadful—this crime wave—people dying left, right and centre. On a personal level, Penny would prefer it if everyone lived happily ever after—of course, she would—but from a purely professional standpoint, Tanner's offer couldn't have come at a better time. Two bodies. Two sets of analyses. Double the paycheque. An opportunity to extricate herself from the debacle that is Craig Tong. A chance to stick it to Noah Cordell.

Another chance to get yourself killed.

"What's that, Yee?"

"Yes, yes, of course, I'd be happy to accept a second contract…an expanded contract."

"Well, don't let's get ahead of ourselves here. Cordell wants the work and he's already on site. I can hold it for you, but only if you can get your arse out here, pronto. I'll give you 20 minutes." He rings off.

Mum is holding court at the yellow bench. Coming away from the window, Penny catches her last comment: "Now Craig, you mustn't worry that my sister's mental illness is hereditary—it's not. I want to make that quite clear. Penny's genes are perfectly sound."

What?

"I'm not a brood mare," Penny hisses under her breath. Even Craig has the grace to look away.

"Now Pandora, Craig's practically family," Mum replies. Penny cringes. Could her voice be any louder? "Well, he will be family just as soon as you two kids stop making woo eyes at each other and get down to business, isn't that right, Hing?"

"Muuum!"

Mum smiles at Craig as if Penny is a wayward child too cute to reprimand. "Penny, really. There's no point denying it. We all saw how you looked at Craig when he stepped out of the elevator just now. Your face lit up. You were like a peach blossom opening in the springtime, wasn't she Craig?"

Penny's mouth fills with a rush of saliva, a wave of reverse peristalsis building in her proximal small intestine. Penny recognises the precursors to vomition. She hides her gag behind her hand. A mistake. As far as Mum's concerned, that Chinese gesture of politeness is a declaration of her love. Craig grins.

Oh no, he thinks I love him too!

Mum barrels on. It's like watching a train wreck, one carriage at a time. Penny looks to Dad, imploring him for help, but he seems oblivious, or worse, complicit.

Where the hell is Matiu when I need him?

"Don't think you can keep secrets from your parents, Pandora," Mum admonishes, taking Penny's chin between her finger and thumb and giving it an affectionate shake. "And come to think of it, we shouldn't be keeping secrets from Craig either. Not when the darling man has gone out of his way to come here and offer you his emotional support."

More saliva floods in. Penny's chemoreceptor trigger zone is on overload.

By the time Penny has got her extramedullary brain centres under control, Mum has turned to Craig and, holding his lapels in her hands, she says: "My sister suffered post-traumatic stress as the result of an event that occurred in her youth, Craig. She was in love, you see, and the boy threw her over. Left her expecting a baby boy. Love, when it's denied, can be a terrible thing."

Her knack for performance is sublime because right at that moment, the baby boy steps out of Whaea Mārama's room.

"Matiu!" Mum calls.

Matiu's head snaps up. Penny catches his smirk. She can only imagine what they must look like: Mum sweeping down the corridor, leading her entourage of faithful subjects like the legendary East Coast chieftainess, Hinematioro. All that's missing is the famous litter. Although, to be fair, if someone were to agree to carry her on a litter, Mum would probably be all for it.

Matiu darts in and gives her a perfunctory peck on the cheek. "Hey Mum, nice to see you." He keeps moving. "I'd stay but I've got an appointment, gotta fly. Hey Dad, Craig. Good to see you, man."

"You're leaving? But you're supposed to be driving me today. I have a case, remember?"

Matiu shrugs. "Sorry, sis. Maybe later."

"But—"

"You'll drive your sister," Dad interjects. "You don't have any pickups: I called the depot earlier and had Carlie reschedule your work for the afternoon."

Putting his hands on his hips, Matiu blows out slowly. "Well, of course, I *could,* but then I'd have to miss my probation meeting."

Penny sighs. Well, that's it then, isn't it? Nothing beats the probation officer argument.

"You know, wherever you need to go, Pandora," Mum says breezily, "I'm sure Craig can drop you off?"

Penny groans silently. Mum just can't pass up an opportunity to throw her at Craig. She looks to Matiu for salvation. Only her brother—that sly piece of work—is already disappearing down the stairwell. How dare he abandon her like this? Just wait until she gets hold of him; she'll skewer him with the pointy end of a fruit kebab.

The elevator pings again.

"About time he turned up," says Mum, waving at the stocky man who is making his way to the nurses' station.

"Who's that, Mum?"

"Dr Banerjee. He's Mārama's GP. I expected him over an hour ago."

At the counter, the doctor clears his throat. The nurse's smile drops. The unicorn horn swings in Penny's direction.

Whoops!

"On second thoughts, I will take you up on your kind offer, Craig. If you don't mind." Grasping him by the elbow, Penny hurries him to the stairs.

CHAPTER 5

- Matiu -

Matiu pulls into the garage, scans the space as the roller door rumbles closed behind him. All around are the shapes of cars covered in thick tarps, trolley jacks and toolboxes, stacks of tyres, vehicle parts and barrels smeared with grease. A few buzzing fluorescents hang on corroded chains from the ceiling, throwing a pallid light across the dark space. Along the back wall there's a temporary spray booth, complete with extractor, compressor, and a trolley loaded with spray-painting air tools. He pulls the car into an empty space and climbs out, opens the back door for Cerberus. The dog extends his front legs, sticks his rump in the air and yawns, before moving off to sniff at a nearby pile of tyres. Matiu lets the leash spool out so the dog can explore but not wander off.

"Yo, Screech."

"Fuck off, we don't want any," calls a voice from down the back.

Matiu grins. A pair of legs can be seen on a car creeper poking out from under the only vehicle not covered in a tarp, a blood-red vintage Camaro. A relic of the days when fuel was cheap, and the hobby of importing niche vehicles for specialist buyers was actually a viable business. Now it's just a rich bastard's game.

"Shit, you don't see many of these around nowadays," Matiu says, impressed.

The creeper slides out, revealing a pair of grimy overalls, hands stained with engine grease, and finally a dirt-smudged face mostly hidden behind a scraggly beard. "Well fuck me days," the beard says. "There's a face I didn't think I'd ever see again. Pretty boy like you, thought they would've eaten you alive on the inside."

Matiu spreads his hands. "Guess I was more than just a pretty face, eh? Good to see you, Screech."

"Good to see you've still got the door code memorised, bro. Even though I change it every month." Screech pushes himself up, tossing a tangle of electronics into a small tub of clear liquid near the toolbox. Hissing yellow smoke bubbles from its surface.

Matiu lifts an eyebrow at the dissolving circuit board. "Man, if you want that shit to be secure, you need to upgrade to an algorithm I can't crack with a phone app. Especially if you're busy cutting out Gee-Pee units before you chop and shop stolen cars in here. So what, you carry a scrambler when you boost the car so the unit can't transmit, then rip it out here and give it a little acid bath for its troubles?"

Screech thumps Matiu in the shoulder. A seventeen-inch wrench dangles from his other hand. "Dude, you got me. Some shit never changes, right?"

Matiu shrugs, and nods at the Camaro. "Nice ride. Someone's baby?"

"Sure was." They regard the sleek lines of the American sports car, brought across the ocean on a cargo ship decades earlier during a surge in popularity among Kiwi revheads for muscle cars, back when shipping was cheap and drag racing was a pastime of the average joe, not the extremely rich. The bonnet bulges with the sweeping curves of the intake, and the polished chrome mags shine even in the garage's gloom. "She's a beauty. 2014 six-point-two litre COPO, concept design. Only ninety-three of these puppies ever made. Check out the twenty-nine inchers on the back axle."

Matiu whistles in appreciation of the oversized rear tyres. "That's extreme, bro."

"Not even street-legal when they built them, strictly drag racers, but someone twisted some arms so they could drive her around our mean streets."

"Bad luck for them they didn't lock it up better, eh?"

"And good luck for me. So, what brings a write-off like Matiu Yee all the way down to Screech's humble vehicle redistribution facility?" Screech turns to look him over, his eyes going to the dog. "Up to your old tricks again as well, eh? Got a few prospects in the rings?"

Matiu smirks half-heartedly, a carefully manufactured expression. "Not likely. You hear about Hanson? Heard his dogs got loose, messed him up real bad. *Real* bad."

Screech shakes his head. "Guy like Hanson I can do without hearing about, you know?"

"No shit. Anyway, I got some panel work needs doing, and a flat tyre. Figured you're the guy to see."

Screech gives Matiu a searching look, before wiping his hands on a rag and wandering towards the Commodore. "Shit, they're a good car, eh? Good call, bringing them back into production when they did." He leans down and regards the bent number plate. "Fleet car. You work for the man now?"

"*The* man. My old man runs cars, keeps me in paid employment. Probation office likes that."

"Company car. Why'd you come to me then? Won't the company wanna use someone they can run their insurance through?" Screech walks down the passenger side of the car, reviewing the damage, then looks back at Matiu. "I'm guessing this is some shit you don't want dear old Dad to know about. The sort of shit the Probation Office might not want to hear about, either?"

Matiu puts on the special smile he reserves for those moments when he really needs someone to just come to the fucking party and not ask any questions at the door. "Screech, my brother. Guy like you, operation like this? Security on the front door that a shit-for-brains like me can crack with his cell phone?" He points at the COPO. "That Camaro's worth over a hundred and fifty gee to buy, so an easy seventy-five for a guy like you once it's had a paint job and some tracing mods. Move one of those every coupla months, oughta keep you in a good living."

"You threatening me?" Screech stares at him hard, the wrench tapping his open palm.

Matiu crumples his face into his best pained expression. "No threats here, bro. I wasn't suggesting anything, just asking a question. What I need is a quick turnaround on some panel work, and a new tyre. Oh, and can you repack the airbag? You've got the tech for that, right?" Screech would have, since some security systems caused the airbags to deploy if they detected a tamper. Sort of tech that's usually controlled by import regulations, given that it deals in explosives. But a guy like Screech, he can be a bit loose with things like regulations. Likes to think of them more like guidelines. "Plus a car to borrow in the meantime. And I haven't got any money, so it's like a favour. I'm hoping you've got it in your heart to help a brother out, like the old days. Bit of nostalgia. Waddya think?"

"I think you're a sneaky little shit is what I think. I don't like smarmy bastards like you driving in off the street and trying it on with me. Tell me why I shouldn't just smack in your fucking skull and dump you in the harbour?"

Picking up on the rising tension, Cerberus starts to growl, low and steady.

"What, you gonna sic your mangy mutt on me?"

Matiu shrugs. "Bro, either you can help me out, and I'll owe you a favour, or you can't."

"Or else? You'll drop the cops on my ass?"

"The cops? Shit no. I'd never do that to a bro." Screech steps around the car, closing in. Matiu doesn't flinch, maintaining the illusion of calm. Screech is all noise and bluster, but there's a reason he works alone. He's got the smarts to boost even the most highly secured cars, and the trade skills to move them, but deep down he's not a thug. He hates fighting, and he can't stand the company of people like Matiu Yee and Simon Kingi. Screech is the guy who turns up *after* the pub brawl, but who was mysteriously absent when the fists were swinging. Push him in the right places, and he'll break. "Guy like Simon Kingi though, he'd love to know where you are these days, the sort of stock you're moving. What's the worth in here? Ten cars, fifty-gee each, give or take? Easy half-mill. Good score for someone who knows how to shift the product without tipping the cops."

Screech stops still, the wrench twitching. "Kingi's inside."

"For real? Funny thing then, since I caught up with him today." He pulls his phone from his pocket and brings up the photo of Kingi Penny took earlier, the one Matiu swiped from her phone while she was fluffing around in the lab with lover-boy Beaker. "Seems he's looking to fill Hanson's shoes, make his mark sort of thing. And after that falling-out you and him had, he'd probably be dead keen to make your acquaintance again, you reckon?"

"You wouldn't do that."

Matiu shakes his head. "Not to a bro, no way." He steps up to Screech, puts both hands on his shoulders. "We look after each other, right?"

Screech nods, paler now.

"So, you do a couple little jobs for me, I'll owe you a favour, *and* I won't tell Kingi where you're set up. Now, which car can I use?"

The Porsche 929-R thrums under his fingertips, the steering wheel feather-light, the car keen to obey. It reminds Matiu of history vids he's watched about Spitfires, back in the war a century ago, planes built of wood and wire that were so sensitive all they needed was a nudge of the stick to throw them into a soaring roll. The Porsche is a bit like that, part of the same legacy, a warplane on wheels. Throw together a combination of speed and an accidental twist of the steering wheel, and this baby would become airborne, and deadly to boot.

So Matiu drives it like he owns it. Can't afford another mess all over the road. Pulling into the parking building, he finds a spot on the fourth level and heads downtown, Cerberus in tow, sunnies on. He's sweating under his leather jacket, but it's better to feel the discomfort of being too hot and humid than the unnatural chills that wrack him every time he thinks about the other shit that's going on. Penny's victim in the park. Simon Kingi on the bridge. Mārama in the hospital. He needs some time to clear his head, focus on real life. Something to distract him from those words:

He will find you.

It's your turn.

The Ministry of Justice offices are in a building adjacent to the Auckland District Court, a faded relic of colonial era pillars and stone façade. Seems, for some reason, that while every other building in the city got a facelift sometime in the last fifty years, they like to leave the courthouse looking ancient. Lends it more weight, maybe. A reminder that the government doesn't care much for fashion, and it's been around a lot longer than you. Matiu has spent too many hours inside that courthouse.

It's not as imposing on the inside as it looks on the outside, just a shabby replica of the fancy courthouses you see on American movies. A tired, worn-out building for a tired, worn-out system.

Leaving his sunnies on and letting Cerberus lead, he enters the MoJ lobby and makes his way carefully to the reception desk.

"I'm sorry sir, you can't bring a dog in here," the cherub-cheeked girl behind the counter says. "You'll have to leave him outside."

Matiu feigns startled shock, turning roughly towards her, but not quite. "My guide dog?"

The girl turns bright red. "Oh, I'm sorry. Who are you here to see—? Ah, who's your appointment with?"

"Erica Langley. I hope I'm not late."

"I'll let her know you're here." She fumbles with her earpiece as she makes the call.

Matiu smiles his friendliest blind man smile, and turns to stare at a blank wall.

Several minutes later, the elevator pings and Erica, all five-foot-nothing of her, hair tied back severely, hints of blonde roots showing through the black dye, storms across the lobby, a charcoal grey tablet clutched under her arm. "Matiu Yee."

Matiu turns to her, grinning widely. It's an odd thing, his smile. Has a strange effect on most women, something he's never really understood. Erica might be immune to his charms, of course, given her demeanour, or maybe she's just good at hiding her feelings. Probably a requisite for her job. "Hey, Erica."

She waves a hand at Cerberus. "You can't bring a dog in here."

"He's my guide dog."

"You're *not blind*," she hisses.

He shrugs. "Never said I was."

"Ditch the bullshit, Matiu. You're wasting my time." She's right in his face now—or she would be, if she wasn't a whole foot shorter, craning her neck back to make eye contact. But what she lacks in height, she makes up for in guts.

"Am I late?"

"Not at all."

"Then how am I wasting your time?"

She waves the tablet under his nose. "Shall we go discuss how you've turned my day into a bloody mess, shall we?"

Matiu frowns, avoiding the confused look from the girl behind the counter. "You know, I have a disability. Talking to me like that could be considered abuse, and I have a witness," he says, utterly deadpan.

Erica takes a step back, folding her arms. "Look. I've missed my lunch already. That makes me shitty. Then I get a call about one of my clients being in a high-speed chase with a known reprobate ending in a pile-up on the Harbour Bridge? That makes me even shittier, and leads to questions I don't have good answers for."

"Oh," Matiu says, heat rising in his cheeks. "That."

"Yes, *that*."

He clutches at the only straw in his grasp. "Well, what if I make it up to you by buying you lunch?"

It's a ploy, of course. A perfunctory distraction that Erica ought to reject, unable to deny he made the offer. But something changes in her face. She looks at him, quirking an eyebrow.

"Fine. I'm starving. Come on."

She heads for the door. Matiu watches her, mildly stunned. Cerberus regards him, ponderous. "Um, right," he says, to no-one in particular. For the sake of the girl behind the counter, he lets Cerberus lead the way. From the corner of his eye, he sees her give a little wave, then drops her hand, embarrassed. No point waving to a blind man.

A lunch date with his probation officer was even less on his plan for the day than confronting a tentacled version of Simon Kingi on the Auckland Harbour Bridge. He's not sure which is more terrifying. He catches her up easy enough, ditching the blind man routine. "How'd you know it was me? I didn't give the receptionist my name."

"Cameras, Matiu. There are cameras everywhere." She turns down a side street and stops at the door to a tiny juice bar squeezed in between a Budget Gift Shop and a place selling cheap knock-off electronics. "You're not bringing that dog inside." She pushes through the door, leaving Matiu regarding the frontage of the juice joint, his heart sinking. It's all fruit-smoothie-this and veggie-juice-that, fat-free, sugar-free, gluten-free, dairy-free, egg-free, soy-free, nut-free, taste-free. Not a burger or chips in sight. What looks like tubs of actual *grass* are growing on top of the chiller display, like a tiny urban interior lawn in need of mowing. He's seen places like this, but never actually been *inside* one. Sighing, he loops Cerberus' leash around a signpost and follows Erica into the store, tucking his sunnies into a pocket.

There's a throng inside, waiting for their mid-afternoon fibre blast. The air is chill with aircon, reeking of fructose and vegetable scraps, like the inside of a fridge. Blenders screech and whine. Matiu finds Erica at the till. "Large Spirulina-Wheatgrass with blueberries, thanks. And whatever he's having." She jerks a thumb at Matiu. "He's paying." Erica swans off to a table in the deepest corner of the narrow shop.

The young guy behind the counter, who's either gone bald early or shaved his head for the sake of hipster fashion, while his beard falls down his chest like a long, plaited rope, nods in the way of übercool baristas everywhere and fixes Matiu with a piercing look.

"Um," Matiu mumbles, glancing at the menu which looks like a vegetarian shopping list. His gaze drifts to the noticeboard beside the blackboard menu. For Sale notices, rooms for rent, bands looking for new members, missing cats, pharmaceutical bargains. A young woman with sad eyes gazes at him from a sun-bleached photograph, her features faded by time, her message for the world almost buried beneath sedimentary layers of community events and phone numbers. Fragments of lives in inkjet splinters pinned over top of one another, like all the people of this city clamouring to be heard above the noise of everyone else. "Two fish and a scoop?"

The barista smiles a condescending smile that doesn't reach his eyes, clearly reserved for those few times when the charms and wards on the front door fail to keep out the riff-raff. There's an awkward moment while the barista waits for Matiu to register that his sense of humour is not appreciated, before he rocks in with a suggestion. "How about a banana milkshake?"

Matiu narrows his eyes. Smart-arse. Like anyone can afford real bananas these days. But whatever it might actually be, a banana milkshake sounds better than the wheatmeal-spirograss-whatever-the-hell-it-is Erica just ordered. "Sure," he says simply, and digs for his wallet. In the far corner of the back bench, he spies a neglected-looking espresso machine. "And a double shot."

Matiu taps his card to pay the bill. "Cheers," he says, ignoring the barista's slick grin that might just as well be a sneer as he turns to work the espresso machine. Until recently, this particular situation might've gone downhill quickly. Those thoughts would've been taken by Makere, amplified, twisted, thrown back at him like so much meat on a butcher's block, hammering at his senses until he snapped. Matiu can see the tips jar beside the till, see himself grabbing it and swinging it, the glass smashing and coinage flying across the room as the barista goes down in a cloud of bloody splinters. That was the Matiu who found himself landed in a ten-foot cell, staring at the wall, with no company but the demon on his back. This Matiu can restrain himself from breaking glass jars on arrogant wankers' skulls, at least when he's on a lunch date with his probation officer, anyway.

The barista slides a thin paper cup across the counter, black and steaming. Matiu grabs it, then recoils from the heat.

"Here," says the barista, grabbing a cup sleeve from behind the till. Matiu barely notices it, except that it's all green and blue and looking healthy enough to eat, like everything in this place. He slides the cup into the sleeve and retreats to the corner table with Erica. She's watching him, like a hawk watches a mouse in a field before diving in, talons outstretched. Matiu feigns oblivion as he drops into a seat, tries to look past her sharp edges, into the Erica Langley that would let a bad day twist her up so bad she'd take it out on her client.

"Client." He chuckles, watching her eyes. "You called me a client."

She flinches. "What?"

"You're my case manager, right? But earlier you said I was your client. That's like a customer. If I'm a customer, then you ought to be selling me something. When did I become a client? When did the whole fucking world become...clients? Can't I just be your ex-con?"

"Shut up, Matiu."

And there it is, that shift behind her eyes. A deep lurking worry, waiting to spill over, or drag her down. Then it's gone as she slaps the folder on the table. "Care to tell me what this is all about?" She swipes her tablet open, revealing a photo of a Ford Mustang with a smashed bonnet splayed across two lanes of the Harbour Bridge, a truck to one side of the picture. "This is all over the newsfeeds. I got a report on the plates, and that's Simon Kingi's car. Guess who paid the registration for the last three years while Kingi was inside? Russell Hanson. The same Russell Hanson that was found dead on his farm, ripped apart by *dogs*, not very long ago." Suddenly having Cerberus in tow doesn't seem like such a good idea. Matiu had hoped having a dog would make Erica see he was taking some responsibility, looking after an animal and wotnot. But all she saw was a weapon. "Hanson who *you used to work for*. What's the connection, Matiu? If I dig into this, am I going to find out you had something to do with Hanson's death?"

Matiu shakes his head slowly. Snakes coil and writhe in his belly. "No, nothing. Penny was meant to go up there and run forensics on the scene—"

"But she couldn't because you somehow got yourselves involved in a shoot-out in the basement of the Museum instead." She skewers him with her glare. An uncomfortable silence stretches between them, mercifully broken by Mr Bald-and-Beard arriving and depositing their drinks on the table. Matiu's is a suspiciously orange shade of yellow for something purporting to be banana, while Erica's is a tall, green monstrosity flecked with purple.

"Enjoy," Bald-and-Beard quips, before disappearing.

"He was mocking me," Matiu says, glaring after the barista. "I'm not sure how, but he was. Swear it."

"What aren't you telling me, Matiu? Would you, and the rest of New Zealand, be safer if I was to advise the Board that you're a danger, and you need to go back inside?"

He sips his drink. It tastes of carrot, yams, kumara, and possibly capsicum. What a dick. "People drink this shit?" He pushes the glass aside and slides his coffee closer. "Erica, I'm working for my sister, who's working for the cops. OK? Means I find myself in some unexpected situations. Doesn't mean I'm responsible for them. Now, what aren't *you* telling *me*?"

"I beg your pardon?"

"You're worried about something and it's eating you up inside."

She stares at him open-mouthed, then leans in and sucks on her blitzed compost. "My worries are none of your business," she says around her straw.

Matiu glances about, taking in the juice joint. "Bullshit. If you'd just wanted to ream me out, you could've back at the office. Look at that crap you're drinking, it's not even lunch."

"It's highly nutritious—"

"Don't change the subject. You came here because you've got shit you need to say away from all those cameras and voice recorders. I'm a violent criminal, so why go outside the safety of the office and risk being alone with me?"

Colour flushes her pale cheeks, and she suddenly seems smaller, but only for a second. She sits up straighter, shoulders ramrod straight, and Matiu has to glance away before he's caught admiring the sudden, distracting thrust of her breasts beneath her blouse. She blanks her tablet and pushes it aside.

"My sister has disappeared."

Matiu blinks. He doesn't know what he was expecting, but this isn't it. "That sucks. Not sure how it involves me."

"She was distant. We were never close, but we were friends, generally speaking. You know how siblings are."

Matiu nods.

"Then, she just started, I don't know, slipping away. We used to talk every couple of weeks, dinner or lunch together at least once a month. Then that stopped. She stopped calling. When I called her, she sounded...far away. Sad. Like she was losing hope. And then, it was weird. She just bounced back. For a little while, she was suddenly full of life again. Kept going on about this thing she was in, this food thing. Had changed her life. I only saw her once more after that, and then...it stopped. Didn't hear from her for ages, but I was so caught up in cases and correspondence and getting to the gym after work that I didn't think about it. When I finally did..." She pauses, sipping more of her drink. Matiu lets the silence stretch out, pretending not to notice the shimmer in her eyes. They're in a dark corner, after all. Hiding from the world.

"Her house was empty. Not empty, not moved out, just...she wasn't there. Hadn't been for ages. Her cat was around, but thin and ragged, and so happy to see me. Dishes in the sink. Laundry in the machine, still wet. The house smelled of rotting clothes. But her car was gone, and she didn't answer her phone. It'd been weeks since I saw her."

Matiu nods. "Let me guess. The cops have been no help at all. Too snowed under with actual murders to worry about another missing person."

"She went out with laundry running in the machine. She *intended* to come home. Charlotte wasn't the sort to just abandon her cat, leave the house in a mess. Something happened to her."

"OK," Matiu says. "So, why me?"

"Because you know people I don't." She reaches across the table and lifts his coffee up to eye level for him to look at more closely. He reads the looping text printed on the sleeve.

Touching the Sun
Micro-gardening for a Healthier You!

"So?"

Erica turns the cup around. Surrounded by blue and green swirls, an eye stares back at him. The same eye that he had seen tattooed on the dead man's wrist, back at the park.

This is why she brought him here.

"This eye symbol. See it?"

"What about it?" He keeps his voice steady, reluctant to reveal any hint of recognition, or weakness. He takes the cup from her, brings the coffee to his lips. Still too hot to drink, and probably too bitter.

"I told you that I saw Charlotte one last time before she disappeared." She stabs a finger at the photo. "She had this symbol tattooed on her arm. Exactly the same eye. And she'd never had a tattoo before in her life."

Matiu pushes the cup away. The eye looks up at him, and blinks. He barely manages to keep his shit together. "I—"

But Erica's all about knowing people's tells, reading a face like a book, and Matiu has never been good at hiding emotion. "You've seen it, haven't you?" She leans in closer, lowering her voice. "Does this joint have something to do with that tattoo?"

Matiu grits his teeth, scratches at the sudden itch under his bandage. This was not how his afternoon was meant to go. "Did she have a new boyfriend?"

Erica glowers, settling back. "Like I said, we weren't that close. If she did, she didn't tell me. Why?"

Matiu shrugs. "Sudden erratic highs and lows, sounds like romance. Always a chance she had a new man, and he might've—"

"Swept her away on an impromptu romantic tour of the country? Maybe they're doing a vineyard a day, all the way down to Otago and back?" Erica looks hopeful.

Matiu's brow furrows. "You read too many cheap novels. I was going to say maybe they had a falling out, an argument that went bad. But that's wild speculation on my part, only because I know people who would do that."

Erica sighs. "She was never a particularly romantic sort anyway. But she only had to meet the right person, eh?"

"Or the *wrong* person. Where does she live?" Matiu asks, gingerly turning the coffee cup so he can see the eye motif again. Little as he wants to look at it, it keeps drawing his gaze, like someone—or something—trying to make eye contact from across a room.

"Mt Albert. Why?"

"Is the house locked? Alarmed?"

"Both, of course, but—"

"Give me a key and the codes if you don't want me breaking any laws to get in, and I'll go take a look around. See if I can find any clues."

Erica considers this. "Why would I trust you to go snooping round her flat? I thought maybe you could just make some phone calls. For all I know, you'll just rob the copper out of the walls."

Matiu doesn't flinch. "Yes. I'm so smart that when my probation officer threatens me with more time in jail if I don't help find her missing sister, I would go and rob said sister's house. I'm that dumb, and that's why you asked for my help." He gives her a withering look. "Fuck's sake, Erica. If you don't trust me, call in sick for the afternoon and come with me. I won't bite."

She stares at him hard, sucking intently on her smoothie. Matiu looks down, only to find the eye looking back up at him. He shivers. Erica pushes her glass away, half-empty, and stands. "Let's go."

"Great," Matiu says. "Any chance we can grab a burger on the way?"

CHAPTER 6

- Pandora -

Penny cracks the window and lifts her face to the stream of warm air. But even with the window down, the aroma in the vehicle is enough to make her gag. She wipes a wisp of hair from her face and breathes through her mouth. It's no use; she still feels queasy and it's not the waft of foul air off the mudflats or the mega-musk of Craig's cologne that are responsible.

It's the stench of expectation.

She thumbs the button and opens the window all the way.

This is Mum's fault—her bloody-minded insistence on match-making Penny with Craig. She'd even implied that they'd been making woo eyes at each other. Woo eyes! Penny had nearly died of embarrassment. *So* not true. It's not. At least, not on Penny's side. If it'd been an option, she would've crawled into the nearest vent shaft, but of course it wasn't. And now, thanks to Mum's meddling, the air between the pair of them is charged with unspoken things, like a nasty rumour whispered over morning coffee that's all over town by the end of the day.

Of course, Dad's behaviour wasn't much better. He isn't as blatant as Mum—no one could be as outrageously blatant as Mum—but he wasn't exactly pushing back either. Wasn't he the one who brought Craig to the hospital? And on a family matter? OK, so technically Craig brought Dad, since this is Craig's car, but do they really expect her to believe that not one vehicle in the entire Yee fleet was available? Penny shakes her head. Mum's the worst, but Dad is definitely complicit. No question.

Whatever. She isn't going to stand by and let her parents thrust her into Craig's lap. If they think he's such a catch, let *them* marry him. It's not as if this is about ensuring Penny's happiness, or a burning desire to have grandchildren or anything. This is all about the bottom line, because Craig has an in with the Transport Minister. For some unfathomable reason, her parents think cosying up to the man will grease the wheels—literally—for the Yee family business.

Do I look like I have the words 'bargaining chip' tattooed on my forehead?

Penny steals a glance at Craig. His lips tight, he's clenching and unclenching his fingers on the steering wheel. She frowns. If he has the warm-fuzzies for her, shouldn't he be happy they're finally alone? Could he be feeling the pressure, too?

Mum and Dad can be pretty intimidating, even for a slick operator like Craig. Has she been reading him wrong?

She wraps her arms around her satchel. Best if she says nothing in case he hasn't made up his mind yet. She wouldn't want him to get the wrong idea. He might think she's encouraging his attention, when all this is, is a ride to work.

Just a few more minutes: we're almost in Karaka.

Turning back to the window, Penny gazes across the swamp marsh, the early afternoon sun blinking off the waxy mangroves. Decades ago, all this area used to be estuary, the picturesque inlet lined with swanky mansions owned by the *nouveau riche*. The mansions and the sprawling walled gardens are still there, although the waterways have all but gone. Now, after years of eutrophication, the mud flats are choked with vegetation, discarded Coke cans and soggy chip packets washing in and out on the tide.

They've nearly made it to the turn off when Craig decides to open the conversation. "So Pandora…"

Penny squirms on the polished white leather seat. Damn. So close. "It's Penny."

His eyes on the road, Craig's mouth turns up. A smirk? Her hackles rise. "What's so funny? Something wrong with my name?"

"No, no, nothing. It's kind of cute, actually. Suits you. It's your baby name, right? I'm pretty sure I've heard Matiu call you that."

She clutches the satchel to her chest. "No. Well yes, Matiu does call me that, but—"

Taking a hand off the wheel, Craig holds up his palm. "Penny, seriously, you don't have to explain. Anyway, it's not the worst name. You should hear what my brother calls me."

"What?"

"Nah." He lifts his shoulders and shivers in mock disgust.

"Craig. You can't do that. You can't say 'you should hear', and then not let me hear."

He squeezes his lips together and shakes his head.

She shrugs. "OK, suit yourself."

He puffs. "It's Kit, OK? There, I said it."

Penny frowns. "I don't get it. What's so bad about Kit?"

Craig checks the rear-view mirror, then slides the vehicle into the left lane. "Nothing at all. Perfectly ordinary. Except when your Chinese middle name is Zheng."

Penny sounds out the words in her head. "Ah." She can't help but smile. "Kitchen tong. That's so lame."

Craig flashes her a grin. "Yeah. What can you do? Brothers, eh?"

"Tell me about it." You know, maybe Craig isn't so bad. He's as much a victim of Mum's manipulation as Penny is, and he didn't have to bring her all the way out here in the middle of the day.

At the bottom of the ramp, Craig turns to her. "Where exactly are we headed?" he asks.

Penny checks her phone. "That way," she says, pointing. "Milano Boulevard. It's on the waterfront." The light changes and they make a right. Craig gives a low whistle as they turn into Milano.

"Fancy postcode."

The road is already chock-full of cars: police vehicles, a couple of media vans, an ambulance. Craig pulls up on a grass verge behind the crowd. She's slipping her phone into her satchel when he touches her gently on the elbow.

"Look, Penny, before you go. What Kiri…what your mother was saying back at the hospital, about the two of us…"

Oh no.

She grapples for the straps of the satchel. "I know, I know," she gibbers. "Mum really shouldn't have asked you to drive me. In her defence, I think she's a bit distraught, you know, about her sister." Desperate, she yanks at the door handle.

"No, that wasn't what—"

Penny pretends not to hear. Her fingers slip on the leather armrest. *Come on, come on...* At last, the door swings open. One hand on the window frame, she scrambles out.

Before she can close the door, Craig leans across the console. "I'll wait for you. You might need a ride back."

No, no, no. This isn't good. If Mum gets wind of it, she'll have the pair of them engaged before dinner. "Craig, really, I can't ask you to do that. I could be ages."

"You didn't ask: I offered."

Penny's heart sinks. She forgot he's a politician.

"Ms Pandora!" Louder than a megaphone, Tanner's voice carries over the chatter of the crowd. He beckons from the mangroves' edge. "Down here."

Thank heavens.

"Someone get her some waders, will you?" Tanner roars. "And for God's sake, confiscate that media drone! I don't want the press leaking images until we've got some answers."

"I'd better go," Penny says. "Duty calls and all that." Giving the side of the car a little pat, she throws Craig what she hopes is a wistful moue. "Thanks, Craig. See you later."

- Matiu -

Matiu climbs from the car and hooks the seat down to let Cerberus out. "Remind me never to own a Porsche and a dog at the same time." He wipes sweat from his neck.

Erica is hunting through her handbag for the key. "Remind me again how you ended up driving a Porsche, anyway?" she says, acid in her voice.

"Like I said, a friend loaned it to me." He trails Cerberus to the nearest spindly tree growing on the verge, where the dog relieves himself noisily.

"Of course they did."

Matiu regards the small townhouse down the narrow driveway. It's a semi-detached flat, sharing a wall with the place next door, a mirror image of each other with a fence dividing the yards and a tiny carport down the back. The grass is getting long, even in this heatwave. The flat looks normal enough, but the windows are foggy, like they need a good clean. Tugging Cerberus along, he follows Erica down the drive. She walks into the tiny back yard, where the grass is growing up around a weathered outdoor table and a stack of fading resin chairs. A barbeque with a sun-bleached cover is jammed against the wall of the house. A washing line, on a bit of a lean, takes up most of the lawn. In the corner, under a ragged pine tree, is a dilapidated tin shed limned with rust. The whole place could benefit from a once-over with a lawnmower and a weedeater. Nothing out of the ordinary, aside from the way that pine looms over everything, throwing its scattered shadow like clawing fingers. Amazing a tree like that has lasted this long, the way Aucklanders are so keen to carve up their backyards, subdivide, build poky little houses on undersized sections, live looking in each other's bathroom windows. Matiu ties Cerberus in the shade of the carport and crosses to the back step.

Erica unlocks the back door and pushes it open. A wave of fetid heat rolls out of the house, smelling of closed rooms, damp carpet, and something rank. The acrid tang of pipes drying out, the air moist and rich, like a greenhouse. Erica steps back, coughing. Matiu holds his breath and steps inside, the hot air crushing him, the smell a sensory assault. Thankfully, it's not the charnel reek of dead bodies. Count the blessings. It's a smell that's weirdly familiar, but which he can't quite place, not yet. The alarm trills a warning, and Erica hurries to disarm it.

He moves through the small laundry and into an open plan lounge and kitchen, breathing through his mouth. "Wow."

"Oh my god," Erica agrees, coming up behind him.

"That's what the smell is, then. Fertiliser. Like a garden centre. Were these here when you came by last?"

Erica shakes her head. "The planters, maybe, but not the plants. They must've been growing from seeds."

Every windowsill is covered in long, narrow planter boxes, from which grow lush green stems, some over a foot high. Tacked to the tops of the windowsills are black pipes. Something hums, and small jets of water puff from the pipes, sparkling rainbow mist drifting down to moisten the stems. All the windows are covered in fine condensation. Matiu traces the line of black piping, tacked artlessly to the walls, back to the kitchen sink. Several hoses converge there, feeding off a manifold from an electric pump sitting on the bench and hooked up to the tap, plugged into the electrical outlet on the wall through a digital timer.

"Weird," Matiu mutters, and proceeds slowly around the lounge. "Looks like she's trying to start her own wheatgrass smoothie shop, like that dodgy place you just took me."

"I don't think that's wheatgrass."

Matiu finds the remote on the coffee table, half-buried under a bag of fertiliser balls and several dried-out tufts of dead vegetation. He flicks the TV on, navigates to the house network and passes the remote to Erica. "Don't suppose you know her password?"

"Maybe," she says, sounding doubtful. She drops onto the couch and uses the remote to open the virtual keyboard, which hovers before her in a pulse of gentle red light, and starts trying different options.

Matiu shakes his head. "I was just being polite." He swipes his phone to life, taps open an app. Seconds later, the locked screen on the TV vanishes and an options menu appears. "Have a look at what she's been doing online. I'm going to check out the rest of the flat."

Erica's glare is something between outrage and relief. "Those apps are illegal."

Matiu shrugs. "Isn't that why you hired me?" He turns to the hallway that leads off the lounge.

"I didn't *hire* you, Matiu Yee. You're not getting paid for this."

"Might be better *not* to remind the violent career criminal that you're blackmailing him, eh?"

She has no response to that, and he drifts into the kitchen, opens the fridge. Besides the milk going sour, a half-empty carton of apple juice, some mouldering cheese and carrots, and several bottles of premix vodka tonic, there's a whole shelf of medicines in glass vials and jars with names he doesn't recognise: Gonal-F, Suprefact, Ovidrel, Crinone. Beside these is a plastic container full of hypodermic needles in sterile bags. He snaps photos of the medicine labels and swipes them into a message to Penny with the simple note: *Hey sis, what are these?* Then he moves into the hallway, towards the bathroom and the bedrooms.

The spare room is filled with boxes and piles of books. Curious, he flips through the stacks that cover the dresser and bed. Well-thumbed paperback romances, those slim, cheap ones you see by the supermarket checkout with ridiculously handsome men on the cover sporting phenomenal abs while sweeping stunned heroines off their feet. "So our girl has a thing for romance novels," Matiu says to himself. He enters the lived-in bedroom. Thankfully, there's no overwhelming rush of something awful here, not like he'd felt in Darius Fletcher's apartment during Penny's last case.

Just the lingering hint of old perfumes, stale sweat on unwashed sheets, and underneath it all, something heady that stirs the blood. The scent of woman. He's intruding. This is someone's private place, and he has a way of knowing things, *seeing* things, that he ought not. Still, a woman is missing, and her disappearance may somehow be connected to the dead body at the park, the one Kingi was interested in. Maybe Matiu can help find her, and keep himself out of prison at the same time. It's worth a little invasion of privacy.

Someone else's privacy.

The queen-sized bed is unmade and the curtains are drawn. A large TV dominates the wall facing the bed, a built-in wardrobe along the other. Matiu circles the bed. The bedside table on the wardrobe side is more cluttered than the other, suggesting this is where Charlotte sleeps. Matiu eases himself into a sitting position on the edge of the bed, like he might if he was Charlotte, rolling out of bed and about to start her day, and places his palms flat on the sheet.

The images wash over him in a rush, snapping his pulse up a series of notches and catching the breath in his throat. A warmth suffuses his groin at the sudden flood of heat, memories of naked skin and stifled moans, creaking timber. Emotions punch him in the gut, a melange of pleasure and desperation. He's invading a moment as deeply primal as it is personal, and he knows he should let go, but something holds him there. He glimpses hands wrapped together, fingers tight and tense, two wrists, so close. Two tattoos.

"Shit," Matiu grunts, pulling himself away from the haunting flashback. He staggers to his feet, crashing into the wardrobe door, stands there, clutching his head.

"Matiu?" Erica appears in the doorway, rushes to his side.

Unspent adrenaline surges through him, the memory of sweaty coitus suffusing his blood, a phantasmal taste of woman in his mouth. He has his hands around Erica before she knows what he's doing, wrapping her up like a lover, an instinctive reflex to relieve what's surging through him, his mouth questing for hers.

The triple puts Matiu on the floor in a second: a heel to the toe, forehead to the chin and elbow to the groin. He collapses, curling into a gangly ball of pain.

"What the hell?" Erica stumbles back, flattening herself against the doorframe, while Matiu lies crumpled, breathing hard.

"Thanks," he says. "I needed that."

"No shit? Want a swift kick in the balls as well?"

"It's not like that. Give me a minute." He rolls into a sitting position, leaning against the bed. "Nice moves, by the way."

"You think you're the first client ever tried it on with me?"

"Wasn't me," he says, grimacing. "It was Charlotte's boyfriend."

Erica stares at him, slackjawed. "Now would be a good time to start making sense."

"I," Matiu stumbles for words, collects some, tries to put them in an order that might not sound completely crazy. Probably fails. "I see things, sometimes. Little curse of mine. I saw your sister in here, and her boyfriend. Getting busy."

Erica glances about, bewildered. "What the hell do you mean, *saw* her? And like I told you, she doesn't *have* a boyfriend."

"Not one she's told you about, is what you said. She sure had *someone*. And it might be the same guy the cops found dead in the park this morning. The case I took Penny to right after breakfast."

Erica shakes her head. "You're so full of shit."

"He had the same tattoo. And all that gear in the lounge, the grass or whatever. That's micro-gardening, indoor hydroponics, same as what the Touching the Sun ad is selling. The tattoos are the same. It's connected, somehow."

"Could just be a coincidence."

"Too small a town for coincidences like that. You find anything?"

"You mean apart from a sexual predator in the bedroom? Nothing. Her browsing history's been erased, along with all her photos and videos, even her Filmtrax account."

"Shit." Matiu gets to his feet. He brushes past Erica, maintaining a safe illusion that his urges were entirely a symptom of the neuro-empathic event. Part of him would still like to put his hands on her, feel her surrender under his grip, but that part of him can go piss off. He doesn't want another elbow to the groin. "Someone else has been here."

Erica follows him to the lounge, where he sits at the virtual keyboard and swipes into the house network's security settings. He scans the display, rubbing at the impossible itch under his bandage. "Shit. Shit. Shit. We need to go."

"Why?"

Matiu waves vaguely at the screen as he gets up and heads for the door. "Whoever came and cleared out the network also put a sniffer on the alarm. As soon as it flagged an activation, or even a deactivation, whoever planted it got notified. They know we're here, knew that eventually someone would come looking and do exactly what we've done. They might be heading this way right now." Could be one of Kingi's associates, someone equally dangerous, he thinks, but doesn't say it out loud. He doesn't need Erica to panic, or to think he's talking it up. "Let's get out of here."

He rushes from the house and unties Cerberus as Erica locks the door. They jog down the drive and get strapped into the car, just as a black van swings around the corner and accelerates towards them. Matiu hits the gas.

CHAPTER 7

- Pandora -

"It's through here." His head ducked to avoid the branches, Tanner holds back the foliage. Slipping by him into the clearing, its trees draped in yellow tape to keep out the rubber-neckers, Penny gets her first look at the body. A Jane Doe. She stifles a gasp.

It's a bog body! Like the ones discovered in peat marshes all over Northern Europe. Penny's heart does a little leap. She damps it down quickly. No matter how historical and thrilling the find, the corpse was once a living, breathing person. She needs to treat the site, and the body, with professional respect.

She takes a breath and examines the scene.

Curled up in a newly-excavated hollow, the dead woman is lying on her side. She's perfectly preserved. Her leathery skin is as dark as Guinness and, in places, folded in on itself like an apple wrinkled with age. She's not wearing any clothes, and there's no jewellery or other adornment to point to her age. Still, something in the woman's features, perhaps the small ears and the delicate nose, suggest she might have been younger, possibly in her thirties. That's all Penny can see for the moment, her view partially blocked by a man wearing waders, crouched beside the body. His back to Penny, he prods gently at the cadaver, trying to lift the woman's head with a wooden spatula.

With a start, Penny recognises the set of his shoulders. She'd been warned, knew he might still be here, but even so her heart races. Beads of sweat spring up on her palms, and her face flushes hotly. Bloody autonomic nervous system. At least he isn't looking her way. But then he does, and his mouth twitches.

I used to kiss that mouth.

With his usual infuriating air of studied nonchalance, Noah Cordell stands up and pushes the fringe of wavy curls off his forehead with the back of his arm.

"Noah."

"Pandora. How nice." His tone suggests it is anything but nice. With a brisk snap of his Nitrile gloves, Cordell turns his back on her and addresses the detective. "What's this about, Tanner? I thought we agreed I'd be the lead scientific consult on this case."

"That's not exactly how I remember it, Cordell. Anyway, you already have fifteen, sixteen cases on your books."

Cordell shrugs. "We could have double the caseload and still handle it. LysisCo has the capacity. My staff are well-trained and our labs are state-of-the-art. We get results…"

Did he always talk like this? As if he were an advertorial?

One arm still holding back the mangrove like a traffic lollipop, Tanner lets the branches go, closing the three of them in the clearing. He folds his arms across his chest. "I see," he says. "So you're implying Ms Pandora here isn't up to the work, is that it? Because you were the one who recommended her. Didn't she do her internship at LysisCo?"

"Well yes, she did," Cordell backtracks smoothly. "I'm certainly not casting aspersions on the validity of Pandora's qualifications, it's just…" He raises an eyebrow. "Shall we say, a lack of experience?"

Penny karate-chops the air between the pair of them. "Um… seeing as I'm here, would you mind if I took a quick a look?"

Tanner puts his hands on his hips. "Dr Cordell?"

Cordell heaves a sigh, then gives a theatrical sweep of his hand as he steps to one side. "Be my guest."

Taking care not to cave in the hollow, Penny steps closer to the body.

Tanner hovers behind her. "I've got to admit, in all my years of policing I've never had a body look like this one. I've seen them come out the water all blown up like balloons, but this is…"

"It's a bog body," Cordell interrupts. "Naturally mummified. Amazing really."

Slipping on her gloves, Penny drops to her haunches. "How was she discovered?"

"The tide made a channel, which uncovered the sink hole, and then someone's dog dug it up. I think she was buried deeper, but the mutt dragged her out of the ditch," Tanner replies.

Penny nods. One of the woman's arms shows evidence of an animal bite. The same arm sports a small tattoo at the wrist. Unlike the one on the body in the park, this tattoo is hard to make out, the ink barely discernible against the woman's darkened skin. Nevertheless, the pattern is unmistakeable: concentric whorls and a central motif resembling an eye. Coincidence? Tanner doesn't think so…

Taking care not to damage the limb, Penny moves to check inside the other wrist.

"There's nothing there. I looked," Tanner says as his phone rings. "Where the hell are you?" he barks. Lifting the tape over his head, he steps out of the clearing to take the call.

Penny continues her observations. The woman's face looks too serene for her to have suffocated, although it's a possibility. There's a blackened mass in the lower abdomen area. Had the victim been eviscerated? Was that how she'd died? Maybe she'd been tortured before death. Or perhaps she'd attempted to carry out her own Caesarean. Penny shudders. She hopes that wasn't what happened. The mass doesn't *look* like a baby and there's no sign of a skeleton. Not that that means anything. The same highly acidic conditions that preserved skin and internal organs would likely have resulted in the break-down of any bone salts. Given that mineralisation of foetal bones peaks late in gestation, the lack of an obvious skeleton wouldn't necessarily rule out an aborted foetus. Penny would have to sample the mass to know more.

"Look, Tanner," Cordell says when Tanner reappears. Engrossed in her work, Penny had forgotten Cordell was there. "I was here first and I'm your lead consultant. My company has both the experience and the means to get the job done. You can't deny, LysisCo gets results."

"Experience," Tanner echoes.

Cordell frowns. "I just said that."

"So, you've carried out analyses on one of these…" Tanner waves a frypan-hand at the corpse in the hollow.

"Bog bodies," Penny and Cordell say together.

"…you've worked on bog bodies before, then?"

"Well, I…" Cordell smacks at an imaginary sand-fly on his neck. "Well, no. Not exactly. No one has. This is the first example of its type ever uncovered in New Zealand."

Taking a sampling bag from her satchel, Penny turns it inside out and scoops up a handful of the substrate surrounding the corpse, speaking while she works. "It's true," she says. "Instances of bog bodies are extremely rare, less than 100 uncovered worldwide, because only a few bodies of water provide exactly the right conditions. Even recreating them under laboratory conditions is problematic. Not only does the substrate need to be anaerobic, it has to be saturated with organic acids and aldehydes, making it highly acidic. Normally, rotting peat provides the organic material. It's what causes the acidity: humic acid released as the vegetation breaks down. I wonder if the decaying mangroves serve the same purpose here…" she says out loud. "But I always thought conditions had to be cold, much colder than New Zealand, typically less than 4°C. That's why bog bodies tend to be found in northern Europe… I'd take an internal temperature reading…" She shakes her head. "Too risky. I'd hate to damage a specimen as scientifically important as this one. Anyway, the site's been uncovered for a while now…"

Tanner turns to Cordell. "So," he says slowly, "what were you saying about there being no experts?"

"Now look, Tanner—"

But Tanner raises his palm, stopping him. "The thing is, Cordell, there's a possibility this body is connected to another one discovered at North Shore."

"The case from this morning? The homeless guy?"

Tanner nods. "The one you were too busy to handle…"

Cordell's eyes narrow. "Not too busy, Tanner. I never said we were too busy, just that the North Shore case didn't require any specialised expertise…" He pauses. "I can't see how this bog body could have any connection to a death that occurred in the past 24 hours. Most bog bodies date from the Iron Age. For all we know, this one might have died before Kupe rowed up in his waka."

Tanner's mouth drops. "You're fucking kidding me." He turns to look at Penny. "Is that true?"

"I'm sorry, what?" Using a pair of tweezers, Penny is concentrating on putting what looks like hair into a sampling bag.

"Could this body really have been here since the Iron Age?"

Her eyes fixed on the fibre, Penny nods. "That's right. The oldest known bog body is Koelbjerg Woman from Denmark. She lived in the Mesolithic period."

"Mesolithic?"

"The Stone Age," replies Cordell.

"Jesus."

"But she was only a skeleton," Penny murmurs. "The oldest fleshed out example dates from the Bronze Age. The thing is, just looking at this body *in situ*, we've no way of knowing how long she's been preserved. It could be as little as one year or as much as a thousand. It would've helped if she'd been wearing clothing, or if she'd been buried with some personal items to give us a hint to her era. I could look at her teeth for dental work, and examining her stomach contents might help."

"But look at her: she's got skin and nails and everything. Can't you just do a DNA test?" Tanner demands.

Sealing the bag, Penny slides the sample into her satchel and stands up. "Assuming her DNA was catalogued somewhere, but I'm guessing they didn't have DNA profiling as far back as the Iron Age. In any case, it's unlikely any DNA will have survived the preservation process. Radiocarbon dating would work, providing the age of the cadaver doesn't go back more than 10 half-lives."

Tanner gives her a blank look. "Ten lives. What is she, a cat?"

Cordell cuts in. "What Pandora is trying to say—and doing rather a poor job of it—is that radiocarbon dating is only accurate up to 50,000 years."

A poor job. A poor job? Penny could happily stab him in the eye with her tweezers.

"LysisCo can handle the carbon dating," Cordell goes on. "I've just upgraded our equipment to include a model 2035 benchtop Quantulus spectrometer."

We interrupt this programme for a brief message from our sponsor.

"Excellent. That's sorted, then. When she's ready, Ms Pandora can send a sample over."

"But—" Cordell stammers, his face a rictus of surprise.

"I'm giving her the case, Cordell."

Penny is overwhelmed by a rush of gratitude for the big detective.

"No need to get too smug, Yee," Tanner says, bringing her back to earth. "You've got 72 hours to see if the two cases are connected. After that, our Jane Doe goes to Cordell."

Gloating isn't professional, so Penny smiles instead. "Is the pathologist on his way? I don't think the body should be left exposed like this. It'll already have started to decompose."

"That was Mather on the phone just now. He doesn't want anything to do with it. Something about preferring his bodies fresh. You'll have to store it. I'll have it bagged up for you to take back to your lab."

"My lab?" Penny mumbles. She hadn't expected to play host to a cadaver.

"Yes. That way, it'll be easier for you to do whatever it is you people do. You've got a cool store, right?"

"Yes—"

But the detective has already departed in a flutter of yellow crime tape and a swish of mangrove branches.

Cordell snaps off his gloves. "Right, Pandora, I'll see you in 72 hours to collect the body. Try not to completely destroy the evidence, will you? I'd like to be able to salvage a modicum of justice for the poor woman, whoever she is."

He turns on his heel, presumably to stomp off, except with all the mud it's more of a squelch off.

When he's gone, Penny gets out her phone and snaps a photo of the tattoo. Hang on. She's missed a message from Matiu. He's sent a bunch of photographs. Penny swipes through the series. Her eyebrows knit. They're medicine labels: Gonal-F, Suprefact, Ovidrel, and Crinone. All prescribed for a woman named Charlotte Langley.

What the hell?

Penny doesn't recognise the others, but Gonal-F is a synthetic version of FSH. Follicle stimulating hormone! A protein that encourages ovarian follicles to grow and release ova. There's only one reason Penny knows for taking that. She sucks in a breath. IVF. Matiu's making plans to be a dad?

Without telling *me*?

But he hasn't said a thing. He hasn't mentioned this Charlotte woman, not even in passing.

Thigh deep in mud, Penny stabs at her phone.

What the FUCK, Matiu? she types.

Then deletes it. That's not the way to approach this, even if he is her brother. Although, maybe it isn't Matiu who's pushing for a family. Ever since high school, girls—Penny's friends included—have been throwing themselves at her little brother—attracted by his decent set of abs and carefully feigned nonchalance. It didn't stop at schoolgirls, either. Women are still chasing him, and Matiu's recent stint in prison—the connections and the facial tattoos he got in there—have only added to his appeal. Penny doesn't really get it. Sure, it's well-documented that women in mid-cycle prefer males they perceive to be hyper-masculine, but not every woman Matiu meets can be mid-cycle! Still, there haven't been any serious relationships. Nothing meaningful. Not as far as Penny's aware.

Omigod. What if this is serious?

No, no, no. She shakes her head. If Matiu was in a serious relationship, if he was in on plans to have a baby, why would he be asking about the drugs? Why wouldn't he already know? Something's off. Instead, she types:

In vitro fertilisation meds? Serious chat due, little brother. Developments at this end: Jane Doe is bog body pulled from mud at Karaka. Tanner right about tattoo, identical to John Doe.

Then she adds a photo of the tattoo to the bottom of her message, as well as a Wikilink about bog bodies, so Matiu understands the significance.

Right, time to wrap up this site investigation. Penny needs to eyeball Matiu and find out if she's about to be an aunty.

- Matiu -

"More of your dodgy mates?" Erica asks, both hands holding onto the seat as Matiu hurtles through a bend, tyres squealing round the corner, and accelerates onto the main road. Cerberus howls as he slides into the doors and the back of the seats.

"Dunno. Would you like me to pull over and ask?" The van has dropped behind, no match for the Porsche. Matiu floors the gas, weaving around a bus and a couple of trucks, a few cars whizzing by the other way. Horn blasts assail them, but Matiu doesn't slow down until the van is gone from his rear view. Then he takes a hard right, zigzags through the backstreets at a more legally acceptable speed, and soon they're cruising along an industrial drive, Matiu scanning the road. They pass a series of looming warehouses, now creaking with neglect, which used to be a hub for national courier companies before the implosion of the transport industry in the wake of the oil crash. He pulls the Porsche into an access way. Down the back are a number of smaller buildings, large tin sheds with roller doors, where the transport companies used to do maintenance on their fleet vehicles. Matiu taps his phone screen and one of the roller doors starts to rise. He drives the Porsche through and swipes his phone, dropping the roller door behind them. He kills the engine as the door shudders closed. For a moment, they sit there in the darkness, the silence broken only by their heavy breathing, the ticking of the engine block cooling, and Cerberus' quiet whines.

Finally, Erica speaks. "And what are we doing here? Wherever *here* is?"

Matiu rests his head against the seat, willing the tension of the past few minutes to drain away. "It's a criminal thing, Erica. We're illegally inside an abandoned building we have no right to be in, which I have illegal access to because people are dipshits when they buy cheap security systems and link them to the internet making them vulnerable to all sorts of hacks. What we're doing here is called lying low, which is what we do when potentially dangerous people are chasing us at high speed through the city because they think we might've uncovered their dodgy dealings and they want to wipe us off the map before we cause them any trouble. Especially when we're in a car as distinctive as this one. Those guys in the van, whoever they are, will have almost certainly called their mates and told them to keep an eye out, so we've got some time to kill. Hope you had nowhere else to be today."

Erica unclips her seatbelt, the coil of it winding up loud in the car's still interior. "What did we find back there, then? What's going on?"

Matiu's phone pings. He glances at it, swipes through to the message. Penny. "Dunno yet, but this is interesting."

"What?"

"Charlotte ever say anything to you about wanting a baby?"

Erica frowns. "No. She didn't even have a boyfriend."

"Well, we know that's not true. Your sister wanted something more in her life, and these were in her fridge." He shows her the photos of the drugs. "Penny says they're IVF meds, in vitro fertilisation. Baby in a bottle stuff."

"I know what IVF is, lughead. No way was she doing that. It's thousands of dollars, and she's on worse money than me."

"Someone else could be paying for it. Her mysterious boyfriend, maybe."

"Why the hell would she be trying to get pregnant? She's not even in a relationship, she's got no money."

"Sometimes people just...need things."

"My sister didn't need a *baby*."

"The evidence suggests otherwise." Christ, he's starting to sound like Penny.

Erica sits back, arms crossed. Even in the gloom, he can see the colour rising in her cheeks. "Why wouldn't she have told me?"

"Because she's not in a relationship and she's got no money and you can be an overbearing, judgemental bitch?"

"What'd you call me?" Erica growls. She twists in her seat, coming up on one knee, her small stature making it easy to move in the cramped car, and slaps Matiu clean across the face.

Stunned only for a heartbeat, Matiu's instincts kick in and he grapples her wrists. He wants to push her away but he's got no leverage, and the pain in his arm flares up, so instead he wrenches her closer, pulling her arms in tight so she can't hit him again. Then her face is pressed against his, her lips striking viper-hot, the moment taking him so completely by surprise he has no response but to let her. The kiss is hard and fierce, and over almost as soon as it began.

Erica draws back, her breath coming in short, hard gasps, a glimmer in her eye. "I'm sorry, I...I shouldn't have done that. Just...something I've been needing to get out of my system for a long time."

Matiu is lost for words, but he manages to string something together as he eases his grip on her wrists. "You needed to assault someone with your mouth? Do I get to elbow you in the ovaries now?"

"Dick," she says, but a flicker of a smile graces her lips. "I've wanted to do that to *you* for a long time. Something about you just...gets under my skin. You're dangerous, and gorgeous, and you give me lip, and that makes me all hot inside. But you're a client, and I'm a professional, and I can't risk creating a conflict of interest, so that's it. No more. I just...had to do that. We can move on now."

Matiu stares at her, blinking like a possum in a spotter's torch. He's holding her arms only lightly now, but she's not pulling away. "You're right. This would be a very bad idea." He releases her wrists and, after a breathy moment, she sinks back into her seat, looking awkwardly out the windows into the dimly lit workshop. "A really bad idea." He lets the words hang in the air, like bait, to see if she bites.

She glances across at him. "Take that look off your face. We're going to pretend this never happened."

"Pretend what never happened?" Matiu says, then climbs from the car and lets Cerberus out behind him. "I'm going to take a look round, see if there's anyone about. Don't go anywhere."

Erica glares up at him, the same old Erica he used to know, the one who will never look quite the same now he's seen a little of the woman beneath the armour. "Don't mind me, I'll just be here, *lying low.*"

CHAPTER 8

- Pandora -

"Ms Yee." A woman pushes through a group of bystanders and rushes at her, a ridiculously narrow pencil skirt forcing her to take tiny staccato footsteps. "You remember me." It isn't a question, although, to be fair, Patisepa Taylor's blazing mane and overstretched leonine expression are hardly circumspect.

"Ms Taylor. Hello."

"So, who's the murder victim?" The real estate agent doesn't bother with preamble— probably because Penny isn't a client.

"Would you mind?" Handing Patisepa her satchel, Penny peels off the waders, pushing the straps off her shoulders one at a time. "Sorry, I'm not at liberty to divulge any information." She steps out of the attached boots, leaving the waders in an upright heap of Land Rover green. It's a relief to get some air on her skin. Even made of breathable BogTex™ fabric, wearing them has been like standing in a sauna.

"Aha! I *knew* it wasn't an accident." Patisepa flaps a handful of glossy brochures at Penny, who's grateful for the extra breeze. "I told the media people, if you were here, then it had to be a murder. You're like their top detective or something, aren't you?"

"Oh no, I'm not actually—"

Patisepa shoves the bag at her. "What sort of murder are we talking about exactly? Something horrendous, I'll bet. A botched drug deal? A gang hit? Maybe a crime of passion? What am I talking about? This is the burbs; it *has* to be a crime of passion. My money's on a lover's spat... and the victim lives on this street. Maybe the *killer* lives on this street..."

Penny slips the satchel over her shoulder. "I'm sorry, Ms Taylor, I really can't—"

Narrowing her eyes, Patisepa draws herself up to the top height of her Jimmy Choos and leans in close. "You don't have to be such a fucking cow, you know," she hisses out of the side of her mouth. "I'm only trying to do my job. It wouldn't hurt you to help a sister out."

Shocked, Penny takes a step back, an officer taking advantage of the moment to swoop in, gather up the soiled waders, and carry them off.

"This is the second time in a month one of your investigations has interfered in my business," Patisepa rails under her breath.

A man and his dog peel off from the group gathered at the edge of the mangroves. As he approaches, Patisepa raises her voice a decibel. "Of course, I'll do everything in my power to help you with your important investigation. Although, I'm really not sure how you expect Taylor and Associates to sell Amber-Leigh William's beautifully appointed 6-bed villa with tennis court and swimming pool when there's a *murder* investigation going on, and right on Amber-Leigh's doorstep!" With a perfectly-timed sideways step, she thrusts a glossy leaflet into the startled man's hand.

He angles sharply away, the Schnauzer in tow. "Um, thanks… come on, boy."

Her audience retreating down the street, the agent lowers her voice. "I lost the sale on the warehouse, you know. That woman—the buyer—she shot through."

Penny nods. "Sandi Kerr." When Penny had last seen her, the Egyptologist had been smack in the middle of a bloody ritualistic sacrifice. Matiu and Cerberus had interrupted her, but the victim and her beloved dog had died anyway, Kerr escaping in the commotion. Despite several weeks of searching air and seaports, there'd been no sign of her.

"Yes, that's her." Patisepa pouts, straightening her over-bleached hair with her fingers. Penny wishes she wouldn't. Even without putting a single fibre under the microscope, it's obvious the cysteine disulphide bridges in her α-keratin helices have been dissociated so many times the mesh is in danger of breaking.

"With the buyer gone, I had to re-list the warehouse," Patisepa says.

"I'm sorry to hear that."

Patisepa stops with the hair-thing, and waves a hand breezily. "As if you care. Not that it matters. With all the noise about the warehouse being the site of Darius Fletcher's, you know, his *death*, and *Dish-It* leaking photos of blood congealing on the floor… the flies all over it… Well, I was inundated with calls." She giggles. "Seriously, I was on the phone so much I wouldn't be surprised if I end up with a tumour from all the radiation."

Actually, Penny would be very surprised: unlike ionising radiation, there's very little evidence linking cancers to radiofrequency energy achieved from sustained cell-phone use— even if Patisepa had been on the phone for years. More likely her ear just got a bit hot.

Still rabbiting on, Patisepa fans her face with the stack of leaflets. "Anyway, with all the publicity, I sold the warehouse in three days."

"You did?"

The agent turned her head to one side and nodded. "Unconditional sale. Twice the original offer."

"That's fantastic." Penny means it. Darius' sister, Rose Fletcher would likely be the sole beneficiary of the sale, after Patisepa's expenses of course, and while the funds wouldn't return Rose's only family to her, it might soften her loss.

"Well, obviously, I don't like to blow my own trumpet, but I'm a very good negotiator. Anyway, the new buyers are from out of town, some guy and his wife planning to run paranormal ghost tours." Patisepa lifts a hand to her ruby-lined mouth and whispers conspiratorially, "Don't tell the Health Department, but they didn't even want me to clean up the blood."

"Um, Ms Taylor, I'm really not sure this conversation is…"

"Gotta go. I think the film crew have rounded up someone who knows something." Smooshing a glossy leaflet into Penny's hand, she teeters off as fast as her pencil skirt will allow.

Someone knows something?

Hitching up her satchel, Penny follows the agent to where a crowd has assembled. Bystanders. Online crews. A couple of vloggers. Penny hovers on the fringes.

The announcer's jeans are even tighter than Patisepa's skirt. "Streaming live now from Karaka, RealEvent has secured an exclusive interview with Dr Noah Cordell, the country's foremost scientific consultant, at the site of what could be the most significant event in recent anthropological history. Dr Cordell, what can you tell us about today's discovery of a perfectly preserved bog body?"

"Well, Xander, it's really too early to say much, other than we believe the victim is female. Anything else would be speculation, although various studies suggest bog bodies are the result of religious sacrifices carried out amongst the high class in certain societies. Other scholars associate them with the punishment of exiled criminals. It's an absolutely fascinating area of study."

Funny, Cordell hadn't mentioned either possibility at the site. Probably Googled bog bodies the second he took his waders off.

Taking a couple of steps towards the crowd, Cordell clears his throat. Penny recognises this part of his performance: he's always loved an audience. "What's vital right now," he says solemnly, "is preserving the specimen as quickly as possible. As you can imagine, decomposition is a big factor, which is why authorities are currently taking steps to remove the body to prevent any further deterioration."

He waves at a departing van bearing the LysisCo logo, as if that particular vehicle were transporting the body. On cue, the phones and cameras all swing in that direction. When the van has pulled away, Cordell continues his soapboxing: "As soon as the body is properly stored, my company, LysisCo Scientific, will conduct the radiocarbon analyses. That's L. Y. S. I. S. Yes, S.I.S. as in *secret service.*"

The crowd titters.

"Speaking of which, there's a naming tradition for bog bodies, isn't there?" Xander asks. "Tollund Man. Keepen Man. Yde Girl. Will they be naming this particular bog body Cordell Woman, after you?"

Penny should have used those tweezers while she had the chance. Cordell Woman? She'd bet her laboratory and every test tube in it that Cordell had suggested the name himself. Better they call her Spot or Max or Rufus after the dog who dug her up!

"Oh, I don't know about that," Cordell says, batting his bloody eyelashes and feigning modesty. "That's not my call. I'm just a researcher. Although Cordell Woman does have a nice ring to it, don't you think?"

"Is it true that the body could predate the Māori?"

Cordell raises an arm and sweeps his hair off his forehead. "Quite possibly, Xander. In fact, this find might force us to re-examine everything we know about the history of mankind in this country…"

The pat on her shoulder makes Penny whirl. Behind her two uniformed police officers are loitering with purpose. "Excuse me, Dr Yee, if you wouldn't mind pointing us to your vehicle, please?"

"I'm sorry?" Penny steps away from the crowd, Cordell's voice fading behind her.

"Your vehicle? Whereabouts is it?" says the officer with the goatee.

Penny blinks. "I haven't got a vehicle."

The second officer rolls his eyes. "Well, how did you get here, then?"

Penny glances down the street. She gulps when she sees Craig has waited for her. "Um, I came in that silver Mercedes over there."

"Right." The two men bend, and it's only then that Penny notices the white plastic bag laying on the ground. One metre by two and a half. Central zipper.

A body bag!

Hefting it by the handles, the men pick up the corpse and haul it towards Craig's car. Even with its flesh preserved, the corpse mustn't weigh much, judging from the way they are hurtling along.

"Wait!" To catch up, Penny breaks into a run, the satchel banging against her hip. "What are you doing? Where are you taking that?"

"Detective Tanner told us you'd be taking the body. He said to put it in your vehicle."

"But… I can't take this. It needs to go in a refrigerated van."

"Sorry. The last van on site was that Cordell-fella's, and it just left." Goatee tilts his bristled chin back towards the crowd. "Probably wasn't refrigerated, anyway. So, unless you can conjure up an ice-cream truck, there's not a lot we can do."

"But we can't just toss it in the back seat of a car."

The second officer rolls his eyes again.

"Please. Just give me a minute to sort this out." Penny glances about, expecting to catch sight of Tanner. Where on earth is he? Normally, the detective is easier to spot than the Sky Tower on New Year's Eve.

"If you're looking for Tanner, he left already," says Goatee. "Got called away. City's in a fucking crime wave. I heard he's got eighteen cases on the go."

Reaching the Mercedes, the pair dump the bag on the grass behind the vehicle, Rolls-his-eyes giving the back of the car a little celebratory thump with the palm of his hand.

"Careful!"

"Sorry. Sign here, please." Goatee hands her a stylus. Penny scratches her name on his phone.

"Hey wait, can you help me put it in the boot?" But the pair are already hightailing it across the grass to catch a ride out. Neither of them looks back.

The car door opens. Penny cringes as Craig gets out. He rounds the Mercedes, holding the too-perfect creases in his pants between pinched fingers. He takes in the body bag and his eyes widen. "Penny? What's going on?"

- Matiu -

"So, can I drop you at your car or something?"

The shadows stretch long as the Porsche hisses down the sun-baked streets, Matiu taking it easy, scanning every corner and side street for signs of danger, or black vans.

Erica gives him a sharp look. "Car? I take the bus. Not all of us can afford fuel, you know."

Matiu shrugs. "Yeah, sorry, I forget. Spend all day driving, eh."

"Lucky for some. The rest of us have to do honest work."

Matiu grimaces and watches the road as the sun drops.

"But I live not far from here, so you can drop me off, if you like."

"Which way?"

Five minutes later, they pull up outside a high-rise council apartment block in a rundown part of New Lynn. Matiu expects to see overturned shopping trollies in the long grass, hobos crowding around a fire burning in an old oil drum, that sort of thing, but the place just has a forlorn, abandoned look about it. "You live here? I know you like being involved in your work, but living next door to your clientele seems a bit much, even for you."

"It's what I can afford," she says, unclipping her seatbelt. "I know who your parents are, Matiu. You've grown up with privilege, and you must've made a bloody hash of it to even know me. But don't go being the *judgemental bitch* about where I live and how I get around, all right?"

He winces. "You want me to walk you to your door?"

Erica smirks. "Why? So you can catch the bus as well? This car won't last a minute in this neighbourhood."

"Erica, I'll find out what I can about your sister."

"Do that. I'll call you. Have some answers."

She gets out of the car and stalks towards the apartment block without so much as a goodbye. Matiu takes a long breath and pulls into the street. Damn her! Messing with his day like this, screwing with his head. Shit, even if she didn't have the whole *Do what I tell you or I can send you back to prison where you belong, you sexy thing* routine going on, Matiu would feel obliged to do something. If *his* sister was missing, he'd stop at nothing to find her. And Charlotte could be pregnant, but what? Was she too scared to tell anyone? And what the hell was going on with all the grass growing inside her house? He shouldn't be getting involved in this sort of shit, but he can't walk away now. There's more to it than just some weird hippy diet thing going on. Erica needs his help, and somewhere low in his gut he has an unexpected urge to co-operate with her. He's been resisting her as long as they've known each other, fighting like dogs, and now suddenly, from that one moment of regrettable contact, his outlook has changed. She's playing him, of course. He's not stupid. She wants him to do this for her, and the kiss, that suggestion of something more, is meant to hook him in. He doesn't want to bite, but there's a woman missing, and he might be able to connect the dots, given the headspace to work it through. Fuck it all.

It's another fifteen minutes across town to Screech's workshop, and the gloom of evening has set in by the time he hacks the roller door open. Parking the Porsche back in its space while the door drops behind him, Matiu lets Cerberus out and walks up the dimly lit aisle between the rows of covered cars. "Yo, Screech?" An eerie silence greets him. The old fluorescents throw a sallow, fizzing glow, casting everything into carved shadow. There's music playing somewhere out back, but no sound of tools clanking. The Commodore's still where he left it, the airbag draped across the front seat like an abandoned wedding dress. "Crap man, you're not done yet? You've had all day!"

Cerberus lets out a low moan as they move around the car, past the Camaro, and head for the office behind the workshop. "Maybe he's ducked out to eat," Matiu mutters, as much to the dog as to himself. Cerberus whines in reply, tugging against him as he moves deeper into the garage. "What's up, boy?" He pauses beside the creeper. It's halfway across the floor, and if Matiu had ever given a flying fuck about health and safety he'd be writing it up as a slip, trip and fall hazard as well as a slapstick routine in waiting. Then he notices the scattering of tools, wrench handles and socket heads lying haphazardly over the concrete. Maybe Screech had stepped on the creeper, gone for a tumble, taking his tools down with him. Maybe he's laid up in the office with a broken wrist or a bad back. Matiu takes a step forward, avoiding the creeper.

Then he sees the blood.

In the bad light, and against the ubiquitous grease-stains that cover every surface, it hadn't been obvious, but as soon as he sees it, Matiu realises why Cerberus is dragging his nails across the floor. As his eyes adjust to the dark, he traces the lines of spatter along the floor, up the walls. There's a good slash of it up the side of the Camaro, the same red as the paint-job. Suddenly his arm is itching again, something fierce.

"Screech?" Matiu steps gingerly over the detritus, ears alert for any sound, any hint of movement. Something scrapes in the room beyond the workshop. The sweat running down his neck turns chill, the shadows jumping with his spiking pulse.

Matiu steps around the corner and looks into the office. Screech is in his chair, and for a second Matiu wonders why a two-bit crook like Screech even needs an office when he sure as shit doesn't do any taxes, before he's struck by a memory of another wheeled office chair, back at Hanson's farm, a man no longer a man creaking forward from the darkness to breathe ice into his world. But Screech isn't Hanson. Screech has been cut, and cut bad. He's strapped to the chair, which sits in a slag of blood and body parts. His overalls are sodden, but it's the face staring back at him that holds Matiu's morbid attention. Suddenly Screech strains against his bonds like there's lightning running through him, thrashing, feet lifting the chair off the floor and slamming it back down. Matiu expects him to be screaming but he can't, because...

Because his tongue is one of the hunks of meat on the floor, discarded there along with an ear, one eye, several fingers. Half of Screech's left cheek is missing, and Matiu can see the ragged stump inside his mouth as it hangs open, a muted hiss of air streaming from his lungs devoid of the howl Matiu can see in the man's remaining eye. But he knows what he's saying, this bloody ravaged thing, this corpse who hasn't accepted he's a corpse yet. He's cursing Matiu for an oathbreaker, for selling him out when he promised he wouldn't. Kingi came here, found Screech. Kingi did this to him, shredded half his body, in some twisted parody of human art. The chopped-up man in the chop-shop. But was it revenge, or torture for the sake of finding out whatever the hell it was Kingi was looking for earlier in the day? Finding out where Matiu Yee was at, or his sister, or the body from the park? Or all of the above?

He backs away as Cerberus growls low under his breath. He ought to get in there, untie Screech, get him to a hospital. Scoop all the dismembered flesh from the floor into a chilly-bin and hope some doctor can work a miracle, but he doubts he'll get that far. Screech still has his teeth, and his face is a twisted mask of insane rage. If Matiu cuts him free, he could go mental, clawing and biting and fuck-knows-what. He's better off getting out and calling 111, leave this shit to the professionals. Matiu is turning away when the shadows move. Cerberus yanks him forward, off his feet. If not for the dog, Matiu might've been struck by the thing that swings from the ceiling. A shape swoops through the light, legs and arms outstretched, hanging from something long and sinuous. Tentacles. The fluorescents swing madly on their chains. Matiu scrambles to his feet and slides across the blood-slick floor, skidding on loose tools. One foot finds the rogue creeper, which scoots out from under him, and he goes down again. Drops the leash.

The air explodes from his lungs, head slamming into the concrete floor. For a second, there's a silhouette over his head, Kingi, reaching for him, twisting limbs writhing black against the swinging lights, then Cerberus leaps over Matiu, and both dog and monster tumble from view. Groggy, ears ringing, Matiu staggers to his feet. The bandage on his arm is sodden with grease and blood. Cerberus is rolling on the floor with the man he'd once called Si. Brothers of a sort, once, him and Simon Kingi. What the fuck had happened, that here they were now, soldiers on opposite sides of some fucked up, invisible war? Dimly, he hears Screech slamming his feet on the floor.

"Cerberus!" Matiu yells, and spins towards the Commodore. Remembers the exploded airbag, the seats covered in powdered chalk. No way can he take that back to Dad. He whips open the Camaro door and Cerberus leaps in without hesitation. Matiu drops into the driver's seat, turns the key and throws it into gear. Kingi stands, flicking a hand, spraying more dark spatter across the floor. With barely enough room to get the car out, Matiu lurches the dragster forward, locking the wheel hard over. Tyre smoke and exhaust fill the tight space. The car was built to burn rubber. It spins up a storm without any help from Matiu. He pulls it into a tight turn to line up the roller door. He won't have time to fuck around with his phone. Matiu lets the clutch out and the Camaro squeals like a banshee towards the closed door.

Kingi moves, faster than blinking. Tentacles lash out, catching the rafters and hurtling him across the workshop, feet catching and tipping over barrels and stacks of tyres as he rushes in. The Camaro's bonnet hits the roller door right as Kingi drops onto the front windshield. The roller door explodes outwards with a shriek of torn metal, and Kingi is dragged backwards out of sight. The car bounces down the driveway and onto the street in a spray of sparks. Matiu hauls the wheel around, showering the street with shattered steel. Oversized rear tyres fishtail in a cloud of black smoke. Then the car leaps forward, the front tyres clearing the road for several seconds before gravity reasserts itself. Matiu watches the speedo rocket higher. He's driven cars before, but never a fucking *rocket*. This is the shit.

"Fuck bro, that was too close," he says to Cerberus, who's laid out in the well behind the driver's seat. "Too fucking close." He dares to take a breath, glad that Screech had the good business sense to locate his dodgy little chop shop in a part of town where the CCTV stranglehold hasn't quite reached yet.

The rear windscreen explodes. Tentacles swarm into the car, hunting.

"Shit!" Matiu yanks the wheel over hard and cranks the handbrake, throwing the car into a spin. The tentacles vanish through the hole as streetlights sweep viciously through Matiu's burning retinas, his head screaming with the pressure. Blackness creeps in. He lets off the gas, and the car slews to a halt. The V8 purrs on, unperturbed. Blinking away the darkness, Matiu looks at the street, where a body moves, getting up. He hits the gas again. The Camaro loves this shit. The bump of the crumpled bonnet pounding Kingi into the road would've almost been satisfying, if what was happening wasn't so fucking terrifying.

Matiu takes the next bend and puts his foot down. Hopefully he's left Kingi behind this time, but he doubts it. If only he had a shotgun handy. One more stop to make before he can get out of here. Two more corners take him around the block, back into the seedy industrial side road where Screech's workshop now lies open to the general public, the roller door a snarled mess of twisted metal, detritus covering the road. He pulls over, yanking the keys from the Camaro and throwing them into the gutter. He and Cerberus jog back up the drive and through the remains of the roller door. Sirens echo somewhere in the distance. Better make this quick. Get Screech, get Dad's car, get the hell out.

Inside, there's a reek of methane. The floor is awash in high-strength corn-based biofuel from an upturned barrel. Matiu holds his shirt over his nose and runs in, past the Commodore and over the scattered tools to the office. Screech isn't moving, his head hanging down. Matiu doesn't waste time figuring out if he's alive, he just wheels the chair from the office. Screech slumps. If he's not dead, he's playing some good possum. Slipping through blood and fuel, Matiu skids up beside the Commodore and jerks the back door open, hunting for his jack-knife to cut the cable ties holding Screech's wrists to the chair.

He's got one arm free, the body falling forward into Matiu's arms, when Cerberus growls again, low and loud. Matiu looks to the broken roller door. There's a figure standing there, and for one awful breath he thinks it's Kingi, back already, but it's not. No tentacles. It's a dark silhouette, broad, imposing. Like a statue drawn out of shadow, a flicker of a shape glimpsed over the shoulder, from the corner of the eye and then gone, but this time the figure remains.

"Matiu," the figure says, and he lifts his hand to his face, the incarnadine glow of a cigarette briefly brightening his sculpted, dour features as he inhales. Smoke wreathes around his face like ghosts in the wind. "Got a sec?"

Matiu's blood runs cold. He wants to throw Screech into the back and get the hell out of here before the cops arrive, but he can't move. Can't breathe. "What do you want, Makere?"

"All I've ever wanted, bro. To help."

Matiu snorts, a bitter sound. "Bullshit. Get the fuck out of my way."

"Don't talk like that," Makere says, taking another ominous drag on the smoke. "We're *whanau*. Used to be real close, you and me."

"You're not real. You can't even *be here*. You're in my head." The itch under his bandage flares up again, maddening.

Makere chuckles. "It's like this, bro. I'm not in your head, never was. That was just a handy place to watch the world from. But now I'm here, not there, and things are out of balance. Someone needs to go back, take my place, or it might all get out of hand, and I can't make any promises that people won't get hurt. So, you're the obvious choice, right? It's your turn."

"I dunno what you mean," he lies. Fear spikes his innards and he wrestles Screech's inert body, his fingers, grimed with blood and oil, slipping on the knife. Screech flops around uncooperatively. Cerberus growls and paws the floor, fuel dripping from his nails.

"You're going to find me someone to send back there, bro, or I'll take you. Or maybe our sweet little *tuahine*, Pandora. We clear?"

Matiu stops. A lead ball sinks through his guts, and he straightens up, dumping Screech back in the chair. He glares at Makere, adrenaline trembling his fingertips, as he judges the distance between them. Weighs the knife in his palm. "Don't you threaten me, and stay the fuck away from Penny." He's tensed to jump, ready to cross the workshop and put Makere down like the dog he is.

"Your choice, bro." Makere takes one last drag on the cigarette.

Matiu's eyes widen. He's seen enough action movies to know what's coming next. He shoves the chair aside, grabs Cerberus' collar and throws him into the car, rips the driver's door open and slides in behind the wheel. Makere, languidly, flicks the glowing cigarette butt from his long, lean fingers to arc end-over-end towards the fuel-soaked floor. Matiu guns the engine as the cigarette lands, the fuel erupting with a *whoompf*, the air suddenly super-hot. Impossible to breathe. He finds reverse and accelerates through the flames, Makere in his rear-view mirror before the Commodore jounces out of the hole left by the Camaro. Flames boil from the doorway, but as the car slows, there's no sign of Makere. Just like the old days, there one moment, gone the next. The sirens are getting closer. Matiu hits the gas, making himself scarce. He has to get to Penny. This shit just turned ugly.

CHAPTER 9

- Pandora -

Close to town, Penny pushes the button to roll up the window. "Thanks for doing this, Craig."

"Hey, no worries. You've given me the greatest story ever to take back to the office. Bog Body in the Boot. It sounds like the title of one of those classic Taika Waititi black comedies."

Penny twiddles the buckle on her satchel, opening and closing the clasp. "Actually, Craig... I'm afraid I'm going to have to ask you to keep this quiet. Until the case is resolved, I'm meant to keep any details confidential. I could lose the account."

"What?" Craig's head whips in her direction. "But the media were all over it back at Karaka."

"Yes, I know. Even so."

"Penny, it's in my car." She nibbles her lip. He looks back at the road. "A dead person in my car..."

"Sorry."

Shaking his head, Craig sighs deeply. They drive a couple of blocks, Craig not saying anything.

"It's the next left," Penny says when they reach the intersection before the lab.

Craig turns into the street where Yee Scientific has its premises. Penny had been lucky to find a place that already had a basic lab fit-out: a tertiary education provider forced to close its doors owing to a lack of bums on seats. Plenty of bums in the neighbourhood, though, the suburb a mish-mash of contemporary apartment developments squeezed in between the empty lots and industrial warehousing.

"You know, Penny, I'm starting to get why your parents have reservations about this science work you've been doing."

"Excuse me? My parents discussed my job with you?"

"It wasn't like that, Penny. You have to understand, if they talked to me, it was only out of concern."

He's right. Penny doesn't understand. She isn't a little girl. She's a grown woman, and her career choices have nothing to do with her parents, Craig, or anyone else for that matter. She grips the buckle of the satchel, letting the pin dig into her palm.

"It feels dodgy," Craig goes on. "You hanging around crime scenes. Have you ever heard that old saying, 'if it smells like shit, it's probably shit'?"

"Pull in here, please."

"Penny—"

"Just here is fine."

Pulling in opposite the fence with its mis-spelled spray-painted slogan BASTARD GOVERMENT ARSEHOLES, Craig cuts the engine, and turns to her.

"Thanks so much for your help, Craig," she says quickly.

"Penny, please. Don't be like that."

"Like what? My lab is here. It's on the second floor." She forces a smile.

Craig breathes out through his nose, his nostrils flaring. "I'll help you move the body then."

"Really, there's no need," Penny insists. "I'll get my colleague to bring down a trolley." She's about to get out of the car, when he lays a hand on her shoulder. "At least, let me get it out of the car for you."

The man has waited in the car half the afternoon in the heat. A refusal would be churlish. She nods. "OK." Opening the door, she steps out on the footpath.

What? Her eyes widen as Cerberus bounds over, his lead dragging on the asphalt behind him.

Cerberus? What are you doing out here on your own?

"Where's Matiu?" she whispers, bending to grab the lead, but Cerberus is too quick for her, loping into the alley at the side of the building. Penny checks over her shoulder to where Craig is busy unloading the bog body. Obscured at the rear of the car, he doesn't appear to have noticed Cerberus.

"Um. No reception," Penny says, waving her phone theatrically. "It's always a bit dodgy on this side of the building. I'll just nip into the alley and use the intercom at the back entrance." Not waiting for Craig's reply, she darts into the alley.

Sucks in a breath.

Matiu is leaned up against the door of Dad's now beaten-up Commodore. The car's paintwork looks like someone has set to it with a Brillo pad and a blowtorch. Matiu must have come through the fires of hell to get here because his jeans are covered in grease and there's a rent in the seam of his leather jacket. Penny rushes over, catching him just before he topples.

"Oh my god, Matiu," she says, getting her shoulder under his and moving him to the wall. "What happened?" He's had a blow to his head; his hair crusted with congealing blood.

"Nothing." He puts a hand on the brickwork, supporting his own weight again.

"This is *not* nothing. You went to see your probation officer. How do you get like this at the probation office? And why does the fleet car look like you've just taken part in a monster derby?"

"Pen, can you please wait until we get inside for the interrogation?" he croaks.

Matiu saying please? Penny's stomach sinks. "Hang on, I'll get Craig."

But before she can properly extricate herself, Matiu grabs her arm. Trembling fingers dig into her skin. "No."

"But he's just around—"

"No!"

Penny pauses. "OK, let me get rid of him, then. Wait here." She hands him Cerberus' lead and punches out a text to Beaker.

"Make it quick, sis," Matiu says tiredly.

It's all Penny can do to leave him there and walk calmly around the corner. By now Craig is leaning against the car, waiting.

Holding up her phone, she flashes him a wide smile. "I've messaged my colleague. He'll be down with the trolley in just a moment."

Craig steps away from the car. "Penny, I really didn't mean to upset you before."

"You didn't." Penny smiles so wide her cheeks ache.Dropping his chin, Craig looks at her from under his lashes. "Penny."

Come on. Go already. Matiu could pass out any second.

"Really. You didn't. I'm just a bit overwhelmed, you know, with Mārama being ill, and getting two consults in one day." She inclines her head to the mountain of white, where the first bog body ever discovered in New Zealand has been plonked unceremoniously on the footpath.

Craig puts his hands in his pockets. "You're sure you're not angry?" He rocks on his heels.

"Not a bit."

"Well, then how about you prove it and have dinner with me tonight?"

Oh.

"Craig, really, that's very kind… it's just, um… I have a lot of work to do." It's as if she's still wading in the bog at Karaka.

Craig runs his hand through slick black hair. "Penny, come on," he coaxes. "You have to eat."

In the alley, Cerberus barks. Craig looks up.

"Dinner would be lovely," Penny blurts, touching her fingers to his sleeve and steering him towards the driver's side. "Eight o'clock sound OK? We can cancel if that's too late—"

Craig grins. "Eight is perfect. See you then."

As soon as the car is out of sight, Penny sprints into the alley.

"What on earth have you been doing, anyway? You know Dad's going to kill you when he sees that car." Somewhere nearby, tyres squeal in sympathy.

"Pen, I'm dying already, can it wait until we get inside?"

She helps him to the front of the building, Matiu wincing with every step. They've only just made it when the front doors open and Beaker steps out with the trolley.

"Thank heavens," Penny says, grasping one of the doors before it can close. "Talk about death warmed over; that body will be warmer now than it was when it was alive. Can you grab the bag please, Beaker, and bring it upstairs to the cooler while I help Matiu." She ushers Matiu through the doors.

"Penny?" Beaker says, puzzled. "What's going on?"

"Oh, it's nothing," she says, trying to sound nonchalant. "Matiu and I were involved in that little fender bender on the motorway this morning, remember?" She gives a little chuckle. "You know how it is, you don't notice the bruises until the adrenalin wears off."

"No, that's not what I mean," Beaker says. "Where's the body?"

"It was just there," Penny wails as the lab doors swing shut behind them. She leads Matiu to the nearest bench, then stomps back to the entrance to hang her satchel on its coat-hook. "Right there on the footpath. And next thing: gone! I can't believe it!"

Beaker giggles. "The thief won't believe it either, when he opens that bag. I mean, a dead body isn't your usual contraband, is it? He was probably hoping for weed."

"Beaker," Penny snaps. "This isn't a joke."

Beaker flares red. "Um no. Of course not. I just…um…I'd better put the trolley away." He hurries off, Cerberus bounding after him.

"That was harsh, sis," Matiu says when Beaker is out of earshot. "None of this is his fault. The poor guy was just trying to lighten the mood."

"Well, it isn't helping. What am I going to do, Matiu? I should phone Tanner and let him know. Only the minute I phone it in, my entire career will be over. Tanner will pull the contracts. I'll be forced to close the lab. Beaker will be out of a job. I can already imagine the glee on Mum and Dad's faces. Not to mention Cordell's."

"Come on. It can't be that bad."

"Matiu, you don't understand. It was a bog body. *A bog body*. Only the most important archaeological discovery in recent history, and I've gone and lost it." She slumps over the bench and lays her head on the epoxy resin, its cool surface strangely soothing. "I'm doomed."

Matiu ruffles her hair. "We'll figure it out, Pen. People don't just steal bodies off the street, so whoever did this has to have known what was in that bag. My guess is they followed you back from Karaka."

"You really think so?"

"Probably not. I'm still a bit woozy. In case you hadn't noticed, I recently took a clout to the head."

"Matiu, I'm serious."

"Pen, Craig's with *Transport*, not the Secret Service; he won't have been watching for a tail. Look, why don't you go and do whatever it is you have to do with your samples, while I take a shower. Nothing's going to happen in the next half hour. We'll decide what to do next when we're all a bit calmer."

"I am calm!"

Matiu draws a lazy circle on the benchtop with his index finger.

She sighs. "OK, so I could be calmer." She hates it when he makes sense. "Come on. Let's get you cleaned up. And when you're done, you can tell me what you've been playing at." Straightening, she drags a plastic BBQ chair into the wet-room and places it underneath the shower rose. Matiu trails her in. Like a shaky toddler, he tacks from one handhold to the next. Bench. Wall. Wall. Doorframe. Eventually, he steadies himself on the back of the chair. Penny flips on the water. "There's a first aid kit out in the lab."

He nods. "OK." One-handed, he tries shrugging off his jacket, his face puckering in pain.

"Here, let me do it." Penny slips it off his shoulders then pulls his t-shirt over his head, hanging both garments on a hook behind the door. It reminds her of when he was little, when she'd help him in and out of his dinosaur pyjamas. She used to fold them and put them under his pillow then, too. *Well, he can drop his own jeans. He's not that blimmin' helpless.* She grabs a fresh towel and lays it on the vanity, catching her reflection before the mirror clouds over. God, she looks a mess. She sucks in a breath. Cordell saw her like this. And that's not the worst of it.

"Matiu," she groans. "I only have until Thursday morning to deliver the body to Noah. He's going to be dating it."

Unzipping his jeans, Matiu arches an eyebrow. "That's a step down, even for him."

"Oh, for goodness' sake. *Carbon* dating. Not dating-dating. Honestly, I don't know why I bother." She whirls on her heel. "The hot water cuts out in fifteen minutes."

- Matiu -

Matiu locks the door and shucks off the rest of his clothes, coated as they are in the dust and grime and soot and blood of a day that has gone entirely not how he had imagined it would when he woke up this morning. The steam is sweet, wrapping him like a blanket, and he steps into the water, resting his weight on the back of the chair and letting the detritus sluice away down the drain. It stings where it runs over his broken skin, and his head still spins, but he stands, letting the simplicity of the moment consume him. Trying not to think, just for a few minutes. Slowly, he unwraps the filthy bandage from his arm and lets it fall in a sodden mass to the shower floor. The healing wound itches like hell, but he resists the urge to scratch, or to look at it.

Time was he would sit in his prison cell, eyes closed, seeking something like zen, a hiding place where Makere couldn't get to him. It hadn't really worked then, but he tries to recapture it now, to find an empty space in his head to just sit and breathe. The shower soaks him, runs through his hair, his eyes closed, his breathing slow and rhythmic, until the water swirling down the plughole runs clean. Then he turns the chair, drags it back under the showerhead, and sits. He can't let Penny know, but standing is an effort. Almost as much of an effort as thinking. The back of his skull alternately aches and tingles in pulsing waves. He just wants to sleep, and he knows enough about hitting people in the head to understand this is a bad sign. Could be a concussion. Could go to sleep and not wake up.

Focus, bro. Get your shit together. So much going on, how does it all fit? The stiff in the park, Erica's missing sister with the crazy grasses inside her house and the baby-making going on, the mysterious black van chasing them, Kingi and his tentacles constantly jumping in front of his car, what happened to Screech, Makere threatening first Mārama and then Penny, this body they pulled out of the mud and which someone then had the balls to steal right off the street. Who the hell would want that smelly thing, anyway? At least the missing body distracted Penny enough that she forgot about the state of the car, or how he got himself all battered and bleeding. Thoughts stream through the empty spaces like the water running over him. Different currents, but somehow connected. Crossing over, combining, but all running down to the same place. Or maybe not connected at all, just intersecting because he happens to be caught in the middle. *It's not all about you, bro.*

Oh, fantastic. No voice in his head anymore, but he's talking to himself like there is. That's progress. If only he could get some sort of short, sharp wake-up call to make everything clear. If only...

Something in the plumbing clicks, and the hot water runs cold.

Matiu yelps, instantly chilled to the bone. He staggers up, slips, goes down on one knee, feels an overwhelming urge to vomit, manages to scramble to the toilet in time to void his stomach, and slumps to the floor against the wall. Shivering, naked, mouth hot with the taste of acid, he watches the water spray down from the shower. All those streams, cascading away from each other, then clashing as they hit the floor, swirling together.

The solution is not that everything's linked. Kingi had nothing to do with Penny's bodies, like Charlotte's disappearance is unrelated to Makere. It doesn't have to be connected, it isn't some sort of fucking jigsaw puzzle that'll all snap together and make sense. Life, the world, are spirals constantly spinning apart and sometimes colliding. Like koru in the bush, rubbing against one another in the wind. Stop looking for patterns in the chaos. Look for the chaos engine instead, what drives the spirals.

Matiu grins, shakily clambering to his feet and flushing the toilet. Deliberately, he steps back under the freezing shower, leaning hard on the chair, lets the water run through his mouth and rinse the taste away. The cold reminds him he's human, vulnerable, and that things can always get suddenly, painfully worse. But if he stands here long enough, he'll go numb, and the pain will go away. When he shuts the water off, the warmth of the air is a relief. Now all he needs is some really good painkillers, and maybe a nice, strong coffee. One thing he can't afford right now is to give in to the need to sleep.

- Pandora -

Back in the lab, Penny takes her lab coat from its designated hook and slips it on. She breathes deeply, her olfactory receptors alert for the fruity nuances of ketones and the cleansing odour of decontaminant. She exhales. Breathes in again, feeling her anxiety leach away. Works every time. The lab is her sanctuary and this lab coat her protective chainmail, even if it is only a 65% polyester: 35% cotton twill mix.

Better start by fixing things with Beak.

The fridge murmurs its approval as she crosses the lab in search of her technician, the soles of her shoes squeaking on the linoleum. Beaker is cowering at the far end of the lab, feeding Cerberus the meat filling from sandwiches left over from lunch.

He jumps to his feet. "Pandora... Penny." Pushing Cerberus' nose aside, Beaker stuffs the empty bread crusts into a container. "Is your brother OK?" He cradles the lunchbox under his arm like a rugby ball.

"He's fine, although the same can't be said for Dad's car."

Beaker grimaces in sympathy. "Ouch. Look, Penny, that joke I made about the body..."

Penny fends off his excuses with a wave. "It's not your fault, Beak. I overreacted. It's been a trying day."

"I'm sure it'll turn up," he says cheerfully, Cerberus nudging him for more of his lunch.

"Hmm." Penny's brow wrinkles.

Beaker hurriedly changes the subject. "I've had a look at the samples from this morning's John Doe."

"Find anything?"

"Nothing notable from the bench seat samples, except to confirm that at some point the North Shore council was using lead-based paint."

Penny guffaws. "Well, that's hardly surprising, is it? That bench seat must have been there since the dawn of time; definitely pre-1980. Anything else?"

"Traces of what looks to be diethylamide of lysergic acid in the skin cells."

"LSD?" Penny nods. "Drug abuse. It would have to have been a massive dose. Still, that fits with my observations at the scene; our John Doe looked to have been living rough."

"It's not *conclusive*, though."

She smiles. "No, not conclusive." Because there were those expensive Saveas. Why hadn't he sold them? "Clark's hoping to convince the pathologist to give me another look at the body. If that happens, I'll make sure we get some additional tissue samples. Blood. Stomach contents… Nothing else of note?"

"Not yet. I still have a few assays to complete."

Penny glances at the readout on the incubator behind him. "It's already nearly five. They can wait until tomorrow."

"I don't mind staying late."

"Beak. Don't make me raise my voice."

Flushing pink, Beaker ducks his head. "OK, OK, I'm going. Night, Boss."

When he's gone, and Matiu is still wallowing in the wet room, Penny goes to the cold store to retrieve the windscreen sample from this morning. Fingerprinting this sample will place Kingi on the bridge, and help prove he followed them from Little Shoal. And if she puts the assay on now, there'll be enough time for the Breadmaker™ to run its full cycle before Craig picks her up for dinner.

Still standing in the cool room, she snaps on a pair of gloves, cuts the sample tape, placing half the sample in a cuvette, then pipettes in the DDT/proteinase solution, primer, and polymerase. That done, she returns to the lab and gives the cuvette a quick spin in the table-top centrifuge. 15,000 RCF should do it. She sets the RPM and listens to the quiet hum as the machine accelerates. Matiu was right. Just a few minutes working, and already she's feeling calmer. Of course, it's well documented that people find comfort in positive routines. Psychology papers cite the classic case of those 33 Chilean miners, victims of a rock fall, who waited months to be rescued. Giving the trapped men work assignments distracted them from their trauma, and instilled them with a sense of purpose. In some cases, it may have helped to maintain their sanity. Those papers were published decades ago now and, let's face it, psychology isn't the hardest science, but clearly there's something to the theory. And happily, no one is asking Penny to move 4,000 tonnes of rock! The situation is still dire—it's not every girl who can discover a bog body and lose it in the same day—but panicking isn't going to change anything. Either the robbers have plans for it, and are keeping it suitably refrigerated until they reveal their purpose, or they'll dispose of it.

Please let them have it safely refrigerated somewhere.

After a minute, the centrifuge pings and she removes the cuvette. The spun down solution is as black as octopus ink. She's holding it up to the light when Matiu comes out of the bathroom, his t-shirt dangling in one hand and his torso bare.

"Penny? A little help?"

"Coming." She slides the cuvette into the Breadmaker™, closes the lid, and presses start. The machine will do the rest: incubating the sample *in situ*, vortexing off the buffer, and carrying out annealing and digestion phases on the eluted DNA. All she has to do is wait. She snaps off her gloves and throws them into the recycling receptacle. Wipes her hands on the back of her lab coat. Time to find out how Matiu mashed up the car.

- Matiu -

"Thanks," Matiu says as Penny helps him into his dirty shirt, regretting he doesn't have a spare stash of clean clothes tucked away in the lab like she always does. The rush of nervous energy has drained away, and now he's just sore, worn down, exhausted. Liquid energy is in order. He fires up the coffee machine, then pulls out the first aid kit from under the bench. Penny follows, a tension in her shoulders like she's walking on rusty nails. "You want a coffee?" he asks.

Penny looks him over like a vet might regard a tortured Rottweiler: beaten animals can seem timid one moment, but might never be more than a heartbeat away from violence. "I'd love one," she says cautiously.

"Excellent, can you make me a long black while you're at it?" He continues to rummage in the first aid kit.

"You're unbelievable," Penny huffs, glaring at him, but as he starts wrapping a clean dressing around his arm, she steps up to the *Caffe Espress* and punches in the commands for their refreshments.

However much Penny might love her lab equipment, the coffee machine was probably her single wisest investment. At times like this, the world might as well end if not for the ready availability of coffee. Thankfully, the shifting climate had allowed growers to cultivate good beans down in the Rimutakas and the Kaimai Ranges after the costs of shipping them from South America made coffee the express domain of the über-wealthy, for a time. Why the hell hadn't he thought to invest in coffee plantations in his youth, instead of boosting cars and selling drugs and generally making a social nuisance of himself? That's hindsight for you.

"So, you want to tell me what happened?" she says, clunking a cup down on the bench beside him and going back to make her own. "Who's been beating you up this time?"

Matiu stifles a raw chuckle. "You should see the other guy." Penny doesn't need to know what happened at the chop shop. Wouldn't believe him anyway. All he needs to do is keep an eye out, watch for Makere, figure what that sly bastard's next move is going to be. Not let Penny out of his sight.

She turns, her knuckles white on the handle of the mug. "Is it something to do with that message about IVF meds? Did you have a run in with the angry relatives, is that it?"

"Who in the what, now? No! That was something else. I was just asking for a friend. Don't go knitting any booties, sis." He cinches off the bandage and scratches Cerberus behind the ears. The dog leans into his legs, whining low and soft. He's got a phone call to make, before he forgets.

"Well, what happened to car 55?"

Matiu throws up a hand. "Place I took the car to get work done had a fire break out. Bad timing is all." He pulls his phone from his pocket and taps at the screen, the coffee staring up at him from the white expanse of the benchtop like a cyclopean black eye.

- Pandora -

"That only explains the car—"

Cerberus howls. The big dog's on his feet and running, nails scratching on the floor. Like a crazed berserker, he skids around the corner towards the lab.

"Cerberus."

Penny dashes after him. The lab is no place for an anxious pooch. It's dangerous in there. There are glass flasks, reagents…

She turns the corner and stops. The BreadMaker™! Her assay! Clouds of grey-green smoke stream from under the lid, the machine's stop-alert whining like a badly played violin, its troubleshooting light blinking over and over, RED-RED-RED-RED-RED. The place reeks of rotting eggs.

No!

The smoke and stench are driving Cerberus wild. With his lips pulled back and teeth bared, the dog growls at the machine, hackles raised. He leaps up to snap at the lid, canines closing down hard on a curl of smoke. His spine twists and he falls back, yelping.

The smoke alarm starts screeching.

Sulphurous gases stinging her eyes, Penny scrubs away tears. Her head pounds with noise. They should evacuate the building. Now. Yet Penny can't help hesitating. Her Breadmaker™! If that goes up in smoke, she can kiss the police work goodbye. It'll be back to routine algae samples and monthly Prothrombin Clotting Time tests. The lab will go under. If there's any chance of salvaging that machine…

I have to turn it off.

She lifts the collar of her lab coat over her nose and mouth and rushes forward, shrieking over the din, "Matiu, get Cerberus out of here!"

Back on his feet, the dog is having none of it. Forcing his bulk between Penny and the machine, the big Lab throws his head back and howls like a wolf, a chilling marrow-shrinking note that carries over the shrill of the alarm.

Out of my way, Cerberus!

But, acting like a true Hound of Hades, Cerberus refuses to let her pass. He tosses his head and snaps at her, saliva dripping from his bared teeth.

"Cerberus, come on, let me through," Penny mutters. The dog's going ape shit. Won't let her near the control panel.

"Matiu, help me," Penny screams. Where the hell is he anyway? She glances back and he's just standing there, eyes glazed as if he's in another world, as if he's just woken from a nightmare. He stares at the Breadmaker™, his face contorted in pain.

Taking a step back, Penny grabs his arm. Gives it a yank. "Matiu, what the fuck! Snap out of it. Take Cerberus, and get the hell out of here."

And suddenly he's back: one hand grabbing Penny by the lab coat, and the other on Cerberus' collar, hauling them both away. "Let's go," he shouts.

"No, not me! I can't. I have to stop the machine." She twists in his grip just as Cerberus lunges. Matiu can't hold them both. He chooses Cerberus, allowing Penny to slip out of his grasp. She dashes for the Breadmaker™, coughing gas, and punches in the abort code. Why isn't it working? The troubleshooter alert is still blinking red. The smoke's still leaching from under the lid, filling the lab with its rotten egg fumes. She has to stop it. Blinking back tears, she punches the code again.

RED-RED-RED...

Again.

Penny could scream with frustration. *Stop!*

Then Matiu is there, yanking the power cord out of the socket. One more step, and he throws the fire alarm to off, sending the automatic FALSE CALL message to the Fire Service. Within seconds, the machine and the alarm wind down to silence.

Penny's head keeps pounding. Why hadn't she thought to stop it at the source? With one hand still grasping a slobbering Cerberus, it's what Matiu must be thinking too because he looks at her as if to say, 'what the heck?', but Penny hasn't got time for explanations. That gas could be toxic. Who knows what it's doing to their lungs? She runs to the windows and flings them open. Switches on the fume hoods. Sets the extractor fans to Def Con 1. Then buries her face behind her collar again. Seconds tick past. At last, the smoke dissipates, albeit leaving behind its putrefying stench.

"I swear, there's something seriously wrong with this machine," Penny says when the smoke has all but cleared. She wipes her forehead with the back of her arm. "That's the second time it's malfunctioned this month. I should drag out the warranty: get the manufacturer to check it out. Still, I'm glad we caught it before it made a bigger mess."

Matiu snorts. "Yeah, just lucky, I guess."

Now that the noise and the smell have died down and Cerberus is calmer, Matiu releases him. The dog pads over to Penny and sits, kneading the floor at her feet. Poor baby. He's looking for reassurance. Penny's heart lurches. He thinks he's done something wrong. Crouching, she puts an arm around his neck and gives him a good scratch under his chin. Sure, he slowed her down, got in the way, but Penny isn't mad at him. He'd sensed a threat and tried to protect her from it, and not for the first time either. Cerberus braved a burning building for her once; since then she's been inclined to trust his instincts. "You're a good boy, Cerberus. Everything's going to be fine now," she murmurs.

Cerberus whimpers and trembles under her fingers—the drifting fumes still making him jittery—so she carries on a little longer.

Matiu's phone rings. "Hey, bro, yeah. Sorry, had a little emergency, just as I dialled your number, you know how it goes. Anyway, I got a favour to ask." Turning his back on Penny, he strides out the fire doors towards the office.

Good. That should give her a few minutes to take a look at the machine.

Giving Cerberus a last pat, she stands up, and, taking a pair of silicone gloves from a hook on the end of the bench, slips them on. The dog watches her, growling softly as she approaches the Breadkmaker™.

"Shhh. It's OK. I'm just taking a quick look. I'll be careful, I promise."

Holding her breath, she lifts the lid. Just as well too, because a last puff of noxious gas whooshes out. Cerberus gives a little whine.

"Shhh," she says again.

Inside, the cuvette is still intact. She lifts it out and holds it to the light. At the bottom of the crucible the sample resembles the blackened flesh of a rotting walnut. The dark mass is puckered and misshapen as if the machine has chewed on the sample, and, finding it indigestible, spat it out. And the results? She can't risk turning the machine back on just yet, so a digital readout is out of the question. But the machine is loaded with paper coated in Bisphenol A, which makes it heat-resistant, so there's a chance…

Penny checks over her shoulder. Matiu's voice carries from the office. "If you find anything, send it through…"

He's still talking. She has time. She un-clips the machine casing and unwinds the feed. The paper is crumpled, but intact. Her pulse skips a beat as she scans the results. What? Those sugars. She closes her eyes and opens them again in case the gas is affecting her.

This *can't* be right.

Cerberus whines again. He edges towards her, his nails clicking.

Using the blade to tear off the read-out, Penny throws a furtive glance towards the office. "We're not going to tell Matiu about this," she whispers to Cerberus. "Not until I've worked it out, OK? So, if he asks, I'm counting on you to keep schtum."

The dog gives a low growl.

"I'll take that as a yes."

Matiu is finishing up his call. *Quick.* Cramming the read-out into her pocket, she throws the immolated sample into the Hazardous Waste, then strips off the gloves and throws them in after it.

She lets her fingers brush the top of Cerberus' head on the way to the office. "Not a word, remember." Closing the fire doors on the stink in the lab. "Who was that on the phone?"

Pocketing the device, Matiu shakes his head. "Just someone I know."

"Sure." Penny veers towards the wet-room.

"Where are you going?"

"Shower. I've got a date in an hour."

"A date? Who with?"

Penny doesn't look back. "Just someone I know."

"Come on. Stop being all huffy. We both know you don't have a date."

Penny spins on him. "Oh really? I can't possibly have a date? Nothing for little Pandora but her lab and her samples and her cleaning wipes, is that how it is? I'm so wedded to my lab, I'm supposed to marry a beaker and have little test tube babies?"

"Umm..." Matiu trails off.

Penny's face burns. "I didn't mean *Beaker*, I meant, you know, a glass beaker, and little test tubes for babies instead of little people, and—"

Her phone rings. Saved by the bell. She checks the screen. Toeva Clark.

Maybe not.

"It's Clark!" She paces the length of the office. "He knows I've lost the body. How could I be so stupid? The first bog body ever found in New Zealand. I'll lose the contract, the lab, everything..."

"Penny, calm down. How can he know? I doubt your thieves will have phoned it in."

"Then what's he calling me for?"

Grimacing, Matiu gives a half shrug. "You won't know until you answer it, will you?"

Penny gives him a glare. She hates it when he's all logical. She takes a deep breath and swipes the phone on. "Officer Clark. Sorry, I was meant to get back to you about the cordon. I'm not going to get back to Little Shoal today."

"That's fine. Tanner made us pack up a couple of hours ago."

"He did? Oh. Then what can I do for you? Please don't tell me there's been another murder. Haha. I've only just got back into the lab after wading thigh-deep through the mud at Karaka," she jokes.

There's silence.

"Clark?"

The police officer coughs quietly. "Actually, there *has* been another murder."

Penny swallows. "Oh no."

"Yep. Afraid so. Brings the current tally to nineteen for the jurisdiction. Detective Inspector Tanner is hitting the roof."

"And here's me being flippant. I'm so sorry. Does Tanner want me to consult on this one, too?"

"No, not this one. There could be a conflict of interest."

A conflict of interest? "I don't see how—"

"That's why I'm calling. I was wondering if your brother is with you?"

Penny's hackles rise. Just because Matiu has a conviction, they suspect him of everything. He can't be everywhere; he's not a Time Lord, for goodness' sake. "Yes, Matiu's here," she says coolly. "But I really don't see what it would have to do with him."

"The dead man is a former acquaintance of your brother's—a fellow known as Screech."

"Screech? I don't know him, and I'm quite certain Matiu hasn't seen him today or any day. I know it's hard to believe, but Matiu's made a clean break from that life, Officer."

Hearing his name spoken, Matiu stands up and takes a step towards her. Penny places her palm on his chest, holding him back. "All he wants to do is put all that behind him..." she says.

Matiu yanks the phone out of her hands.

"Clark. Yee, here."

What the heck? Penny tries to snatch the phone back, but Matiu turns away from her, blocking her out. She runs around him. "Matiu," she hisses, her hands on her hips.

Matiu sighs. The phone held painfully above his head, he switches it to speaker, then puts a finger to his lips. His meaning is clear: she can listen, but she has to shut up.

Penny doesn't like it; she nods anyway.

"Did you happen to see Will Strickland earlier today?" Clark asks, his voice sounding tinny and far off.

"Yes sir, I did," Matiu replies.

Penny's heart skids. He did? When? Matiu, what the hell have you done? Her legs wobbly, she sits heavily on the office sofa.

"I dropped off a fleet car at his workshop to get some panel work done," Matiu says. "Little scrape on the Harbour Bridge this morning. In fact, it was right after we left Little Shoal Bay. The left wheel rim and passenger doors were dinged up pretty bad, so after we stopped by the hospital, I asked Screech to take a look at it."

"Was the vehicle a...metallic blue Commodore, registration 2YEE4590?"

"Yes, that's the one."

"You took it to him?"

"Yes, sir."

"Why?"

"I just told you. To get it repaired."

"Yes, by why take it to him? To Screech. It's one of your father's fleet cars, isn't it? Doesn't the Yee company have a preferred supplier for repairs? I would have expected your parents to deal with a bigger outfit, someplace more...reputable. For insurance purposes."

"Well, yeah. About that. That was my decision, taking the car to Screech. I wasn't too keen on the old man seeing the car messed up like that."

"I understand. You thought if you came back with a damaged car, you'd be fired, putting your probation in jeopardy. And your chances of getting another job would be slim to nothing if your own father won't employ you..."

"No." There's an edge to his voice. "No that's *not* it. I don't give a rat's arse about the job." He lowers his voice. "Look Clark, the reason I went to Screech was because of Pandora."

Penny whips her head up. *Me? What has this got to do with me? Don't you go blaming this on me, Matiu Yee. And don't call me Pandora!*

"The thing is," Matiu goes on, "as far as our parents are concerned, Pandora is their little princess."

Little princess, my foot. Penny makes chop-chop gestures at her neck, but Matiu barrels on. "They're very protective. Over-protective, some might say. They don't want their little girl exposed to any risk. It's why they have me driving her — why it's *always* me driving her—when they have an entire fleet of drivers at their disposal. It's because they trust me to do everything I can to look after my sister. So, you understand why I couldn't take the car to our regular automotive company. My parents were going to find out we'd been in an accident because the airbag deployed. I figured I could get the damage fixed before they saw it—assuming it was something Screech could sort over a lunch hour—and that way the olds couldn't make a big deal of it. Because if my parents even *suspected* this science consult job was putting my sister at risk, they'd call in their loan, Pandora would be out of a job, and you, the police, would be down one very fine scientific consultant."

In spite of everything, Penny can't help but smile. She clasps her hands to her heart and mouths, 'VERY FINE.'

Matiu turns his back to her. "And you know what? Even if that hadn't been the case, even without Pandora, I probably still would've taken the car to Screech. He's a good guy. Does good work when he can get it. Only there's a lot of folk out there who aren't willing to give an ex-con the benefit of the doubt, you know? Anyway, I wasn't there long. In and out in about half an hour. Turns out he had too much work on to help me out today. Maybe I'll drop the car back in tomorrow."

On the other end of the phone, Clark is quiet.

"Right," he says after a moment, his voice slightly muffled. "Unfortunately, your friend Screech isn't going to be able to service the vehicle, because he's dead."

Penny checks Matiu's reaction. His face is as stony as a Queen Victoria statue. The hairs on her neck rise. This was a friend of Matiu's, or at least an acquaintance, someone he'd spoken to only hours ago, and yet apart from a ripple at his jaw, there's no shock.

He knew! Matiu already knew Screech was dead. All of a sudden, Penny feels like throwing up.

"OK, that all makes sense," a tinny Clark says. "I have Screech's…Mr Strickland's work order filled out for the Commodore, with time in today at 11:15am and your name in the client box, so your story checks out. Thank goodness for fire sprinklers, right? Just for the record, can you account for your whereabouts since then? You weren't with Ms Pandora because she was out at Karaka. Tanner was out there, and he said you weren't with her."

"I was seeing my probation officer. Erica Langley."

"The entire time?"

"We had a lot to talk about. Going straight isn't as straightforward as you might think."

"You realise I'll have to call her and verify."

"Of course."

"OK, well that's it," Clark says. "My apologies for the inquisition."

"You're just doing your job, sir."

"Please give my regards to Dr Yee," Clark says.

Matiu swipes the phone off and hands it back to her. "That's the five-oh off your back for another ten minutes. Can't you *ever* stay out of trouble with the cops?"

Penny glares at him. Hard.

Matiu backs up against the wall, his hands raised in the air as if Penny were a Pinkerton and he the two-bit bandit. Not so far off, given the circumstances.

"I thought you said you needed a shower," Matiu blubs. "Social life, remember?" He sniffs loudly and makes a show of crinkling his nose. "I'm not convinced Craig Tong will appreciate your current perfume, sis. Whatever you had baking in your Breadmaker, it wasn't exactly wheatgrain and rye."

Penny can't help grabbing the end of her ponytail and holding it to her nose. Eeew. He's right. She reeks of decomposing eggs. She flips the ponytail over her shoulder. "Who said I was going out with Craig, anyway?"

Matiu lifts his chin. "Well, you are, aren't you?"

Who's she trying to kid? He's already guessed. Resigned, Penny lets her shoulders slump. "I didn't have any choice. I had to get rid of him. You were in the alley. I couldn't have him seeing you and reporting back to Mum and Dad that you'd been brawling. But I guess I misjudged you, Matiu. Here was me jumping to conclusions, thinking you'd got into an altercation with the disgruntled relatives of some girl you'd knocked up, when instead, you were busy hanging out *at the scene of a murder!*" She spits the last words, her hands firmly on her hips.

Matiu shakes his head. Nostrils flaring, he pushes past her and sits on the tiny sofa, resting his elbows on his knees. "Pen, you've got it all wrong."

"Tell that to the judge. Dad's money isn't going to soften the blow a second time."

"I didn't kill anyone!" His hands clench into fists.

"You were there though, weren't you?" Penny says softly. "You lied to Clark."

"I have an alibi."

Penny folds her arms across her chest.

"Yes, OK, so I was there. But I didn't kill him."

"I should hope not. But it doesn't really matter, does it? Not if the police can place you—an ex-con—at the scene."

"I didn't do it."

"Like I said, I'm sure the judge will buy it."

"It was Kingi, alright? He did it. And while he was at it, he made sure Screech wouldn't breathe a word to anyone..." Matiu's breath catches. "Kingi tortured him, Pen. Cut the poor bastard's tongue out. The man was covered in blood. It was everywhere. Great gluts of it. A fucking sea of blood, and Screech's tongue quivering and twitching on the floor like a fish caught in the shallows. I wanted to save him. Tried. Cerberus... we..." His fingers stroke the dog's ruff. Penny bites her own tongue while she waits for him to continue. "Screech was the bait, you see. Kingi was after me...I had no choice. Had to leave him." Matiu drops his head and buries his face in his hands.

This time, it's Penny's turn to ruffle his hair. Her baby brother puts his arms around her waist and hugs her close, his cheek against her lab coat. Penny could swear Cerberus senses his pain too because he rests his doggy head on Matiu's knee.

After a while, Penny disengages herself and perches alongside Matiu on the sofa. "What's going on?" she asks softly. "What does Kingi want with you?"

He tips his head back, his eyes closed. "You're not going to like it."

"I don't care. Just so long as it doesn't get you locked away."

Matiu grins, but there's something off about it. Penny's skin prickles with goose bumps. He opens his eyes. Looks at her. "There was a time I knew Kingi. We were mates of a sort. Once in a while, we'd kick around together after a job, have a few drinks. He wasn't all bad, and he was smart enough. I reckon he might've made something of himself if his dad hadn't screwed him up, beating the living daylights out of him. Si used to say his dad was the meanest son of a bitch he ever knew, and that was saying something. The old man broke every bone in Simon's puny body over the years. And each time, the namby-pambies at Social Welfare would patch him up and send his skinny arse back home for another round. That kind of abuse day after day; it does something to a guy's head, and Si was just a kid. He split before he turned 14, lived rough until he hooked up with Hanson and his gang, and sometimes even after that. There wasn't much kindness in Simon Kingi's life."

"I don't understand why you're telling me this. You just told me Kingi murdered Screech."

"It wasn't him."

Penny takes his face in her hands. "Matiu, honey, you're not making any sense. A minute ago, you said Kingi murdered Screech and now you're saying he didn't." She brushes his hair off his forehead. "Have you been feeling sleepy, at all? I think you might have a concussion."

But Matiu shoves her hands away. "Penny, listen, the creature that killed Screech; it only *looked* like Kingi. It had *tentacles* coiling from its back. Just like Hanson did. And its eyes, I swear, they were as black as a fucking sink hole..."

"Stop! Stop it. That's enough."

"It's happening again."

Penny shakes her head. "No. It is not."

"Yes, it is. Sacrifices, raising the dead; I don't know how, but it's happening again and somehow your John Doe from this morning is mixed up in it."

Penny jumps up, turning on him. "No! I don't believe it. I refuse to listen to any more of your stories about rampaging Cthulhus. There are no such things as demons. People simply do not go around with tentacles sprouting from their backs. It's all fantasy. Fiction. You've got a concussion, Matiu. It's what happens when you decide to waltz with a concrete floor—"

Dark eyes blazing, Matiu stands up and grabs her face in his hands. "OK, let's say I didn't see a man I used to know morph into some kind of otherworld monster. What was in your Breadmaker, Pen? Tell me, honestly: a sample from your John Doe?"

Sucking in a breath, Penny pushes him away. She straightens her back and looks him straight in the eye. "No, it wasn't actually."

CHAPTER 10

- Pandora -

The water runs cold.

Bloody hell, Matiu.

Shivering, Penny turns it off. At least the cold has given her some clarity. Wringing the water from her hair, she steps out from under the shower rose and buries her face in a towel. Enveloped in soothing wafts of 3,7-dimethyl-1,6-octadien-3yl acetate from her lavender laundry detergent, it's easy to tell herself there's no such thing as monsters.

That's because there isn't. There is no such thing as monsters. There's *always* a rational explanation.

She dries herself off and slips on some clean underwear. What Matiu described has no basis in fact. None whatsoever. He must have been hallucinating. Except Penny had looked him straight in the eye and checked his pupils. Neither one had been more dilated than the other. She struggles a moment with the clasp of her bra. Equal-sized pupils doesn't necessarily mean anything. Like Beaker says, it's not conclusive. Matiu could still have a concussion. Although, a mild concussion wouldn't normally cause hallucinations. Shock would, though. And post-traumatic stress disorder. Earlier this afternoon Matiu had witnessed the brutal murder of a friend. He'd even tried to intervene. Under the circumstances, anyone would suffer hallucinations.

The clasp sorted, Penny pulls the hair dryer out of the drawer and turns it on, flipping her hair to dry underneath. Warm air tickling her nape, the hairdryer whirrs in her ear. *And what about the sample in the Breadmaker™?* it goads.

Penny separates her hair with her fingers, increasing the surface area for drying. "The apparatus must have been faulty. I'll get the manufacturer to look at it. It should still be covered; I haven't had it a year yet."

The hairdryer hums. A shift in pitch.

"OK, OK, so there's nothing wrong with the machine. But the read-out was…well, there was clearly some sort of error. Most likely the sample was contaminated. I took it from an accident site. Off a broken windscreen. Anything could've got in there."

The whirring escalates. *Anything?*

"No. I know what you're suggesting and I'm not even going to entertain the idea. It's ludicrous. Yes, I concede that the salvaged readout showed the presence of xenonucleic, rather than deoxyribose or ribose sugars, and that corroborates Matiu's tale of otherworld intruders. Yes, it's another observation, but even then it's not conclusive. There'll be some other *less fanciful* reason for the machine to have detected unnatural sugars."

More humming, softer this time. *Cerberus didn't like it either.*

"Cerberus is a dog. Dogs are sensitive to smells. Of course he was going to get agitated. That was one unholy stink. What is it with the machines in this lab, anyway? First, it's the bloody fridge giving me an earful, and now you. Do none of you realise that you are not sentient?"

A whoosh of hot air hits her full in the face.

Enough. Penny pulls the plug on any further conversation. Giving her hair a final fluff, she steps across to her locker and takes out a black wrap dress. Her *date* dress. From back in the days when she went on dates. Don't be ridiculous, Penny. This isn't a date. The man has admitted to spying for your parents. *Which is why I have to go.*

Slipping the dress on, she cinches it at the waist, double knotting the ties. She gives the skirt a little swish and checks out her reflection. She looks as if she's been hauled from the grave. Technically speaking, it's the truth. Happily, she keeps some supermarket makeup rolling around in the top drawer of the vanity for when the landlord drops by. She goes for a smoky effect, a look which blends nicely with the dark smudges under her eyes. Still, there'll be no need to let the evening drag on. She'd only agreed to the date to get Craig off her back…

Hang on. What if she sends Noah the samples she has already? He doesn't need the entire cadaver to carry out the carbon dating. Handing Cordell her samples would be like mining leaders giving the buried Chilean miners daily tasks to prevent them from stressing. Performing the analyses should distract his attention from the bog body, giving Penny more time to recover it. Perfect. She'll get Matiu to run the samples over this evening.

Taking one last look in the mirror, Penny puts the cap back on the eye-liner and throws it in the drawer. Some perfume on her wrists and the towel in the hamper, she slips on her heels and steps out of the wet-room.

"Hey sis," Matiu shouts through the door, "you decent? Got something I need you to see."

- Matiu -

On his phone is a message, which he swipes open so Penny can see. Good old Scour, always coming through for the boys. Matiu will have to send that man a dozen. Beers, maybe, or strippers. He'll check the finances first.

"What is it?" Penny says.

"It's a VamPN link, a sort of backdoor into a network." Matiu taps the link, and a browser window opens. Instantly, the screen fills with tiny thumbnails, like photos of urban street scenes, except they're moving. Matiu swipes down a search bar and types in their address. The montage of images filters down to just two. In one of them, the edge of the lab building is visible in the dusky streetlight. Matiu taps it open.

"Are these traffic cameras?"

Matiu shrugs. "More like the safety network. Meant to be there to deter crime but hey, we know how well that works." He expands the screen and toggles a control bar, starts scrolling. Sure enough, Penny and Beak appear, walking backwards like manic headless chickens, then disappear. A vehicle rolls past, winding back to the spot where it had pulled up while everyone's back was turned.

Matiu's gut drops. A black van. One of those electric models that businesses aiming for the corporate responsibility look go for, despite the massive environmental costs that came with trying to supply the whole planet in enough lithium to replace the world's aging fleet of internal combustion engines. Whole mountain ranges levelled by strip mining and still the batteries needed replacing every five years. What a mess that turned out to be. "Shit," he mutters, as the images spool back. Two figures load the white bag into the van in reverse. He pauses the playback. No way to know for sure, but it looks a lot like the van that was following them from Charlotte's place. And what's that on the roof? A refrigeration unit?

"Who the hell are they?" Penny says. "Can you zoom in?"

Could Penny's bog body somehow be related to Charlotte's disappearance? Matiu zooms the image, but in the poor light, through a grimy lens, the picture doesn't get any better. "I don't know, but it's not the first time I've seen that van today, I think."

"What?" Penny stares at him. "What else haven't you told me?"

Matiu takes a long breath. "OK, so you know how I went to see my probation officer today?"

"Oh god, it's her isn't it? You've got her pregnant and that's her vindictive brother in the van and now he's out to get revenge on you by stealing my work?" Penny shakes her head. "I know that sounds crazy, so tell me something that makes some sense."

Matiu shrugs. "Erica's got a sister, Charlotte. She's gone missing." Then he runs through everything he saw at Charlotte's house, and the van that followed them.

Penny looks haunted. "What is it?" Matiu says.

"The bog body, it showed signs of abdominal damage. Like, possibly the victim was pregnant, and the foetus had been cut out."

Matiu represses a shiver in the suddenly frigid air. "Charlotte was trying to get pregnant, and now she's disappeared, and the same people who were watching her house just stole your dead body."

"Our evidence. Shit," says Penny.

"Yep," Matiu agrees. "Shit. Look at that though, on top of the van."

Penny looks closer. "Might be a refrigeration unit. I hope it is, I really do."

"Someone who knows what they're doing, then. Narrows down what we have to look for." Matiu digs his phone out of his pocket again, swipes a call up. Penny goes to speak but he holds up a hand. She glares at him in frustration. "Yo, Scour, it's Grendel. That's the shit, right there. Hey, any of those cameras running IVA?"

"Most the network, bro. Why, whattup?"

"Reckon you can whip up a little tracking algo?"

"Depends what you're after. The cops have a bunch of templated subroutines that a highly-paid professional like yours truly just might know how to tap into. What's a brother need?"

"I'll send you a link. Talk in a bit, bro." Swiping out of the call, Matiu loses himself in pulling up the video feed properties, timestamp and geolocators, and swiping them all into an email.

"First it's IVF, now you've moved on to IVA? Matiu, what are you up to?"

Matiu waves vaguely. "Intelligent Video Analytics. Smart cameras. You can tell them to look for things for you, they do the hard work. If Scour is as shit-hot as he claims, he should be able to get the camera network to track that van, and if it goes through a set of lights with a plate-reader, then the network can find it again even if it disappears for a while, then tell us where it pops up again."

Penny stares, dumbfounded. "Our public safety CCTV system can do all that?"

He looks at her as he hits send. "Only for important people, like the cops, and the SIS, and people with friends like Scour."

Watching her face crumple in disappointment is almost hilarious, if it wasn't so tragic. "It's totally illegal, isn't it?"

Matiu shrugs. "Your taxpayer dollars at work, sis." He knocks back the dregs of his coffee.

Penny turns away, throwing up her hands. "I'd rather not know. Anyway, can you take these samples over to Cordell's for me? That way he can't accuse me of total incompetence."

Matiu cocks an eyebrow at her retreating back. "But, aren't I driving you...?"

"No, Matiu, you're not. Craig is picking me up. You just go do whatever criminal little things you need to do, and keep telling yourself that you're not mixed up in that world anymore, and I'll keep pretending like I can't see." She disappears into the cool room, emerging a moment later with a sample bag. She drops it in his lap. "And the dog needs to pee."

"Sure," he grumbles, as Penny strides purposefully towards the door. "Course I'll run your errands and hunt down your thieves for you while you swan off and have dinner with Greasy Tong." The door snicks shut behind her. Matiu gives her a few moments, then calls a whining Cerberus to heel. "Like I'm going to let her go off alone into the night, at a time like this, eh boy? Come on." Not with Makere out there, biding his time. Waiting for the shadows to lay thick and heavy across the city, for the eyelids to droop. Tensing to pounce. Yeah, fuck *that*. Dog at his heel, he heads out into the soupy warm evening.

- Pandora -

Hairs prickle at her nape as if there's a breeze blowing off the ocean, a glorious breath of cool air, a gift from the sea gods to calm the stifling city. Chance would be a fine thing. Already eight and it's still hotter than a witch's cauldron here on the waterfront. Penny raises her hand to her neck, lifting her hair away from her skin. No, not even a whiff of a breeze. This prickly feeling has nothing to do with the heat. It's been with her ever since she left the lab, a sense of foreboding, forcing her parasympathetic nerve receptors on alert and making her jumpy. It's got to the point she's seeing black vans on every corner.

Still a better theory than otherworld invaders.

There it is again. That creepy-crawly sensation down her back, as if she's stepped into a cobweb and released a nest of spiders. Someone behind her? Penny glances back, but there's only Craig in his perfectly pressed vintage Armani dress suit complete with lilac tie, pungent cologne, and a vaguely feline smile.

Nothing creepy there.

The building's air conditioning gives them a frosty welcome. Penny shivers, hugging her bare arms as they cross the lobby to the lift.

"Too cold?" Craig asks, while they wait for the car.

"It won't take long to adjust," she replies.

When the lift arrives, Craig places his hand on the small of her back to guide her in. The doors close behind them.

"Penthouse, ninth floor. The Sedge, please," Craig says, and the lift moves off. "I think you're going to love this place. They say the chef is *hors pair*. A pioneer of micro-fusion cuisine—the flagship. Rave reviews everywhere. I had to pull a few strings to get us a table. Having Ministry connections helps…"

Penny nods. The cloying dread has followed them, the lift's too-bright light and mirrored walls making her queasy, although that could be the multiple Craigs confronting her from every angle.

Fourth floor... More likely it's just the worry of today piling up. Along with the pile of bodies. And finding out that Matiu-dearest has been clinging to his underbelly connections. Didn't he learn anything the last time? That stint inside nearly killed him: his sanity flying perilously close to the wind, as brittle and fragile as Mārama's...

Sixth floor... Penny could be in that opening scene from Macbeth, the one with the witches—*fair is foul and foul is fair*—her Spidey senses telling her that trouble's bubbling and nothing good can come from it.

They've almost reached the eighth floor when Penny glimpses someone in the mirrored angle at the corner of the lift. There. The flash is so fast she almost misses it. But he was there. Solid and undeniable. A man's back. Penny squeezes her eyes tight and opens them again. The angle is empty.

"Did you see that?" Her voice is shaky.

"See what?" Of course Craig hasn't seen anything other than his own reflection; too busy perfecting his already perfect Hanover knot.

"I don't know," Penny says quietly. "For a moment, I thought there was someone else in the lift with us. It was quick, though. I wondered if maybe it was one of those holograms."

"Could be," Craig muses, still fiddling with that knot. "I wouldn't rule it out. The Sedge is pretty *avant garde*: stands to reason they'd have some progressive marketing on the go."

"But why so quick? It couldn't have lasted more than a micro-second."

Adjusting his cuffs, Craig shrugs. "Subliminal programming. Tapping into your subconscious. It's a common enough marketing technique..."

But in the lift on the way up to the restaurant? Surely, that's just preaching to the converted?

The light flickers and Penny spies the figure again. It's a man, a moko on his face like Matiu's. This time he's looking at her, his smile cruel and calculating.

Like a rapist's.

She blinks and he's vanished.

Penny draws in a breath and closes her eyes again, searching for his imprint on the back of her eyelids, but the flash had been too quick, too fleeting. Even so, she hadn't missed everything: there was no mistaking the burning mockery in his eyes or the nonchalance of his stance, as if their meeting was inevitable.

Get a grip, Penny. You sucked up some of that gas that spewed out of the Breadmaker™ earlier and it's fogging up your brain.

"Penny? You've gone a bit pale."

See? Even Craig's noticed.

Penny gives him a wide smile. "It's nothing. I think it's this lift—all these mirrors are creeping me out."

Ninth floor. The lift pings for the penthouse. "Welcome to The Sedge," declares the sultry voiceover.

"Let's get you out of here, then," Craig says. "You'll feel better once you've eaten." Turning to leave, he checks his reflection one last time before they step into the restaurant.

Whoever owns The Sedge has spent a fortune on outfitting. The restaurant is a temple of glass and chrome. The entire back wall houses a ceiling-to-floor wine display, while at the front, panoramic picture windows offer an unobstructed vista of the Hauraki Gulf.

"Mr Tong. Good evening. This way, please. Your table is ready."

They follow the hostess to their seats by the window, Penny catching sight of what looks like Patisepa Taylor's blonde bouffant at a secluded booth. When they're seated, the hostess lights the candle—a real one—then scurries away to see to their drinks order.

Penny gazes out the window, across the bay, where the suburbs are winking to life, a string of golden fairy lights against a soft rose twilight. All at once, the foreboding she felt in the lift melts away. "Craig, this is lovely."

Craig straightens his tie. "I'm glad you like it."

"I do." She means it. It's been so long since she's had an evening out.

Even more of a surprise is The Sedge's menu. She'd expected Craig to go for a restaurant where the options were heavy on rib-eye and peppercorn sauce. Instead, the dishes appear fresh and original, all comprising micro-greens in some form or other. Penny orders a salad of char-roasted beets and pistachio, garnished with Swiss chard, topped with pomegranate foam, and served on a rustic rye biscuit. "What's this about a sensory cushion?"

"They bring your meal to you on a sage infused pillow, so when you cut into it, a puff of sage accompanies every bite."

Penny arches an eyebrow. "You've got to be kidding."

"Like I said, the chef's an artist. It's all about creating a full sensory experience for his diners."

For the second time today, Penny wonders if she's misjudged Craig Tong. Perhaps Mum and Dad's instincts are better than she'd thought?

"The business model is innovative, too. My counterpart in the Business Ministry was telling me that all the produce served here is sourced from local micro-producers," Craig goes on. "And the restaurant has its own rooftop garden, where the sous chefs grow some of their own ingredients. It's a bit of a gimmick, but it's really rather nice up there. We can take our wine and have a look while we're waiting on our meals, if you like?"

"Actually, I would like that."

Craig pulls out her chair for her, and they take the stairs to the rooftop where the entire surface area is a quilt-work of raised beds, all brimming with fragrant micro-produce, holographic labels proclaiming the name of each crop. There's amaranth, red vein sorrel, gold endame shoots, garlic chive sprouts with their tiny black nodules…

The only guests on the roof, they amble among the raised beds, Penny running her fingers over the tiny fronds, stopping here and there to inhale the peppery scent. Beyond the rooftop, on the horizon, the ocean and the sky have fused to a warm indigo, the bridge spanning the bay like a sparkly tiara. Penny can't believe it. She's having fun. With Craig Tong.

Suddenly, her phone rings, the sound brash in the stillness of the roof.

Cordell.

Penny's heart lurches. "I'm so sorry, Craig. I have to take this. Work. It's… um…confidential."

"Of course." Taking her glass from her, he steps to the edge of the rooftop, giving her some privacy.

"What's this about, Noah?"

"Good evening to you, too."

"What do you want? I'm on a date."

There's a pause. Oh, for goodness' sake. Why is it so hard to believe she has a life? Switching her phone to FaceFlix, Penny angles the screen to include Craig, so there's no doubt she's on a date.

Noah's eyebrows twitch. "The rooftop at The Sedge. Very nice."

"Can you hurry up? Our meals are about to arrive."

"It's these samples the courier dropped off this evening."

"What about them?"

"They're just samples, Pandora. It isn't what we arranged."

Does he know? Penny's palms go clammy. No, how can he know? Unless he's the one who sent the black van? No, he wouldn't. No. Even Noah wouldn't stoop that far.

She lifts her chin. "I think you'll find Tanner said 'samples'."

"Pandora, really." He rolls his eyes as if he's the parent of an unruly teen out past curfew. "You do know how petty and obstructive you're being, don't you?

Whatever it was Tanner said, we both know what he meant. It's imperative that LysisCo is provided—"

"Are you telling me your company isn't able to conduct the analyses?" she says, stopping his advertorial midstream.

"Of course, not. That would be ridiculous. LysisCo is the country's foremost—"

"Great. Let me know when they're done."

Before she can slip the phone back into her purse, it rings again.

Mum.

Penny groans inwardly. She doesn't dare ignore it. What if Mārama's had another turn? Mouthing 'sorry' to Craig, she swipes it on. "Mum, is everything OK? How's Whaea Mārama?"

"She's fine, dear. She was sleeping when your father and I left the hospital, although she worked herself into a bit of a state this afternoon. Kept tossing and turning and shouting for Matiu. Pulling at her hair. The backs of her hands are covered in scratches where she's raked them with her fingernails. In the end, the doctors had to give her a sedative in case she hurt herself. I was hoping to talk to Matiu about it. Is he there with you?"

"No, he's not with me."

"Well, where is he? He's not answering his phone."

"I don't know, Mum."

What am I? My brother's keeper?

"He didn't return the fleet car for refuelling this evening," Mum says. "He's only gone and taken it off the grid again. You know how your father gets when Matiu does that. If you see him, tell him he's not to do it anymore, will you? It puts your father's blood pressure through the roof, and right now I have quite enough on my plate with your aunt's histrionics. You're sure Matiu's not there at the lab?"

"I'm not at the lab, Mum. I'm on a date."

Mum falls silent.

Honestly, why does everyone insist on doing this? I have a life!

The hostess appears at the top of the stairs. "Mr Tong? If you and your partner would come this way please, your meals are ready now."

Penny's heart sinks like a stiletto heel in sand. On the other end of the phone, Mum coos. "Pandora!"

CHAPTER 11

- Matiu -

Matiu drums his fingers on the steering wheel, the red lights on the empty intersection looking back at him like the eyes of so many nocturnal beasts. Through the speakers, Penny cuts the conversation with their mother short, and her footsteps become muffled as the phone disappears back into her pocket, or her purse, or wherever. Other voices, Craig Tong maybe, or the wait staff. Matiu picks up words here and there, but nothing of interest. Enough to know Penny is safe for the moment, but what the hell was that about seeing someone in the elevator? That'd sent a shiver through him, sparking images of so much of his life, seeing someone over his shoulder, in his periphery, but never *there*. Can Makere talk to her? He isn't sure how that works. Maybe you really have to *believe* in him for him to be able to whisper in your ear. No-one else believes in Makere, but if there's anyone who *might*, given enough proof, it'll be Penny.

The lights change, and Matiu pulls away. It had been easy enough to tap into her phone and slip the microphone malware into her background settings while she was in the shower. He's only doing it for her own good, so he can keep an ear out for her when he isn't around. Bloody glad he'd done it too, since she'd then ditched him. Luckily he knows people who could drop things off for him, or it would've taken him half the night to get those samples to Cordell. Probably some issues around chain of evidence, handing them off to Young Shiv to deliver, but Penny should've thought about that before agreeing to have dinner with Craig Tong. Now, through his phone, he can listen in on anything that might happen around her and locate her if he has to. She might wonder why her battery's running down faster than usual, that's all. In any case, he's cruising around the block, stalker-style, watching the other cars on the street, the people walking the waterfront. Nothing creepy about that at all. But if Makere turns up for Penny, he doubts Craig Tong is going to be the right guy to keep her safe. And Dad will kill Matiu if he lets anything bad happen to their little girl.

To his left, the historic ferry building is dwarfed by the Apirana Ngata Convention Centre that dominates the Captain Cook Wharf, a leviathan of sweeping glass and chrome, meant to portray wind and waves against the sky, but really just suggesting that the builders couldn't find their spirit levels that day. Even in these days of state-mandated power conservation, someone has managed to get sign-off to leave the funky architectural lights running on this visual monstrosity. More than once, Matiu had wondered what his chances would be of driving up those curving steel waves fast enough to get airborne. Oh, the things he would've done if he was younger, dumber.

His phone rings, muting Penny's feed. Mum's been trying to reach him, as has Carlie at the depot, but he's ignored those calls. They'll want to know why the GeePee's not pinging in to despatch. Easy answer is he disconnected the battery. Shit load of use a GeePee is without any power to transmit, and the last thing he needs tonight is the third degree from any *more* of the women in his life. But it isn't Mum or work, it's another call he's been equal parts dreading and, reluctantly, hoping for. Screw it. He answers. "The lovely Erica Langley, how are you this fine evening?"

"Matiu, she called."

"What? Who? Charlotte?"

"Yes, Charlotte, who else?"

"And? What'd she say?"

"Nothing, she didn't have time. The call cut out."

Matiu frowns, hanging another right in his constant sweeping circle of the HSBC tower building, where The Sedge occupies pride of place on the penthouse floor. "So how'd you know it was her? Was it her phone? Maybe someone found it and tried to use it to make a call?"

"It wasn't her cell phone. The call came from inside our father's apartment."

Matiu waits, but Erica doesn't offer any more. "And that's significant because?"

"There are only three keytags to that apartment. Dad has one, I have one, and so does Charlotte. Dad keeps the apartment in the city for when he's here on business, but he's only up three or four times a year, so it's empty most the time."

"Wait, so there's an empty apartment in the middle of the city, just down the road from your work, and you live in that dump?"

"We're not here to debate how much I want to be beholden to favours from my parents, Matiu. I'm sure *you* can appreciate that."

"Righto, whatever. So what are you thinking?"

"She was there, but something happened. I need someone to go and take a look."

"And that someone would be me, I take it? I'm sort of right in the middle of something right now."

"Matiu."

He grinds his teeth. "Whereabouts?"

"PWC Tower, Lower Albert Street. Down by the ferry terminal."

"You're kidding," he says, looking up. The PWC Tower looms even taller than the HSBC in the dark. High-rise waterfront apartment living. Holy shit. "What does your dad do for a living?"

"He's a lawyer."

"Of course. When did the call come in?"

"Right before I called you. Why?"

"I'm at the waterfront now. Text me the apartment number. I'll call you back."

"Matiu—"

He swipes the call off and accelerates around the block again, pulling in to a service alley. Cerberus bounds out after him, keen to have a run and a stretch. "Heel," Matiu barks, snapping his fingers. The back door doesn't quite latch properly, but hopefully he won't be long. He slips his earpiece on, so he can continue to eavesdrop on Penny's dinner date, and runs up the wireless security cracker app on his phone. Adopting the sunnies-and-guide-dog look once more, he crosses the road. The front doors of the PWC breeze open for him just as natural as you please as his phone tags him through, then hiss shut behind him. The crisp, cool air of the lobby hits him full force. *Guess the rich bastards who can afford waterfront apartments can afford air con, too, eh?*

The guard station behind reception is unoccupied. Either the guard's doing his rounds, or he's ducked out for a puff. Good timing. His phone pings, a message from Erica. He hits the button for the 26th floor.

The lift pings, and Matiu steps in, Cerberus at his side. Breathes deep and slow as the doors snap shut, boxing him inside. He's had a thing about confined spaces ever since his time in the slam. The lights flicker as they ascend, panic raising its ugly head for a heartbeat as Matiu falls in eyeblink snatches into the dark again, the tight pitch black of his tiny cell on a moonless night. Those were the worst, alone in the dark with Makere, his voice scraping across his ears, driving him to nightmare. He presses against the wall, heart thundering, breath short and sharp, fighting the black rising around him. His arm burns with the itch. For a long moment, he fears he's going to lose it, going to fall, and when he falls, he'll fall down into eternal black. Cerberus senses his unease, and whines low in his throat, ears laid back.

The lift pings open. Matiu staggers out, fighting for ragged breaths. Must be the knock to the head, setting him off like this. He probably needs to sleep, but he can't afford to. He'll take the stairs back down, thanks very much. After a moment spent catching his balance, he turns to regard the corridor he has emerged into, looking for apartment 2613. From somewhere nearby comes an electronic beeping. Following the brass numbers on the walls and doors, Matiu moves down the hall, his steps bringing him closer to the sharp, annoying tone. He's heard the sound before, a security-monitored door left open for too long. Rounding a corner, it all falls together.

Sure enough, the door to apartment 2613 is ajar, something wedging it open. A shoe. Oh hell. Matiu nudges the door wider, Cerberus growling now, and sees that the shoe is on a foot, attached to a leg. There's a body sprawled in the entryway, black pants and grey shirt. The security guard.

"Shit," Matiu mutters, pushing the door fully open with his shoulder and dropping to his knees to check for signs of life. Thankfully, he's breathing, just knocked out. There's a sticky patch of blood on his head. Because they really didn't need *another* dead body popping up to complicate matters even further.

"OK boy, leave no fingerprints," he tells Cerberus, trying to piece together what might've happened. In the spill of light coming through the full-length windows with their view across the harbour, the apartment looks trashed. Matiu edges inside, careful not to touch anything. Charlotte came to the apartment, but someone came after her. She tried to call Erica. Matiu spies the phone, on the floor in a corner, the battery ripped out. Violent intervention, then. So what next? Don't these rooms have panic buttons? Charlotte must've got to the button, which is what brought the guard up, but the intruder took down the guard and has left with Charlotte. Probably only minutes ago.

Matiu crosses to the window, looking down onto Albert Street, across the roof of the HSBC and what looks like a freaking *garden*. No-one's dragging a girl across the street, but there's something else. Just around the corner from where he parked, in the service alley between the HSBC and its neighbours, are two black vans. Two figures are wrangling someone into the back of one of them, someone who's struggling and who looks very, very pregnant. "No fucking way," Matiu says, eyes wide, as the van doors are slammed shut and it reverses out, turns hard, and speeds down the alley.

- Pandora -

Penny is warm right down to her toes. The flickering candlelight, the drifting scent of sage, soft music, conversation… She may have been cornered into coming out tonight, but it's been really nice. Craig can be quite the charmer when he wants to be. And *attentive*: pulling out her chair, checking the air con isn't causing a draught at her back, ensuring her wine glass is topped up. Although perhaps it'd be better if she slowed down a little on the wine. Just her second glass and already the lights of Devonport are beginning to pixelate. Little wonder. She hadn't eaten anything since breakfast, and the perfume of her meal when it arrived nearly knocked her out with hunger. But all that's behind her now. Despite its exquisite presentation, Penny practically wolfed her dinner down. It's not hard to see why The Sedge enjoys rave reviews. The food is fantastic, so much so she let Craig order her dessert, a crystallised rosewater and sugar basket, served on a gooseberry foam tower. The waitress said it would take fifteen minutes to construct. In the meantime, they've got time to talk.

"You know how it is with family," Craig says, while twiddling the stem of his glass.

Penny smiles. "I believe you've met mine."

"Chinese families, especially."

"Tell me about it," Penny replies, even though, technically, only Dad is full Chinese. Mum and Mārama are Māori and Matiu is…

Well, there's no point in splitting hairs, is there?

Taking up her invitation, Craig launches a tirade. "Since Dad passed away, Mum's been living with me and it's been awful. Two rooms allocated to her, but that hasn't stopped her taking over my space. She insists on feeding me, doing my laundry, cleaning the apartment. She treats me like I'm a ten-year-old. I love her to bits of course, but the woman is smothering me alive. I've told her I'm quite capable of doing those things for myself, and you know what she does? She stands on her tippy-toes, flattens my lapels with her palms, and says, 'Tong Zheng, you're an important man and it's the least I can do'. Honestly, her meddling's got so bad that these days, I avoid going home."

Penny definitely knows *that* feeling.

"I even suggested she live half-time with my brother—after all, he's an important man too, has a lovely tree-top apartment in Titirangi—but he won't hear of it. Privileges of the first-born, he says." Craig shakes his head and takes a sip from his glass. "I could kill him."

Pushing a stray rye crumb about the table, Penny replies. "I know how you feel. Matiu's the same." She brushes off her hands. "Half the time his phone is off, and the other half, he filters Mum's calls out. So, when she wants to speak to him, she calls me…well, you saw it for yourself when she called me on the rooftop."

Craig lifts his dessert spoon and checks out his reflection in the concave. "If it's a pity party you're looking for, then I'm sorry, Penny, but there's simply no way you can win."

"Oh, I think I can give you—"

Craig holds the spoon as if it were a gavel. "Nope, I'm telling you, nothing trumps this: last week, I found a bucket of 100-year salted eggs percolating in my laundry cupboard. That is, it used to be my laundry cupboard until my mother turned it into an ancient Chinese apothecary!"

Penny giggles. "They're yummy, though."

"That's not the point." Craig brings the spoon down, tapping the table with it to make his case.

"You're lucky she bothers. Not many people still make century eggs. Did you know that in the old days, after they'd been soaked, the eggs were wrapped in salted clay and rice husks for preserving? It took months. These days, a roll of cling film will do the trick—that and a bit of basic chemistry. I expect your mum has her eggs soaking in a solution of salt, calcium hydroxide, and sodium carbonate."

"You see? It sounds like something that should be carried out in your lab, not my laundry cupboard."

Penny grins. "I imagine they're pretty smelly."

"Like you wouldn't believe." Miming disgust, Craig waves a hand in front of his nose. "There's a reason the Thai call them horse urine eggs, you know. No kidding, if my Body Corporate gets wind of it, I'm going to be looking for somewhere new to live, and then see how my brother likes it—" Craig's anecdote is interrupted by Penny's phone.

She checks the screen and groans. "It's my mum again." It's only the third time Mum's buzzed since they sat down for dinner.

"Just go ahead and answer it, Penny."

"She's being nosy."

"Go on, take the call. I don't mind. If Kiri's anything like my mother, if you don't answer, you'll never hear the end of it. Tell you what, if you like, I'll even let you toss a glass of water over me to throw her off the scent."

Penny laughs. "Don't tempt me." She swipes the phone on.

"Pandora!" Mum's voice is like breaking glass. "I need to get hold of Matiu. Mārama has gone missing from the hospital!"

"What? That's…but how? Don't they have security?"

"Not anymore; your father has them all out with the fleet combing the streets for her. I don't mean to spoil your date, but I can't find Matiu anywhere. I've been calling and calling. Mārama was asking for him this afternoon, and I'm afraid she's trying to look for him."

"Mum, just sit tight, OK? I promise, I'll…" She looks up.

Matiu, his sunnies pushed to the top of his head and his face like thunder, is storming through the restaurant as if he's the hero in the last scene of every romantic comedy ever made. Patisepa Taylor gives him the once-over as he passes. Craig gets to his feet.

"…find him." She switches her phone off and wipes the corner of her mouth with her napkin. "Matiu, Mum said she couldn't get—"

She doesn't even get her sentence out. He bowls up and seizes her by the elbow. "Sorry Craig, I'm going to have to steal my sister away. Family emergency, you understand. Pandora promises to have that dessert with you some other evening. You won't mind picking up the bill, will you? Save us some time." Not waiting for a response, he yanks Penny's chair out and manhandles her away from the table, Penny barely having time to snatch up her purse before he drags her towards the lift.

"Matiu, that was rude."

"We have to hurry. I left Cerberus downstairs in a no park zone." He jabs at the button. "Fuck this!" He gives it another stab. And another.

"Stop that. It isn't going to get here any faster."

"Pen, Mārama's missing."

"And the hospital security staff and all of Dad's fleet are out looking for her. She's wearing a hospital gown; *someone* will find her. They probably already have."

Matiu doesn't say anything, but his jaw ripples with tension.

The car arrives. They wait while two guests step out. Matiu clenches his fists. Finally, the lift is empty, and they get in, Penny turning to wave goodbye to Craig as the doors close.

His elbow above his head, pressed hard against the mirrored glass, Matiu punches the button for the lobby. "Anyway, you should thank me."

"*Thank* you?"

"For rescuing you from the ultimate date disaster. You really have no idea how to seduce a man, do you, sis? Did you really think you were going to have him foaming at the mouth talking about calcium carbonate and hydroxy salts?"

"It's calcium hydroxide and sodium carbonate…oh my god, you were *listening*?"

- Matiu -

Matiu tugs out the earpiece and stuffs it in a pocket, like that might somehow undo the damage. Can't just keep his big mouth shut, can he? "Not listening in, just keeping tabs. I'm meant to look after you, remember?"

"No, you're meant to drive me places, that's all. Not chaperone me. You're not my freaking *bodyguard*."

Oh Penny, if only you knew...

"Hell, how many times have you left me in the lurch when you should've been there, yet you manage to spy on me the one time in *forever* I'm having a dinner date? Do you even realise how disturbed that is?"

"Look, there's—" He wants to tell her everything, that Makere is hunting her, that he'll be there, in the shadows, in the mirrors, in the dark places behind her eyes when she closes them. Will she listen? Something flickers in the corner of his eye, a darkness corrupting the elevator's shiny glass and chrome. *Go on, tell her,* says a voice in his head, though whether it's Makere or just his own fear speaking, he can't tell anymore. *Tell her about me. Tell her what's coming for her. Tear away any doubt she may have had that you're coming completely unhinged.* "I've got my reasons, all right? You're not safe."

"Matiu, your paranoia might be really sweet but it doesn't give you the right to eavesdrop on my dinner date. What, were you watching from the lobby or something?" Her cheeks redden. "How many speed limits did you break dropping off those samples and getting back here so quickly? I thought you were trying to stay *out* of jail."

If Train X leaves Station A with 12 passengers at 7.35pm travelling at 165 kilometres per hour... Trust Penny to crunch the maths on that. Also not a conversation he wants to get into, in case she gets all precious about things like *chain of evidence.* But she hasn't guessed it's her phone he's tapped. That's handy. Better divert the conversation. "You saw him, didn't you?"

"What? Who? Don't change the subject."

"Makere. You saw him in the lift."

She stares. The lift car settles, and the door pings open. "Stop it, Matiu."

He meets her gaze, neither of them moving. "Didn't you?"

"I'm not doing this. All right?"

So much he wants to say, but he doesn't. A couple dressed for a swanky night out are standing in the lobby, regarding them awkwardly. "Excuse me," says the well-coiffed woman, ripe with sarcasm, "but are you planning on standing there all night, or might we use the lift when you're done? Not that we would dare interrupt this," she waves vaguely at the tableau of Penny and Matiu, "whatever *this* is."

The lift starts to close. Penny slaps the door to hold it open and storms across the lobby. Matiu trails after, giving the couple a mock bow on the way past. "The salmon puffs are particularly good tonight," he advises, ignoring their bewildered stares. "Tip your waiter."

Cerberus bounds against the window at Penny's approach, tail wagging like mad, tongue slobbering all over the window. Penny wrenches the passenger door open, her rage at being dragged from her dinner clearly lending her the strength to defeat the jammed handle which had beaten her on the bridge earlier in the day. She attempts to dust the chalk off the seat, slides into the car around the folds of the airbag, and is instantly assailed by the lovable, treacherous hound.

"What the hell is this?" Penny asks, simultaneously trying to firmly but affectionately convince Cerberus to settle, and nudging the small black box in the footwell trailing wires and plastic connectors.

Matiu gets behind the wheel and pulls into the street. "Research."

"You just can't help yourself, can you?"

"Penny, forget that. We need to find Mārama."

She growls in frustration. "Aargh! I told you, Dad has police and all sorts looking for her. She's on foot, wandering the streets of Greenlane. They'll find her. You didn't need to ruin my evening for this."

"You sound awfully put out about this dinner date you didn't even want to go on, and I quote, 'I didn't really have a choice, I had to get him off my back.' Or words to that effect. Anyway, I know where Mārama is. And she won't be on foot."

She gives him an acid look. "You *know* where she is? Please, do go on."

"OK, put it this way: I know where she *probably* is, which is nowhere Dad will think to look, and if she's there, then that's all good, and you can help me get her home, but if she's not, then I'll *really* need your help to find her."

Parnell rolls past the windows as Matiu heads for the motorway on-ramp.

"We can't take her home. We have to take her back to the hospital."

"In this car? And explain to Dad what happened to his precious Commodore? What part of 'lying low' don't you get?"

"All of it! I'm not the one in the family that feels the need to *lie low*. That's *all* you. You're the one who gets us into car accidents and has known associates turning up dead as often as you change your underwear. And what is *this*?" She lifts the black box, presenting it as if it were evidence in a murder trial.

"Ah that," Matiu says. "You'll like this. You know that black van, the one that stole your smelly body?"

Suddenly, Penny's interested. The angry wine-fuelled fog lifts from her eyes. "Yes?"

"Turns out there's more than one of them, and they happened to be parked up outside the very same restaurant where you were just dining, and they're the ones who've got Erica's sister."

"Wait...what?"

"I just got a call, saw a few things. They've kidnapped her, maybe she escaped them and was calling for help, but they found her and took her back, or something. I'm sketchy on the details. But the thing you're holding is gonna tell us where they come and go from all day, so hopefully it can lead us to her."

"You stole the GeePee unit?"

"Had a look in the back too, but alas, no body bag. Just trays of leafy greens."

Penny gapes. "I don't want to know how you took a look inside, do I?"

"Nope."

CHAPTER 12

- Pandora -

Penny's sigh is muffled by the car's rattling as Matiu takes the on-ramp. Death rattles. It'll be interesting to see which holds out longer: the fender or her patience.

"So, let me get this straight," she says, running a finger along the edge of the black box. "We now believe that Touching the Sun is a fertility cult hiding behind a successful micro-gardening enterprise?"

"Yup. Your Touching the Sun subscription buys you a houseful of grass and a tattoo on your wrist."

"And the cult runs its empire from the back of a fleet of refrigerated vans which it also uses to transport kidnapped girls and hijacked bog bodies."

"Both of which might be pregnant."

"Both of *whom* might be pregnant. Which means my bog body might not be an artefact from the Iron Age at all; instead it's far more recent. A woman killed by accident or misadventure. Perhaps in the last year."

Checking the rear-view mirror, Matiu changes lanes. "You sound disappointed."

Penny turns to look at him. "*Disappointed?* Matiu, if we're right, then a young mother died, possibly while giving birth, and your green-grass-and-bloody-sunshine cult covered it up by burying the body in the mangroves at Karaka."

His eyes back on the road, Matiu nods. "That'd explain why the cult was forced to swoop in and steal the body back when it was discovered."

"Then how do we explain this morning's John Doe? He was a believer. Why did he die?"

"Maybe he knew too much? What if he was trying to blackmail them? The man had a penchant for expensive shoes, remember?"

"I suppose so." Penny squeezes the bridge of her nose, hoping to pinch away the beginnings of a headache. "The evidence would support that. Beaker says he found LSD in one of the samples." She screws up her eyes, blocking out the oncoming headlights. "But what I don't get is, why. What's the cult's motivation?"

Matiu clucks. "Um. Not getting closed down for being a bunch of charlatans?"

"No, that's not what I mean. I'm not talking about why they hid the body. I mean what's their motivation for helping childless couples?"

"I would've thought that was obvious: to populate the world with rosy-cheeked little cherubs," Matiu says, clapping a hand to his chest. "Desperate people will go to any lengths to have a baby, Pen, even as far as joining a health food cult. Because nobody would eat that grass-shit, otherwise."

"That's just my point. Touching the Sun's multiple producer model is already making them money, so why bother to go into the baby business? Why spend money when you can make it? Didn't you tell me earlier that Erica's sister wasn't likely to have had the cash for repeated IVF treatments?"

"I did, but I'm not so sure about that now. Turns out their old man is a fancy-pants lawyer with deep pockets. Maybe he had a hankering to bounce a grandkid on his knee."

"You should probably ask your probation officer to call her dad and find out."

"I'll phone her as soon as we've found Mārama."

Penny wraps her arms around the box. "After that, we'll go somewhere quiet and torture this GeePee unit into telling us everything it knows."

Matiu arches an eyebrow. "Pandora, I'm surprised. You do know what you're suggesting isn't entirely above board."

She stares at a distant tail-light until it bleeds. "Doesn't matter," she says. "We don't have a choice. If our theory about John Doe is right, and Erica's sister knows something about the Karaka death, then Charlotte's life could be in danger."

- Matiu -

"That's some great parking," Matiu says, as he swings the Commodore into a space beside a red Honda Horizon LEV, its door hanging open, one wheel up on the curbing. He yanks on the handbrake and jumps from the car, Cerberus scrambling over the seats to get out as well. Ducking into the open door of the haphazardly parked car, he quickly scans the dangle of wiring under the steering wheel.

"How can you know this car has anything to do with Whaea Mārama?" Penny says, struggling to scoop up Cerberus' lead as the dog leaps about, yipping and scampering.

Matiu shoots her a puzzled look. "Because it's too far to walk, obviously." He straightens up, looking around the carpark, and up the walkway towards the stabbing finger of the obelisk that crowns One Tree Hill. Auckland sprawls below them, scrolling lines of light, the rippling horizon of the volcanic field where two million people make their homes, the dark of the harbours that surround the city on all sides.

He sets off up the path towards the monument. Cerberus tries to launch into a run, forcing Penny to haul back on the leash and scramble to keep up. "I hear you, boy," Matiu agrees, and breaks into a jog.

"There'd better not be any broken glass up here," Penny groans, kicking her heels off into the grass beside the path. "You're jumping to conclusions, both of you. What makes you think Whaea Mārama knows how to steal a car?"

"Who do you think taught me?"

"Seriously, Matiu. And why would she come here anyway?"

"This is where we used to come, some Saturdays, those times she was having a good day, and the weather was decent. Didn't happen often, but it did. Our special place sort-of-thing, if you want to be sappy about it. Mārama would buy us ice-creams, we'd drive up here, sit at the lookout and scope out the city. She likes being able to sit and see to every horizon. Used to be Maungakiekie Pā, three-hundred-odd years ago. Good place for a fort, easy to defend and hard to sneak up on with the hillsides and the view in all directions." Cerberus' excited yips turn suddenly to growls, and he yanks forward more urgently than before. "Yeah boy, I feel it too."

Matiu bursts into a sprint. His head throbs, but he can taste the violence in the air. The Honda Horizon wasn't the only car in the carpark. The air is thick, and it oozes a different heat, something he can sense without seeing. The scent of predators closing in on prey. He drops the lead, lets Cerberus charge ahead. Penny'll just have to catch up.

He tops the rise, sees the crowd. Cerberus ploughs into them, but they're already running. Vapour floodlights bathe the scene in sickly yellow, turning the blood a rusty shade of brown. Youths in shabby clothes—maybe homeless or maybe just going for the desolate urban look—scatter from the woman standing in the halo, her fingers gripping a steering-wheel lock like a warhammer, hospital gown spattered with red. She's standing over the brass wreath inlaid in concrete at the obelisk's base, surrounded by a low metal fence. Two forms are laid out at her feet, crawling away while clutching their battered heads, and yet another rolls around in a panic as Cerberus snaps and savages at their face. The fleeing youths disperse, see Matiu bearing down on them, and disappear over the railings and down the hillside. The brassy gaze of a lone Māori warrior looks down on the scene from the base of the obelisk.

Matiu leaps the fence to reach Mārama, grabbing Cerberus' lead and tearing him from his victim. The dog's muzzle is wet with blood. Broken and bleeding, the three remaining hooligans pick each other up and stagger away with all the speed they can muster. Matiu turns to Mārama, holds out his hand for the steering-wheel lock. "What'd you use to open that? Hairpin? Old school."

Mārama nods, the fierce look in her eye fading as Matiu takes the weapon and pulls her close to him. "This isn't a safe place, this time of night," he says. "People are worried about you."

"Nowhere's safe." She shakes her head. "I had to see, had to see the oceans. See the horizon. See if it's come yet." She sags against him, the wild, frenzied strength draining from her limbs like air rushing from a punctured tyre.

"See what? What are you looking for?" Gently, awkwardly, adjusting the steering wheel lock so he won't drop it, he gets his arms under her knees and armpits and hoists her. She's lighter than balsa, and Matiu can almost feel her wafer-thin bones through the hospital gown, wearing away at her skin from the inside. He heads away from the monument, towards the carpark.

"You know," she says, and Matiu hears the change in her voice, that shift in tone which tells him she's already moved on, diverted to something less upsetting, "they used to call this a memorial. Built it to remember. White man paid five thousand pounds to build a memorial to the Māori, so we wouldn't be forgotten when we were gone. *Gone*, Matiu. That man," she points back at the wreath, the smaller memorial in the shadow of the towering obelisk, "they buried him here, so he wouldn't be forgotten either."

"But we're not gone, are we? We showed him. So let's not worry about it. Not right now." He steps over the fence as Penny finally appears, out of breath and bewildered.

"We're not dead, we're not forgotten," Mārama goes on. "We fight on. We have to keep fighting. They keep coming, closing in, from all sides."

Matiu meets Penny's wide-eyed stare. "Hey look," he says with more calm than he feels, "it's Penny. See, lots of people worry when you go off on your own like this. We don't want to worry people, do we?" Matiu hands Penny Cerberus' lead.

"Our monsters," Mārama continues, unfazed, "they're here. All around us, inside us. Others, they forget, they stop fighting. We can't forget, Matiu. They're coming. We can't stop fighting."

- Pandora -

Matiu comes over the ridge, Mārama in his arms, a steering wheel lock hooked in the crook of his elbow. Gasping, Penny rushes forward, ignoring the stones biting at the soles of her feet. A few stones are nothing; her aunt's hospital smock is spattered with blood. Great gobs of it. There's a spot on her chin…

"Hold your panic," Matiu says, putting their aunt down gently and tilting his head back towards the crater. "The blood's not hers."

Breathing out her anxiety, Penny peers into the hollow where two men are still sprawled on the ground, one haemorrhaging from his nose. Crouched before them, Cerberus is protecting his pack, his muzzle matted pink with blood. He bares his teeth and growls at the pair scrambling to their feet.

"Is that…are they…did she…?"

"Yep, and there were others. They took off when I arrived, but they won't be far away. Let's get out of here before they regroup. Come on, Cerberus."

The dog backs away, his eyes not leaving the men, who are now limping towards the edge of the park.

Penny ducks under Mārama's arm, taking her weight, leaving Matiu's hands free in case their aunt's attackers decide to come back for another round. Although why anyone would want to mug a woman in a hospital gown is beyond her. What could they possibly have to gain? Penny staggers, slightly unbalanced as Mārama leans heavily against her, the adrenalin that had fuelled her aunt's little escapade obviously wearing off and leaving her shaky. "It's OK, I've got you," Penny murmurs gently in her ear. "You're safe now. We're here."

"And Penny dragged herself away from a hot date to be here, too," Matiu says.

Penny glares at him. "Well, we can't have Whaea Mārama taking on entire gangs of street kids on her own now, can we?" she says, patting her aunt's hand.

But Matiu isn't listening, his eyes drawn to the shadows beneath a line of trees swallowed in the valley to their left. Suddenly, Cerberus throws his head back and keens like a wolf, his bloodied muzzle pointed at the near full moon. The hair on the back of Penny's neck rises as the menace of his cry echoes through the park. Next thing she knows, the stupid animal is charging across the park towards the trees.

"Cerberus! Come back. Oh, you've got to be joking. He has to pick this moment to go chasing bunnies?"

"I don't think it's bunnies," Matiu says, his eyes narrowing. Pulling his shoulders back, he lifts the steering wheel lock, his knuckles whitening around the metal. "Back in a tick," he says, striding into the darkness after the hound.

Mārama moans, her fingernails nearly breaking the skin of Penny's forearm. "No…" she breathes.

"Get a move on, Pen," Matiu calls over his shoulder. "Get Mārama back to the car. And whatever you do, lock the fucking doors."

Her heart galloping, Penny hustles her aunt down the path to the car and settles her into the back seat. Then she snatches up her shoes from beside the path, gets into the passenger seat, locks the doors, and they wait.

The car is airless and hot, the moon outside bathing the asphalt in silvery sweat. Penny holds her breath, while Mārama rocks in place, humming something Penny doesn't recognise.

"Matiu said he'd be back in a second, just as soon as he catches up with Cerberus," Penny says to fill the silence.

Mārama's humming goes up a half note.

The minutes tick by.

"Penny," Mārama shouts, making her jump. "You have to look after Matiu."

"Of course," Penny soothes. "You know I will. Haven't I always looked out for him?"

"Yes, yes," she says, calming a little. "Kiri's *tamāhine*. You're a good girl, my son's sister." She cups her hands against the window and leans against the glass, staring into the grey-green gloom where Matiu and Cerberus disappeared. "You know, the monsters are coming for him again," she whispers. "They come, seeping up from the darkest places. Hovering in the shadows. They know I'm weak. They tested me and saw me falter. Now, they're breaking through! Slipping sideways through the spaces. Searching for Matiu. They'll torture him, you know, like they tortured me, like they still do. My son is stubborn: he'll fight back until he knows nothing but fighting, nothing but pain... Penny," she shouts. She pulls away from the window, her breath leaving a sphere of condensation on the glass, her eyes brimming with tears. She claws at the back of the seat. "They always find the weakness. It's the easiest thing. They come after the thing you love."

Penny puts her arm through the gap beneath the headrest and strokes her aunt's face. "Whaea Mārama, I'll look after Matiu. I promise. I won't let anyone hurt him."

Mārama nods, and begins her rocking again. The poor thing. Who knows what demons lurk inside her brain, eating away at her reason? Sometimes, Penny wonders if those same demons haven't taken up residence in Matiu's brain too. Just a half hour ago he mentioned Makere again, even tried to suggest to Penny that *she'd* seen his imaginary friend. Maybe that's what Mārama meant when she said the monsters were breaking through again. What had she said exactly? Slipping sideways through the spaces? Getting into Matiu's brain. Like the figure she'd glimpsed in the corner of the elevator at The Sedge building? She shakes her head. No. That was a hologram. Subliminal messaging by the restaurant to drum up business. Demons, holograms, either way it was messing with your head. Like this waiting.

Come on. Where are you? Penny's scalp tingles with fear. Please, let them be all right. She's not sure exactly which gods she's beseeching. It doesn't matter. *Any* gods. Just let them be safe. Maybe she should go and look? But Matiu said to lock the doors. What if he's in trouble? *When isn't he in trouble?*

Penny is still wrestling with herself when the pair of them burst from the trees, sprinting like they've got the Four Horsemen of the Apocalypse on their heels. Cerberus is ahead, the dog's ears pinned back and his tongue lolling out the side of his mouth. Matiu races after him, breathing hard. Someone's after them. The gang's regrouped! Penny leans over, fumbling with the driver door lock. Stuck. She tries it again, throwing the door open just as Cerberus reaches the car. He leaps in, his paws barely touching the seat before he joins Mārama in the back seat, Matiu sliding into the driver's seat a split second later. The doors slam shut. Matiu thrusts the steering wheel lock at Penny. "Take this."

"What happened?"

"Not now!" He throws the car into reverse, screaming out of the parking spot, then powers forward, the wheels kicking up stones. "Seatbelts!" he bellows.

The vehicle may be beaten to shit, but the Commodore's engine is far from dead; the four of them roar into the night. But as they pass through the park gates, Penny glances back and spies a perfect silhouette standing in the centre of the public car park: it's Kingi, his chest heaving and his wild dreadlocks undulating like tentacles in the moonlight.

It doesn't look like anyone's following them but, just in case, Matiu circles the streets for a half hour before driving them into the underground carpark beneath Penny's apartment. He pulls into her allocated space—the first vehicle ever to park there—and cuts the engine. The Commodore rattles to a stop. Matiu leans his head back against the headrest and exhales heavily.

When her pulse has slowed and her breathing is back to normal, Penny phones Mum to put her out of her misery. "We found Mārama," Penny tells her. "You were right; she was looking for Matiu." She holds the phone away from her ear while Mum cycles through Elisabeth Kübler-Ross' five stages of grief.

It could've been a lot worse. In the back seat, Mārama has nodded off, her upper body slumped sideways. She's curled around Cerberus, the pair of them snoring softly.

"She's sleeping now, Mum," Penny says, when the verbal deluge has slowed to a torrent. "Probably best to let her rest. We'll bring her in tomorrow. Yes, I promise, one of us will be with her the whole time." She swipes the phone off and turns to Matiu. "Mum's calling off the search posse. She says she'll let the hospital know."

They share a look. If Mum has anything to do with it, the hospital's going to know *all* about it.

"You didn't tell her about the blood?" Matiu asks. Penny doesn't answer, making a point of studying the dashboard instead. "Good call."

"You should probably contact Erica."

"I texted her while you were on the phone to Mum. She said she'll get back to me when she has the information we need."

"You didn't mention our theory?"

"What do you think?"

"Yeah, good decision. We should wait until we know what's in this box. Worrying her isn't going to help."

While Penny slips her shoes on—there's no way she's setting her bare feet on this greasy concrete floor—Matiu climbs out of the car. The way he's moving, he could be Dad. Or Sisyphus pushing his bloody great boulder up the hill.

He catches her watching him. "Right, let's get Mārama upstairs and into bed," he says with all the false enthusiasm of an afterschool TV host. "Bring the GeePee unit, will you?" He's about to open the rear door and scoop up Mārama, when his Thunderbirds ringtone goes off. Frowning, he lifts his phone to his ear. "Yes? Oh hello, Ms Taylor."

Carrying the GeePee unit, Penny teeters in her tracks. *Patisepa Taylor?* Why would she be calling Matiu?

"Yes, of course, I remember you…"

Damn. Looks like Penny isn't going to find out because Matiu turns his back on her, walking into the concrete gloom at the far end of the building. After a few minutes, he charges back.

"Get in," he says, swinging into the driver's seat and slamming the door.

Penny pokes her head through the passenger window. "What?"

"You heard me, get in."

"But I thought—"

"Penny, I know where the warehouse is."

"What?"

"Stop staying what. It's bad manners."

"Matiu," Penny hisses, not wanting to wake Mārama. "You tell me what the fuck is going on, right now."

"You coming?" Matiu's dark eyes blaze. "Because I'm leaving whether you're in the car or not."

"What about Mārama?"

Matiu glances back with a shrug. "Apparently she's fine to go for a drive. Just get in."

Yanking the door open, Penny thrusts the GeePee unit into the footwell and scrambles in after it, the skirt of her date dress getting caught up in the process—it'll probably be covered in grease—but there's nothing she can do because Matiu is already pulling into the street. Penny looks left and right. Happily, there are no black vans lurking in the vicinity. She unclenches her teeth.

"Patisepa Taylor saw me at the restaurant," Matiu says when they've driven a block.

"Yeah, she saw me at the restaurant, too. I didn't get a phone call."

"Aw, is widdle Penny jeawous?" he mocks, turning sharply to shoot up a one-way alley.

"Just shut up and tell me what's going on," Penny whispers at the top of her voice.

Matiu grins. "Seeing me reminded the lovely Patisepa that we're still looking for Sandi Kerr."

"For your information, I reminded her that *the police* were still looking for Kerr when we spoke this afternoon."

"Yes, but why would she tell you anything when you're not a police officer?"

"I hate to break this to you, Matiu, but you're not a police officer either."

"Ms Taylor doesn't know that. Apparently, she thinks I'm an undercover operative."

Folding her arms across her chest, Penny snorts. "It figures. Maybe you can employ an undercover lawyer when you get arrested for impersonating an undercover police officer."

"She might've had information about Charlotte's whereabouts. I thought it was worth the risk."

Penny clamps her lips shut. He's right. Penny doesn't know her, but she can only imagine how terrified the woman must be. For herself, and for her baby. If they're to have a chance of finding her alive, they need to consider every possibility.

"After she saw us in the restaurant, Patisepa got on her real estate spy site and looked up *other* warehouses with similar dimensions and in the same cost bracket as the Fletcher property," Matiu says.

Penny sits up. Why hadn't she thought to ask Patisepa that? "And?"

"Two similar properties were sold in that same week: the first to the Wyatt Family Trust—"

"The truck from this morning. Wyatt Couriers."

"Yes, the company have expanded recently and were looking for more warehousing space. They bought a site over in Glendowie. The Yee Family does business with them under Dad's corporates and cartage partnership scheme. Everything seems legit there."

Which would explain why we're not heading east to Glendowie

"And the other site?"

"It's in Grey Lynn, so fairly central. Sold to a private individual. A woman."

Penny whips her head in his direction. "And you're thinking it could be Sandi Kerr?"

Matiu shrugs.

"It's pure fantasy, Matiu. No one has seen hide nor hair of her since the murders at the Museum. There's no way Sandi Kerr is tied up in all this."

Matiu drums his fingers on the steering wheel. "But what if she is?"

"She isn't."

"You don't know that."

"She isn't."

"Penny."

Penny turns to gaze out the window, a warehouse apartment block whizzing by in a flash of rust brick. "It just feels too, too…convenient, somehow," she whispers.

"Look, the timing makes sense. All she'd have needed to do is colour her hair and use a new name. Estate agents don't give a rat's arse about the moniker you use, as long as you're good for the money." *Patisepa Taylor remembered yours though, didn't she?*

"She'd have to be brazen. The whole city has been looking for her."

"Tanner and his boys have eighteen cases on the books. They can't be everywhere."

That's true. The department is short-staffed at the moment.

"But the thing is," Matiu continues, "if Kerr's involved, then it's because of Hanson, isn't it? It's because of what she was trying to achieve."

"I'm not listening."

"Penny, you saw it happen. She was trying to revive the dead, to make contact with the other side…"

"No, I didn't. She wasn't…"

"For Christ's sake!" He pulls over, stamping on the brake and jerking them to a stop. In the back seat, Cerberus whines in his sleep. Matiu turns on her, his face twisted in fury. "I knew when Simon Kingi followed us that he had to be tangled up in your case somehow. Well, this proves it."

Penny glares at him. *Why hasn't anyone invented laser vision contact lenses?* "It doesn't prove diddly-squat. We both know the real reason Simon Kingi is tangled up in my case," Penny says deliberately, "is because *you*…" She jabs him with her finger. "…are also tangled up in my case."

"Penny—"

She shows him the palm of her hand. "Before we add two and two and make six, let's just see if this warehouse parking lot is full of black vans, shall we?"

CHAPTER 13

- Matiu -

They drive a little further in silence. Clearly, it's pointless arguing with Penny. She refuses to believe what can't be laid out in front of her, which only leaves Matiu one choice: he'll *need* to lay it out in front of her.

They pull up about fifty metres shy of a warehouse with a yard surrounded by chain link fence. The tattoo stares back at them. Plastic signs emblazoned with the eye logo, its lid resembling a rising sun, hang on the fence, declaring to all the world that this is the logistics centre for Touching the Sun. Alongside these, plenty more stating *Private Property*, *No Entry*, and *Electric Fence*. There are no vehicles in the yard. "They really don't want anyone going in there," he says, but Penny is already out of the car, slamming the door, before Matiu can stop her. It's awkward, stomping in high heels, but she manages it. Matiu watches her cross through the highbeams, her good black dinner dress covered in muck and tattered at the edges. This night really hasn't gone the way she'd anticipated. But even putting aside the need to step in and save not just one but two victims—Mārama and Charlotte—at least he got her out of having dinner with Craig Tong. She'd have to be happy about that, wouldn't she?

Wouldn't she?

Matiu scans the fence line and the roof, noting the convenient yet ominous lack of security lighting, and trying not to think about Simon Kingi, a whirling shadow, darting through the bush of Maungakiekie. *Push him back, just long enough, buy some time to get back to the car, get the hell out.* He turns to Cerberus, who raises his head but doesn't get up, Mārama's arm draped over him. "You look after her, OK?" Then he grabs the steering wheel lock and steps out of the car, locking it behind him, and strides after Penny, catching up with her at the gate. She's eyeing a padlock that binds a chain through the bars.

"Looks new," Matiu says, glancing around. "Probably means the electronic controls are disconnected."

"Why assume that?" Penny says.

He points to the electric gate controller. "If someone remotely starts the gate opening and there's a chain holding it closed, the motor will pull the gate straight off the rollers. That's annoying, and expensive to fix. Someone wants old school security, the sort that can't be hacked with a cellphone. Can't see any cameras, either. No point collecting evidence of your own crimes, right?"

Penny looks up. "That's good, though, isn't it? No electronic security?"

"Maybe." He gestures to the multiple signs along the fence warning of high voltage. "Guess it depends if those signs are for real or just to scare people off." He steps back, gripping the steering wheel lock by its thick rubber handle and extending it towards the barbed wire that crowns the fence. White light arcs and crackles from the barbed wire to the blood-spattered lock. Matiu drops it, the paint seared and smoking.

Penny takes a careful step backwards. "So how do we get in?"

"You're the scientist." He shrugs, scooping up the scorched lock. "Can you short it out? Interrupt the circuit? Can't be that hard, surely. It's just electricity." His phone buzzes. "It's Erica. Be back in a sec. Don't do anything I wouldn't do. Yo," he says into the phone, stepping away.

"For fuck's sake, Matiu, what's happening? Why did I just get a call from my dad saying there are police in his apartment? Did you find Charlotte or not?"

"Relax. I'm on it."

"Dad says the place is trashed, and they've had to take a security guard to hospital. What did you *do*? And don't bullshit me. They're reviewing CCTV footage now to see what happened."

Fantastic. Placed at the scene of a crime yet again. "Did you happen to ask your dad if he's given your sister money recently, for the fertility treatments?"

"Strangely enough, Matiu, with my sister missing and now possibly involved in a violent abduction, money wasn't really on my mind."

"Always follow the money."

"What?"

"Look, I'm working on tracking down the people who have her, but you need to know there's some bad shit going down and Charlotte is somehow mixed up in it. If we can work out who's got her on that medication, we're going to be closer to knowing what they're planning and why. If it's not your dad paying, then I need to know who."

"Fine, I'll try and find out. But you better not be wasting my time."

"Why not? You know how much I like it when you're angry with me."

"Watch yourself, Matiu Yee." The line goes dead.

Matiu stands still, staring into the darkness for a long time after she hangs up. Tries not to think about the way her smell still lingers from that brief, too-close moment that never happened.

Then a bang and a crackle thump through the night, along with a white flash that lights up the sky, and he's turning, looking for Penny.

- Pandora -

Damn.

Penny's best pair of heels sink into the cracks in the verge. The leather will be scraping off the backs. They'll be ruined. She follows the chain link fence line around the site anyway, weaving between the saplings the council has planted in a recent beautifying scheme. On the western perimeter, she finds the compact black box which feeds the fence its current. There's no earth wire running along the bottom of the structure. Excellent: an old school set up, where the earth is the earth. Now all she needs is a metal pole of some sort. Her toes pinching in her shoes, she hurries back to the last sapling in the row. Yes, she'd remembered correctly: secured with garden tape, the tiny tree is supported by a hefty metal waratah stake.

She grabs the steel stake with both hands, but it barely budges, stuck fast in the dry ground. She leans on it, then pulls back with all her weight, her heels digging into the dirt. There's no point grieving over a pair of heels when a woman's life could be in danger. She leans on the stake again. Pulls. Leans. Pulls. On the fourth lean, the stake gives. Just a little more should do it. Penny keeps up her push-me-pull-you wiggling until there's sufficient space for her to yank the pole free. She gives it a final heave and hauls the spike out, dirt raining over her date dress and into her shoes. Penny kicks the grit out from under her soles. She only hopes Charlotte appreciates the lengths she's going to...

Right, let's short this fence.

Holding the waratah upright, she pauses to ensure it's not touching her body anywhere, then drops it against the fence. Sparks fly, but not for long, the arcing easing like the dying sizzle of a hotplate. Not a massive conflagration, but still, it might've attracted unwanted attention. Penny glances up, checking the warehouse for signs of life, but no lights go on and there's no movement. Good. Time to breach this fence and find out what Touching the Sun is all about. Now, in theory, this section between the waratah and the black box is still live, the metal stake closing out the circuit, which means the fence to the right of it should be safe to climb over.

In theory.

Approaching the chain link, Penny listens for the hum of electricity. It *sounds* safe. She can't feel any static in the air either. She plucks some dry grass and holds it near the chain link. Bracing herself to drop the grass, she squints her eyes and touches the blade to the fence. No tingling. It worked!

Don't celebrate too soon, Penny, you still have to get over the fence.

She selects a spot where there are some barbs missing, bunches the hem of her dress over her palms, then pokes the toes of her shoes into the chain webbing and climbs. She's nearly managed to negotiate the barbed wire, her dress only torn in a couple of places, when Matiu hisses at her from the bottom. "Penny, what the hell are you doing?"

"Isn't it obvious? Finding out if Charlotte is here."

Matiu grabs the chain link with both hands.

"Careful," Penny squeaks. "If that waratah slips sideways, we're both toast."

"I'm coming over."

"No. Matiu, you have to stay there."

"Not happening, sis."

But Penny is already picking her way down the other side. "You have to. I promised Mum that one of us would stay with Mārama." She jumps the last metre to the ground. "If Mārama wakes up and wanders off, are you prepared to deal with the fallout from Mum?"

Matiu hesitates.

It's only a split second, but Penny seizes the advantage, spinning on her heel and scurrying across the carpark. "Thought not," she calls over her shoulder. "I'll be back in five minutes."

"Penny—"

But Penny's already closing on the darkened warehouse, slipping into its shadowy flanks, where she flattens herself against the corrugated iron cladding. She checks the side door first. Locked. The top third is window, but it's made of that pimpled opaque glass with wire running through it. Penny tiptoes for a look-see anyway. Just as she thought: impossible to discern anything, apart from the fact there are lights on inside. She'll just have to keep looking. She risked an electrified fence to get here. She's not leaving without more information.

Trailing her fingertips across the corrugated cladding, she sneaks to the front of the building and peeks out. There. Beyond the wide roller doors. A window in the top right-hand corner of the building. Perhaps there's a mezzanine on that level. Is that an office window, and is Charlotte in there, languishing like a princess in a tower?

Penny needs to get a look inside.

But if she runs past the roller doors, there's a chance she could be seen.

There's a chance she might not.

What if she gets caught?

What if she doesn't?

And while she's standing here dithering, what if Charlotte has run out of choices?

No time like the present. Penny dashes past the roller doors and whips around the corner of the building, her heart pounding with dread. But the dash was worth it because on the way past, she'd spied the downpipe. It looked sturdy enough to climb, too.

She starts picking at the double knot at her waist, then changes her mind. The dress fabric is far too gauzy to be helpful. Instead, she pronates sharply, first her right foot, then her left, stamping down heavily to break the heels off her beloved shoes. Who is she kidding? They were never going to make it, anyway. After flinging the broken heels away into the grass, she stoops to buckle the two ankle straps together. Then, grimacing with disgust, she spits on her hands, and, stepping out to the front of the building, she grasps the pipe with two hands and shimmies up using the ankle straps for traction.

Well, not quite shimmies. It isn't a graceful process. Inching would be a better word. There's this dress to contend with, and the smooth soles of her shoes are making it hard to grip the plastic downpipe. Her stomach is burning, half from exertion and the other half from the stress of possibly being discovered. Because if she comes a cropper and ends up sprawled on the asphalt, and if these people *do* have Charlotte, what might they do to her?

Penny's just a metre from the window, when a roller door grinds. The noise gives her such a fright she nearly loses her grip. Gasping, she clutches to the plastic pipe with clammy palms. The smell of freshly cut grass drifts up from the open door and, below her, two armed guards spill into the night.

"I don't see why we have to patrol," grumbles the first man, who could light the Third World with the moonlight gleaming off his bald head.

"You're getting well paid for it," the other says.

"Don't get me wrong, Ray, I'm not complaining," Moonbeam stops to light a cigarette, the flame illuminating the bottom half of his face. "There aren't many gigs offering this kind of coin, but they don't half want a pound of flesh for it, do they? Demanding that we step the patrols up to every 20 minutes. For fuck's sake." He exhales. A long stream of dirty air. "What's that all about, anyway? It's not like Cinderella is even on the premises anymore. There's only the stiff the police dug out of the swamp and it's in the cold-room, not going anywhere."

Penny's ears prick. Matiu was right. The stiff. They have the bog body! Which means Cinderella *has* to be Charlotte. In her head, Beaker admonishes her for extrapolating from insufficient data. Ignoring him, Penny clenches her knees, straining not to lose purchase on the slippery pipe, and concentrates hard on what the men are saying.

"Not so sure about that. Seems the Sunshine Queen wants the stiff moved toot-sweet. She's called for increased security—" Ray says.

"—and what the boss lady wants, she gets," Moonbeam replies, taking another drag on his cancer stick.

"Which means we're all going to be on our best behaviour until her meeting at the flagship with the Big Kahuna Sun Priest tomorrow night."

Tomorrow? Sun Priest?

"What's that all about then?" Moonbeams asks the question for her.

Ray shrugs. "Expecting a promotion maybe?"

They move off. "Something's got her all in a tizzy, that's for sure."

"You ever meet the supreme commander?" Ray asks.

"Not me…"

The voices fade as the men round the corner, heading clockwise around the building. It'll only take them a few minutes to complete the circuit. If she's still here when they come back around the building, they'll see her.

Shit.

Penny abandons the idea of looking through the window. If what Moonbeam and Ray were saying is true, then Charlotte isn't up there anyway. Instead, Penny scrambles down the drainpipe as fast as she can, her hands chafing and her shins scraping cruelly on the brackets.

After a millennium, her feet touch the ground. She hesitates, her pulse thundering in her ears. If she follows Ray and Moonbeam, she'll pass right by the open roller door. But if she goes the other way, she could run right into them.

They have guns.

Roller doors it is.

She takes a deep breath and sprints through the beam of light and past the open doorway. But not without glancing inside.

Ohmigod.

The warehouse is full to bursting. Rows on rows of micro-green beds, stacked in layers and reaching to the ceiling on one side of the warehouse. And on the other? A fleet of black vans. That's all she sees because already she's on the other side of the roller doors. Ray and Moonbeam will be back soon. Keeping to the shadows, she slinks around the corner.

What? The guards are coming back the same way they left!

Not far from Penny's head, their torchlight glances off the crenelated walls of the warehouse. Penny dives to the ground, hitting the asphalt hard and grazing her already ravaged knees. Her palms burn. It's all she can do not to scream in pain. They're coming. She lies still, hardly daring to breathe. A helpless rabbit, frozen in its tracks, while two keen-eyed hawks circle. Surely, they'll see her. Even if they don't, her heart's thumping so loud, they have to hear her. Penny waits for their shout. But, striding for the warehouse doors, Ray and Moonbeam have other things on their mind.

"Fucking kids and their fucking waratah," Moonbeam curses.

"Maybe we could call the police," Ray suggests. Penny holds her breath.

"Are you fucking kidding me? Do you want to lose us this job? *We're* the security here. We'll turn the fences off. It'll only take us a minute to nip back and get rid of that blasted stake. No one has to know."

"We'd better make it fast then," Ray says. "If the boss finds out, she'll have our guts for garters."

"She ain't exactly sweetness and light, is she?" In her peripheral vision, Penny glimpses Moonbeam's shiny dome.

"Why do you think she wants that girl's baby, then?" Ray asks.

Moonbeam gives him a look. He grins. "Maternal instincts?"

The pair guffaw loudly. They're still laughing when they turn the corner.

Penny is lying on the asphalt, still paralysed with fright when it dawns on her: Ray and Moonbeam had been on the way back *to turn off the fence*. Once they've done that, they'll remove the waratah and along with it any chance of her escaping undiscovered. She has to go *now*. She winces. Why is it impossible to get up without using either your hands or your knees? Her knees are slightly worse for wear, so she puts a hand out to steady herself against the wall. Clambers to her feet. With her body battered and bleeding, she limps for the fence on her broken shoes. She doesn't look back, just thrusts her toes into the webbing and climbs. She's forgotten to wrap her hands, the barbed wire at the top of the fence stabbing the webbing of her thumb. There are more barbs here, the dress tearing again and again, ruined like her shoes. Like the skin under her arm, a stray barb dragging a gouge into her flesh as she scrambles between the wires.

Voices carry through the night.

They're coming! No, no, no. Hurry. Are they on their way out, or have they already retrieved the waratah? Are they on their way back to the warehouse? About to flick the switch back on? Please don't let them flick that switch. Panicking, she struggles on, but every handhold carries a barb, every empty space is bordered with metal thorns that pierce and slice. Her hair is twisted in the wire. She bites down and tastes blood. That 16kV jolt will come soon, filling her nostrils with the smell of her own roasting flesh. How will it feel when her heart skips and fails? The barbs tighten around her.

Suddenly Matiu is there, on the other side. How he knew to come here, she has no idea. "I've got you," he murmurs and Penny dives forward.

"Charlotte's not here," she says as she drops into his arms.

Matiu staggers backwards a step under her weight, carrying her away from the fence to set her gently on the ground. Blood dribbles down her shins, and her scalp tingles where her hair has been torn out.

"Matiu, something's going to happen…Kerr, she's some sort of priestess, and there's another one, someone higher up—"

Matiu puts a finger to her lips. "Shh, let's just get you home, Pen. You can tell me on the way."

CHAPTER 14

- Matiu -

He drives. His head is buzzing with it all, the streetlights arcing across the windscreen, and shit is he hungry or what? When did he last eat? He grips the wheel hard, fighting to keep his thoughts clear, his vision straight. No rest for the wicked and all that. He can sleep when this is over. Or when he's dead. Sounds like a radio tune.

Penny talks, and he takes some of it in, in snatches. Her words run over him like water, stirred to a flurry by her own panic, the rush of cooling adrenalin. Pretty Penny, climbing electric fences, breaking and entering. Mum and Dad were right. He *is* a bad influence on her. Get herself in trouble, that girl will.

It's your turn.

He shakes his head, wants to dislodge the voice that suddenly curls inside his ear. Just a stray thought, a misplaced memory, not someone creeping into his head to tell him what to do. That's over. Makere isn't in his head anymore. He *left*.

But he said he was coming for Penny, and now what? Here she is, breaking the law.

"No!" Matiu snarls, grinding his teeth. "No fucking way!"

Penny gapes at him. "What? We have to talk to *someone*, so why not him?"

Matiu glances at her, abashed. "Sorry sis, lost in my own little world there for a minute. What'd you say?"

"I said we ought to talk to your friend Scour and see if he can trace the van you saw tonight using the traffic camera thingy you showed me before. That should lead us to Charlotte."

Of course. Here they are chasing shadows when the answer has been right in front of them the whole time. Distracted by finding Mārama, he'd completely forgotten about the camera network. And nowhere is as heavily covered by CCTV as Auckland Central. He thumbs his phone to unlock it and passes it to her. "Search for Lower Albert Street and Quay Street. That's the last intersection I saw the van go through. Scroll back to around 9pm."

Never mind that she's pulling herself deeper into exactly the sort of shit she keeps going off at him for being involved in. Who's whispering in her ear? Definitely not the angel who's always lived on her shoulder.

Penny loses herself in the screen for a minute, and Matiu's eyes drift to the houses and shops floating by the window. A light misty rain coats the windscreen, the wipers scraping two rainbow-shaped apertures in the grime, smearing dust back and forth across the windscreen. Matiu drives, and Matiu breathes. The tyres hiss on the damp road, and Cerberus snores and huffs, a slumbering dragon in the back seat carefully guarding their precious cargo, Mārama.

He's got everyone he cares about, right here, right now. Screw Erica, and Makere, and Sandi Kerr, and Craig Tong and Mum and Dad and Beak and all of them. He could keep driving. He's thought about it before. Leave this shithole of a city behind. No reason not to. Does he have the balls?

Drive away, and what happens to Charlotte? Some chick he's never even met, mixed up in all the wrong crap when all she wanted was...what? So? It happens all the time. Why the hell did it become his problem?

Because if we stop fighting, they win.

We have to keep fighting.

He did his time, and that was meant to make him better, somehow. Elevate his moral fortitude and all that, and damn he'd tried. But it's more than that. It's about the itch on his arm. The wound that hasn't healed, but keeps weeping and quietly bleeding, driving him slowly insane. The wound he suffered *over there*, which doesn't abide by the laws of this world. If it was going to simply heal on its own, like everyone keeps saying it will, it would've by now. It won't heal until the source of the infection is gone, and the source is somewhere on the other side of the veil, scratching around for a way in.

Matiu can't run away, not because this shit will follow him wherever he turns, but because it's inside him now, eating him from within, and the only way he'll ever be free of it is to follow the infection back to the core and burn it out. That's why he has to find Charlotte, and Sandi Kerr.

They're his way through.

- Pandora -

While Penny crosses her apartment to close the blinds and give them some privacy from the creepy neighbour across the way, Matiu drops the GeePee unit on the kitchen island and heads to the bathroom.

Meanwhile, the two sleeping beauties, who've been snoring in the back seat for the better part of an hour, are now wide awake. Full of energy, Cerberus runs about the apartment, reacquainting himself with the place as if he'd not seen it in years, his tail thumping against the hallway wall, the couch, the kitchen island. Finally, the big softie sidles up to Mārama, rubbing his body against her bare legs, begging for her attention. Mārama indulges him, sinking her hands into his fur and scratching behind his ears.

With blood all over Cerberus' muzzle, and more of it staining Mārama's hospital gown, the pair of them could've stepped straight out of a B-grade spatter movie. But, lowering the blind, Penny glimpses her own reflection in the sliding door. She doesn't look much better herself. Her dress is in tatters, she's bleeding from her scalp, and pale yellow ooze is seeping from the grazes on her knees. Tiny beads, like raindrops on a branch, reveal a scratch on her cheek.

Well, that's what you get when you insist on trespassing on private property.

"Penny?" Mārama says quietly. "I think the puppy's hungry."

Of course he's hungry. He's a Lab. When are they not hungry? But it's just like her aunt to think of the dog. Perceptive to the point of pain, it's as if she takes on others' suffering, absorbing it into herself. She probably hasn't had dinner either, running about in the dark fending off Kingi and his minions.

"Let's feed him then, shall we?" Penny says, taking a sack of dog biscuits out of the cupboard and shaking some into a bowl. Cerberus is bolting them down when Matiu emerges from the bathroom. Patting Mārama's shoulders as he passes, he sinks into the couch and closes his eyes. He doesn't look too hot either. His skin is grey, and his hair hangs in damp tendrils where he's splashed water on his face.

Letting him rest there for a moment, Penny shepherds Mārama up the hall. "If you have a shower, Mārama, I'll make you something to eat while you're getting cleaned up. How does that sound?"

Mārama nods. "You're a good girl, Penny."

"There are fresh towels in the vanity. Shout if you need me." Closing the bathroom door, Penny slips into the bedroom and rummages in her drawers for something for Mārama to wear. Somewhere in here there should be an old nightie that Mum bought for her—the one Penny calls her contraceptive nightie because it buttons to the neck. But it's roomy and comfortable on Penny, so it should fit Mārama. She finds it two drawers down, squashed in at the back. Shaking it out, Penny shuts the drawer closed with her foot, then grabs up her dressing gown from the back of the chair.

Knocking first, she hangs the clothes on the back of the bathroom door. In the shower, Mārama is humming.

"I found a fresh nightie for you, Mārama," Penny calls through the frosted glass. "Just throw the gown on the floor when you're done."

"Hey, how come you never let me throw my clothes on the floor?" Matiu says when she returns to the lounge.

"Because you ought to know better. Look, she'll be out soon. Can we agree to not talk about the case—*cases*—while she's in the room?"

"We talked in the car."

"When she was *asleep*. Come on, Matiu, she's traumatised enough as it is. How's she going to react when she hears about Charlotte? Even a stranger's suffering could push her over the edge. And she might be a bit addled at times, but she didn't come down in the last shower of rain. How long do you think it'll take her to work out that by going after Charlotte's kidnappers, we'll be putting ourselves in harm's way?"

"Penny, what I don't think you realise is—"

"Matiu," Penny cuts him off. "Just don't talk about the case in front of Mārama. Please." With that, she stalks past the kitchen island, gets out the toasted sandwich maker and slides it onto the counter. Switching it on, she fishes in the fridge for bread, butter, cheese, tomatoes, and a jar of Marmite, assembling a couple of sandwiches and placing them on the platter to toast.

In the bathroom, the water cuts out. Matiu gets up and helps himself to a beer from the fridge.

"Are you sure you should be drinking? You bumped your head earlier when you—"

Matiu nudges her. "Shh. Mārama's coming."

They look up. Coming down the hall dressed in Penny's nightwear, their aunt looks like a little girl up too late and still insisting on hearing a bedtime story. The only thing missing is the teddy bear.

"Mārama," Penny says cheerily. "Feeling better? Come sit down and have something to eat. It's only a toastie, but it'll fill the gap."

Shuffling over to take a seat at the table, Mārama flashes her a rare smile. "That's OK. I don't mind toasties."

"Well, that's perfect, then," Penny says, cutting a toasted sandwich in half and circling the island to bring it to her, Cerberus loitering hopefully at her feet.

Matiu joins them at the table, having already helped himself to the other toastie. He bites into it, steam rising from the crust. "Ow, that's hot."

Mārama pats Penny's hand. "Aren't you eating with us?"

"I ate earlier," Penny says. *Omigod.* With everything that's happened this evening, she's forgotten to call Craig. Leaning against the kitchen island, she gets out her phone and types him a text: 'Mārama found safe.' Except, when they'd found her, she was anything but safe. Penny scrolls backwards and deletes the word 'found'. There, that's more accurate. She adds, 'Thanks for a lovely meal', and presses SEND. The message whooshes off. A second later, he replies with a smiley emoticon.

Penny grins.

"You really need to learn to cook," Matiu says, licking melted cheese off his fingers. "How are you ever going to seduce Craig when your culinary skills are limited to cheese toasties? I thought cooking and chemistry were supposed to be the same thing."

He's right, cooking is a form of chemistry—simple methodologies using bulk reagents—but for the life of her Penny's never quite mastered it. Maybe because really great chefs improvise, altering the ratio of ingredients, adding a hint of something here, and a pinch of something there, adapting the recipe in unfathomable ways that enable them to produce something tasty. The times Penny's tried it, the results were barely edible.

OK, so they were foul.

"Ooh, Pen," Matiu mocks. "You forgot to be pissed at me for mentioning Craig." He offers Cerberus a piece of his crust. The dog swallows it whole. "Does that mean the date passed muster, then? Has Craig wormed his way into your affections, wriggled under your skin and into your—"

"Matiu!" Penny snatches up his empty plate, carrying it to the kitchen island. "That's enough!" She rinses the plate and stacks it in the washer. "I'm not going to discuss my date with Craig."

Glancing at Mārama, Matiu arches a brow. "So what *are* we allowed to talk about?"

"I don't know. Current events?"

Matiu smirks.

"Oh for goodness' sake. I'm going to have a shower. You make Mārama a cup of tea," Penny says.

When she returns, Mārama and Cerberus are gone, the kitchen looks like a bombsite, and Matiu is sitting at the kitchen island dismantling the GeePee unit with one of her kitchen knives.

"Don't panic," he says, when he sees her looking left and right. "I put Mārama to bed in your spare room. Her new best friend is in there with her."

"What happened to my kitchen?"

"I had another toastie."

"So I see."

"Don't start, Pen. It's only a bit messy."

"Well, clean it up, then."

"Can't. It's a Friday. You know very well it's not my dishes night."

Penny rolls her eyes. "Don't give me that. That roster was defunct years ago."

"Can you do it? Please?" He pulls the puppy-dog face he used to make when he was trying to get out of the dishes back when they were kids.

Penny snorts. "Why should I?"

"Because I'm trying to work out where Touching the Sun have hidden Charlotte," he says, immediately making her feel like shit.

Sighing, Penny gives in. Moving to the other side of the kitchen island, she wipes out the sandwich maker and rinses the dishes. There are no uneaten crusts to throw away. Matiu must have fed them all to Cerberus. When the kitchen's tidy, she flicks the kettle on, then takes two cups from the cupboard, dropping a teabag into each one. "You know, I've been thinking about what Ray and Moonbeam were saying earlier."

"Who?"

"Security detail for Touching the Sun. I think Charlotte might be OK. The way they were talking, their boss—"

"Sandi Kerr."

Penny frowns. "We don't know that."

"It's her."

"Well, *whoever* it was that ordered the abduction has plans for Charlotte's baby, which means she should be safe, possibly even well cared for, until the baby's born. How close to term do you think she is?" Penny asks, pouring hot water over the bags and causing woody lapsang souchong steam to spool from the cups.

"I didn't see her up close," Matiu replies. "But she looked pretty pregnant to me. 'Two cushions up her jumper' big. And we already know Kerr's posed as a counsellor before, what's to stop her pretending to be a nurse and administering a dose of whatever it is the doctors use to induce a birth?"

"Oxytocin," Penny says. "Or a synthetic alternative. The hormone softens the cervix and improves—" Penny stops mid-sentence, bringing hands to her face, her stomach dropping into her slippers.

Matiu's head whips up. "What??"

"That'd only be if the kidnappers cared about the mother."

"Shit." Matiu steps up his attack on the GeePee unit.

"Matiu," Penny whispers. "I'm scared. This is getting too big for us. We need to tell Tanner and Clark. They're the policemen. We have to let them handle this."

Matiu taps the knife on the edge of the box. "And what exactly are we going to tell them, Pen? That a woman's being held hostage by a bunch of lettuce-munching greenies? Even if they believe us, which I doubt, they'll never get a search warrant. Not without hard evidence, *which we can't give them*, not given the way we acquired the information."

"You're talking about stealing the GPS unit?"

"That and trespassing on private land, sabotage, not to mention deliberate tampering with private property…"

Now it's Penny's turn to swear. "We need to find her, Matiu, and we need to do it before tomorrow night."

CHAPTER 15

- Pandora -

Penny drifts awake, the living room lights blinding her. She must have nodded off on the sofa. How long was she asleep? She rubs the grit out of her eyes. A while. Long enough for the milky surface of her tea to crack. Has Matiu been working on that box all this time? He must be exhausted. She looks across the living room. Blinks. There are two figures in her kitchen. The one on the left is Matiu—she'd know him anywhere—but the man leaning close and murmuring in Matiu's ear looks familiar, too. His friend Scour? But Penny's never met him. Unless she has and didn't know it. Either way, Penny must've been dead to the world because she didn't hear Matiu buzz him in.

"Matiu?" she says.

"Yup." He doesn't bother to turn around.

"Did you find anything?"

"Not yet. Don't wait up, Pen. I'll let you know when I find it."

She's about to stand up and head off to bed, when the man beside Matiu turns. Penny's blood freezes. It's the hologram. The one with the moko like Matiu's. The one from the lift.

Except they're not in the lift.

He leans back against her kitchen island, his arms folded across his chest, looking her straight in the eye and giving her that lecherous Hannibal Lector smile.

"Penny," he mouths.

Gripping the sofa armrests, Penny blinks again. Opens her eyes. He's still there. She runs through all the reasons she might be seeing someone who isn't actually there.

No. 1: She's still asleep and doesn't know it.

No. 2: She's overtired and hallucinating.

No 3: It's delayed shock.

No. 4: She's totally cray-cray.

The man touches a finger to his nose. *"I know you see me."* His voice is hollow inside her skull. Penny's intestines shrivel. She shakes her head. *No!*

"Denial, I love it."

"You're…you're impossible."

"You're the one who's impossible," Matiu murmurs.

The stranger strokes his chin. *"Except you see me. How are you going to rationalise me away, then, Little Ms Scientist?"*

Penny's mind races. Little Ms Scientist. Science. Systematic study of the world through observation and experiment. There's a rational explanation, she just has to find it. So, what does she know? What observations can she make? Firstly, the lift was full of mirrors and she only saw him for a split second. As far as she's aware, Craig didn't see a thing and Matiu isn't seeing him now, although to be fair, he hasn't looked up lately. The man *could* still be a hologram, but it's improbable because, apart from limited military use, distance wireless hologram projections are still a few years away.

Gleeful, the intruder shakes his head, enjoying himself.

Penny barrels on. The last time she'd seen him, he'd been in the corner of the lift, reflected in the mirror on two sides. She draws in a breath. What if he exists in a single plane? He could be 2-dimensional. A living hologram. Is that even possible? Why not? People didn't believe in micro-organisms until the 1670s when Antonie van Leeuwenhoek developed lenses, allowing scientists to see his animalcules for themselves. What if that's the case here? Why *couldn't* he exist in another dimension? Suddenly, something Mārama said explodes in her head, about people slipping sideways into the spaces…

The stranger shifts his weight forward, his brow furrowing.

Matiu swivels on the barstool. Facing her, he arches his back and stretches his arms above his head. "Stop your babbling and go to bed, will you? I can't concentrate."

Penny blinks. The man has gone. Disappeared. Or perhaps he slipped sideways through a portal to some other dimension…

"Pen, you OK? You look a bit spaced out."

"What? Oh, it's nothing. I'm just tired."

He nods. "Night then. OK if I make myself a coffee?"

"Sure." When she looks back from the hall, Matiu's alone in the kitchen.

It was nothing. Just her brain working overtime. A waking dream. She glances into the spare room. The dim shaft of light from the hall reveals everything is as it should be: Mārama huddled under the duvet and Cerberus on his mat at the base of the bed. The hound growls softly in his sleep, sensing her presence in that uncanny way animals do. "Shh, boy. It's just me," she whispers.

The moon glints through a tiny gap in the blinds. Far off, in the distance, a siren wails, sounding sad and hopeless. All at once, Penny doesn't want to be alone. Crossing the room, she scuffs off her slippers, lifts the duvet, and snuggles in beside Mārama.

- Matiu -

He stares at the wall of numbers loading on his tablet's screen. People earn their living doing this sort of shit, trying to make sense of pages full of numbers. How the hell do they do it? Matiu's head is spinning already, and he only just started the download. Hacking the GeePee's history had been simple enough once he'd found the model and firmware numbers printed on the circuit board, but what to do with it now that it's flooding out like digital diarrhoea? The back of his skull throbs and his eyes ache, but he resists the urge to shut them, even for a minute. He goes to the coffee machine, makes caffeine happen. Big heap of sugar. The smell is like a kick in the jaw from a friendly horse, the taste even better. *Ain't no rest for the wicked.*

He slips in his earpiece and thumb-dials Scour. The phone rings several times—more than Matiu would expect—before it picks up. There's laboured breathing on the end of the line. "What?"

"Yo, Scour, it's Grendel. The fuck, man, are you *running*?"

"Fuck no, I'm screwing your sister."

"If you were, you wouldn't have answered, and I'd be able to hear you in the other room, plus that's just a stupid thing to say so shut the fuck up. How'd you go with tracking that van?"

"That van? That fucking *van*? Dude, why do you think I'm running?"

A chill sweeps Matiu. "Enlighten me, bro."

"Whoever owns those vans had a sniffer running on the traffic monitoring server. Soon as the van passed a plate cam and my worm pinged the result back to me, I picked up another ping: the sniffer tracing my worm back."

"No shit?" It made sense to leave a sniffer on Charlotte's home TV, but holy crap, the traffic network? Not only are Touching the Sun paranoid as all fuck, they've got the forethought to anticipate a move like this and be ready to react.

"Who are these guys, bro? What shit have you dumped me in? Because not five minutes after the flashback ping, I hear a vehicle coming down the street and I look out the window and there's a fucking black van pulling up outside, and two guys are getting out, carrying guns. Guns, bro. Is this some more of your badass gangland bullshit? Because if it is, I really don't fucking appreciate being dragged into it!"

"What'd you do?"

"What you think? I flicked the killswitch and ran, bro."

"Heavy," Matiu says. "Killswitch, that's serious shit."

"Most my data's stashed in proxies anyway, so I haven't lost much. I'm more worried about the dudes with the fucking guns who are out here somewhere looking for me. Shit, gotta go."

The line drops out. Matiu sits for a long minute watching the data scroll down his screen, listening to the ghostly silence on the other end of the phone. Did he just lead a bunch of killers to his mate's doorstep? Shit. How the hell did someone as professional as Scour manage to get caught by a two-bit IP sniffer? It's looking more and more like Touching the Sun are beyond amateur, and Scour's fallen afoul of them only because he was doing Matiu a favour. This is on him, dammit. At least Scour's got street smarts, and he knows his local back alleys which hopefully these Touching the Sun arseholes don't. He'll have a bolthole somewhere, a drainpipe to scurry up like a rat. The sort of contingency you plan out when you're working for volatile motherfuckers like Hanson. Meanwhile, Matiu needs to track these bastards down and burn them to the ground.

But first he'll have to overcome the demon right in front of him: this seemingly infinite dump of numbers. He's faced off against monsters and ghosts. He won't be beaten by a freaking *spreadsheet*. Even if he has no idea where to start, he knows someone who will. He thumbs his phone again. It buzzes in his ear, three, four times.

"Hello? Matiu? Is that you?" The voice on the line is puzzled, almost confused. "Has something happened? Is Pandora OK?"

"Hey Beak," Matiu says, putting on his smoothest voice. "Sorry to call you so late, but I need a favour. You got a minute?"

Matiu doesn't really care how, but now the numbers are near to making sense. Deleting nonconsecutive duplicates, sorting the rows, subtotalling and grouping the data to create blocks of time, conditionally colour-coding these to show where those times lasted the longest or recurred most frequently. It was a blur, but less of a blur than it had been twenty minutes ago. He hadn't given Beak the details of what he was looking at or why, just enough vague instruction to help him figure out which buttons Matiu should be clicking. Poor lad will be stumped, but since that's pretty much his general state of existence, no change there. He sends the lovestruck lab-monkey back to bed and dials up some decent, loud music in his earpiece to keep him pumping. His hands tremble over the screen as caffeine and exhaustion vie for dominance. Scour is out there in the dark somewhere, running from a bunch of murderous psychopaths, and this is his fault.

Grabbing co-ordinates from the top of the list, starting with the most frequent locations, he swipes them into a map of Auckland and collects the addresses on a text pad. There's the warehouse they just came from, as well as a whole raft of restaurants, cafes and retailers around the city, including The Sedge and that damned hippy juice bar. Despair settles in as he works down the list. Nothing about the pattern of the van's movements suggests anything more than the activities of a legitimate business running its normal delivery operations.

Matiu slugs back the dregs of his coffee and rubs his eyes, the thump of bass and drums violent in his ear. Every time he snags a lead, the enemy yanks it away. These well-funded loonies have a secret game-plan and an end goal which they think justifies kidnapping and murder; they're not rational, stable people. They'll have made a mistake. Mistakes are the chinks in the dragon's armour.

He resumes his scrolling, copying, pasting.

The map jumps to the southwest, centring on Puketutu Island, a spit of land jutting out into Manukau Harbour, not far from the sewage treatment plant, and joined to Mangere by a narrow causeway appropriately dubbed Island Road. The map returns a street address, but no business name. Matiu frowns. He pastes the address into a search, which returns some defunct web pages suggesting the old estate on the island used to be the site of a function centre and boutique fruit winery, but it's been closed a long time. Another victim of the economic downturn. Apart from that, no mention of what might be transpiring on the island these days. But looking at the timestamps, the van he stole this GeePee from visits the island a couple times a week, at least. Head office, maybe? Cash pay packets?

A nervous burn fires in Matiu's gut. That could be the place. Surrounded by water on all sides, hard to sneak up on, easy to watch everyone who comes and goes. Bit like Maungakiekie. Lots of empty space to hide whatever evil crap you're doing from the watching world, but not too far from the city. If Sandi Kerr can afford to own an island, even a small one, then paying for IVF treatments and network sniffers and hired goons with guns should be well within her financial reach. That's where they'll find Charlotte, for sure.

He sits back, closes his eyes, lets the exhaustion sweep over him. Confused half-images of falling light slip sideways across his eyelids, music the pounding beat of war drums in his skull. Just for a second, he's sure, he rides the spiralling colours down, down into the well, spinning voidwise.

His phone chirps in his ear, the music dropping off suddenly, snapping him back up into a groggy half-dream. He swipes at air, confused, tries to answer his phone, fumbling at the screen. It takes him a moment to realise he can't answer because it's not *his* phone ringing. *"Hello?"* Penny's voice in his ear, thick with sleep. The mic malware. He hasn't turned it off since interrupting her date with Tong.

What the fuck? He glances at the clock on Penny's microwave. Midnight, exactly.

You're dreaming, another voice croons, *beautiful child, e tuahine. Keep sleeping. Keep dreaming. We'll be together soon.*

That voice. That motherfucking voice. Matiu lurches up, stumbles for Penny's door.

"What? What time is it?"

I've been waiting a long, long time for us to be together, Pandora. This will be a dream come true for me. So long, too long. It will be beautiful. Like a dream.

"Penny!" Matiu throws her door open, fumbling for the light.

"Matiu, is that you?"

No Penny. Crap. She's in the spare room, with Mārama. Matiu spins and bolts across the hall.

"What the hell, Matiu? Who do you think you are, waking me up in the middle of the night?"

Tāu hāmua.

"Matiu?"

"Penny!" He flicks the light on and slides across the bed, snatching the phone from her hand. *Caller ID Unknown,* the screen declares. He swipes the call away. Cerberus barks, a staccato chatter to violate the still of the night.

"What the hell? Why did you call me?"

"I didn't—" Matiu chokes on the words. "That's not my voice."

Penny shakes her head to clear away the fog of sleep. "That was *totally* your voice. And you said *tāu hāmua.* Weird thing to say but only you'd say that. Have you even been to sleep yet?"

Tāu hāmua.

"I've been...I've been busy. Shit's happening, Pen. Crime doesn't sleep, you know."

"No, but we need to. Go, find some blankets, shut your eyes for a while. Please?"

Surreptitiously, Matiu holds down the power button on the phone until the screen blanks out. "Yeah, good idea." He stands, and in moments Penny is gone again, back into the well of sleep, nestling closer to Mārama, who hasn't stirred despite the commotion. Cerberus regards Matiu quizzically, then settles back where he was. The dog doesn't close his eyes.

Matiu watches his sister for a minute, her breathing deep and even. Thinks about Charlotte, about Scour, and what the voice on the phone said. Of all the awful, terrifying things Makere ever whispered in his ear over all those long years, none was ever as frightening as what he just said to Penny:

Tāu hāmua.

Your brother.

CHAPTER 16

- Pandora -

Penny wakes, her head buzzing and her body aching like she'd overnighted on a medieval rack. She was so tired she'd hardly slept. And when she did doze off, talk about weird dreams. Freud would have a field day. She peels herself away from her still slumbering aunt and gets out of bed. The buzzing isn't in her head. Her phone? It isn't anywhere near the bed. Finally, her brain makes the connection. The front door!

She punches her feet into her slippers and rushes through the hall into the living room, the smell of frying butter hitting her full in the face. A quick glance into the kitchen reveals Matiu standing over the fry pan, his earbuds crammed in his ears, and waving the spatula like a conductor's baton. She groans out loud. Talk about a mess! On one side, her kitchen looks as if Tanner's SWAT team have combed through it, systematically yanking things out of the cupboards, searching for contraband in amongst a sack of flour, a tower of mixing bowls, a tub of cream of tartar. The entire counter, and some of the floor, glistens with a fine film of crystal sugar. Meanwhile, the kitchen island is laid out like a Hong Kong electronics shop: with two black casings discarded at one end, a screen and the solid-state thingy at the other, while the space in between is littered with screws, washers and micro-chips—not to mention four empty coffee cups and their accompanying coffee rings.

Oblivious to her look of horror, Matiu boogies on.

The door buzzes again. Insistent. Whoever Penny's visitor is, they're the lean-on-the-buzzer type. Cerberus is already waiting to welcome them, treading the carpet, his tail wagging. At least *someone* likes early-morning visitors.

Snatching a throw off the sofa, Penny wraps it around her shoulders and steps up to the Voxcom. "Yes?"

Her mother's nose fills the screen. "Pandora? Your father and I have come to pick up your aunt Mārama."

Omigod. Her parents. This early?

Out of sight of the camera, Penny waves frantically at Matiu but, swept up in his opus and his pancakes, he doesn't catch the movement.

"Mum, good morning," Penny stalls, still flapping frenetically in Matiu's direction. Cerberus runs off, following the movement, thinking she's thrown something for him to fetch. "I hope you slept OK? No doubt, you were worried sick about Mārama. She's fine, of course. A bit tired, which is to be expected. Um… the thing is, she's still in bed right now."

"That's all very well, Pandora, but we need to get her up. Your father used the leverage from yesterday's security fiasco to wangle an appointment with a top-notch visiting specialist. An off-country expert. The problem is she's only here another two days, and, who knows, with the fuel shortage, she's not likely to be back on this side of the globe for another decade, so we really need to make the most of the opportunity."

"Wow. An off-country specialist. That's fantastic, Mum. Would I know her?"

On screen, Mum's nose bobs from side to side. "Oh no. I don't think so, dear. She's a world-renowned practitioner. Has as an entire alphabet after her name. Her fees alone would be enough to give Hawaii back to the Polynesians. Not that the cost matters to us, of course, since Auckland Hospital Board will be footing the bill… Is that a bruise I see on your head?"

Penny slaps her hand to her forehead. "What this? Oh, it's nothing."

"Pandora." It's still Mum's nose in the picture, but this time the voice is distinctly Dad's.

"Yes, Dad?"

"Your mother and I have no intention of interfering in your love life. We simply wish to pick up your aunt, so if this stalling is because you have a young man with you…"

"That isn't… I wasn't—"

"Then open the door."

Fuck. She punches enter, unlocks the door, then flies across the room to where Matiu is flipping… Cthulhu pancakes? She yanks his earbuds out by the cord. "Mum and Dad are on their way upstairs!"

"Shit! Why didn't you warn me?"

"I tried, but you were too busy rehearsing with the Philharmonic."

"Huh?"

"Never mind. Quick, help me hide the GeePee before they get here."

Using her forearm, she sweeps the miscellaneous flotsam off the kitchen island and into a mixing bowl. Meanwhile, Matiu stuffs the metal casings in a cupboard above the fridge and Cerberus deals to the sugar on the floor. She thrusts the mixing bowl and the solid-state thingy into the pantry just as the door opens.

"Mum, Dad," Matiu says, placing a stack of hot pancakes down on the table. "You're just in time for breakfast."

Hanging her triple-stitched Savea handbag on back of the couch—and well out of reach of Cerberus' slobber—Mum pulls out a chair. "Thank you, dear. It's good to see *one* of my children up and organised." The withering look suggests to Penny that child isn't her.

She forces a smile. "You do know it's a Saturday, Mum."

"And yours is a fledgling business, Pandora," Dad says. "When you're established, when you're in the black, that's when you can afford to waltz around in your pyjamas all morning." He arches a brow. "Even if it is a Saturday."

"I thought you didn't like me working for the police."

"I'm talking about demonstrating a certain work ethic, Pandora. Do you think I got where I am without working the odd weekend?"

"We were up late," Penny stammers. "Looking after Mārama." She could scream. How is it that her parents always succeed in making her sound like a petulant teenager?

Pouring a thick dollop of Golden Syrup on her pancake, Mum says, "Well, it didn't stop your brother getting dressed and sorting breakfast, now did it?"

And there it is. Every. Single. Time.

Practically skipping to the table with a pot of hot tea, Matiu throws Penny a sideways smirk. Seriously, she could kill him.

"I'll just go and wake up Whaea Mārama, then shall I?" she says tightly.

"Thank you, dear."

By the time Mārama is dressed in a loose sun frock and a pair of Penny's summer flats, Mum and Dad have polished off a couple of pancakes and their second cup of tea.

Dad stands up, his arms wide. "Here she is," he says, full of bonhomie in front of his crazy sister-in-law. "Good to see you looking so much better, Mārama."

Her arms wide, Mum crosses the living room to sweep her sister into a Cannes Film Festival hug. "Mārama, my darling! You gave us such a fright."

Dad pushes his chair under the table, upsetting Cerberus, who's planted himself there in the hope that someone might drop a piece of pancake. "Right, we'll be off, then."

"Wait. You can't go yet. Whaea Mārama hasn't had anything to eat."

"Ooh, Hing, do you think she should? What if the doctor gives her a prescription?"

"I really don't think—"

"Don't interrupt, Pandora. We're talking about a proper medical doctor. Not one of your doctorettes."

Flabbergasted, Penny almost swallows her tongue.

Dad checks his watch. "We haven't got time to dally if we're going to get Mārama back to Greenlane for this appointment. Besides, Pandora has a business to run."

Whaea Mārama opens her mouth, but she doesn't get a chance to say anything because Dad is already bustling the two women to the door. Mum barely has time to snaffle up her Savea bag. Matiu slips Mārama a water carton.

"Keep us posted on how things go then, won't you?" Penny says as the door closes behind them.

She's about to carry the plates to the dishwasher when Matiu hands over her cell phone.

"What were you doing with my phone?"

"It was snoring so I turned it off," he quips.

She arches a brow.

"You were sleeping, OK? I didn't want it to wake you."

"Oh. OK. Thanks." Penny checks her messages. One missed call from Toeva Clark. He can't know about the bog body—nobody will know, Touching the Sun are too careful—but still Penny's heart pounds.

She presses connect: "Officer Clark, good morning," she says, all sing-songy and Saturday-morningy. "Penny Yee here. You left a message for me?"

"Ah yes, Dr Yee. Sorry to bother you on the weekend, only you asked about getting another look at yesterday's John Doe. The pathologist's given us the green light if you can get here this morning."

Penny looks over at Matiu, but he has his back to her, pouring cereal into a bowl for Cerberus. Was he able to hack into the GeePee? Penny didn't get a chance to ask.

"This morning? I—"

"Unfortunately, there's no other time." Clark is apologetic. "Pathology's pushed as it is, what with the current case backlog…"

"And crime never sleeps, does it? Of course, I'll come straight away," Penny says. "Can I meet you there, say, in 40 minutes?"

Forty minutes! What is she thinking?

"Great. I'll keep an eye out."

"Matiu, quick, bring the car round," Penny shrieks. Abandoning the mess, she sprints to get dressed.

CHAPTER 17

- Matiu -

"Drop me at the mortuary," Penny says, pulling her door closed and clipping her seatbelt. "We've got, like, less than half an hour to get across town."

"No can do, sis," Matiu says, his fingers thrumming on the steering wheel as he bumps out of the car park and onto the street. "Pretty sure I found out where they're keeping Charlotte." His ears hum. The world is vibrant, pulsating. Ringing. Buildings sweep past in a morning-bright haze. He can taste the harmonics of the skyscrapers bending against the sky, and it's yellow and cinnamon. Usually it takes weird drugs to get a window on reality that slips and slides like this, but Matiu is simply riding the wave of not having slept, and the possibility that his brain is still bleeding, just a little. Perception keeps popping in and out, and he hasn't felt more alive in a long time.

"Matiu!"

He blinks, hits the brakes for the red light. Not that there's anyone else on the road. Penny and her little panics. "We're cool. So there's this island—"

"Are you even listening to me? I have to get to the mortuary before they put my John Doe on ice and then I don't have a case, I don't have a job. Why don't you get that?"

Matiu blinks again. The light will turn green any second now. Better not miss that. "But your guy's dead already, right? We can't change that. Charlotte though, she's not dead yet, and we've got a chance to do the right thing here, save her like we didn't save Screech and Tikau and—"

"It's not up to us to save Charlotte. That's a job for the police. And anyway, they're not going to kill her, they need her alive—"

"We don't know that."

"—but if I lose this case then not only will I be shutting up shop, you'll be out of a job too, because I'll be telling Dad that you're going off the rails and can't even do the simple job you've been given which is to take me where the hell I tell you to take me when I tell you!"

"Penny, there's no need to shout." The light turns green. He hits the gas, drops the clutch, and the Commodore wheelspins out into the intersection, slewing right.

"The mortuary is *that way!*" Penny growls, pointing left, and yanks on the handbrake.

Matiu is tossed sideways in his seat as the car spins around, coming to a sudden stop in a cloud of smoke. "Penny! That was *very* dangerous." The fire in her eyes crawls down her face, dripping off her nose, filling the car with a weird stink like burning hair. "Trippy," he says. Someone's horn is blaring. Matiu's phone rings. "Excuse me a minute. I better get this." He releases the handbrake, manoeuvres the car back into a sensible alignment with the layout of road markings and cement footpath, and swipes the call to answer. "Hey, Erica."

"Am I on speaker?"

"Yip. Say hi, Penny."

"Hi Penny," says Penny. Such a hoot.

"Matiu, can you take me off speaker?"

"Nope. Driving. Health and safety SOPs, you know how it is." Penny doesn't rage at him any further, so presumably he's going the way she wants him to. That's good. He doesn't want any more of that nasty smell in the car. The sky is a rippling shade of caramel ice cream. Neat. "How about I meet you for breakfast? That place we like so much." There's a reason he has to go back there. Not sure what, but his subconscious is screaming at him, and probably not for want of a wheatgrass smoothie.

"You mean our *regular?*" Her voice drips sarcasm. Matiu can see it running off his phone in big, iridescent globs, steaming where it hits the upholstery. He waggles his eyebrows at Penny and gives her a thumbs-up.

"Totes. Gotta drop Pandora somewhere. She's *such* a pain in the arse. But I'll head straight over. Shit, have I got a scoop for your morning edition or what? And that's not a euphemism. Well, I guess it is, but it's not one of those other things. Innuendo. Not that."

"Sure, meet you in an hour," Erica says, and swipes off.

"Matiu," Penny says carefully, the ire gone from her voice and replaced with something wary, concerned. "How late were you up last night?"

Matiu grins, his face broken up by the sunstrike which splinters the windows into spearheads of golden light. The grin might scream lunacy in small doses.

"How much sleep did you get?"

"How long is a piece of string? Anyway, before you got all high and mighty back there with the handbrake and the squealing and the being crazy and dangerous and all, we were talking about priorities."

"Yes, *Dad*, we were, and my *priority* is at the mortuary, slowly decaying. *Your* priority is to take me there, right now. The last time I let you take me off somewhere other than where you were supposed to take me, I ended up with a dead body on my hands. And the time before that, I ended up *on top of* a dead body. You can't just keep dragging me off into your bullshit at the expense of my career, Matiu."

"No worries. We'll just do it at the expense of someone else's life. That good with you?"

Penny shuts up. Flights of manta rays drift through the caramel-whip sky. It reminds Matiu of the monsters, shit Penny can't see, *won't* see. Monsters like Makere, calling her in the middle of the night. Giving a guy like Matiu a reason to pace the apartment all night, watching the windows, the door, the broken dreaming spaces between the shadows and the buzz of coffee in his veins, waiting for the insane thing from inside his head to try and force its way through the walls. The only other constants of the night gone, besides his pacing, were those big green eyes in the dark. Cerberus, watching over them through the long dark hours. Every time he stood at the door and looked in on the sleeping women, the dog's eyes met his, a bond of brothers, warriors of battles past. "Just take Cerberus. The dog has got your back, OK? Trust me."

"No! It's the city mortuary. I can't take a dog into a sterile environment."

"You let him in your laboratory."

"That's different," she retorts, except it isn't.

"OK, how about this? There's this girl and if things go well I just might find myself totally on the straight and narrow. But guess what? She's allergic to dogs. So if I take Cerby with me, I can kiss that chance goodbye, and that'll be on you."

"Erica? You think this whole Charlotte thing is some sort of means to a romantic entanglement with your probation officer? You're nuts."

"Am I?"

"I'm not taking the dog."

"You will. Wanna hear about this island?"

"Sure. But I'm not taking the dog."

- Pandora -

Penny steps out of the car into a wall of humidity, Cerberus scuttling over the central aisle and onto the footpath. Penny seizes the lead just before he gallops off, firing Matiu a withering glare. She gives the dog a little slack in case he needs the bathroom, and he sets about investigating the posts holding up the sign that says Gate Four. Shading her eyes against the glare, she examines the slice of grey sky between the office towers. A storm on the horizon? She wouldn't say no to a break in this interminable heat. It's been weeks.

"Gonna go catch us some kidnappers. It'll be epic," Matiu says.

"Dr Yee!" Toeva Clark waves from the steps of the hospital's LabPlus Building.

Penny sighs. She doesn't have time to argue. Closing the car door, she winds Cerberus' lead around her wrist and steps up to the open window. "OK, but no rescue attempts," she says through the gap.

"I'll do whatever I can."

"No, you won't. You'll scope out the island, take a photo, a recording, anything that'll prove to the police she's in there, but you will *not* go charging in like some kind of comic book superhero."

Darkness flits across his face and his lips curl upwards. She knows that look. "I mean it, Matiu. Promise me you won't attempt anything on your own."

He drops his head and looks out from underneath his lashes. "OK, I promise."

Penny stoops, intending to check the steering wheel in case he's got his fingers crossed, but already he's rolling up the window. He gives her a wave as he pulls away from the curb. Honestly, having him as a brother is as infuriating as being stuck in a bedroom with a mosquito!

Adjusting her satchel, she plasters on her professional face and hurries towards the entrance. "Officer Clark, sorry to keep you waiting."

"Not at all," Clark says. "Just thought I'd wait out of the heat." He gestures to the revolving doors, allowing Penny and Cerberus to pass through first.

"Insufferable, isn't it?" Penny replies when the officer emerges into the cool of the lobby.

"No kidding," he says, guiding her towards the basement stairs. "Although, I'm told the forecast is for thunderstorms this evening."

Penny snorts. "They said that last week. Lately, I think we'd be better off sacrificing a few goats and consulting the entrails." Actually, that's not exactly fair. Meteorological science has come a long way in the past decade, even if there's still an element of unpredictability.

"Well, if it's entrails you're after, looks like you're going to get your chance," Clark replies, grimly. "This is us here."

The sign on the wall reads: Forensic Pathology—Brendon Mather.

They swing open the doors and step inside. Penny shivers. The air in here is freezing.

A man in blue scrubs, presumably Mather, turns to look at them, deep crows' feet around his eyes. His icy glare causes the temperature to spiral even further downwards. He pulls his mask down, revealing a fashionable 5 o'clock shadow. "You can't bring a dog in here."

I know! It's so unprofessional.

Embarrassed, Penny can't think what to say. "His name is Cerberus," she stammers. "He could be Hades himself, he still doesn't come in my lab."

Clark clears his throat. "I'll take him, Dr Yee. We'll be waiting outside in the corridor. Come on, boy. Let's go charm some nurses, shall we?" The doors close behind them.

"You're here to look at the cadaver that came in yesterday," Mather states. "Caucasian male, mid-thirties, possible suicide, picked up yesterday morning from Little Shoal Bay."

"Yes, that's correct. I'm the consultant on record. Penny Yee, from Yee Scientific."

"Yeah, I don't care who you are. Nothing personal, but I've got six cases on my dance card today—two homicides, two suicides, a medical misadventure, and a wretched sudden infant death—my chances of salvaging some weekend were close to nil, and that was before your Detective Inspector demanded I put the corpse back on ice and fritter the morning away waiting for you."

"I'll try not to keep you any longer than I have to, then." Penny's voice is as frosty as his stare. "Scrubs and gloves?"

"On the wall." He tilts his head.

Penny stalks over and gets herself kitted up, while Mather transfers the body from the refrigeration cabinet to the stainless autopsy table. Talk about bells and whistles: it's one of those rotating, recirculating, elevating, pedestal models. Mather touches a button and, like a car seat, it automatically orients to his position. He pulls back the shrouding and Penny recognises the John Doe from yesterday. Against the steel of the table, the body looks even more emaciated. Now that he's naked, several pustules and patchy skin lesions are evident on his legs and torso. She hadn't seen those while examining him in the park, although skin conditions aren't unusual in people who live rough.

Penny checks the label tied to his hallux and is surprised to read a name: Antony Jendoubi. Age 34. Accountant.

"You were able to identify him, then."

"Turns out Jendoubi here didn't always live on the streets. Some years ago he had some expensive dental work done which allowed us to identify him. Census records gave us the rest."

"Address?"

"Nothing current. Formerly of Ponsonby."

"Family?"

"Clark's got some uniforms on it."

"What do you make of it?"

"The body's in a pretty poor state, which is consistent with him living rough. And given he was reasonably affluent not so long ago, a fall from grace might imply suicide. Or death by misadventure." He folds his arms across his chest. "No doubt you'll let us know when you've completed the analyses."

"And your gut feeling?"

"You're asking me to speculate."

"I'm asking for your best guess. As an expert."

He shrugs. "The latter seems plausible. Simple benchtop tests point to some kind of home-baked LSD."

Penny nods. Beaker had said as much. "You noted this discolouration of his fingers?"

"Of course. I made a note in my preliminary report although only for completeness. It'll be incidental to any eventual findings. Looks like some sort of ink."

No shit, Sherlock.

"Any other cadavers present with ink on their fingers recently?"

"None that have been across my table. I was thinking: maybe he was working as a printer. There's been a resurgence in print media lately. I hear there's big money in new-release first editions."

Penny wrinkles her nose. "Hmm. That doesn't quite fit with Jendoubi's living on the street."

"OK, so maybe he was hungry and caught himself an octopus. Maybe his girlfriend dyes her hair with henna or he fancied himself as a tattoo artist. I don't know."

He's being deliberately flippant, but a couple of Mather's suggestions aren't so far-fetched. Penny turns Jendoubi's arm over. The Touching the Sun tattoo appears on his forearm like a Deatheaters' Dark Mark from the old Harry Potter tales. What if, disillusioned with life as an accountant, he discovered the cult and made a career switch to become their resident tattooist? Penny wouldn't put it past Touching the Sun with their touchy-feely earth mother philosophy to use cephalopod ink, a basic food colouring, as the basis of their tattoo art. Perhaps the change to their hippy grass-inspired lifestyle wasn't what Jendoubi was looking for and, still disillusioned, he chose to overdose.

She didn't have time to take samples of the digits at the site. "Do you mind if I take a couple of additional skin samples?"

"Be my guest." He hands her a scalpel and she prepares the samples, suspending the skin specimens in various buffers, then tucks the fixed samples in her satchel to take back to the lab for later.

The phone again.

"Excuse me," Penny says, as she plucks it out of her satchel.

Shaking his head, Mather heaves a sigh.

Penny lifts the device to her ear. "What exactly are you playing at, Pandora?"

"Noah? Playing? I'm not sure what you mean."

Through the phone, Cordell's snort is muffled. "Bad enough you refuse to deliver the cadaver as we'd arranged, but this is beyond the pale, even for you."

Turning her body away from Mather, Penny keeps her voice even. "Noah, we've already been over this. Tanner said 'samples': samples which were duly delivered and well ahead of the cut-off time."

"Yes, and I've already told you that your stance is completely unacceptable and somewhat juvenile. LysisCo is the foremost scientific consultancy in the country. Far more appropriate that initial observations be conducted by my staff. We have the experience and the equip—"

Penny tightens her fingers around the phone. She's sick to the teeth of being condescended to. So her business operates in direct competition with LysisCo. Cordell can suck it up for all she cares. "Noah," she interrupts. "Was there a particular reason for your call?"

"There is. With usual efficiency, LysisCo have completed our carbon dating analyses." Cordell pauses for effect.

"Yes?" says Penny, no choice but to provide the requisite prompt.

"Well, quite apart from the fact that the body is naturally mummified, the results are entirely unremarkable."

Which explains why you aren't referring to her as Cordell Woman any more.

But Noah has launched into full lecture mode. "...I suspect there'll be some academic interest by bog body scholars regarding the unusual conditions contributing to the mummification process. Our climate is, after all, much warmer than the Nordic examples—"

Penny grits her teeth. "Noah, what do the results say?"

"It isn't old at all. Not Iron Age. Nor Bronze either. In fact, my people estimate that your Jane Doe has barely been in the ground long enough to exhibit this level of preservation."

So she and Matiu had been right. "How long?"

"Eighteen months to two years at best. More than likely an accidental death. We're speculating a prostitute or an addict. A vagrant perhaps. Fallen into the bog and too wasted to pull herself out."

That doesn't make sense. If Jane Doe was a down-on-her-luck who'd had a few too many and tumbled into the estuary, she'd still be wearing clothes. At the very least, there'd be fibres clinging to the body, and yet there'd been nothing. No, they had to have been removed, but if she'd done it herself, why weren't they found somewhere nearby, by Tanner's officers, or the nosy dog who discovered the body in the first place. More likely, any clothing had been removed from the scene to prevent her from being identified.

By the Touching the Sun cult. Who have a penchant for kidnapping pregnant young women. What do they want with the babies? A high-class adoption ring? Slave trafficking?

"Are you even listening to me, Pandora?" Noah shrills.

Whoops. Penny had tuned him out while he rabbited in her ear about quality control and margins of error. "Sorry, the connection dropped out briefly." Only partly a lie. "Can you repeat that?"

Sluicing out a mortuary pan at the sink, Mather chuckles.

"I said, what do you intend to do about my machine?"

Penny's heart clenches. Machine? What machine? What's he on about? But the way her pulse is racing, she has an inkling.

"Since the body is no longer of any historic importance..." Cordell's voice drips with impatience, "...we took it upon ourselves to conduct the regular tests."

You took it upon yourself to steal the contract out from underneath me, but please, do go on.

"Now, I'm well aware that acidic bog water alters genetic material, but given the body went into the bog only recently, I suspected there might still be enough intact DNA for a viable fingerprint. And given prostitutes and drug addicts have a proclivity for appearing on police databases, there'd be a good chance of identifying her. So, I had my people run a test on one of the samples, and it blew up my DNA analyser!"

Penny's knees soften. "Which sample?"

"The one from the girl's abdomen."

Penny goes cold, and it's nothing to do with the chill of the mortuary.

"Don't try and wiggle out of this, Pandora. I had you pegged for a vindictive bitch, but I never dreamed you could be this callous. This calculating. It exploded, you know. Shrapnel everywhere. Windows broken. People could've been killed. Did you even think of that?"

Me?

"Luckily, the staff were on break at the time and no one was injured, but my analyser, and my lab, are out of commission. Who knows for how long? The Chemical Spill Squad have closed us down for the foreseeable future. I have sixteen cases pending with the police, let alone all our other contracts. The fallout is going to cost me a fortune. Not that you could care less," Noah breaks off.

"I'm pleased to hear no one was hurt," she says, "and it's a shame about your facilities, but I really don't see how this has anything to do with me."

"Nothing to do with you? You've got to be kidding me!" His fury is so intense, Penny can almost feel it. "I have the evidence right here in my hand. The DNA results were still intact in the processor. I'll bet you didn't count on that, did you? Admittedly, it'd been thrown across the room and was pretty mangled, but investigators salvaged it and the results were…well, it isn't normal DNA, is it? It's XNA. XNA! I don't know what the hell you think you're playing at: contaminating the sample with synthetic DNA. That's deliberate sabotage, Pandora. I won't stand for it. I'm holding you liable: you and your ridiculous little company."

It takes every last pennyweight of sangfroid to keep her voice steady. "I'm sorry, Noah, but I don't see that Yee Scientific has any liability here. That sample had no business being in your DNA analyser: it was delivered to you for carbon dating. Anything else was done on your initiative."

Across the other side of the lab, Brendon Mather raises an eyebrow.

"Well, someone has to pay for my machine!" Noah roars down the phone.

"I'm sure you have insurance. In the meantime, I have a little Breadmaker, a bench-top DNA-typing machine. Granted, it doesn't have the speed of your analyser, and its capacity is limited, but I'm only too happy to offer its services to help out a colleague—that is, should you find yourself getting behind and needing to subcontract."

Noah splutters. He might be saying something but the words are incoherent.

Cocking an eyebrow, Mather points to the autopsy timer.

Penny nods vigorously.

Mather presses a button, eliciting a stream of loud beeping.

"Sorry Noah, that'll be my assay," Penny lies into the phone. "I'm sure I don't need to explain the importance of taking down an experiment in a timely way, so if you'll excuse me." Swiping the phone off, she slumps against the wall, grinning. "Thanks for that."

"No worries," Mather replies. "Noah Cordell is an arse. Now can we get this examination over with?"

- Matiu -

"I know the place," Erica says, around a mouthful of gluten-free bagel layered with something green that looks like it used to be a vegetable but has since melted, or maybe just decomposed, while the yellow stuff dripping off it must be a symptom of whatever infection killed it. "Used to be people got married out there, corporate Christmas functions, that sort of thing. But that was years ago. There were some houses on the island too, but after a spate of arsons, no-one wanted to buy or build out there."

"Convenient." He slurps on his wheatgrass spirulina smoothie. Makes a face like it's much worse than it really is.

"How did you not hear about that?"

Matiu shrugs, fixated on the bagel, waiting for it to blink at him. "Too busy holding up bottle shops for cigarette money I guess."

"Matiu, if you want one just order a spinach bagel with hollandaise. Right there at the counter. Are you sure you're OK?"

"I'm good, charged up, I'm on fire," he nods, a touch manically. "Does it come with a side of cheeseburger?"

"You know that what you call beef is mostly synthesised seaweed, don't you? The actual meat content in New Zealand beef mince is marginal at best. And don't get me started on how they manufacture 'chicken' from mass-farmed crickets."

"Shut up. I'm comfortable in my delusions." Strange how clear some things become in the haze of sleep deprivation. If only the reason for his being here would make itself as clear.

"So this Puketutu Island," Erica presses. "How'd you find out about it?"

"I got sources. Better if you don't know. You being you and doing what you do and all."

"Fine. So what are you thinking?"

"Take a drive, look around. Lay of the land sort of thing. And soon."

Erica nods. "Absolutely." There's a quiver in her voice. Like wind rippling over an inlet.

Inlet, why does that thought keep coming to him?

"You can drive us there?"

He shoots her a look. "Us?"

"Yes, us. Since I can't seem to trust you to do anything on your own."

He looks at her, hard. How long has he spent looking at this woman, her face, and not really seen her, until now? Until... Did she really make a move on him yesterday? Maybe. Or maybe he imagined it. For a long moment he studies her face, the height of her cheekbones, the pulse of blood in her neck, the determination chiselled across her brow. The flint in her eyes, dark and waiting to strike a spark. Everything about Erica Langley speaks of hidden strength. But what is it about those features that drew him back to this place, with her, something in the back of his mind shrieking at him to open his fucking eyes and take notice? "Does Charlotte look like you?"

"What?"

"Do you look similar? The same hair, eyes, nose? Like chips off the old block, you know? Or is she a blazing redhead with hands good for slapping a bass guitar and a great face for radio?"

"We...we look similar, I guess, as sisters go. Why?"

Matiu stands slowly, still framing her face for his reptilian hind-brain to absorb, make the connections he can't seem to make. He drifts to the noticeboard. Starts lifting pages here, there, pushing aside notices selling suspiciously cheap power tools and overpriced guitar lessons, until she appears. She'd been there, waiting to be found. He'd seen her, last time they were here, but it hadn't mattered then. Hadn't meant anything. Until now.

"Who is she?"

Matiu tugs the Missing Person notice from the noticeboard. The face looking up at them isn't Erica, nor is it Charlotte. The text underneath the sun-faded photo of the young woman with her soft smile and sad eyes reads:

Have You Seen Jaime Sutherland?

Jaime has been missing since February 14th, 2044. Her family fears for her safety.

Jaime is pregnant and has been suffering from bouts of depression.

If you know Jaime's whereabouts, please call at the number below.

Matiu holds the photo up for Erica to see. The resemblance isn't so close as to be uncanny, but there are strong commonalities. The dark hair, the high cheekbones. "Almost two years ago. Pregnant woman goes missing." Of course Erica doesn't make the connection. She doesn't know about the bog body.

Erica shakes her head. "What, so Charlotte's not the first? And whoever took Charlotte likes women of my phenotype?"

"Come on," Matiu says, and as he heads for the door he can't feel the floor under his feet. He's floating, dreaming he walks on air, runs against time. He thumb-dials Penny, but the call goes straight to messaging. "Penny," he says, hoping Erica is keeping up, with that gorgeous perfectly sculpted face of hers that the demons from beyond have a taste for. "I've got a name for your bog body."

CHAPTER 18

- Pandora -

The heat whips at them like a wet tea towel the second they pass through the revolving doors.

Behind Penny, Clark says, "Just a couple of years old? So it's not the amazing archaeological bonanza the press is claiming, then?" Penny had filled him in on the less controversial parts of Cordell's call on their way up the stairs.

"No, it was a young woman. Someone who's likely to have been missed. Someone with a Touching the Sun tattoo like the one you and I saw on yesterday's victim."

"Well, that should narrow things down a bit. I'll check the missing persons' database when I get back—"

Penny's phone buzzes. Juggling Cerberus' lead, Penny rummages in her satchel. "Here, let me take the dog."

She hands Clark the lead, unearths the phone, and checks the number. "It's my brother." She taps the voice to text request, and his message pops up. "Actually, I might be able to save you that Missing Persons' search," she says, showing Clark the screen.

He nods. "Let me make a call," he says, handing the lead back again. When Penny has been sweating on the stairs for what seems like forever, he swipes the phone off. "Seems this Jaime Sutherland is still missing. They've sent me through the file. How are you getting back to the lab?" he asks.

"I... my brother... I'll have to call him. He's seeing his probation officer."

"Maybe you could accompany me to visit Jaime Sutherland's family. I could drive you back to Yee Scientific afterwards."

Penny raises an eyebrow. "You want me to go with you on official police business? I might get the idea I was a sworn-in detective," she teases.

But Clark's expression is sombre. "The Sutherland family hasn't heard anything about their daughter for close to two years. Learning that we *might* have found Jaime is going to come as a shock. They might not take it well. I'd appreciate your support."

Ashamed of her flippancy, Penny swallows hard. "Of course."

"My car's this way," Clark says.

The car is hotter than an inner-city Rhumba class. Penny lets Cerberus into the back seat, while Clark cranks the air-con to maximum. He checks the file for the parents' address then switches his phone to GPS.

"Good afternoon, angels! At Gate 4 turn right onto Grafton Road," the GPS says in the voice of Charles Townsend from the 1970s detective show.

"Sorry," Clark says. "It's been like that since the vehicles were serviced. No one knows how to turn it off."

He turns right, slowing at the first set of lights. "Didn't your brother see his probation officer yesterday?" His thumbs drum on the steering wheel.

"Um, yes, you're right, he did." Penny helps herself to Clark's notebook from the console, and uses it as a fan, the cool air wafting down her cleavage. *Don't ask, don't ask.*

"He in some kind of trouble?"

Policework is all about observations and Clark is too good an officer to let it go, but still Penny is caught out. *Quick, think of something. Anything.* "Um... I suspect it's the news about his friend dying like that yesterday, and just minutes after Matiu had seen him. That kind of thing will throw you."

"Hmm."

"Survivor's guilt and all that."

Clark's nostrils twitch.

"And Matiu's extremely sensitive."

Clark says nothing.

"You just have to get to know him."

Damn. He's doing that thing and she's falling for it. Everything you say can be used against you... Penny stops talking.

"That Erica Langley is a dedicated probation officer to make a second appointment in two days," Clark observes.

Penny shrugs. Waves her makeshift fan.

"Don't Corrections have social workers to deal with trauma?"

Clever. *Asking a direct question so she has to answer.* In the back seat, Cerberus pants loudly, his doggie breath fogging the windows.

"All I know is Matiu didn't sleep much last night, so he called her. They already have a rapport. You know how it is."

Clark nods. "I guess so."

"Nice work, angels," GPS Charlie says. "You've arrived."

- Matiu -

Puketutu Island doesn't look like much from the road, low and flat and bristling with pine trees. Under the swirling ice-cream clouds, gravid with the promise of rain, which look more like whipped liquorice than salted caramel as the day goes on, the island is something of an afterthought, a burp of ancient ejecta jutting into Manukau Harbour. Another failed volcano on a plateau of fire. Matiu squints across the long black strip of Island Road and the wastewater reservoir that runs its length between Mangere and Puketutu, looking for signs of life. Guards, or parked vehicles maybe. Good chance the road is covered by a camera. Even if he can't see anything beyond the fenced-off pipelines flowing by the car windows, it's unlikely there's no-one watching.

"Pretty isolated," Erica says, holding her sleeve across her nose. "And it reeks. Can't blame people for not wanting to live out here."

"All that poop has to go somewhere," Matiu says with a half-cocked grin, breathing through his mouth as the wastewater plant with its open evaporation ponds roll past on the left. "At least they turn it into something useful." Beyond the wastewater plant, the turbines that burn up the solid waste from Auckland's sewage system and turn it back into precious electricity bleed thin trails of pungent smoke skyward. "Plus I think they grow mushrooms around here somewhere."

"Don't play your cunning mushroom-poop word-association mind games on me, Matiu Yee. Eating mushrooms does not mean I'm eating human faeces."

"Just sayin'."

"You were lucky at the apartment, you know."

"Why's that?"

"Whoever broke in had hacked the building CCTV. Crashed the server before they went in. Cameras were down for the whole thing."

Matiu nods. "Sounds about right. They're smarter than I'd like."

"Any thoughts on how we're going to get out there? I don't fancy swimming through the outfall, but if that's what it takes to get to my sister, I will."

"I'm thinking about it," Matiu says, veering around a tight bend and heading away from the island to loop around the block. "It'll come to me." He frowns. "What's the time?"

Erica checks her phone. "Going on 10.30. Why?"

Matiu hits the brakes hard, then throws the car into a tight U-turn and accelerates back the way they'd come, taking the corner at speed. The battered Commodore groans. Erica grips the dash. "Care to share?"

"I spent hours last night looking at where that bloody van went, but I was only really paying attention to the places it stopped. I guess some part of my brain was keeping track of the other details, like the time, but it didn't matter before."

Matiu's knuckles are white on the wheel as he throws the car around another corner, hoping like hell these crazy bastards are as psychotic about routine as they are about kidnapping young mothers.

"Is that...?" Erica leans forward, peering down the long straight road ahead.

"A black van? Yip."

"And what are you planning on doing with it?" Erica asks, nervously fingering the limp remains of the airbag draped over her legs.

"Not much," Matiu says, slapping down a gear and coaxing a throaty growl from the engine. "Maybe a little game of chicken."

"Matiu?"

The Commodore veers over the centre line with a graceful ease that belies the punishment it's taken over the past day. Matiu holds steady down the median strip. The headlamps on the oncoming van flash.

"Killing us would be slightly counterproductive right now, you know."

Matiu eases the wheel over further, bearing into a collision course with the van. The space between them snarls up into a panicked mash of nerves and exhaust fumes, then the van swerves hard as Matiu twists the wheel away, hitting the brakes, jamming on the handbrake and spinning the car about in a shredding of rubbery smoke. The van clatters up onto the grassy verge in a streak of tyre treads, all brake lights and gouges in the dirt. Already the driver is angling the wheels around, trying to get back to the road, but Matiu is faster. The Commodore slams across the road and bounces up onto the verge, blocking the van in. He's light as air as he jumps out his door.

"What the hell, man! You got issues or what?" the driver shouts from his window, but Matiu isn't interested in discussing the psychological breakdown behind his road rage. He jerks the door open and drags the bewildered courier from his seat, shoving him onto the Commodore's bonnet. The freedom of letting loose floods him, the rush that used to get him through the old days, his reason for walking the streets. A chance to unleash the violence that had built up behind his eyes, a fire stoked by Makere and given an outlet by Hanson. He raises a fist, ready to bring it down on this weedy little loser's nose, break something, make him regret falling in with crooks like Touching the Sun.

Erica's face through the windscreen gives him pause. She's his probation officer. It's her job to monitor his behaviour, keep him on the straight and narrow, and here he is about to commit grievous bodily harm right in front of her. But her eyes are alight. A tight smile curves her lips, at once entrancing and utterly terrifying. She's never looked hotter. What the hell is wrong with her, with him, with *them*? His fist snaps down, but he pulls the punch, plants it just so in the centre of the forehead, and the kid goes slack in his grip.

He meets Erica's eye. Whatever he just saw, the wall has fallen back in place. She winds her window down. "Now what, Sherlock?"

Matiu gestures at the idling van. "Princess, your chariot awaits."

- Pandora -

The Sutherland's property is a former state house from the 20s, two-storey cell-crete construction with the house dominating a section not much larger than a paper towel. A 1.8m fence surrounds the house on three sides and there's a tidy concrete pad out the front for the wheelie bin. If it were on the market, Patisepa Taylor would likely describe the property as the 'cutest little button of a house' or 'affordable urban living' with a caveat about getting in quick since it 'won't last long at this price'.

Clark knocks. The man who opens the door is slightly built, bordering on skinny. "Mr Sutherland?" Clark asks.

Still clutching the door, the man nods. "Dominic. You the police?"

Clark shows him his badge. "Toeva Clark, and this is my colleague, Pandora Yee."

"Please, call me Penny. This is Cerberus. I hope you don't mind…"

The Sutherlands are obviously not bothered by dogs, because he opens the door wider to allow them through. Clean-shaven with a receding hairline, monochrome attire, and a lacklustre manner, Jaime's dad is one of those forgettable face-in-the-crowd sorts. His handshake, like his appearance, is nondescript. He leads them through to a small ground-floor living room, where the teal accessories are straight out of the 2020 home catalogue. "My wife will be down in a second. She's… naturally, she's shaken. We haven't heard anything about Jaime for so long."

"Of course," says Clark.

A surly girl with a mousy cardboard complexion, who Penny guesses is around thirteen, carries a tray through from the kitchen and serves lukewarm tea in thick ceramic mugs. Following her with a plastic biscuit box of store-bought Gingernuts, Dominic Sutherland says, "This is Jaime's sister."

Jaime's sister. No identity of her own. Just an appendage of her missing sibling. That's got to be tough. Penny gives her a warm smile. "Sorry, I didn't catch your name?"

The girl examines her feet. "Frances."

"Thank you for the tea, Frances," Penny says, declining Sutherland's Gingernut with a shake of her head.

"Can I pet the dog?" she asks.

"I think he'd really like that."

Depositing the tray on the coffee table, the teen kneels on the carpet and scratches Cerberus under his chin. "What's his name?"

"Cerberus." Although Judas would work just as nicely, since the dog has already forsaken Penny for the teenager. His jaw open and his tongue hanging out, Cerberus rolls onto his back, Frances obliging him with a good rub on his belly.

"Cerberus. Like the monster-hound who guards the gates of Hell? The one who stops the dead from escaping into the world? I don't believe it. You're too much of a big softie, aren't you, boy? A big softie…" The girl grins, her face lighting up.

Not so cardboard, then.

Mrs Sutherland sweeps into the room. Unlike her wishy-washy husband, she's beautiful. Not flashy, just striking. Penny's taken aback by the mismatch. It's as if Geppetto has hooked up with Pocahontas. Ever the gentleman, Clark stands up.

"Darling," Sutherland says, moving to his wife's side. "These officers have come to talk to us about Jaime."

Even before Penny and Clark are introduced, Mrs Sutherland launches into a barrage of questions. "What can you tell us? Where did you find her? Can we see her?" Question after question, like a tennis ball ejector gone mad.

"We're not certain we *have* found her," Clark says when he can get a word in.

"But you've found someone?" Sutherland asks.

"Um…"

"A body? Someone who you think could be Jaime," the wife insists.

Clark coughs awkwardly. "Yes, that's correct."

Mrs Sutherland buckles at the knees. Her husband rushes to her and the two men help her into an armchair.

"So is Jaime dead, then?" Frances gazes up at Penny, her fingers curled in Cerberus' fur.

Omigod, what am I supposed to say? What are the rules? Penny doesn't know the first thing about teenagers, hasn't had anything to do with them since she was one herself. How's she supposed to tell Frances that yes, the odds are that her big sister is dead and has been mouldering in a swamp for the past two years?

She opts for the truth. "It's a possibility, Frances. Something you'll need to be prepared for."

Frances' chin wrinkles. She nods. "I kind of knew. If Jaime was alive, she would've come home." Hearing her say it, Mrs Sutherland does one of those sniff-in sniffs and buries her face in her hands.

"Is that true?" Clark asks. "Jamie's disappearance was unexpected?"

Sutherland perches on the arm of the chair, his arm about his wife's shoulders. "Nothing was bothering her, if that's what you mean."

"She'd never run away before?"

"She was twenty, an adult, not some teenager acting out!" Mrs Sutherland snaps. "We told the police all this when we reported her missing."

Clark flushes red.

"I'm sorry if Officer Clark's questions seem obtuse," Penny says quietly, "but it's vitally important that we ask again. Things can change during the course of an investigation, new information that comes to light later which can alter people's understanding of events."

"There's nothing new," Mrs Sutherland says bitterly. "There's just nothing." Her eyes stray to the window.

Flashing Penny a look of gratitude, Clark turns to Mr Sutherland. "The flyers you distributed mentioned Jaime was prone to bouts of depression?" Clark turns the statement into a question.

"Well yes, she'd been depressed as a teen, so we wondered if it was a possibility. Her therapist thought it prudent to include it on the flyers."

"But she wasn't depressed when she went missing?"

"No. Just the opposite. Everything was going well for her. She was in love and they were having a baby."

"What about the baby's father? How did he react to her disappearance?"

"Tony? The poor boy was distraught. When the police investigation turned up nothing, he wouldn't give up. He kept on looking on his own dime. Spent all his savings on it, the deposit he and Jaime had been putting together for a house. He said, what was the point, if Jaime wasn't there to share it with him?"

"So he's still looking for her?"

Mr Sutherland kneads his wife's shoulders. "We're all still looking for her. Have you ever had someone you love go missing, Officer? You see them everywhere…" he trails off.

"What about the partner? Do you still see him?" Clark prompts.

"We did, but after a while he stopped coming around."

Clark says nothing.

"This whole thing took its toll on him, didn't it? The lad wasn't coping. A couple of times he came here drunk and smelling like a rubbish tip. I think he might have been living rough."

"We were worried he would upset Frances," Mrs Sutherland adds.

Frances looks at Penny and rolls her eyes. A kindred spirit. Penny stifles a smile. *I hear you, sister.*

"You asked your daughter's partner to stop coming," Clark states. No question this time.

"It wasn't like that!" Sutherland raises his voice. "He was welcome to come back just as soon as he'd cleaned himself up."

"He ended up on the streets," Frances butts in.

"What are you talking about, Frances?" the girl's father says.

"Be quiet. You don't know anything," her mother chips in.

"I do so! I saw him from the bus once, on my way to school. He was lying in a doorway, but I recognised him."

Penny cuts across the family squabble, "What do you know about Jaime's involvement with the Touching the Sun cult?"

"Cult? They're not a cult." Mrs Sutherland's eyes are beautiful, but hard. "Touching the Sun is a holistic health movement. They focus on whole body wellness. They promote the nourishment of self with natural ingredients to foster wellbeing and fecundity. Where do you people get your information from? Why on earth would you think they were a cult?"

"I beg your pardon. I spoke out of turn," Penny backtracks. "I'm new to the case. It was just the way members have tattoos on their wrists: it made me think of something a gang might do. Like a patch."

Mrs Sutherland scoffs. "They're nothing like that. Jaime loved Touching the Sun, positively raved about them. It's where she and Tony met."

"Jaime said joining the group helped her to have a baby," Frances says. Cerberus is draped across her body.

"Was there a problem?" Penny asks, trying to ignore the adoration on Cerberus' doggie-face. Feckless animal.

Frances nods. "Jaime was sick."

"Sick?" His tea resting on his knee, Clark scrolls one-handed through the file on his phone. "That isn't on the file."

Mrs Sutherland sighs. "It's because it wasn't anyone's business. Jaime didn't want people knowing."

Clark lifts his chin. "Mrs Sutherland, any information you can give us might help us to locate her."

"She had throat cancer, OK?" Sutherland blurts. "Her doctors treated it with permanent brachytherapy. It was the reason she got depressed. Jaime didn't believe in mainstream medicine. She claimed we were letting them poison her."

Penny's pulse skips a beat. At last, something useful.

Clark looks blank.

"Permanent brachytherapy involves taking irradiated capsules and injecting them into the tumour site," she explains. Over time the radiation dissipates and the inert seeds are left *in situ*."

Clark's eyebrows come together. Penny's going to have to spell it out for him. "Brachytherapy capsules are covered in titanium and are about the size of a grain of wheat. They're *never removed* from the patient's body," she says deliberately.

"Oh," Clark says, and for the briefest instant his face lifts. "Right, well, I think we've got enough for the moment." He sets his tea cup on the table and gets to his feet. "Dr Yee and I will get back to you as soon as we have more information."

"You mean, you'll let us know if the body you're holding is Jaime!" Mrs Sutherland shouts. Her eyes flashing, she lunges from her seat and storms out of the room. Moments later footsteps thump up the stairs.

Clark flicks an imaginary piece of lint off his shirt cuff while Penny gathers up Cerberus' lead. To her surprise, the dog pads over, allowing her to clip it to his collar without any fuss.

Frances moves to stand next to her father.

"Please excuse my wife," says Sutherland. "You're just doing your job, we know. It's just all this, learning that Jaime might be dead… We'd prepared ourselves for the worst, but even so…it's very hard." Frances leans into her dad's chest. He puts his arm around her.

"Just one more thing," Penny asks.

Clark raises an eyebrow. "Dr Yee, perhaps it can wait—"

Sutherland waves his hand wearily. "You're here. May as well ask."

"It might help us if we could talk to your daughter's partner. You said his name was Tony?"

"Jaime called him Tony. His real name is Antony, Antony Jendoubi."

CHAPTER 19

- Matiu –

The electric van drives like a lumbering beast, swaying around the corners, gutless when he puts his foot down. But Matiu isn't looking for power or speed, just the illusion of belonging. The kid's plain black cap is drawn down to cover most of Matiu's face in an attempt to conceal the ink on his cheeks. In the back of the van there are trays of greens and, now, a delivery driver hogtied with Matiu's tow rope and wrapped in a dirty boot liner tarpaulin. No hog body, no Charlotte. That would've been too easy.

"You know we're walking into the dragon's jaws, don't you?" Erica says, from where she's crammed her small frame down into the footwell in front of the passenger seat.

"Isn't this what you wanted?"

"Let's just be careful, all right. No point getting in there and never coming out again."

Matiu has no idea what they're going to find, or what they'll do when they find it. He's rushing headlong into the unknown, the skies singing in his ears, as the clouds swell and buckle and bleed with the promise of violence. There's a storm coming, many storms, and he's in the eye of it all.

He turns into the causeway road. On the left the long flat stretch of the wastewater reservoir runs parallel to the asphalt, beyond which lie the southern reaches of Manukau Harbour. Off to the right, the choppy tidal flats of Mangere Inlet, patches of shiny mangrove mud exposed by the falling tide alongside deep swift channels. Mats of algal bloom variously drift in the current or lie stinking on the flats, curling in the heat. Ahead, the twin humps of Puketutu thrust upward like the misshapen horns of some lurking *taniwha*. So many monsters, everywhere he looks. If he closes his eyes, the lights slide past in glittering rainbows, falling into darkness.

"Matiu!"

Matiu jerks awake at the sudden pain of a horsebite to the knee, and wrenches the weaving van back into line. "What?"

"Should I drive?"

He shakes his head to clear the fog.

"Then stay awake, for fuck's sake."

"Roger roger."

The road curves around to the south, pine trees looming along the horizon. Dilapidated signs point towards the old function centre, and Matiu turns up the driveway. "Here goes nothing," he mutters. Up ahead, a dark green Subaru is parked halfway across the drive. Resting his butt on the bonnet with a serious-looking semi-automatic shotgun cradled in his tattooed beefcake arms waits the sort of guard Matiu would've expected to meet around one of Hanson's old dog-fight rings rather than on a winery. He slows the van, gives a little fist-bump wave. His hopes the guard will wave him through are dashed when he gets up and saunters into the middle of the drive, giving him a slow-down hand signal. Matiu obliges and winds his window down. Erica tugs Matiu's black jacket over her and keeps still.

"You late, bro," the guard says, coming up alongside the window, looking comically at a watch he isn't wearing. "Three minutes. Tut tut. You stop for a little bit of loving with Miss Palmer and her five daughters on the way?"

Matiu keeps his head down. If the sunnies and hat don't camouflage him from this pair of prying eyes, they've got trouble. Hopefully, their other drivers indulge in a bit of moko on their cheeks as well. "Road closed over by the airport. Had to detour." Chances are slim Matiu can take the guard before he gets a round or two off with that assault weapon, so bluff, bluster and bullshit are his best weapons for the moment. The guard gives the cab a glance before slapping the door. "Haul ass, bro."

"Chur." Matiu drives on, checking his mirror as he veers around the Subaru. The guard is talking into his hand, probably advising someone up the track they're on their way. There goes the element of surprise, then.

Through the trees, a grand old estate house comes into view. In its day, it must have been a sight to behold, and even though the paint is peeling and the place looks neglected, the mansion projects an air of the grandiose, of greatness fallen into shadow. "Guessing we don't drive up to the front door," Matiu says, the mansion's dark windows following the van like sunken eyes in a Dadaist skull. The drive dips and curves around the hill, past overgrown gardens and choked lawns, and through a sturdy set of rusting steel gates into a yard surrounded by pine trees and a chain-link perimeter fence. Another black van is parked on an induction fast-charging pad in front of a corrugated iron warehouse that stretches the length of the fence-line. A taller roller door stands open behind the van. "Don't know what we've found, but we found something," Matiu says, swinging round in a wide arc and backing up alongside the other vehicle. "Be ready."

"For what?"

"No idea."

Matiu cranks the handbrake and swings out of the van, ducking his head and scoping the scene. There's no-one around, although the sound of electric machinery whines from the shed. He takes a tray from the back of the van and wanders towards the roller door. Matiu sidles up behind a stack of empty pallets piled near the entrance, and peeks around them. Row upon row of racks fill the space, each holding several pallets loaded with trays of greenery. At the far end of the shed, an electric hoist whirs and beeps, shuffling pallets and trolleys, and beyond that, a wall of clear plastic curtain, blurring whatever lies on the other side. Matiu whips back as the hoist operator swings the machine around.

"Matiu!" Erica hisses, suddenly behind him. "What are you doing?"

"Me? What the hell are *you* doing? You're meant to be waiting in the van."

"We never agreed to that, you chauvinistic arse. What's over there?"

Matiu looks where she's pointing, to a solid metal door under a mezzanine. "Looks like a chiller."

"Or a cell?"

Matiu sets the tray down on the floor, waits for the hoist operator to swing out of their line of sight, and dashes across the shed to the metal door. It's cold to the touch, but the handle cracks open when he tugs it. Mist rolls out around their feet. "Chiller," Matiu say. "Quick, inside." Erica glances at the hoist swinging back their way and, with a glare, slips through the door, Matiu close behind. The chiller extends several meters, full of racks of white trays and buckets. Even in the frigid air, Matiu can smell the slow rot.

"What the hell?" Erica says, leaning over one of the trays. "Is that... Is that a cat?"

Matiu moves down the chiller, glancing in the containers. "Cats, dogs, seagulls, rats. Strays, pests. Look, a possum. I thought they'd been eradicated."

"Who the hell keeps a freezer full of dead animals?"

"Nutters."

"Why?" Erica pushes the tray away, shuddering. "This isn't what we came for. We need to get inside that house."

Something catches Matiu's eye towards the rear of the chiller, where the overhead fluorescent light fizzes and flickers. Something large and black, vaguely person-sized. He edges closer, Erica's complaints momentarily forgotten as he recalls the video footage of the black van outside Penny's lab, the bundle they stole off the footpath. The body bag.

"Let's go," Erica says, and pushes the door open a crack to look out.

"Who...?" The door is wrenched fully open from the outside, the hoist driver framed in tendrils of freezer mist. "Who are you? Shit!"

Erica raises a calming hand. "Relax, buddy," she says, in her sternest Dealing-With-Difficult-Customers voice, "we're with Security. Spot check, you know how it is. Making sure everyone's doing their job, staying vigilant. Gold star, you."

Matiu walks back up the chiller, heart a pulsing tourniquet in his throat. "I'm Grendel," he says in a bold voice, layering his words with overtones which suggest this young buck ought to know exactly who he is already. "Here to fix this fuck-up someone made. You can help. Come here."

The hoist driver gapes from one to the other in bewilderment. "Umm..." he manages.

Matiu points to the body bag. "That's the wrong one, it shouldn't be here. Give me a hand with it. Don't just stand there with your finger up your arse, get on with it."

Like a puppet on jerky strings, the storeman enters the chiller, following Matiu as he trudges back to where the body bag lies. "Don't worry, it's light," Matiu says, and his unwitting accomplice lifts one end of the bag while Matiu takes the other. His breath steams in the cold. "Why the hell they thought this was meant to come here I don't know. Communication, eh? Sucks around this place."

Erica keeps her lips tight, shooting Matiu a perplexed look as they manhandle the body bag out through the chiller door. Matiu just gives her a tiny nod. At the back of the van, Matiu gets the driver to unload all the plants onto a pallet, then loads the body bag into the back. "Here, you're meant to have this one," he says, nudging the trussed-up courier with his toe. "Give me a hand. It's a bit heavier."

Grunting with the extra weight, they walk back through the warehouse. "Then we've got a special delivery, for the girl. You know, the girl? Where's she?"

The storeman frowns. "Look man, I just run the warehouse, I load pallets and move stuff around when they tell me to. I'm like a mushroom, kept in the dark and fed shit."

Matiu grinds his teeth. "But you know, the girl. She's pretty important."

A light seems to go on in the storeman's dull eyes. "Well, I did hear someone talking this morning about how someone would be taking some girl somewhere today for what they called 'the main event'. And then a few cars went by, coming up through the road to the old housing estate through the trees. I was on a smoke break then, you know, but mostly, I don't see much."

"Righto, never mind, I'll make a call. Watch your back there."

The storeman navigates the chiller door backwards, past Erica who is waiting just outside the freezer with a look like thunder on her brow. "Cheers," he says, just as the load they are carrying starts to squirm and cough. "What the hell?" He drops his end, and the courier shouts in pain.

"Damn," Matiu says, stepping in with a lashing fist, a striking viper. "Sorry about this, bud." The storeman keels over, skidding across the floor, and Matiu backs out of the chiller, slamming the door hard behind him.

Erica puts a hand on his chest. "You can't leave them in there. They'll freeze to death, and much as I'm sure they're the shit of the earth, I won't be complicit in murder."

"Don't sweat it," Matiu says, flicking off the circuit breaker mounted on the outside of the chiller unit. "They'll warm up soon enough, and even better, they'll have plenty to eat until someone finds them."

"You mean dead missing pets and roadkill?"

"Yeah, what's that all about, right?" Matiu asks, and pushes past her, back to the van. He starts the engine and listens as the cooling unit on the roof hums into life, checks the battery levels. Still good. Ignoring the muffled yells coming from inside the chiller, Matiu crosses the warehouse towards the curtained-off area.

"Where are you going now?"

Matiu flicks her a shrug. "Do we want to figure out what the hell these guys are doing?"

He pushes through the plastic curtain beside the electric hoist, stepping into a wall of moisture and heat. Stacked to the ceiling are rack upon rack of grassy plants, similar to those growing in Charlotte's flat. The air is thick with fine mist, jetting in intermittent hissing bursts from overhead lines, and the warehouse is muggy as a bulldog's armpit. Erica sidles in behind him, frowning as she takes it in. Matiu whips out his phone and snaps some photos, before grabbing one of the closest trays and turning away. "Let's go find Charlotte," he says, dumping the tray in the front seat of the van and heading towards the path that leads from the warehouse towards the old manse.

"You think this is all related, don't you?" Erica says, matching his stride. "The growing operation, the kidnapping. What the hell was that you put in the back of the van?"

"No idea how they're related except that they are. And what I put in the van is all that's left of the last Charlotte."

"The last Charlotte? What's that supposed to mean?"

"This isn't the first time they've done this. Bet your lunch-money the thing in the back of the van is Jaime Sutherland."

"The missing girl from the café? How can you know that?"

Matiu spins on her. "How about you start sounding less like Penny and more like someone who trusts me to find her sister when no-one could because I'm not looking in the same places? How about that?"

Erica regards him coolly, the shadows of the pines casting her face into scattered shadow. She reaches up and puts a hand to his cheek. "Just because I trust you doesn't mean I can't also think you're bat-shit crazy, all right?"

Matiu grins. "Story of my life."

Matiu and Erica catch themselves just in time to not walk out into full view of the armed guard sucking on a cigarette by the mansion's back entrance. The deck is spacious, and nearby stand the remains of a pagoda long since fallen into disrepair. It was probably all quite lovely back in the day, when people came out here to get married and the smells of the catering overwhelmed the underlying reek of sewage. The guard has an unobstructed view of the mansion's grounds, and despite how overgrown they may be, there's no way of sneaking up on him. Matiu scans the exterior of the building, spies two discreet dome housings on the walls.

"This could be tricky," he says to Erica, pointing out the domes through the bushes. "Cameras, probably with full PTZ movement. Could be running set tours, but we can't see where the camera's looking at any given moment because they're hard to see inside the dome cover. Might or might not be monitored by a guard inside. Could be linked to the intruder system or not."

"And? Can you get us in?"

Matiu shrugs. "Risky. Let me take a look." He pulls out his phone and brings up his alarm-cracking app. "You didn't see this, did you?"

"Didn't see what?"

The alarm's interface pops up on his screen, and he reviews it quickly. "Most of the zones are unset, but there are a few that are alarmed. Hey, this is good. It's got interface with the CCTV." He taps the screen again, bringing up the camera configurations. "Older units, but they're smart. Linked to the alarm zones." A grin blooms. "Piece of cake, then." Dropping back into the alarm interface, he locates a zone marked as set, and taps it into tamper mode.

From the house, a siren blares. The guard tosses his cigarette and runs inside.

"People will insist on being able to monitor their alarms off a network," he whispers to Erica. "Makes shit like this easy. Come on," Matiu sprints across the lawn and skids over the deck, sliding through the back door. Inside, he looks left and right. Which way to go?

Erica appears behind him moments later. "A little warning next time?"

"Keep up, sweetie." Matiu darts down a corridor, ducking along the wall and past doorways until he hears the tell-tale hum of server racks. Phone in one hand, he swipes the tamper away, and the siren falls off into welcome quiet.

Beyond the door, someone is talking. "Don't know, bro. Nothing on scopes... I know the siren was going, and it looked like there was a tamper in the south bathroom, but it's gone now... Yeah, so you've checked it and it's glitching, that's all. I'll log it. Over."

Matiu pushes the door open silently and crosses the small control room, light as air with the rush of adrenalin and exhaustion in his blood. Barely sees the operator as he wraps his arm around his neck and constricts his carotid artery, gently, lovingly. Ignores the scraping and flailing as his victim claws at his arm, his face. Less than half a minute before it stops, and the operator slumps in his grip. Letting the unconscious body slide to the floor, Matiu jumps into his chair and slides his fingers across the operator's screen, bringing up cameras and quickly finding the one that covers the back of the house.

Erica puts her back to the door, peering surreptitiously around the corner. "I don't think you've got long."

"All good," Matiu says, "they didn't see us. The cameras were linked to the alarm, and they tried to get a look at the zone we tripped. All they saw was wall. Anyway, this is what we want." Matiu rewinds the camera footage, a view of the front entrance to the mansion. A handful of vehicles roll backwards through the screen, but there's only one that catches Matiu's eye. The only car to park outside the front door. A silver Ford Falcon. "Shit," he mutters. Part of him had hoped he would be wrong, that this would prove it, but it's not to be.

"What?" Erica looks over his shoulder, as the footage rolls in reverse, and a struggling woman is dragged from the car to the house. "That's Charlotte!"

Matiu stops the feed, scrubs it forward. Watches as two beefy security goons manhandle Charlotte down the front steps and force her into the car. Her hands are bound, and it looks like there are shackles around her ankles as well. After her first escape, they're not taking any chances. Then *she's* there, blonde and statuesque, brutal in her hard beauty, sauntering past the guards to get into her car.

Sandi Kerr.

"We have to get out of here," he says. "Now!"

"Derek?" someone calls from down the hallway. "You got that tamper sorted?"

Matiu swipes his thumb over his phone again, and the siren screams once more. The camera monitor jumps to the smart cameras trying to get a bead on the non-existent intruder.

"Oh for fuck's sake," the guard in the hall says, but his footsteps quickly retreat. Protocols are protocols after all.

Erica doesn't wait for Matiu, and he follows her back the way they came, across the deck and down the garden path, feet thumping the broken concrete. They reach the warehouse and slide into the van. Matiu heads up the drive as sedately as possible, while Erica buries herself in the footwell. "Might get dicey," Matiu says as they pass the manse, the squeal of the siren loud in the cicada-hot morning. The green Subaru comes into view, the guard with the shotgun holding a hand to his ear as if trying to hear someone talking over the racket of the alarm. Matiu gives him the same good-natured fist pump and drives on by.

"Well, that could've been worse," Matiu says, glancing in his mirror in time to see the guard's eyes narrow and the gun swing up to his shoulder. "Or maybe not." He hits the accelerator and jinks the wheel, just as the air erupts with the roar of a gunshot and shattering glass. "Don't suppose you feel like getting your seatbelt on?"

Erica scrambles up into the seat and clips herself in. "So much for our discreet exit, then?"

"Exeunt with motherfucking trumpets, more like. Hold on, we've got about thirty seconds before that Subie catches us up, and then we're toast."

Matiu throws the van around the corner into the main causeway road, glimpsing moving green in his wing mirror. More like ten seconds then. Can't outrun 'em, can't outgun 'em. He hauls the wheel left, swinging up a tiny access road he'd noticed on the way in, as overwhelmed with overgrowth as the rest of the estate,and slams on the brakes.

"We can't just hide here!" Erica says.

"Course not," Matiu says, and jams the gearstick into reverse. The van hurtles back down the access drive, bouncing onto the road just as the Subaru sweeps around the corner. The impact is deafening as the front of the sports car crumples, and the rest of it spins in a mangled wreck to the side of the road. Matiu grinds brakes and gears and sets off across the causeway again, in a clattering of smashed panelwork and a shriek of protesting wheels.

"And that," Matiu says, rubbing his neck "is the trouble with crumple zones."

CHAPTER 20

- Pandora -

"Hello again, angels. I have a new mission for you. In zero-point-two kilometres, turn left onto Grant Street, then continue straight for zero-point-five kilometres."

When Toeva Clark pulls the car into the traffic, he's as chipper as the GPS Charlie. "Two cases resolved in barely two days. That has to be a bit of a record. Tanner'll be impressed."

"I still have to do the tests. For the moment, all we've got is some wild conjecture," Penny says. Beaker would be proud of her.

Clark grins. "Exactly how many people have radioactive seeds in their bodies?"

"Quite a few, actually. It's a very effective therapy," Penny says.

"Yeah, right. And how many of those are also female, pregnant, and went missing two years ago?" Penny has to concede the odds are good that the bog body is Jaime Sutherland. If there are seeds in the cadaver's throat, it should be easy enough to confirm her identity from the manufacturer's batch numbers etched into the titanium capsules.

That is, providing Penny can get the bog body back from the thugs at Touching the Sun.

"If it is Jaime, we still don't know how she ended up in the Karaka swamp," she says.

"Now angels, take the onramp..." the GPS says in the background.

Pausing first while Charlie completes his mansplaining, Clark continues, "The Sutherlands played it down, but it's clear their daughter was prone to depression. And Jendoubi doesn't sound as if he was too stable either. Maybe the pair made a suicide pact."

Penny arches an eyebrow. "Suicide? Two years and an entire city apart."

"It's just a possibility."

"If there was a pact, why would Jendoubi wait to kill himself, and why then spend months looking for her?"

"We don't know that he did look for her. Maybe that was just a story he concocted for the parents. It's what they'd expect from their daughter's grieving lover."

Penny shakes her head. "I'm just not buying it."

"OK, let's say he knew nothing about Jaime's decision. She was pregnant and had a history of depression: her hormones would've been as chaotic as a Picasso painting. Maybe she had a low moment and took things a step too far."

Penny gives the police officer a sidelong glance.

Clark shrugs. "I'm not claiming to be an expert. All I know is when Mrs Clark was expecting our son, she was a Mumzilla. I didn't know which way to jump; one minute she was ecstatic, sewing pastel bunting and wallpapering the spare room, and the next thing she was all doom and gloom and art house movie, questioning the sanity of bringing a child into the world the way society was going. And you have to admit, she had a point. Look at us now, with eighteen murder cases on our books…"

Fiddling with the strap of her satchel, Penny nods. "If Jaime decided to take her own life, it stands to reason that Jendoubi would move heaven and earth to look for her."

"And when he couldn't find her, he succumbed to despair."

"Enough to take his own life?"

Clark slows for the traffic lights. "I don't know. Fortunately, I still have Mrs Clark."

Yes, if his sweetheart and his baby went missing Jendoubi may well have wandered the streets looking for her, turning to drugs to curb the pain and eventually overdosing. Brendon Mather will likely recommend that the coroner cite death by misadventure in his autopsy report. But what caused her death? Because, contrary to what Clark believes, Jaime Sutherland didn't commit suicide, she was murdered, and Touching the Sun, with their sunshiney clean-green holistic hoopla, were all over it. Should she tell Clark about their theory? About the danger to Charlotte? Penny bites her lip. Clark's a good guy. Reasonable. But he's also a police officer, and when it comes to the law, the ends don't justify the means. All he'll see are the offences. Once again, Penny uses Clark's notebook to fan herself.

No, she needs some solid evidence before spilling the beans.

Like what?

Penny can't put her finger on it. It's as if she's being anaesthetised; counting backwards from ten, liquid darkness seeping in. She clutches at the blurry images at the edge of her vision, willing them to explain. What is she missing? Not Matiu's edge-of-reality hocus pocus about tentacled demons emerging from the underworld to dance on the graves of innocents either, but a logical, rational link between the successful micro-gardening business, Jaime, Jendoubi and now Charlotte. There has to be something that connects them. What did the Touching the Sun group want with Jaime, and what do they have planned for Charlotte?

Penny's head throbs. Dehydration. It's this awful heat getting to her, sapping her energy. A drink of water would help. Maybe then she'd be able to work out what it is that's eluding her.

"Nice job, angels. Time to go to work."

Penny looks up. They're outside her lab. Lost in thought for the second half of the journey, she realises Clark's been quiet, too. She unclips her safety belt. "Thanks for the lift, Toeva, and for letting me in on the meeting with Jaime's family. That was really useful. With labwork, it can be hit and miss, so it saves a lot of time having an inkling of where to look." *Just like having an inkling of where to find the body could save my career.* "I'll get back to you as soon as my colleague and I have completed the analyses."

She gathers up her satchel and steps out of the car.

"That'd be great. At the very least, it should give some closure to the Sutherlands."

"I hope so."

"I expect Tanner will be assigning you a lot more work too, now that Cordell's lab's been compromised."

Two DNA analysers exploded; it has to be a coincidence… Penny opens the back door for Cerberus.

Clark twists in his seat. "Dr Yee?" He rubs his chin. "If Mrs Clark ever finds out I called her a Mumzilla…"

Penny grins. "My lips are sealed."

- Matiu -

The lightness is gone, replaced with the same bone-weary gravity that hangs in the sky, those dark rumbling clouds weighing on his body, his soul. Whatever has kept Matiu running this long, it's just about burned up, and now he struggles to remember why he had to stay awake, alert, vigilant. But he hasn't cracked it yet. This shit ain't over 'til it's over.

Matiu hauls the boot open, and Erica helps him carry the body bag into the lab. She doesn't speak. They haven't talked since they transferred the body into the Commodore and pushed the van off the road into the inlet. Can't blame her really. She just saw her sister literally in chains, being dragged into a car, and now she's complicit in any number of crimes. Not good for a woman in her position. Yet Matiu's bigger concern, it must seem to her, is for this cadaver, and that's annoyed her. "It's the link," he'd insisted as they drove north up the potholed motorway, "if we can extract some clues from this body, we'll know where to look for Charlotte next." But they're running out of time, and if they can't locate Charlotte before nightfall, then maybe they never will.

They deposit the body bag onto an empty lab bench. "Merry Christmas, Beak," he says, as the lab tech looks at them in confusion, a test tube in each gloved hand. "Where's Penny at?"

"Um, she'll be back soon. What's this?"

"Overtime for you, bro. Don't mind us. We're starving and we need a coffee. You know if Penny still keeps a stash of Weet-bix in the cupboard?"

Beak gives a little wave as Matiu heads to the kitchen and fires up the coffee machine. "Tell me you drink coffee, because I don't have any of that wheatgrass bullshit around here."

Erica shakes her head. "Coffee is good. And yes, you do. We kept that tray of rye grass, or whatever. It's in the back seat."

Matiu grins. "Ah yeah, but that's evidence. Penny needs to see that, too."

"Why?"

"Dunno. That's why she does all the actual sciencey stuff." He puts two cups under the spouts and sets the machine to run, then wanders out to the car, through the oppressive heat beneath the glowering stormclouds, and returns with the tray of grasses. The coffee is ready and he sucks at it greedily, waiting for the kick to dispel the threatening wall of sleep.

"Matiu? Is this what I think it is?" Beak calls from the lab.

"If you think it's a cheeseburger and fries with a milkshake, then no," Matiu replies. "But if you think it's Penny's missing bog body, then yes. She can thank me later."

"Have you... Have you looked at it?"

Sighing, Matiu shares a look with Erica, sets his coffee down beside the tray of greenery, and they go back into the lab. Beak has opened the bag, exposing the withered, petrified thing within. It's a husk, a shell of a person long gone. The eyes are sunken hollows, the mouth stretched back in a toothy rictus, a silent and eternal scream. Matiu advances on the body slowly, a hissing susurrus building in his ears as he nears. The walls draw in tight, and Beak is talking but Matiu can't hear him. Sunken eyes, fingers curled into claws, reaching out. Knees drawn up to a belly torn open, left empty. So much pain bound up in this frozen tableau, this moment of time captured forever in the torment of death. The lightness returns, but for a different reason this time. The blood rushes from Matiu's head, and he struggles to put one foot in front of the other. The hands are reaching out to him, lips begging to impart their secrets. To share with him this tale of misery, of the awful chilling moments that led to what now lies before him.

His fingers brush the cold, dead hands, and the world falls away. Someone is screaming, it might be him, or it might be the animal cries of a mother in the agonal throes of childbirth. There is a taste of blood and lightning on his tongue, a rage against the futility of it all. There is sky, endless boiling clouds, and behind them a void through which something comes, something twisting and coiling and *hungry*. Pain clenches and tears at this body Matiu has fallen into, but the terror is the worse part, fractured splinters of nightmare driving into his eyes, the razor edges of insanity cutting away at his mind in precise, methodical slices. This thing, this writhing shadow, is coming for her. Coming for her baby. She *trusted* these people, and this is where it has led her?

The coiling mass finds her, caresses her naked skin, and if she thought she had known pain before, it is nothing as exquisite as the perfect cold that burns through her at that touch. There's a ripping sound, and far away someone cries out in protest, that no, this is not how it is meant to be. The baby is *not* the sacrifice. But Jaime can no longer hear, her body consumed by pain. Her skin is growing brittle, cracking and drying, and there is something inside her, taking her apart, pulling the life—the *lives*—from within.

Matiu hits the floor. Voices rise and fall around him, but the words make no sense, so short and finite against the lingering glimpse of that vast overwhelming emptiness. There are no walls around him, only the ramrod silhouettes of towers angled against the horizon, all crumbling black sand, and everyone is gone but for one shadow, hunkered just beyond his shoulder.

Very interesting, Makere breathes, and fades out as the skyline disintegrates, and Matiu is back on the lab floor, twitching.

"Matiu? What happened?"

Penny's voice. That's good, then. Penny will know how to fix it. Penny always does. The dark presses in at last, and drowns him in its warm embrace.

- Pandora -

Upstairs in the lab, all hell has broken loose. Beaker is jabbering nineteen-to-the-dozen, and Cerberus is racing about howling like a category 5 cyclone, some strange woman dashing about after him trying to catch hold of his lead. Penny ignores all of it because her baby brother Matiu is collapsed on the floor, his body limper than yesterday's leeks.

Slinging her satchel on the bench, Penny rushes over. "Beaker, what the hell happened?" She drops to her knees beside Matiu.

"I don't know. He just freaked out. I thought he might like to see the body—"

"What? What body?" Penny checks Matiu's pulse. Thin and rapid. Just fainted, not dead. Although, if he were, Cerberus is barking loud enough to wake him. "Cerberus," she screams, "shut up!"

"Here, boy," the stranger croons.

"The bog body," Beaker says. Quivering and downcast, the poor man looks like he just wet his pants in class. "Matiu and his friend bought it back. I thought they might want to take a quick look, it being a historical artefact…"

Penny nods. It was the sight of the body that did it.

She gathers him in her arms. He opens his eyes, fathomless anguish in his gaze, and Penny is hiked back in time to when she was eight and she'd come across him in the basement cleaning cupboard, his knees bunched to his chest, the bulging grey coils of pool hoses around his puny little body. He'd been shaking in terror, physically trembling, his hands crammed over his ears to block out…what exactly? He couldn't tell her, his four-year-old vocabulary unable to articulate whatever unspeakable thing was haunting him. That day, she'd somehow fixed everything by touching her lips to the graze on his knee. Today, with his head cradled in her lap, she kisses his forehead. "It's OK, sweetie, I'm here."

"Pen." His fingers grip her forearm. "They're coming for us."

"No one's coming, Matiu." She smooths his hair. "It's nothing. Just one of your silly nightmares."

"No, it's Makere."

"Oh him," she scoffs. "I already told him to go away."

His eyes flutter, the whites full. "He came when you were sleeping."

When I was sleeping? Matiu was still up when she'd slipped into bed with Mārama, and he'd been up cooking pancakes when Mum and Dad staged their home invasion this morning. "Matiu, when did you last sleep?"

"I've always been asleep. Mārama tried to warn me…" He struggles in her arms, attempting to free himself. "I have to get up."

"No honey, you need to take a nap. Everything's going to be fine. I promise to stay awake. I'll stand guard with Cerberus. Beak, give me a hand to get him into the office, will you?"

Matiu's heavy, so they slide him along the linoleum into the office, only lifting him onto the couch when they get there, his upper body first, then his feet.

"Cerberus. Stand guard." Matiu's giggle is wild, maniacal.

They tiptoe out into the lab.

That giggle has unnerved Beaker because he says, "Shall I call a doctor?"

"No need, Beak. It's just a panic attack. He used to have them a lot when he was little. He lost a friend yesterday, and there was the prang in the morning, plus I don't think he slept very well…"

"I doubt he slept at all. He called me around 3am, asked me to run some numbers for him. I did wonder what it was all about…"

Probably best if you don't know.

Penny rests a hand on his shoulder. "I expect sleep-deprived paranoia was what it was all about, Beak."

He pinkens. "Yeah, probably." Running a fingertip over the digital window on the Breadmaker™, he wipes away a smear. What had Matiu said to get him to stay up half the night?

"I'm sorry he bothered you."

"Hey, no worries." He clears his throat. "So how did it go with Mather?"

"Amazing. I got a call from Cordell while I was there. He'd completed the carbon dating on the samples. Turns out the bog body isn't the find of the millennia, just a well-preserved woman who went missing two years ago."

"Inconsiderate of her," Beaker says.

"Cordell was a little ruffled."

"Not surprised. There goes his speaking tour."

"Beaker!"

"Well, we were both thinking it. What about the John Doe from the park? Anything new there?"

"Oh I forgot, I've got some skin samples from the victim's fingertips. They were stained purple, like he'd dipped his fingers in a jar of permanganate. Mather hadn't seen anything like it before either. He's going to specify death by misadventure on the report, but I'd like us to run the assays anyway, just to be thorough. The samples are in my satchel."

She turns to pick up her satchel from where she'd flung it on the way in…

She stops. With all the drama she'd forgotten the mystery woman. Matiu's probation officer, no doubt. With dark hair, high cheekbones and a stunning figure, if not overly tall, she looks more like someone Matiu would date than a civil servant. And she's dishevelled, as if she's spent the night on the back seat of a car—another feature of Matiu's former girlfriends.

"This is Matiu's…um…friend," Beaker splutters. "Sorry, I thought you knew each other…she helped Matiu carry the evidence bag upstairs."

The woman holds out her hand. "Erica Langley."

Penny returns the handshake. "Penny Yee. We can probably let Cerberus off the lead now."

"Oh yes. Of course." Erica hands the lead to Penny, who unclips him and lets him run free. "Excuse the intrusion, I was with Matiu when…well, when he fell, I couldn't just leave…" She looks at Beaker, then nibbles at her lip.

Beaker takes the hint. "Um, if you ladies will excuse me, I'd better get these assays underway."

"I had no idea," Erica says, when Beaker has loped away.

Penny folds her arms. Another one whose perception of Matiu is based entirely on appearances. On what's written in his file. The ink on his face. To Erica, Matiu's just some wise-cracking, leather-clad ex-con, a scrapper from the city's underbelly. Useful. Malleable. Expendable.

"I'd never have dragged him into all this if I'd known," Erica says softly.

Penny purses her lips, says nothing.

"OK, you're right," Erica concedes. "I still would've asked him. My baby sister's in trouble: I had to do something. Matiu was the only person I knew with the right connections. Well, the only one I trusted not to fuck me over."

Well, she's honest.

Erica crosses her arms over her heart. "Is he ill?"

Penny sighs. "No, not ill exactly. Matiu's…he's a *matakite* of sorts. He sees things. Call it premonitions, a sixth sense, intuition, whatever you like. Our aunt— Matiu's biological mum—is the same. She sees things, too."

"What kind of things?"

"I don't know, but they're bat-shit scary."

CHAPTER 21

- Pandora -

Penny and Erica creep into the office and make themselves coffee, speaking low so as not to wake Matiu.

"Did you two find out anything about Charlotte?"

Gripping her coffee mug, Erica bites her lip. "Nothing we can use. Those Touching the Sun arseholes had her locked up somewhere on that bloody island. They want her for something, or maybe the baby, I don't know, but they have assault guns, their cars look like hearses, and they have freezers full of dead animals. Whatever's going on out there, it isn't a fucking ladies' day spa."

Freezers full of dead animals? Hang on...

Erica glances towards the door and drops her voice even further. "Matiu said the girl in the body bag was *the last Charlotte*. You said he sees things. Is that the kind of thing he sees? Are my sister and her baby going to die? Because one of the men on the island told Matiu the 'main event' was taking place today."

Oh jeepers.

"Main event," Erica goes on, her voice shaking. "What does that even mean? Whatever it is, my sister's going to be the main course. It could be happening right now, and I'm not there to rescue her." Tears well in her eyes. She turns away.

Penny's brain shifts into hyperdrive: dead animals, main event, the last Charlotte... Touching the Sun, micro-greens, Sandi Kern... "Shit. What day is it?"

"What?" Turning, Erica scrubs at her face.

"What day is it?" Penny fumbles with her phone, thumbing through the apps for a calendar. She stares at the screen. Bingo! "I think...Let me make a call." She speed dials the number. It clicks through straight away.

"Penny!" She can just imagine the look on his face. "This is a surprise."

Penny makes a wide Duchenne smile while she speaks because studies have shown a listener can tell the extent of a speaker's smile from the tone of their voice. "Craig, hi, sorry to call you at work, but I was wondering if there was any chance we could reschedule that dessert."

Erica Langley gapes in disbelief, but Penny hasn't got time to explain. Keeping her smile plastered in place, she shakes her head, hoping Erica will catch on.

"Really? That's great," Craig says. "It's late notice, but I can usually get a table at Kai. Shall we say nine o'clock?"

"Oh, Kai. That's a shame. I was so looking forward to that rosewater sugar basket and picking up where we left off last night."

"It did look fantastic, didn't it? But Penny, I'm not sure I'll be able to get a reservation for The Sedge tonight. Their bookings are crazy."

"Didn't you say you had a colleague at the Business Ministry?" Penny twists her fingers through her hair. No studies on that, but you never know, and right now she could use any advantage.

"Well, I guess I could ask him…"

"Would you?" Penny bats her eyelids. In for a penny, in for a pound. "I've got the evening free tonight. Who knows when I'll be free again? It'd be nice to be able to finish our date, you know, *properly*."

"Can you hold the line a moment?"

Erica Langley cocks an eyebrow. "What are you up to?" she asks.

Craig comes back on the line. "Penny I'm sorry, The Sedge is closed tonight for a private function. I can still call the Kai. They keep a table free for me on the off-chance I'll be made Minister for Transport." No study on that either, but Penny pictures him straightening his Windsor knot.

"Oh pooh. I had my sights set on The Sedge. Maybe another time? When you can get a booking?"

"I'll get onto it," he says.

Penny swipes the phone off. "The 'main event' is tonight at The Sedge."

"And how do you figure that?"

"Because it's the micro-green industry's flagship restaurant. What other key venue does Touching the Sun have access to? Somewhere unlikely to draw suspicion where they can hold an important meeting with their supreme commander."

She doesn't tell Erica the rest: talk of dead animals reminding Penny that Kerr had already slaughtered a bunch of dogs and murdered several people in her crazy-arsed attempts to raise the dead. So Kerr went to ground, it doesn't mean she put a stop to her activities.

Erica frowns. "Just how sure are you? Because Charlotte's life depends on us getting this right."

Where better to hold a human sacrifice than a rooftop at full moon?

"I'd bet my lab on it."

"Right then, I'd better go and call my office."

Penny blocks the door. "What for? What are you going to tell them?"

Erica smiles. "Just that I'm out of the office all day with a client. Don't worry, I'm in this as deep as you are." She steps out into the corridor to make her call.

Matiu must detect the movement because he turns over in his sleep. Penny smooths his hair, slow strokes in time with his breathing. Let him sleep, because tonight they're going to get Charlotte back. Pity they're too late for Jaime. "Thank you for finding Jaime and bringing her back, Matiu. Just for that I'm going to let you off this Friday's dishes."

"Rest of the year," he murmurs.

"Don't push it, buster," she says, but he's already gone back to sleep.

- Matiu -

The sky is a twisting pattern of red and black, fire and night. Matiu blinks, his eyelids as heavy as his bones, bones solid as stone, weighing him down. How long has he slept, and where is he now? He looks around, pushing himself up, feeling every ache, every splitting pain, every itch. His head, his arm, his back. Like he's been through a fight pit, or a meat grinder.

Beneath him, barren rock, brushed with dark sand. Filling the horizon, the sea. Water that ripples, something artificial in its symmetry. Behind him, hills march into mountains, their faces lost in shadow. There is no sun, just the glow of an angry star burning behind the horizon. Matiu stands, with difficulty. The land is punctured by a river which flows into the sea. He hasn't seen this place before, but there's something horribly familiar about it, like he should know it. And yet, he's an intruder.

Movement catches his eye, far below on the river. Something floats, dragged towards the sea. A waka. In the waka, a body.

There's no way down this cliff, but Matiu follows the waka's progress. Something's not right. And then, where the river meets the sea, the body stirs, takes up the paddle, rises.

Mārama. She comes to her knees, stares into the place where the sun has fallen away, strikes out against the currents. Matiu stumbles and staggers, slipping on the jagged rocks and the fine black sand that covers everything. "Mārama!" he shouts, but his voice is choked, muffled in his throat.

Then someone is standing before him, and he skids to a stop. A figure that looms, shadow within shadow, a peripheral silhouette thrown into black relief by the alien light. Matiu takes a step back, fists clenching. "Get the fuck out of my way, Makere," he hisses.

"Of course," Makere croons, standing aside and gesturing to the path that winds down the bank, down to the beach of black sand where the dark waves lap, where Matiu may still, if he's fast, plunge into the ocean and swim out to the waka, bring her back to shore. "You go ahead."

Matiu hesitates. If he's learnt anything from years of struggling against this shadow which is as much a part of himself as the pulse of his own heart against his ribs, it's that Makere offers nothing without a price. Everything is a trap. "What's down there?"

"Your destiny, of course." The sea starts to ripple and break. A vastness surges beneath the surface, rushing towards the waka. The blazing sky shudders and shimmers, heralding the beast's approach. "Jump in the sea, Matiu. This is where you belong."

Matiu glances around. The ramparts of hill and mountain now appear as the shapes of buildings, spires and towers and bridges and houses. If he peers hard enough, he may be able to see another world beyond the shadows, one he knows but can't reach. Like he's slipped through the curtain and is trying to find his way back.

He turns to Makere. There's a face now, within the black. A face far too familiar, despite how different the ink on Makere's face may be. His nemesis' *moko* are sharp and angular, suggestions of torturous blades and crushing fists, but the face...

Matiu knows that face as well as he knows his own. He takes a step back, patting at his chest for the comfortable weight in his jacket pocket, the jack-knife he's never quite been able to leave behind. But he's not wearing his jacket. And with every breath, Mārama draws further out to sea, nearer to the approaching mass.

Makere advances, forcing Matiu back, drawing his attention away from the breaking wake on the sea below, so close yet so far out of reach as to be another world. His bare feet slip on the sand, the cliff edge perilously close.

"It's your turn," Makere growls. "I've been here long enough, and now you've given me what I need to trade places. You opened a window, you know that? You showed me the way through. But I can't stay, not until someone comes over to take my place."

Who took his jacket? Nor does he have his boots on. It's like someone's undressed him, laid him on a couch somewhere, wrapped him in a blanket. His arms are bound, and he tries to scream again, but nothing comes out, just sand and saltwater and the taste of despair. He's caught in a nightmare, but it's more than that, he's fallen through the window into this place, Makere's place, and if he doesn't find a way out...

The beast breaks the surface, and even from here, Matiu hears Mārama's war cry as she raises the paddle over her head like a *taiaha*, shrieking her defiance at the true nightmare of gaping maw that breaches and swells to fill the sky, a leviathan, primordial and heartless, the *taniwha* come to claim its due. Beneath that descending maelstrom of teeth, Mārama shines bright, a tiny spark raging against the vicious, angry dark.

Makere lunges, and Matiu finds it, the blanket that wraps him, clutches it and whirls it around, blocking out all sight of both ghost and beast, and he slips, falls, falls...

Matiu hits the floor with a crunch, tangled in a blanket, crying out. He thrashes like a beached fish, kicking furniture, struggling to pull himself out of the nightmare and back to reality.

But it was more than a nightmare. It was too *real*. Something bad is happening to Mārama. He sits up, as the door opens and light floods in, a silhouette in the doorway. Matiu cowers, flashes of Makere filling him with renewed terror.

"Matiu?"

Erica.

His phone rings. Where? He pats himself down, but no jacket. "Where's my phone?" he mumbles, mouth thick and dry. His head is full of wet sand. It's hard to think through it.

"Matiu, you're meant to be sleeping." She tries to help him back onto the couch, but he pushes her away. She's got *her* jacket on. Where's his?

"Sleep when I'm dead," he says, his sardonic reflex kicking in even if the rest of his brain isn't functioning quite right. "Someone's calling me. Might be Mārama." He pulls himself up on the edge of the office desk, fumbles for the lamp. Blinks in the sudden light.

Penny appears in the doorway. She's got *her* jacket on too. Why the hell has everyone else got their jackets on but him? Are they going somewhere? "Matiu, lie back down this instant." There, on the chair. He whips up his jacket and digs through the pockets to find his phone, now silent. One missed call.

Penny's phone rings.

Matiu glares at her as she pulls it out. "It's Mum, isn't it?" he says. "Something's happened to Mārama."

Penny pales as she answers. "Hi Mum," she says. Their mother's panicked shrieking can be heard across the room, a tinny, incoherent scramble of words. "Mum, calm down, take a breath. Start again. Slowly."

Matiu turns away, looking for his boots. Erica's hand is on his shoulder and she drags his face around to look at her. "We think we know where they're going to be, with Charlotte."

"Somewhere high," Matiu says, "a tower. A rooftop."

Erica regards him coolly. "How do you know that?"

Matiu shrugs into his jacket. "Were you going to go, just the two of you, without me?"

"You're in no state for anything. You're running on fumes, a danger to yourself and everyone around you."

"And how were you going to get there? Catch the bus?" He glances at Penny as he edges away from Erica and sits on the couch, dragging on his boots. "Or were you planning to call in a favour from Craig Tong? Get that good boy mixed up in all this bad shit?"

Penny lowers her phone. "Someone's taken Mārama."

Matiu and Erica both turn to stare. "What do you mean, *taken*?"

"The orderlies took her for a walk through the gardens. Someone assaulted the hospital staff and dragged her into a car. Police are at the hospital now, looking into witness claims that there was a man with huge dreadlocks in the carpark just before the abduction."

"They're wasting their time," Matiu says. "You say you know where Charlotte is, right?"

Erica nods. "We think so. The rooftop of The Sedge."

"That's where we need to be then. Let's go."

Penny holds up a hand. "The two are *not* connected, Matiu. I don't know why they've taken Mārama but there's no evidence to suggest that whatever's going on with Mārama and your mate Simon Kingi could possibly have anything to do with Charlotte."

"The link is Makere."

Penny looks from Matiu to Erica and back again, then crooks a finger at her brother. "A quiet word?"

Matiu glowers, glancing at Erica, but follows her to the kitchen.

"Matiu, Makere isn't real!" she hisses.

"You willing to bet Mārama's life on that?" Matiu stalks past Penny to the coffee machine and punches buttons. The machine grinds and hisses in pleasure.

"I'm not going to risk her life based on your sleep-deprived fantasies." Is that a flicker of doubt in her voice? She ignored the warnings last time, and look where that got them. She doesn't need much more of a push, if he knows his sister.

"Well, that's convenient, isn't it? Because we're going to leave the police to look for Mārama while we go and save Charlotte, right? And Mum and Dad will be happy because you're leaving the police work to the police and not putting your precious self in danger. So everyone wins." He scoops up his coffee and takes a wicked slug, burning his lips and throat but relishing the pain regardless. "So, shall we go?"

CHAPTER 22

- Pandora -

On the way to the docks, it starts to rain. Lightly at first, then the sky opens, the gods rumble, and the storm that's been threatening for weeks finally breaks, sheets of grey water pummelling the windscreen. Within minutes, Penny is soaked, warm rain dribbling onto her skirt through the mangled side panel. She shifts her legs out of the way, but the water is the least of their worries; whatever goes down tonight, Dad's going to murder them when he sees this banged-up car.

That is, if Touching the Sun's henchmen don't kill them first.

Matiu pulls into the curb two blocks from the HSBC, the embattled Commodore dragging to a stop, its engine droning down like the spin cycle on a washing machine. "Hang on," he warns. He whips out his phone and makes a call. "Yo, Grendel here," he says down the phone. "You shake those psychos off in the end?"

The voice at the other end is tinny and far off; Penny can barely make it out over the pelting rain. "Yeah, no thanks to you."

"Lucky you're a resourceful bastard, right? Anyway, if you're back online, I'm going to need you to take out some cameras for me."

"Around the HSBC building," the man says.

Matiu's eyes widen. "You know where I am?"

"Course, man. Got you on Track My Fucking Friends."

Matiu snorts. "Figures. Think you can blind some of the eyes on us? Usual six-pack applies."

"Yeah, yeah. Although after yesterday, the price has gone up, but lemme see what I can do."

Matiu puts the phone in his pocket. "We're going to need to sit tight for a bit."

Five minutes go by. Ten. Fat droplets commit hare kare on the windscreen. *Splat, splat, splat.*

Matiu says nothing, just stares straight ahead, his teeth clenched. Penny shakes her legs, brushing off some of the water. Pity the same can't be said for her nerves. Even Cerberus is jittery.

"Fuck this." Erica throws open the door and runs down the street, her feet kicking up water. She pulls up at the southern end of the building, taking a quick peek around the corner.

Forcing the jammed passenger door open, by the time Penny reaches Erica she's stepping back from the corner. Meanwhile, Matiu is still sliding on his sunnies and letting Cerberus out of the back.

"What have we got?" Penny asks.

"Two guards," Erica states. "Rent-a-cops by the look of it. How are we going to get past them without alerting the people upstairs? They've got Charlotte. We can't let anything happen to her."

Penny looks for herself; peeking around the corner at the guards, squinting against the rain. Moonbeam and Ray. *Excellent.*

"Follow my lead." She strides across the courtyard to the main doors.

"Sorry, lady," Ray says, as she approaches. "I'm going to have to turn you around. The building's closed this evening."

"We have a booking upstairs at The Sedge."

He smirks, checking out Penny's skirt where it clings to her legs. "Well, it looks like there's been some mistake, sweetheart. The Sedge is closed to the public this evening. Private function."

"I have an invite."

Moonbeam shakes his head. "No can do. As far as we know, everyone's up there. The guest list is closed." He makes a show of slipping his hand into his jacket, the soggy fabric gaping open to reveal a handgun...

Penny's heart veers. A gun. But she can't afford to back down now. Charlotte's life is on the line. Stiffening her backbone, she steps forward and flicks a bit of fluff off Moonbeam's jacket. "Well, that's your call, isn't it? Although I wouldn't count on the boss lady being too happy when she finds out. Especially since the two of you are already skating on thin ice."

Frowning, Ray steps between them. "What's that supposed to mean?"

Penny puts her hands on her hips. "Hello? The security perimeter. That was you two on duty out at the Grey Lynn warehouse last night? You didn't really think she was going to let that pass, did you?"

"Shit. She knows about that?"

Penny raises an eyebrow.

"But how the hell did she—"

Matiu barrels along, staring blindly ahead, and barges past Moonbeam. "Can we talk about this later, guys? We're on a bit of a timetable here." He makes a show of fumbling the doors open, Cerberus surging ahead as he makes for the lift. Penny and Erica follow the trail of droplets across the lobby.

The lift car takes an age to arrive. While they wait, Penny keeps her eyes on the two out front. Given their frantic gesturing, the pair are still arguing about how the boss got their number. Good. At least while they're bickering, they're not phoning upstairs.

The car arrives and they get in, Matiu ignoring the voice control and hitting the button for the ninth floor instead. In the mirrors, infinite Matius do the same. The car ascends. Cerberus gives himself a good shake, spraying water everywhere and blurring their reflections. It doesn't matter, all the Pennys looked sad and bedraggled anyway, and a multitude of washed-out Ericas hadn't looked much better. The only saving grace is that the fogged-up glass hides any chance of her spying Subliminal Men lurking in the angles; Penny has enough to deal with in the here and now without worrying about imaginary people stepping through the cracks at the corners of the universe.

"So, do we have a plan?" Erica asks as they pass through the fifth floor.

Omigod. Penny's heart drops into her shoes. She buries her face in her hands. A plan. All her thoughts had been focused on getting them to the restaurant rooftop before midnight; she hadn't even considered what they might do when they got here. "Matiu, what do we do? These people are armed. Those two downstairs had guns. I saw them!"

Erica's eyes are wild with anxiety. "They had assault rifles at the island, too. Oh my god, they're going to shoot Charlotte, aren't they? I haven't seen her for months, and when I do it'll be to watch a bunch of lunatic grocers mow her down in cold blood." She steadies herself against the wall, her hand smudging the steamed-up glass.

Penny doesn't have the heart to tell her a clean shot from a rifle would be a kinder fate than the one Kerr and her cronies have in store for Charlotte and her baby.

Eighth floor!

Penny tugs at Matiu's sleeve. "Matiu, we need to get through that hatch and on top of the lift, now! Whoever's in the restaurant is going to shoot us down the minute the doors open. We'll be sitting ducks. We haven't even got a weapon!"

Checking out his image in the mirrors, Matiu opens his leather jacket exposing Moonbeam's gun, which is tucked neatly in the waistband of his jeans. "I wouldn't say that," he says.

Erica sucks in her breath.

The lift pings and the doors slide open.

- Matiu -

The weight of the gun brings back memories of shit he'd rather not have done, memories he'd rather not have bubbling to the surface right now. Tonight's going to be another of those nights, isn't it? He can feel it in the pit of his bowels, as the lift doors slide open like stage curtains pulling apart on the final act of a sinister, unscripted theatre piece, and him standing in the spotlight with no idea of his lines.

He snaps off the safety and raises the gun, bracing it firmly in both hands, sweeping left to right, scanning for a target.

The Sedge is empty.

Aside from the gilded sign positioned dutifully before the maître d's station declaring in bold lettering that the restaurant is closed for a private function, the place is deserted. No bar staff polishing glassware, no wait staff standing by to offer him a tall-stemmed glass of bubbles or those little prunes wrapped in bacon, no rattle and hum from the kitchen. Matiu steps out of the lift, gestures toward the kitchen. "Go that way, find the fire extinguishers."

"What the hell for?" Erica protests.

"You wanted a plan, didn't you? Preferably one that doesn't get too much blood on your hands?"

He moves towards the staircase that leads up to the roof and the thrum of rain. The glass wall flickers with a nearby lance of lightning, followed by the bone-deep roar of thunder. The noise almost mutes the thump of feet in the stairwell, but not quite. Matiu steps around the corner, gun raised, and sights his target. Always sight the target. Especially when your probation officer is a potential witness at your next court appearance.

Two men in suits, so caught up in their Secret Service masquerade they're still wearing their sunglasses, inside, at night. Not great for actually *seeing* threats before they take you down. The gun barks twice, the discharge deafening in the confined space. Both men collapse, one with a shattered kneecap, the other's collarbone punctured by hot lead. Momentum carries them down the steps in a confusion of blood and strangled cries. They'll live. Last thing he needs is a murder rap. Pausing to scoop up both dropped handguns and stuff them in his belt, Matiu scoots halfway up the staircase, the windows beside him streaked with rain, and waits. Below him, wounded men groaning, bleeding. Above, more madness wrought by the hand of the diabolical Sandi Kerr and her quest for what? Immortality? So he might catch ten years inside for putting her crazy arse away for good. He can live with that.

Almost convinced no-one else is coming down right away, Matiu is about to carry on up the stairs when another flash of lightning arcs across the Auckland skyline, drawing his eye, through the window, across the road. Only a fleeting glimpse, but it's there. On top of the PWC tower, something moves. Something with snapping, flailing appendages. And beside it, another body, staked out in the rain like a crucifixion.

As the thunder crashes through him, Matiu's world falls away.

Mārama. It's Kingi, he took her and now he has her there, atop one of the tallest buildings in the city in the middle of a thunderstorm. Why? It's the connection he's been waiting for, but there's no time for questions and answers. Matiu spins down the stairwell, vaulting the bleeding men at the bottom right as Erica and Penny appear, each bearing a fire extinguisher, his sister struggling to hold onto Cerberus as well as the cumbersome appliance. "Go," he says, waving vaguely. "Shock and awe, right? Hit them before they know they've been hit."

"Where are you going?" Penny says, the colour draining from her face.

"I'm going to, ah, flank them. Yeah. I'll come up the fire escape. Hit them from the other side. Go!"

Ignoring the bewildered cries that trail him, Matiu hits the emergency exit to the building's central stairwell and races down the steps two at a time, dreading that the next bolt of lightning may be the last for Mārama.

- Pandora -

"Matiu—" Penny starts. She turns to follow him down the stairs.

"Let him go," Erica says, blocking her descent. "We haven't got time. Charlotte's up there and she needs us." With that, the probation officer belts the fire extinguisher on the railing, smashing off the pin, to hell with the sound. Anyone upstairs has to know they're coming: if Matiu's gunshots weren't enough, the shrieks of the injured men are louder than a banshee. Whatever he's up to, Matiu will just have to handle himself.

Erica moves to charge past her, but Penny stops her with a hand to her shoulder. "Ever been up here?"

"Are you kidding? On my salary?"

"It's an actual garden, runs the length of the building, with raised beds laid out in two lanes. You take the left lane, and I'll take the right. Stay out of sight until we get the lie of the land. Touching the Sun could have all the Orcs of Middle Earth up there. The last thing we need is to lose Charlotte in the crossfire."

A shadow passes over Erica's face, but she nods. She tilts her head towards Cerberus. "What about the dog? You can't take him. He'll just get in the way."

Penny shakes her head. Leave Cerberus behind? Not on your life. Cerberus has a sixth sense when it comes to Sandi Kerr.

"He's going to ruin everything," Erica insists.

Penny tunes her out, stepping onto the roof where the storm hits her full in the face. After a long hot vacation, the weather god, Tāwhirimātea, is gathering his children to celebrate the full moon. They're all here: the terrible wind squalls of Apū-hau to the mighty rains of Ua-nui. Even the gentle mist Tōmairangi has joined the party. Penny smiles. Someone on their side at last. The men downstairs can scream their lungs out, their warnings will be drowned out by Tāwhirimātea's revelry.

Signalling to Erica, Penny ducks to the right and follows the outer lane of beds, Cerberus on her heels.

Where are they? Kerr and Charlotte, and whoever else was on the guest list— the Big Kahuna Sun Priest that Moonbeam mentioned? Penny can barely see a thing. Sheets of water lash her face. Her hair whips about her. She wipes the wet strands out of her eyes with her forearm and sneaks forward. Finally, at the northern end of the rooftop, she spies something.

Kerr.

The cheeky cow is dressed in doctor's scrubs! Well, she did do a gig as a consultant psychotherapist, luring depressed cancer patients into her confidence. Perhaps that's how she was able to gain the cult members' trust?

Over the din of the storm, Penny catches a low groan.

Behind Kerr, a heavily pregnant Charlotte is sitting on the ground, her back to one of the raised beds. She rocks forward over her belly, clearly wracked in pain.

She's in labour.

Penny ignores Erica's urgent gesture. They can't move yet. Kerr might have other henchmen lurking nearby. They need to get closer. Pointing to the next set of planters, Penny darts forward, taking cover behind the raised bed, the last in the row. On the opposite side of the roof, Erica does the same. And it was a good call because there *is* someone else. Concealed behind a bed of wind-battered sweet peas is a large man with massive horn-rimmed glasses, dressed in white robes. Penny shudders.

Like the Ku Klux Klan.

This must be the Big Kahuna Sun Priest, with Kerr as his priestess. Penny's close enough to Kerr now to observe the Touching the Sun priestess in all her malevolent, manic glory. Her lips moving incessantly and her eyes closed, Kerr raises a bowl to the sky where the full moon is barely a yellow glow behind the clouds. She sways in time to some inaudible music, her expression beatific in spite of the deluge.

Suddenly turning, she thrusts the bowl to Charlotte's lips, forcing something down her throat, and Penny's transported to another place, this time in a darkened chamber deep in the bowels of the earth where another woman is slumped, with another bowl, the sweet smell of bitter almonds, and Kerr's blade…

No!

Tāwhirimātea's thunder clap drags her from her waking nightmare…into another. An arc of orange lightning slashes through the gloom and the priest turns away from Kerr's ritual, his eyes looking northwards towards the storm. Penny leaps up. Releasing Cerberus, she sprints at the priest, the fire extinguisher at her shoulder.

Alerted by the movement, he draws a gun from beneath the folds of his robe.

Shoots!

Penny dives away as the bullet hits the metal extinguisher, sending up a chemical geyser. A cloud of white blossoms before her.

The thwack of the bullet drives Penny's breath from her lungs, the force hurling her backwards. She smashes against the balustrade, hard. Pain flares in the back of her head.

Wow, I'm actually seeing stars. Funny, how they move in concentric patterns...

The wind Apū-hau sweeps in to carry away the chemical cloud, just in time for Penny to see Cerberus leap at the priest, the hound looking for all the world like his lupine forebears, his fur on end, jaws wide, curved white incisors angling for the priest's throat. She prays to any god who'll have her that the priest doesn't fire. And all the while Cerberus descends in slow-motion, gracefully, like a ballet dancer.

Vaguely, Penny's aware that Erica is on her feet, screaming, running, spraying wet chemical foam in Kerr's face. These extinguishers are meant to blanket fat fires. They're chock-full of alkali salts. Potassium carbonate or maybe potassium acetate. Assorted GHS hazard pictograms crowd Penny's mind. High pH chemicals penetrate nicely so that's got to sting, maybe even blind. Penny hasn't the least bit of sympathy: not so long ago that bitch cut Buchanan's eyes out.

The priest is screaming, tumbling backwards, firing wildly. Cerberus—*omigod, Cerberus*—lands on all fours on the priest's chest. He's going for the man's throat, ripping at his robes in a Cujo frenzy. The priest fires again and Penny's heart clenches. Sooner or later that bastard is going to kill her dog. She can't just sit here; she has to do something. Using the empty extinguisher as a crutch, Penny struggles to her feet, her head spinning. She drags the canister upright. Stumbles forward. Lifts it.

More firing.

Cerberus!

The hound reads her mind, he has to have, because he scoots away. Penny doesn't hesitate: she thunks the empty extinguisher on the man's head. His glasses splinter, his mouth gaping open and he flops to one side. Prone, he lays still on the ground, his broken spectacles spilling across the roof in shining shards.

Did I kill him?

"Penny!"

Dropping the extinguisher, Penny whirls. Kerr has Erica! Even blinded, the priestess is no helpless damsel. One hand twisted in Erica's hair, she yanks the probation officer backwards, her arm wrapped tightly around Erica's neck, squeezing on her windpipe.

Instinctively, Erica brings her fingers to her throat, straining to free herself from Kerr's stranglehold. She staggers backwards, hoping to reduce the pressure, but Kerr retreats until her back is against the wall. Erica's face is turning red, her muffled protests becoming urgent. She rakes Kerr's forearm with her fingernails, and kicks back with her feet, but with no force behind them, the kicks aren't likely to raise even a bruise. Kerr laughs.

Penny shouts, "Let her go, you crazy bitch," then quietly moves to the right, the roar of the storm muffling her footsteps. Still struggling, Erica follows Penny with her eyes.

"Let her go?" Kerr snorts. "I don't think so, Yee. That would be crazy, wouldn't it? When she's my ticket out of here."

Penny's reply is Campus Self Defence 101: a low hard kick, delivered to the outside of Kerr's knee, the dull crack of bone surprisingly satisfying.

Caught unawares, the priestess howls and releases Erica, who leaps clear. As Kerr crumples against the wall, Penny stomps hard on her foot, heel first. "Get Charlotte," she shrieks to Erica, while thrusting an elbow upwards into Kerr's diaphragm, then quickly steps away herself. Kerr would put her stranglehold on Penny, if she could reach her. Instead, the priestess grasps at air. Blinded and winded, she slides the rest of the way down the wall.

"You fucking bitch, Yee! You'll pay for this," she pants. She can't see a thing, her eyes directed at the spot where Penny had been standing just seconds ago.

Trembling at her own violence, Penny turns away, scanning the rooftop. Nearby, Erica is crouched beside her sister, her arms under Charlotte's armpits, trying to move her to safety. Then Penny's eyes fall on a furry mass on the ground.

Omigod, Cerberus!

She scrambles forward. The priest had been firing. Did he hit Cerberus? He has to be hit. A dark ache grasps her by the bones. Water sluices down her cheeks, mingling with her tears. *Please, not Cerberus. Not this big old hound.* They haven't been friends long, but he's wormed his way into her heart.

"Cerberus." Sliding in on her knees, she scoops up his lead, pulling him to her, and runs her hands over his coat, checking for wounds. The dog yelps and twists. "Shhh, baby. It's okay."

It *is* okay. She can't find anything. Not so much as a broken rib. Her pulse slows. Probably stunned, he's bruised and shaken, but he's alive. Penny almost sobs. Cerberus whines and nuzzles her neck.

Then, suddenly, he's twisting away, rushing to the balcony where he puts his paws on the wall and howls into the wind.

"What is it, boy? Is that Matiu coming up the fire escape?" Penny follows Cerberus' gaze, steadying herself against the wall as lightning bursts across the heavens.

Oh. So, that's what you're barking at.

On the roof of the building next door, a woman is lashed to the lightning rod. There's no need to ask where her brother is headed.

Behind her, Charlotte's scream makes her blood curdle.

CHAPTER 23

- Matiu -

Matiu pounds across the lobby of the HSBC just as the two guards on the front door turn towards him, responding to something in their earpieces. Thankfully, he already has one of the three guns he's picked up tonight in hand. He raises the weapon and fires over their heads. Glass shatters, and the guards duck for cover. Matiu charges on, lowering his head, bracing himself and leaping shoulder-first into the spider-webbed remains of the front door. Shards like raining diamonds spray the footpath as he bursts through, skidding on wet splinters for a second before he gathers his feet and turns, sprinting towards the street. The two-bit security detail isn't sure what the hell just hit them, some blind guy running around with a gun, firing wildly, and Matiu is halfway across the road before they've recovered their wits. Another flash of lightning, this one mighty close, and all the streetlights wink out at once, plunging Matiu into darkness.

The front door of the PWC Tower stands open, despite the hour and the weather, its flickering light suddenly ominous. He enters the lobby, wondering if that low growl humming across the floor is the building's emergency generators or something worse. Once again, in an eerie repeat of his last visit, the security desk is unoccupied. Matiu stuffs the gun beneath his jacket as he approaches the stairs. The other two rest uncomfortably against his back where he's jammed them into his belt.

One of the lift doors hisses open, like the jaws of an alligator stretching wide for a foolish fish to swim inside. Lifts shouldn't be running, not in a blackout. A hot wind rolls from the open door. The itch in his arm flares once more. No way should he get in that lift, but it'll take him too long to run up thirty-odd flights of stairs. He needs to reach Mārama. Scratching at the sudden burn, Matiu steps into the lift and hits the button for the roof access. Should be a security-controlled level, at least a swipe card if not an old-school lock-switch. But the door slides shut, and the lift ascends.

Proving that elevator designers haven't had an original idea in about a hundred years since the HSBC lift cars are exactly the same, the mirrors on opposite walls plunge away into twisted infinities, and as Matiu leans against the back wall, gripping the gun until his fingers ache, all he can see out the corner of his eye is Makere's profile, repeated *ad infinitum*, leaning back and grinning in manic triumph. Matiu rises, and the world sinks away, and he has wings, brittle and burnt, and when he falls, they will not save him. Not from what he's going to face. He resists the urge to grab another of the guns in his belt, toting one in each hand like some big-budget zero-brainer action hero. Bullshit like that just smacks of desperation, and he's not desperate, not yet. He scratches at his arm again, biting his cheek against the irritation, racking up to agony.

A second before the lift reels to a stop and the doors ping open, the infinity of recurring faces in his periphery fades, leaving only the black of the storm beyond. Not only is Makere gone, so is Matiu.

He has left himself behind.

The doors open, and the space beyond is not concrete and steel, not glass and girders, but stone, russet as blood. Running through the cracks and joins are long, dark streaks of black sand, carried by the hammering rain. Pushing away from the glass wall at his back, only a misty handprint remains to signify he ever existed.

Matiu emerges as lightning shreds the clouds, and thunder cackles in delight. Another staircase, this one carved into the side of the tower, leads to the roof. Rain drenches him, like stepping through a curtain, and Matiu hesitates, fighting the urge to rub at his itchy arm yet again. Traps have a certain feeling when you walk into them, and this has that all over, but he can't back out. Raising the gun, he ascends the steps, Auckland stretching around him like a blurry landscape painting smeared with swathes of stalking rain. In another flash of lightning, the dark spire of the Sky Tower stabs the skyline like a needle.

The mast catches his eye first. Whatever has corrupted this place, turning concrete to stone, it has also changed the lightning rod that crowns the tower. The rooftop should be cluttered with solar panels, aircon units, elevator motors, cell transmitters and satellite dishes, but everything is gone. All that remains is a single, massive rod of black metal piercing the clouds. Matiu ascends the stairs, and the scene reveals itself in its awful completeness.

Mārama is bound to the rod as it tempts the fire of the skies, and between Matiu and his mother stands Simon Kingi, grinning, tentacles writhing and snapping at his back.

"Matiu Fucking Yee," Kingi grins, his words slurred by the bloated tongue that scrapes against a mouth full of pointed teeth. "I've missed you, bro. Have we got some shit to talk about or what?"

"Yeah, motherfucker, let's talk," Matiu says. He raises the gun, and fires.

- Pandora -

"Penny," Erica shouts. "Help me!"

Penny whirls. Kerr is crawling away on her hands and knees. Flinging the extinguisher to one side, Erica has abandoned the priestess to crouch over her sister.

Penny scrambles over to them. The storm has risen to a crescendo with driving rain and gale force winds. Penny hunkers in front of Charlotte with her back to the storm, providing the sisters some protection from the wind. Charlotte looks close to death. Sickly white, her hair slicks down her face in sorry tendrils, her lashes wet with rain and tears and her arms wrapped around her belly. She moans, the anguish deep and primal. It's her shivering that alarms Penny most. Is that hypothermia, shock, a normal symptom of impending labour? Penny doesn't know. One thing she does know is that while they're out here, the threat of a lightning strike hovers over them like a serpent curled around a branch, its forked tongue poised to lash from the sky and obliterate them all. "We need to get Charlotte out of this weather. It's too wild out here."

"I've already tried. She won't move," Erica shrieks over the wind. "I think there's something wrong."

"With the baby?"

"No, with Charlotte. God knows what they've done to her. She keeps babbling about octopus monsters raining from the sky."

Octopus monsters? For Christ's sake.

"Let me see." Gently, Penny lifts Charlotte's chin and checks her pupils. They're enormous. Surely that's to be expected? Dilation of the pupils is a typical adrenergic reaction to pain, and Charlotte's in labour, possibly second stage, where the pain ramps up from visceral to somatic. Her pain has to be acute. Charlotte's eyelids flutter and she pulls away. Penny wishes she had something to ease her suffering.

"I think it's fine. Just a physiological response to labour," Penny says. "Between the two of us, we should be able to get her inside, out of the wind."

"No," Erica says, reaching out to grab Penny on the forearm. "That's *not* it. It's more than that. It's as if she doesn't even recognise me. As if she's *high*."

High?

There was that liquid Kerr had forced down Charlotte's throat. Did Kerr poison her? Penny's breath catches. Kerr hadn't shied from poisoning poor Annie Hillsden in the basement of the museum. Penny had tried to save her, she'd tried so hard, and still she'd been too late…

Not this time.

Snatching up the bowl, Penny stalks across the rooftop to where Kerr is scrabbling, blindly searching for the stairs. Shoving her backwards, Penny forces the bowl under her nose. "What's in this bowl?"

Kerr scuttles backwards like a crab. With nowhere to go, she hits the far wall.

"What's in it?" Penny shouts this time.

Her eyes streaming, Kerr can't see and still she smirks at Penny. "If you're so interested, why don't you taste it?"

"I've got a better idea. Why don't *you*?" Penny closes her hand over Kerr's face and crams the bowl to her lips, forcing the liquid into her mouth. Struggling, Kerr clamps her lips shut, but not before swallowing a mouthful. Her eyes dart and she thrashes her arms, her fingers grasping for a weapon. Bracing herself against the wall, she kicks out at Penny. The kick connects.

Ooaf.

Winded, Penny staggers backwards. Dark tendrils like drifting smoke curl about her. Penny longs to lose herself in their embrace, to give herself over to the whispers that tell her Kerr deserves it. A quick death is more than the woman ever offered her victims. She's blind, her eyelids all but swollen together. It wouldn't take much for Penny to close her fingers around her throat and squeeze. *Do it...*

Cerberus' howl startles her. Across the bay, thunder rumbles off the slopes of Rangitoto. Penny blinks. She stares at the little bowl in her hand. What the hell? What is she doing? If this is poison, Penny might have killed the woman.

But Kerr lifts her chin and cackles like a storybook witch.

No, if this were poison, Kerr would be begging for the antidote...

"Penny, leave her. I need your help." Erica is sitting splay-legged behind her sister, supporting her weight. "Any idea how to deliver a baby? Because I've got nothing."

Her chin on her chest, her head thrown back on her sister's shoulder, Charlotte is lost in oblivion. Breathing slow, she's acting on instinct as women have done through millennia.

"I think her waters have broken," Erica says, although how she can tell in this deluge, Penny has no idea. "Help me get her inside."

Penny lifts Charlotte's skirt and takes a peek. "I think it's too late for that."

"Oh lordy," Erica says. Her eyes, wide with panic, beseech Penny to do something, *anything*. "Charlotte, honey, you're doing great. The baby's nearly here..."

Cerberus howls in concert with Charlotte's wails. Or perhaps it has nothing to do with Charlotte. Perhaps it's because a hundred metres to the north, in the midst of swirling wind, the lightning rod rises, a ship's mast in the storm with Mārama its living figurehead.

Penny glances toward the PWC Tower. Her aunt looks tiny, frozen there on the edge of an abyss, her life suspended, like an intake of breath. Penny can't bear it. At any second, a billion-joule pitchfork could explode from the sky at 300,000 kilometres per hour to blast Mārama and everything near her into nothingness.

Please, no. Please let Matiu get to her in time. Don't let them die...

Charlotte screams.

"It's okay, Charlotte, darling. You can do this. My friend Penny is going to help. She knows about these things. She's a doctor..."

At the mention of her name, Penny pulls her eyes away from the tower back to the two women huddled before her. Matiu will have to manage without her. Right now, she needs to deliver a baby. Her nerves stretched taut, every adrenoceptor on overload, Penny drags her attention back to the job at hand.

Charlotte and Erica sit cheek to cheek, Erica gripping her sister's hand, whispering inane yet poignant nothings about their shared childhood, while Charlotte's body strains with effort. Penny's heart aches with the raw beauty of their connection. Together, they have thrown down a challenge to the universe to *bring it on* because nothing is more important than this moment, this struggle, this child... Erica's eyes meet Penny's and for an instant she feels it, too. It's as if that most fearsome carer of souls, Hine-nui-te-po, the earth mother's own granddaughter, has looked down upon them and recognised in them her own defiance.

They are safe from the storm. She will not allow them to be harmed.

"Charlotte, you're doing so great. Nearly there. One more push..."

In the end, nature takes it course, and the baby slides into Penny's arms, blue and mottled and absolutely beautiful.

Beaming at Penny, Erica kisses her sister on the forehead. "Charlotte, you clever thing! It's a girl."

Something to cut the cord! Penny scans the rain-soaked rooftop, and snatches up the broken lens from the priest's huge eyeglasses. When the cord is cut and the placenta delivered, Penny catches sight of a plastic tarpaulin, folded neatly in a corner of the rooftop. Still on her knees, she drags it over mother and baby, sheltering them from the storm.

She's euphoric. Charlotte and her baby are alive, saved from Kerr and her henchman...

Hang on, the Sun Priest had been lying right there, beside his broken glasses.

Penny spins, squinting through the rain to scan the rooftop, but Kerr, too, has disappeared.

CHAPTER 24

- Matiu -

The first bullet twists Kingi around, the second spins him, and Matiu dashes across the slick wet stone, grabbing the jack-knife from his pocket and popping the blade open in an easy, practised motion. Ignoring Kingi, he stuffs the gun back into his waistband and slices the plastic ties that bind Mārama to the lighting rod, catching her as she slumps into his arms.

"*E Tama*," she croaks, her voice rasp-harsh, "it's a trap. The baby, you have to stop him..." She dissolves into a fit of coughing as Matiu hooks an arm under hers and turns towards the stairs.

"Not my baby, not my problem," he says. "Let's get you down to the car. It's on the street. Stay with me now."

The shape comes at him from the darkness in a blur, and Matiu barely has time to throw himself sideways as Kingi whirls past in a deluge of snapping tentacles and foaming rain. Matiu and Mārama fall heavily, tangled, and Matiu crabs around to face the thing coiling for another strike. Shit, this guy got hit by a fucking *truck* and got back up, what the hell did Matiu think a couple of poxy bullets were going to do? He hoists Mārama to her feet and nudges her away. "Go! Get to the car! I'll deal with this!" How exactly, he doesn't know, but he will.

"Matiu! Makere wants the baby. He needs it, to come through. And if he does, I'll lose you!"

Matiu tenses his shoulders, squaring off against Kingi, the jack-knife in his hand a flimsy defence against this monster. But now he understands: Mārama was the bait, the diversion. Makere sent Kingi to take Mārama not because they want her, but because they want Matiu to be somewhere else when this shit with the baby goes does. *It's your turn*, Makere had said. And somehow Penny's a part of it, and she's not here, she's *there*. Makere understands what Kerr is up to, using the baby as a means of bringing something diabolical through the veil, just like she tried with Darius Fletcher, Annie Hillsden, and Jaime Sutherland, and Makere is going to hijack the ritual. Whatever Kerr has started, Makere is going to finish, and when he does, Matiu will be sucked into that red-sky world of black sand and ocean.

- Pandora -

Penny needs to get out of here. She needs to get to the PWC. She needs to call Clark, Tanner, Dad, *anyone* who can help Matiu. But first, she has to get Erica and her sister off this rooftop.

They've nearly reached the stairwell when Charlotte grasps Penny by the forearm. Her eyes widen, the dark pupils far away and fathomless. "That man. The laughing man. He's going to steal my baby."

"He's gone, sweetheart," Erica says soothingly. "There's nothing to worry about. Penny brained him with a fire extinguisher and he ran off."

Charlotte shakes her head. "No. Not that one. The laughing man." Her brow creases and she looks puzzled. "He was here."

Whatever Kerr made her swallow has addled her brain, which was probably the point. Kerr didn't want to kill Charlotte, not immediately. She just needed Charlotte pliable enough to deliver the baby. Add in pain, shock, and hypothermia, and Charlotte simply doesn't know what she's saying.

"It's over now, Charlotte," Erica says. "Let's get you inside in the warm, shall we? And you can introduce us properly to your wee girl."

A crack splits the air. Penny whirls.

Please no. Not the lightning rod. Not Mārama!

She abandons Erica and Charlotte and runs, weaving through the garden beds, to the edge of the rooftop. Cerberus is already there, his paws on the ledge. They stand side by side, looking out at Tāwhirimātea's rooftop light and sound show.

And Matiu and Kingi at centre stage.

It's as if Penny and Cerberus have come to watch their favourite team play in the finale, but could only afford the cheapest tickets, right at the top of the stadium. And from where they're standing, the home team's chances don't look good. A tough side, their opponents have the advantage. It's the last play. Only seconds remain in the game.

Her arm around Cerberus, Penny lays her cheek against his neck and cries stupid helpless tears. There's nothing she can do.

"He's going to die, you know. They're both going to die."

That voice. Penny turns. It's the man from the lift, the one from her dreams. Charlotte's laughing man. The man with Matiu's voice and Matiu's moko. They might be the same person except this one's moko speaks of ancient curved weapons and runnels of blood, whereas Matiu's has always reminded her of ocean waves and ferns on the forest floor...

"You can save them, Pandora."

"What are you talking about? And who the fuck are you, anyway?"

His grin is pure Joker. *"Let's not be coy. You know who I am. And what I'm suggesting is that you offer up your life for theirs. It's really that simple. The natural order of things."*

Yes, she knows who he is. In her heart, she knows, although every cell, every over-stretched neuron, shies from the knowledge. Makere. Matiu's imaginary friend. Perhaps even more... She glances to her right, through the storm, where a rooftop away Matiu is doing battle with a man she saw hit by a truck yesterday and for all intents and purposes should be dead. "There's nothing natural about any of this."

"Ah yes, the science thing is a nuisance, isn't it? But your beliefs are irrelevant here. If you can put them aside for just a moment, you have the power to make it all go away."

His tone is beguiling, as subtle and tempting as the sage that wafts from the pillows they serve in the restaurant downstairs. If what he's saying is true, Matiu could live, and Mārama too. And she'd be rescuing Mum as well, because, let's face it, Matiu and Mārama are Kiri's reason for being.

Cerberus growls low in his throat as Penny steps away from the parapet. "I die and they live. And that'd be the end of it?"

Makere nods. *"The end of it."*

An eye for an eye. A life for a life. Except Penny's life will count for two. It makes sense any way you do the math.

Makere has Kerr's bowl in one hand, a blade in the other. He offers her the bowl, and she's reminded of Disney's Snow White and that perfect red apple.

"There's no need for you to feel any pain."

No pain, but so much loss. She'll never see her family again. Never win the Nobel Prize. Smiling sadly, she reaches for Cerberus, to give him a last scratch between his ears.

The dog snarls, pulling back his lips and baring his teeth. Not at Penny, but at this anomaly, this man capable of slipping sideways through space. Cerberus makes no move to attack. Penny can understand it. Matiu's nemesis is shadowy, but he's familiar, too. If he'd lived, he could have been Matiu's brother, and Penny his sister. Circumstances had been otherwise, but that wasn't Makere's fault.

Pushing the dog away with her knee. Penny takes the bowl. She holds it in two hands. Such a plain little object, which is strangely fitting. A dribble of liquid rolls in the bottom. It's a coward's way, but what if she flinches under the blade? Penny lifts it to her lips.

Screams spread across the night, like sheet lightning across the sky. No, not screams. Gunfire.

- Matiu -

"Why me?" Matiu shouts, not taking his eyes off Kingi as the two circle, looking for another opening to strike.

But Mārama doesn't answer. Matiu dares a glance her way. Her eyes have drifted, her face a mask of horror beneath the roiling sky. "We're here," she says. "We're already here."

Kingi doesn't miss the distraction and hurls himself forward. Matiu sidesteps and grabs an arm, sticking out a leg and hoping to throw him over, but tentacles wrap around his arm and squeeze, pain erupting down his limb where the itch flares fire-hot under Kingi's touch. Still, they're tumbling, falling, and he has the knife, raises it to stab...

The gunshot roars like thunder, muzzle flash bright as lightning, and the tangled pair spin around, tossed by the impact of the bullet. Matiu glimpses Mārama through the rain, drenched and glorious, the gun she must have lifted from his belt smoking in her hands, before Kingi slams into the lightning rod.

"*Tāwhirimātea!*" she howls above the descant of the storm, and the sky lights up.

Thunder claps with the flare of lightning striking the rod, as if summoned by Mārama's desperate cry, sheets of rolling light cascading across the saturated rooftop. Matiu feels the blow, slammed in the back by a freight train, momentarily blinded, heat lashing through him. Then he's airborne, falling, and his wings are burned and broken. Tangled with Kingi, ejected from the rooftop by the power of the storm, they spin, and arc, and tumble toward the stone-dark streets below.

- Pandora -

Penny whirls to see Matiu fall. He's miles away, and yet she drops the bowl, her hands reaching for him, grasping at empty air. And just like that, he's gone. Disappeared. Dead probably. She didn't have a chance to say goodbye.

But Mārama's no longer lashed to the lightning rod. She's escaped! Penny could escape, too. With Matiu gone and Mārama free, why sacrifice herself? Makere must realise it because he spins on his heel and storms towards her, the steel blade glinting.

CHAPTER 25

- Matiu -

Five seconds of falling through nothing, the street rushing up to pulverise them. Matiu counts them, punctuates each deadly beat with a thrust of the blade, consumed in these last seconds of his mortal life with driving the knife into Kingi. The abomination shrieks and twists and cackles insanely as they fall, its coiling limbs wrapping Matiu's legs and lashing at his face while Matiu stabs and slices and severs, determined to finish this thing that can survive trucks and bullets and a fucking *lightning bolt* with his little old switchblade.

Kingi snaps out a tentacle, wrapping around a lamppost, and the falling pair whip to a sudden stop with a bone-jarring crunch. Swinging eight metres above the street, rain pummelling them, smelling like burnt seafood, Kingi squeezes. Matiu cries out, the knife falling from his fingers as something inside him snaps.

"Dunno about you, bro, but I'm having a blast," Kingi quips. "Been too long since we hung out together, eh?" He bares his teeth, his breath a stink of ozone and scorched flesh.

Matiu twists in his grip, struggling to breathe. "Bro, I'd love to trade witty comebacks with you, but I've got other shit I need to be doing right now." He wrestles one of the two pistols free of his belt, lifts it to the tentacle holding them aloft and pulls the trigger once, twice, three times. The tentacle ruptures. They fall, Matiu tipping his weight forward to twist on top of his opponent, bringing his elbow down into Kingi's nose with a satisfying wet crunch as they hit the road. Matiu rolls away, staggering to his feet, still gripping the handgun as rainwater sluices around his boots, pain blazing across his abdomen with the sick familiarity of broken ribs. But holy shit, he fell from like 400 metres and he's still walking. What the actual *fuck*?

He stumbles backwards down the deserted street, the harbour behind him, not taking his eyes off Kingi, who's already pushing to his feet, rolling his neck, blood drenching his face, hands, chest. Several of his appendages hang limp at his back, only a few still weaving in dangerous coils behind him. When Kingi turns to advance on Matiu, at least this time the motherfucker is limping. So he *can* be hurt. That's something. Fumbling in his belt, Matiu retrieves the other gun, brandishing both the stolen weapons in that classic Antonio Banderas cliché pose he so scorns, and hoping like hell the cops don't choose this moment to sweep the scene. That'll be him back to prison for sure, and he hasn't even had the satisfaction of taking down Sandi Kerr. Or Kingi, for that matter.

"It didn't need to come to this," Kingi shouts, plodding implacably forward. "You've made shit real hard on yourself."

Matiu retreats, the guns shaking in his hands. "You didn't give me a lot of choice, bro. You ever heard of the phone? Could've just given me a call if you wanted to get together and chill like old times."

"Old times? *Old times*?" Kingi laughs, a broken sound like rusty knives scraping over broken concrete. "Bro, the old times are gone, and the old times are here. All at once. How fucked up is that? But you, you're not meant to be here anymore. You're part of this. You're the key. You unlock the door." Kingi treads forward, Matiu backing onto the esplanade, towards the low wall that runs the length of the waterfront. Behind him, the storm churns the harbour to froth.

"Go on, tell me more," Matiu shouts back, letting Kingi get closer, closer. Maybe this guy is preternaturally indestructible because of whatever has taken possession of him from the other side, but can he survive a bullet to the head?

"Your dad wants to meet you. Family reunion time."

Matiu frowns, a sudden chill in his veins. "Now I know you're tripping. I see my dad most days, we have dinner at least every couple weeks." Closer, closer.

"Hah! Don't pretend you're that stupid, Yee." Kingi's voice has changed, grown deeper, echoing up from an abyss, reaching him across times and distances he dare not comprehend. "Didn't that woman ever tell you who your father is? Your *real* father?"

A knot corkscrews from his gut up into his throat. He tries to reply but the words turn to sand in his mouth. *It was an awful time in her life*, is all Mum ever says about Mārama's getting pregnant with Matiu. A disturbed and vulnerable woman preyed upon by the cruelty of the world. Nothing more, and Matiu has never questioned further. It's hard enough just maintaining the illusion of normalcy with Mārama, without trying to dredge up memories best left buried.

"Nothing to do with you, bro." Closer...

"You're wrong. It's got *everything* to do with me." Kingi's hollow voice rings with awful truth as he steps onto the esplanade.

Point blank range. Matiu raises the guns, and Kingi tenses, utterly fearless of the paltry mortal weapons, arms and tentacles splaying out wide as he prepares to leap. Time seems to crawl, as through the mist a crumpled white shape hurtles toward them, throwing up a curtain of rain in its wake. Matiu instinctively hurls himself aside as the Commodore roars across the intersection, Mārama dimly visible behind the wheel. Then he's sliding on wet concrete. The Commodore hits the curb at high speed, the front end snaps up, the bumper collecting Kingi as the car's momentum carries it up and over the barrier wall.

Matiu lurches toward the wall in time to see the car hit the water, nose first, and start to sink. Battered as it is, it'll take no time to fill with water. Matiu takes a few steps back, runs and leaps into the roiling water, letting the guns fall as he hits the surface and goes under, into the black.

- Pandora -

Penny backs away. "No! I've changed my mind."

Makere ignores her, lifting the blade to plunge it into her heart. Suddenly, he is less ghostly and more solid. Less Pinocchio and more real boy. *"Pinch and a punch, sis,"* he says and he sounds so much like Matiu. *"Too late. I've come too far now…"*

"No!" Penny feels behind her for the garden bed, desperate for a handful of dirt, *anything*, to thrust in his face.

Suddenly, Cerberus is there, snapping at Makere's ankles. A mere inconvenience, Makere kicks him, a swift brutal jab that sends Cerberus yelping and rolling into the wall. But Cerberus' distraction has given Penny the time she needs. Her fingers have closed on a garden fork, its prongs slipped snuggly into the earth and the handle upright, as if it's been growing there. She grips the handle. Lunges. Stabbing upwards with the fork. She drives the prong deep, putting all her weight behind it, feeling the flesh separate, then metal scrape on bone as she buries it in Makere's eye. He howls, black blood dribbling down his face so like Matiu's it's uncanny.

Matiu!

Makere yanks out the fork and flings it away. Rain runs down his face, sluicing away the blood. When he gets to his feet, his grin is chilling.

Penny's own blood pools in her veins. It isn't enough. She's slowed him down, nothing more.

But Cerberus hasn't given up. Makere might look like Matiu, but the hound isn't fooled. His body slung low, the dog steps between them, his eyes glowing and his hackles raised. The growl he makes is so deep Penny's hair stands on end. Cerberus. The guardian of the underworld, he who keeps the dead from returning to haunt the living.

"Pandora. Call off the hound. It's not too late. Do this for me, and I'll get Matiu back for you—" His voice beckons and the words are so sweet…

Makere steps toward her and Cerberus leaps. This time there's nothing graceful about it: the dog's jaws close over Makere's throat, teeth sinking deep into muscle.

He clamps down hard, black blood dribbling between drawn-back lips. He tosses Makere from side to side, the movement so fast Penny could swear there are three of him. Cerberus must have severed Makere's spine, because Makere flops uselessly. Cerberus drags him onto the nearest raised garden bed, then, his shoulder muscles bunched, the hound flings the body over the edge.

Even as he falls, Makere laughs.

CHAPTER 26

- Matiu -

Lungs burning, Matiu rises into the light, waking from drowning.

Matiu.

The light is white, and cold, and too bright.

Matiu.

The dead lie beneath, driven under, waiting.

Matiu.

Heartbeats like the flutter of wings trapped against a cage. Like rain against stone.

"Matiu."

Breath—a heavy, heady reminder of life. Fills his mouth with sweet emptiness. He can still taste salt, and sand, and blood. He opens his eyes.

"Oh good, you're awake," Mum says, gripping her hand in his like if she lets go he might fall again, into the sea, or into the shadows beneath the bed where the dark things lurk, a place from where he may never return.

"I'm awake," he mutters. "I'm just ignoring you."

"Matiu." He focuses, looks around. Dad, too, with a face like that thunderstorm Matiu was just out playing in. Excellent. Probably ready to do an incident report to ascertain how the fuck, exactly, did his fleet car end up on the seabed in Auckland Harbour, young man?

And then in walks Penny with the cops. Great, the gang's all here. "Tanner wants a word," she says, eyes flashing a warning he's not quite awake enough to fully interpret from body language alone. Man, but his head hurts, and his ribcage aches, and his arm... His arm... He rubs at the itchy patch. It's painful, but the irritation is gone. Must be on the good drugs.

"It's all good," Matiu says. "I was ignoring him, too."

"Not helping."

"How I roll," he croaks. "Water?"

Penny helps him sip from a straw. The cold running through him focuses his thoughts. How long has he been out? What was happening? He remembers pulling Mārama from the water, but what about Kingi, and Makere, and Charlotte and Kerr? It's all a blur, on his knees on the pier in the downpour, pumping her chest and listening for a breath that just wouldn't come while the sirens closed in. Shit. "Mārama?" he whispers to Penny, but his voice is louder than he wished.

"What a good idea," Mum says. "We'll go check on her, shall we, Hing? Give Matiu a chance to explain to these nice policemen how this is all just a strange misunderstanding, hmm?" Patting Matiu's hand once more before leaving his side, she bustles their father from the hospital ward, leaving Matiu alone with Penny and the dastardly duo of Tanner and Clark.

"Matiu Yee," Tanner says, advancing with notebook in hand.

Matiu waves. "Gents." Damn. They've caught him flatfooted. Hasn't had a chance to synch his story with Penny's. What do they know? How many bodies does he have to explain?

"When I heard it was you out there, doing CPR in the pissing rain, I had to check it out for myself. Seems trouble follows you like a bad smell. Care to tell us how you got there?"

Matiu purses his lips, nods a little. "I jumped."

"Funny," Tanner says, sitting on the end of the bed and facing him. "But you'll appreciate that I'm a busy guy, and I like you about as much as I trust you, despite all the assurances your lovely sister gives us that you're a decent bloke. So cut the bullshit and give me a straight answer. Day before yesterday you're placed at a murder scene, then your biological mother is abducted, and you turn up in a part of town where all the city CCTV has mysteriously gone on the fritz, and your car is in the drink. We're hauling it out now, you know. What do you think we might find? Oh, fancy that. Firearms, maybe." He flashes Matiu a photo on his phone of two handguns in plastic bags, coated in mud. "But, because you're such a stand-up guy, I'd like to hear it from you. Horse's mouth and all that."

Matiu shrugs. "Simon Kingi, you know that already, you've got his car impounded, haven't you? Tried to run us off the bridge the other day. He's one of Hanson's old crowd, and with Hanson out of the picture, he's trying to stamp his mark. Make himself something. Trying to put the acid on me to fall back in with him, *or else*, sort of shit. But I'm not into it, right? So he goes after Screech to scare me, but I don't scare easy. But when he snatched Mārama?" Matiu shakes his head, his throat tight at the very thought, at the memory of her hung out like a crucifixion in the rain. "That's a step too far. And Mārama, she's not stable. She got away from Kingi, is all, because she's tough like that. I left the car, probably didn't lock it because my head wasn't in a good place, eh? Just wanted to find Mārama. I went running along the waterfront looking for her, cos Kingi called and said that's where we'd find her. I knew it was some sort of trap, but what was I meant to do? Penny went the other way—no idea what she was doing—missed all this shit. I saw Mārama down by the ferry terminal, like she was going to throw herself in. Done with it, all of it, the bad dreams and the medicines and everything, because sometimes we try to do so much to look after the ones we love when all they really want is to escape, for good sometimes. And she did. Didn't even jump, just fell. I ran towards her, that's when I saw the car coming at me. Kingi must've boosted it, and next thing I know I'm dodging a flying car and we're all in the drink, and all I've got eyes for is Mārama. Kingi can sort his own shit out. I didn't see him come out of the water, anyway. Hopefully he's still down there."

Tanner looks at him hard for a long moment. "That's it. That's your story?"

Matiu nods again. "Yip. Would you like me to make some shit up instead? Something more dramatic?"

"Matiu," Penny warns. Her phone starts blinging, and she moves away to take the call.

"What about these?" He waves the picture of the guns in front of him again. Those fucking guns. But not to worry. Won't be a shit-show of getting a print off either of them, and any trace of GSR on his hands is long gone. He should be fine. Until they find his knife on the road, covered in blood and whatever other freaky shit came out of Kingi when he was slicing and dicing him, unless the rain has washed it all away. Or the other gun, Moonbeam's, the one he and Mārama both shot Kingi with, on the PWC rooftop. Where the hell is that? "Never seen them before," he says.

"That right?"

"That's right." Thank fuck he's not on a heart monitor. "Any more questions?"

"Not right now," Tanner says. "Not for you." He turns to Penny. "Ms Pandora."

- Pandora -

"Sorry, Beaker, gotta go." Penny stuffs her phone into her pocket and turns to face the detective, her heart thumping at what he might ask her. "Yes?"

"Officer Clark here tells me you've identified the bog body and simultaneously closed a missing person cold case."

Penny feels a surge of pride. "Yes. We located a brachytherapy bead in the bog body. Actually, that was my assistant on the phone just now. We still have to check the barcode number with her doctors, but we're confident it's Jaime Sutherland."

Tanner hooks his fingers into the loops of his trousers. "Not a big call for radiotherapy treatments in the Iron Age, then?"

"Apparently not."

His eyes creasing at the edges, Tanner stands to leave. "Good work, Yee."

"Except Jaime was murdered."

Tanner stops. He turns to look at her.

Penny draws in a breath. "Sandi Kerr and her Touching the Sun cult made a sacrifice of her."

"Kerr? But she's gone to ground. No one's seen hide nor hair of her. What makes you think she had anything to do with it?"

"Because she's tried it before," Matiu says.

"Because last night we stopped her from doing it again."

Tanner points at Matiu. "You and him?"

"Me and Erica Langley."

"The probation officer?"

Penny nods. "Erica's sister Charlotte was a Touching the Sun acolyte. Kerr tried to murder her last night on the rooftop of The Sedge. Happily, she didn't succeed."

"And this all happened at the same time and practically the same place as your brother's shenanigans on the waterfront? How coincidental."

"We like to streamline our crises," Matiu says. "More convenience than coincidence, really. We're a very well-organised family like that."

"*Matiu*," Penny growls.

Tanner gives him a dark look before flicking his attention back to Penny. "What happened to her?"

"She had a beautiful baby girl."

"Penny," Matiu says, giving her a quick nudge. "He means, what happened to Kerr."

"Oh." A wave of heat creeps up Penny's neck. "Um, unfortunately Kerr got away. We were busy delivering the baby. There was the storm—"

"Touching the Sun. Is that what the tattoos on the wrists were about?"

"Yes, that's right, boss," Clark replies. "I ran some searches—the cult runs an extensive micro-greens industry with sites across the city. It's a key part of their holistic, wholesome approach to living."

Tanner blanches. "I'd hardly call human sacrifices wholesome, Clark." He hitches up his trousers. "I assume you have evidence to support your conclusions, Miss Yee?"

"There are still a couple of tests to complete, but yes, I believe so. Jaime's body contained ergot alkaloids."

Tanner stares at her blankly.

"Sorry. Ergotamine is a metabolite derived from the spore of rye fungus *Claviceps purpurea*. Different varieties of the fungus exist on other grasses and cereals like sorghum, millet, barley, but essentially—"

"It's bad stuff that grows on micro-greens," Matiu cuts in.

"—it's hallucinogenic," Penny continues, "induces labour, and it's been associated with ritualistic fertility rites and sacrifices. Kerr's obsessed with sacrifices. I suspect Jaime was her first victim, followed by Fletcher, Hillsden and Potaka. She's been using the ergotamine substances to control her followers. Naturally, her rituals didn't work—there's no such thing as a backdoor to the underworld—but Kerr must have decided the reason she'd failed was because those early victims were all cancer sufferers. Perhaps that's why she went after a sacrificial offering with more promise..."

"A newborn." Tanner shudders. "Fuck. I'm chasing serial killers sweeter than this woman."

Clark rubs his hands across the back of his neck. "She *is* a serial killer, and the Touching the Sun cult gave her a ready supply of victims, first Jaime and then this Charlotte."

"Exactly. Which brings us to the John Doe at the park—"

"I have the pathologist's report for Jendoubi on my desk," Tanner interrupts. "He's calling it death by misadventure."

Penny shakes her head. "Jendoubi died of ergot poisoning, too. Only in his case the alkaloid was delivered over a long period, possibly several months. I can understand why Dr Mather missed it; I almost missed it myself. Jendoubi's blood showed the presence of lysergic acid. It's a precursor of LSD, so we both assumed Jendoubi was taking a crude street form of the drug. Instead, we needed to go back a step and consider lysergic acid as a breakdown product of ergotamine."

"You getting this, Clark?"

"I think so, boss. Ergot has a long history. Some scholars have attributed it to things like the hysteria surrounding the Salem witch trials, and the Great Fear that preceded the French Revolution. Others say the poetic saga *Beowulf* was a hallucinogenic masterpiece written under the influence of the substance, like a hipster poet tripping on home-brewed acid, but whether deliberately or otherwise is unknown. The name *Beowulf* comes from the German for 'barley wolf', and is sometimes translated as 'teeth of the wolf.' Freaky stuff, since ergot grows on barley stems, among other grasses and plants, and it can be quite nasty, like a wolf. But, you know, that's all by the by really."

Tanner regards him, mystified. "Freaky that you know this sort of shit, Clark."

"Passing interest in classical literature at varsity, boss."

"Well, better make sure we put a flow chart in the report."

"There were other clues to the ergot poisoning," Penny goes on, with a sideways glance at Clark. "Like Jendoubi's purple fingertips, which we'd mistaken for some kind of ink, possibly to do with the tattoo. But ergotamine causes blood vessels to constrict. Taken over a period of time, the extremities can become gangrenous. Jendoubi's fingers weren't stained, they were necrotic."

"Well, that tells us how he died, but there's no reason to suspect murder. It could still be misadventure."

"Maybe not," Clark says. "Jendoubi was a member of the cult too, and the Sutherlands said he was desperate to find Jaime."

"Young love, eh?" says Matiu.

Clark ignores him. "What if he got too close to the truth, and the cult helped him along a bit? Made sure he got his three square meals a day…"

"And a dose of oblivion…" Matiu adds.

"Kerr was probably keeping him supplied with the drug while pretending to help him search for the woman she'd already killed," Penny says, "even after she'd dumped her body in the mangroves."

Tanner puts his hands on his hips and arches his back in a stretch. "Well, this is all very nice isn't it, but we still don't have Kerr."

"We have enough for a warrant to search Touching the Sun's premises, though, boss. You never know, we might turn up something."

"Right, well, get on it, Clark. Let's see if we can't put some of these cases to bed. Ms Pandora, I'll expect your report on my desk tomorrow."

- Matiu -

He watches the cops' backs until they're gone, absently rubbing at the spot on his arm that used to itch. He didn't realise it was a habit until now. Finally, he bows to the weight of Penny's eyes on him. "What?" he says.

She lowers her voice. "Well, care to tell *me* what happened?"

Matiu glances at the open door. "But I told the cops everything." He drops his voice into an equally conspiratorial tone. "And how do I know you're not just their mole, plying me for information. Sheesh, could've at least bought me a drink first."

Glaring, she helps him sip more water. "Matiu, I saw you on the rooftop. I saw you *fall*. You and Kingi, you..." She struggles for words. "You got hit by *lightning*, and you got blasted off that roof and dammit I *saw you fall*. PWC is twenty-nine stories high. What the hell? Did you sprout wings or something? You should be dead. Instead, I get down to the street and there are cop cars swarming the place because someone in one of the apartments reported gunfire, and there you are on the waterfront pumping water out of Mārama's chest and how the hell did you even end up in the water? You were falling straight down!"

Matiu shrugs. "I can see this is a struggle for you. But it's possible to survive a fall like that, if you know how to land. I read it on the internet."

"Not without breaking every bone in your body!"

"I had something soft to land on."

"Yes, a body that should've been plastered across the street, but there are no bodies. The police are investigating this as a disturbance, thunder mistaken for gunfire, probably only because *you're* involved. They don't have any bodies. Not even Makere. And Cerberus threw Makere off the top of The Sedge, so he should've been right there beside Kingi. And *you*."

Matiu's gut clenches. "Wait, what?"

Penny sags. "Yeah, I don't know how he's managed to keep himself hidden all this time, tormenting you without my seeing him, but I met Makere last night for the first time. Christ, he looks just like you, doesn't he?"

"He came for you." *Like he told me he would. He's stepped through from there to here, coming into this world one tortured step at a time.*

"He wanted to trade. My life for yours. But he didn't count on Cerberus. Anyway, I guess I'm...sorry for not taking you seriously all this time. We really need to know who he is, though. We can get Clark to look into it, get a non-contact order or something written up so if he tries this again they can put out an arrest warrant."

"They won't find him," Matiu sighs, sinking back into the pillows. "He doesn't really live around here."

"But do you know any more about him? Do you know who he is?"

Matiu nods. "Yeah, I think I do. He's the twin brother I never had."

Penny regards him, with her most critical look. "You don't have a brother. *We* don't have a brother."

"You sure? Were you there? It's the only explanation that fits."

"There'll be a rational explanation. He looks a lot like you but he's not your twin. Maybe he just knows about your childhood imaginary friend and has used that to get to you. To get inside your head."

Matiu closes his eyes and lets the darkness settle heavy on his lids. "Whatever you need to tell yourself, sister."

CHAPTER 27

- Pandora -

When Penny lets herself into Mārama's room, her aunt is asleep. She looks so peaceful with her dark hair spread out on the pillow and her chest rising and falling gently. Penny envies her. After last night, she's so tired, she could sleep forever.

Pulling up an armchair that looks every bit as tired as she feels, Penny sits down and lays her head on the bed. Just the touch of her cheek on the crisp bedclothes releases a wave of emotion, the full horror of last night's drama rushing in on her like a mudslide, burying her under a mountain of dark earth and squeezing the breath out of her. "I really thought I was going to lose you both, Mārama," she whispers. "When I saw you lashed to that lightning pole, and then Matiu falling... I can only imagine what it was like for you, firing the gun... Matiu and Kingi toppling over the edge. You must have thought you killed him. Your own son..."

A nurse opens the door, pokes her head in, looks both ways, and goes out again. When the door has fully shut, Mārama's hand closes on hers. It's cool and dry.

Penny smiles, trying not to wince at the bandages on Mārama's wrists where they were rubbed raw by the plastic zip ties. "You're awake."

"Sometimes it's hard to tell when I'm dreaming and when I'm not."

"Dozing then."

"I suppose so."

She strokes her aunt's forehead. "I'm so sorry I didn't keep my promise to you. I wasn't there when you and Matiu needed me."

Mārama takes her hand and kisses it. "You were there when it counted. You're here now," she says.

Penny pulls the chair closer to the bed. "Mārama, about Matiu's imaginary friend, Makere. I met him. Turns out he's as real as you and me. Matiu says he's not from here, which means he's gone to a lot of effort to bully Matiu all these years."

Her aunt's fingers tighten on Penny's hand. "He's a bad one."

"Matiu claims he's his brother."

Mārama's eyes flutter.

Penny's ashamed of herself. She shouldn't have done that. Mārama's far too fragile for confrontation at the best of times, and after the night she's had...

"It's OK," Penny soothes. "You don't have to tell me. Maybe he's your son, maybe not. If he is, I'm guessing he's *whāngai*, like Matiu. And if you kept it from us then, you had your reasons. But just so you know, I saw Makere fall from the rooftop last night. They haven't found his body yet."

Penny sees the rise and fall of her aunt's chest falter: Mārama's holding her breath.

"He might be OK!" Penny says quickly. "Matiu survived the fall, so maybe he did, too."

Exhaling slowly, Mārama gazes out the window. Penny follows her eyes: wisps of cloud in a blue sky, an orange crane on the skyline. After a night of bluster, today Tāwhirimātea and his children are resting. Her aunt sighs. "I saw that big international doctor yesterday. She reckons I'm crazy. She used a lot of fancy words, but that's what she meant." Mārama stares at Penny, her eyes full of tears. "I'm not crazy. I'm just tired. Dog tired. You understand that, don't you? I've fought it and fought it, and I just can't do it anymore. I can't. And I can't run from the nightmares, any more than I can stop them happening." Her eyelids flicker.

Penny's heart clenches. Poor Mārama. Penny understands because she's tired, too. Bone tired. And like her aunt, she's burdened with things she can't tell anyone. Things which would label her as crazy.

Like Kingi's blood from the windshield being XNA, so not even *of this world*.

Like Cordell finding XNA in Jaime's baby.

People dying and their bodies disappearing.

If she were to hypothesise, she'd say something is trying to get through from the other side. She'd even go so far as to say it was already here. Except she's a card-carrying logic-loving practical down-to-earth *scientist* and she doesn't believe that shit. She doesn't!

I'm crazy as Mārama.

"You're a good girl, Penny," Mārama murmurs, close to sleep.

Penny kicks her shoes off and climbs into bed behind her, wrapping her arm around her aunt's waist. Tucking Penny's hand under her neck, Mārama traps her there.

Penny should really extricate herself. She can't be lying here all day: Cerberus is tied up in the shade outside and she needs to get back to the lab and help Beaker finish up the analyses. Still, a moment won't hurt. It's been a long night. She closes her eyes and lets her aunt's warmth soothe her.

They were lucky this time. She hasn't pieced it all together yet, but something uncanny is afoot. Between them, Kerr and Kingi and Makere have unleashed something dark and terrifying. It may be fledgling still, but its power is growing, and when it comes, as she knows it must, there will be no rest.

Glossary of Māori and local terms

boot	Kiwi name for a vehicle's trunk
CBD	Central Business District, colloquially 'ceebeedee'
chur	Kiwi slang for choice, cool, sweet, awesome
(to) come a cropper	an unexpected and embarrassing failure
comms	Emergency despatch service covering Police, Fire, Ambulance
deal to	Kiwi idiom which means to take control of, sort out, or manage
FSH	Follicle Stimulating Hormone
Horsebite	a sudden grab and squeeze causing a horsebite-like bruise
IVF	In Vitro Fertilisation
kai	food
koru	spiral shape of fern frond, symbol of new life
kōwhai	Sophora, native tree with brilliant yellow flowers
Kupe	First Polynesian to discover New Zealand, based on tribal lore
mānukā	teatree
Marama	clear, light, lucid
matakite	Māori seer or soothsayer, one who sees into the future
moko	traditional Māori facial tattoo
prang	(colloq) minor traffic accident
ropeable	Aus/NZ fit to be tied, angry to the point of needing restraint
slaters	woodlice
taiaha	traditional Māori war staff
tama	son, or e tama, an expression of surprise
tamāhine	daughter

taniwha	Māori spirit or monster
tuahine	sister of a brother
tāu hāmua	brother
Tāwhirimātea	Māori god of the weather whose children include the wind squalls, Apū-hau, heavy rain, Ua-nui, and the mist, Tōmairangi
ute	(colloq) short for utility vehicle
waka	traditional Māori canoe
waratah	steel fence post or T-post
whānau	family
whāngai	fostering, adoption, usually by a relative
whaea	aunt
Weet-bix	Weet-A-Bix
wotnot	suchlike

About the Authors

Lee Murray is a multi-award-winning writer and editor of fantasy, science fiction, and horror (Sir Julius Vogel, Australian Shadows). The co-author of *Hounds of the Underworld*, prequel to *Teeth of the Wolf,* her solo titles include the bestselling military thriller *Into the Mist* and its sequel *Into the Sounds* (Severed Press). She is proud to have co-edited nine anthologies of speculative fiction, one of which won her an Australian Shadows Award for Best Edited Work (with Dan Rabarts) in 2014. Lee lives with her family in the Land of the Long White Cloud, where she conjures up stories for readers of all ages from her office on the overlooking a cow paddock. www.leemurray.info

Dan Rabarts is an award-winning short fiction author and editor, recipient of New Zealand's Sir Julius Vogel Award for Best New Talent in 2014, and the Paul Haines Award for Long Fiction as part of the Australian Shadows Awards in 2017. His science fiction, dark fantasy and horror short stories have been published in numerous venues around the world, including *Beneath Ceaseless Skies, The Mammoth Book of Dieselpunk*, and *StarShipSofa*. Together with Lee Murray, he co-edited the anthologies *Baby Teeth - Bite-sized Tales of Terror*, winner of the 2014 SJV for Best Collected Work and the 2014 Australian Shadows Award for Best Edited Work, and *At The Edge*, a collection of Antipodean dark fiction. Find out more at dan.rabarts.com.

CPSIA information can be obtained
at www.ICGtesting.com
Printed in the USA
LVHW03s1451280918
591716LV00002B/455/P